# MORTAL

'If Heaven had a heart, even
Heaven would be mortal.'

Li Ho

# MORTAL MASK

Stephen Marley

CENTURY
A LEGEND BOOK
LONDON SYDNEY AUCKLAND JOHANNESBURG

Copyright © Stephen Marley 1991

*All Rights Reserved*

The right of Stephen Marley to be identified as the author of this
work has been asserted by him in accordance with the Copyright,
Designs and Patents Act 1988.

All translations © Stephen Marley 1991

First published in the UK in December 1991 by Legend,
an imprint of
Random Century Group
20 Vauxhall Bridge Road,
London SW1V 2SA

Random Century South Africa (Pty) Ltd
PO Box 337, Bergvlei 2012
South Africa

Random Century Australia Pty Ltd
20 Alfred Street, Milsons Point, Sydney, NSW 2061
Australia

Random Century New Zealand Ltd
PO Box 40–086, Glenfield, Auckland 10
New Zealand

The catalogue data record for this book is available from the
British Library

ISBN: 0 7126 5108 X
0 7126 5108 9 (Ppr)

Typeset by Deltatype Ltd, Ellesmere Port
Printed in Great Britain by

# Dedication

In memory of Linda Holland;

and in the hope that Wong En-yin,
chief inspiration of the Chia novels,
is more than a memory.

# Acknowledgements

With thanks to Jane Judd, my miracle-working literary agent, for making so much possible; Deborah Beale and Charon Wood, my editors, for their remarkable faith, hope and clarity, along with my special regards to all the staff at Legend; Rachel Hore, for all the hard work and much appreciated effort; Naheeda, who paid the highest price for placing love above religion; Patrick, Desmond and James, for the misfortune of having me as a brother; Maggie, for the listening ear; Enya, for the music; Anita, for the massages and bondage. To all those readers who have forked out hard-earned money for one of my books – a special thanks. And finally, regards to Nastassja Kinski – just in case she happens to read this and is interested in meeting a home-owning, unattached professional writer, with a view to friendship.

Han Dynasty China
Year 164 of the House of Eastern
Han: 189AD
The Fourth Moon
Twelfth Day

It was a wound in nature.

It ripped the night air with the keen wind of its spiral flight. Defying the logic of body and spirit, it tore its phantom heart in two, seeking to shed its phantom blood. It was ghost flesh, spectre blood, spiritual paradox.

And it soared from Celestial Buddha Temple in a spiral of confusion, a whirlwind within a whirlwind, running in contrary gyres as it sought to spin a body from the winds and weave a cloak of air. It was a dangerous nonsense in the night: Wind Flesh – with killing intent.

Earth and sky rotated as the Wind Flesh roiled above the Forest of the Ancestors and the high walls of Celestial Buddha Temple. It heard a faint call from beyond the southern forest, the summons of warm flesh to cold spirit. The rotation of moon and trees slowed above the Forest of the Ancestors. And halted upside-down: the sky below, the earth above.

The Wind Flesh found itself in accord with the upside-down vista.

Forest above.

Moon below.


Hua Shan's mind was full of trees. All day, and deep into the night, nothing but trees wherever he looked, wherever he walked. So close to the end of his long search – and he had to lose his way in this damned forest.

He knew that the woman he searched for was no more than a few hours' travel to the north, in Celestial Buddha

3

Temple. A few hours, that is, on a good, straight road. But the Forest of the Ancestors had led him so astray that Chia Black Dragon – the infamous Woman in Black – might as well have been on the other side of China.

For months he'd dreaded finding the Woman in Black. Now he would have welcomed even her in preference to this quiet night forest.

He had been warned about using the Forest of the Ancestors as a short-cut to Celestial Buddha Temple in San Lung Region. Superstitious villagers to the west of the woods had urged him to take the longer path that wound south of the trees before curving north to San Lung. 'Stay clear of the forest,' one old woman had pleaded. 'Souls perch in its branches. Bad souls.'

But Hua Shan had laughed off the warnings with a shrug and a confident remark: 'The vision in my mind will be my lantern in the night forest.'

Easy to be brave in bright daylight while huddled over a fire and bubbling cooking pot in the middle of a friendly village. Not so easy now. There was no vision of light in his head. Now his mind was as dark and tangled as the thickets between the black congregations of the trees. He stiffened as he suddenly caught a distant rumbling from the north. That was where Chia was supposed to be. Was she causing some more of the mayhem for which she was renowned? And the noise – was the noise getting louder?

A frown slowly creased the crescent scar on his brow.

The ominous rumble seemed to be coming his way.

Forest of the Ancestors above.

Moon and Stars below.

The Wind Flesh set sail between sky and earth, drawn south by the warm flesh.

It was slow at first, skimming over the pines that hung above like black stalactites pointing down at the stars. But the further it flew, the faster it flew. The leafy canopy

4

flashed overhead in continuous streaks of moonlight on dark. And the faster it flew, the more it found its voice.

It was a multitude voice, a hundred maledictions scrambled together in the teeth of the gale. A hundred voices growling in unison: *'Chhhhiiiaaa . . .'*

It swerved up to the forest roof and zigzagged like forked lightning through its labyrinth of trunks and branches, twig-fingers tearing its impossible flesh of wind. *'Die, Chhhiiiaaa . . .'* it roared as it scudded over the soggy loam of the forest floor. *'Join me, Chhhiiiaaa . . .'* it invited as it darted between innumerable branches clutching at the moon beneath it.

Hua Shan flattened his back against the gnarled bole of an oak and drew a short sword from under his long brown cloak.

'Something's coming,' he whispered to himself, peering north into the dense shadows.

From nervous habit, he adjusted the strap of the leather pack hung crossways from his shoulder. Amongst its contents was a note – a message for Chia Black Dragon, the green-eyed sorceress. Teacher Sung, the head of Hua Shan's temple, had entrusted him with the mission of journeying the four thousand li from Melodious Temple in Silver Music Bay to Chia's hidden valley in Black Dragon Mountain. Hua Shan had trudged four thousand li through war-ripped China only to find that Chia had left Black Dragon Mountain just two days before his arrival. Frustrated, he had retraced his steps for three thousand li, following the rumours and corpses that Chia left in her wake. In the last few days all the rumours indicated that Chia was near, very near, in Celestial Buddha Temple, north of the forest . . .

The commotion to the north mounted as it came closer. The sword's length glittered in the twig-netted moon as he aimed its point at the remote source of the noise, blade trembling in his sweating grasp. What was

5

coming? A dark forest spirit? Something dead that wouldn't lie down?

The ghost-gale was up and about in the forest, shaking the life out of the trees.

The call from the south was nearer now, its attraction stronger. And the spirit-wind at last became aware of wrongness, of anomaly: earth above, moon below. It tilted sharply, and the earth was a wall on the right facing the wall of night on the left. Another tilt, and the moon was above and the earth below. For a time, it was less eager for havoc. For a space, it glided over the damp soil, skirting with ease each tree that blocked its path.

Then it remembered what Chia had done to it. Chia of the green eyes. Chia Black Dragon. The Woman in Black.

The branches trembled from its bellow as it surged forward, wrath and momentum regained.

The angle of the ground tilted crazily from side to side as the wind fury veered round tree after tree, swift as thought in its southward rush. Mossy boles hurtled past, mere smears of speed.

Boughs shattered with the anger of its passing. Soil erupted in the swathe of its onrush, throwing slapdash patterns of mud on the ravaged branches.

It swept up to an ancestral shrine on a hillock and burst its crude masonry asunder. Wooden figurines, wilted flowers, broken statues and delicate bronze bells rained down on the forest.

It swooped down the final li to its goal, wrenching oaks and elms from their roots as it drove a straight path to the Glade of Five Faces.

Nothing would stop it reaching its goal.

Nothing *could* stop it.

Not even itself.

'What's coming?' Hua Shan muttered, as the muffled rumbling from the north magnified.

A cold breeze fanned his battle-marked face and ruffled his trailing locks of lank hair. The breeze rose to a wind, and the wind strengthened with each frail cloud of breath from his lungs. His nervous hand brushed the crescent scar on his forehead as if it were a talisman embedded in skin, a blue half-moon, gift of war. The scar felt chill in the rising bluster.

*The air itself is in flight. The wind flees the coming spirit thunder.*

Hua Shan decided he had better run with the wind. Nature knew best. Who was he to argue? He sheathed the sword in its leather scabbard and ran. Dodging and ducking, he barely avoided colliding with tree trunks and jutting branches. The thorns that tore into his legs above the protection of the leather boots were easily ignored: the thought of the storm devil at his back was more than enough to distract him.

As the approaching forest thunder roared louder, he threw aside his last scrap of caution and plunged headlong into the clumped undergrowth and the leafy slap of slender branches, panic making his legs fleet and his heart reckless.

But as fast as Hua Shan ran, he couldn't outrun the devil at his back.

The Wind Flesh had tasted rage in its rampage through the forest. Now it tasted fear. Its own fear.

Fear made it roar all the louder. Fear made it rip wood from earth all the more savagely. Although it now struggled to return north, the warmth of its summoning flesh compelled it south.

It strove to arrest its progress by clutching trees, but the crackling might of its wind claws blasted the wood to splinters. Impossible to delay the force dragging it south, for it was the spirit rejoining the flesh, the breath rejoining the body. That breath was now poison to the body.

When body and breath met, there would be an end to both.

Hua Shan had been running in panic for so long that at first he didn't register the thinning of the trees.

He fled with such blind haste that he wasn't aware of the ground dropping away from him until it was too late.

He toppled headlong down a steep slope, arms threshing and legs kicking as he tumbled through the long punishment of gorse and briar to land with a soft thump on a pliant bed of shrubs. He lay there for a few moments, gulping harsh breaths that burned his strained lungs. The sight of the open sky was a vast relief. Ignoring the protests of his aching muscles and lacerated skin, he staggered to his feet, his keen ears catching, all too clearly, the vast bellow from the sweep of oaks and elms at the top of the slope.

Was he safe, now that he was clear of the forest? He turned south, and his heart died within him.

He wasn't clear of the trees. He was in a circular glade, floored with weeds, walled with high forest.

A huge mound swelled from the middle of the natural arena. A burial mound, as choked with weeds as the floor of the glade. The door at its base was sculpted in the likeness of a gaping mouth. And crowning the burial dome was a massive, rectangular slab of stone, at least as tall as four men. On the two sides of the stone which were visible to him were carved identical round faces, wider in span than two men. The giant visages were like moons with mouth apertures lips pouting in the malicious glee of a madman.

And – he found his wits spinning as he tried to identify the element of dread in the carven features – they were owl visages – or a toad – or –

He shook his head; the images evaded comprehension. Each visage was an impossible amalgam of beasts, unified in a convoluted symmetry. Faces within faces.

He shuddered and pulled his gaze from the mad moon faces, feeling that their round eyes were staring straight at him.

It was then he discerned the figures in the glade. Silver-grey shapes in a silver-grey glade, they were difficult to distinguish at first, but gradually they came into focus. Solemn moonlight illuminated a hundred and more silver-masked, grey-mantled men spread in a loose circle around the burial mound. They stood still as stone, their masked faces upturned to the monolith.

Hua Shan's hand was straying to his sword hilt when he sensed something askew in the balance of his body; a lack of weight to one side . . .

He groaned aloud. The pack was gone from his shoulder. Somewhere, in his flight, he had dropped the leather bundle with its precious message and proof of identity. He had lost the message imploring Chia to come to the aid of Teacher Sung in Silver Music Bay.

Praying for a miracle, he looked up the slope. There was a chance that the pack had slipped free in the long fall.

His prayer to the T'ao-tsang was answered, but not in quite the way he'd hoped. The pack dangled from the barbs of a thicket halfway up the sharp incline. And beside it stood a grey-mantled figure in a silver mask. Swirls of grey hair billowed from the mask's crown in the wind from the forest, the streaming hair almost as long as the figure was tall, a cloak of hair that merged with the hue of the ragged mantle, grey on grey.

A gauntleted hand emerged from under the mantles of fabric and hair and plucked the leather pack from the thicket, holding it aloft in what seemed an imperious gesture.

As he held the precious bundle in upraised fist, the forest that reared behind him exploded in a tumult of ravaged trees and violated air. And something as invisible as thought, and every bit as deadly, swooped down the slope.

Hua Shan dropped to his knees in terror. The devil had come for him.

*

9

It was wrenched into the Glade of Five Faces, raging at the woman who had sent it on its journey to its warm flesh in the tomb – the woman called Chia, the Woman in Black. Chia – may she be damned, damned to a very special hell.

The spirit whirlwind roared above the monolith that surmounted the burial mound. It saw the four stone faces that gazed east, south, west and north – and the fifth face on top of the monolith, staring up at the sky, mouth aperture yawning . . .

The wind-spirit plummeted to the mouth of stone. And the mouth gulped it down. Down into stair after stair, zigzagging wildly at each corner as the turbulent spirit hurtled down the rocky passages.

Deep under the earth, it burst into the domed vault that housed its body, its warm flesh, in a stone sarcophagus. Its emaciated, naked shape, head covered by a silver mask, threshed with fear. The flesh in the sarcophagus knew that its descending spirit brought destruction; it sensed it in the marrow of its bones; in its blood, muscles and skin. The destruction it brought was knowledge, dire knowledge.

The masked body heaved in a last convulsion. Then spirit and flesh were one.

Spiritual knowledge coursed through the labyrinth of veins. The heart swelled with unwelcome revelation; a revelation too expansive for the body to contain:

*I – am – mortal.*

The skin stretched over the expanding heart. The burgeoning brain cracked the skull. Blood spurted from distending pores. The taut skin began to rip.

And the bulging body burst asunder, expelling the spirit from the ruins of its flesh home. A fountain of blood and viscera soared from the stone sarcophagus and rained on the floor of the torch-lit vault.

The spirit ascended through the hot red rain.

The silver mask spun in the air and clattered to the damp flagstones.

10

The wall torches flared in a lurid blaze, then quickly guttered.

Darkness and silence filled the vault.

Hua Shan stumbled as the ground trembled under his feet. A rending crash behind him made him look over his shoulder. Some vast violence was tearing into the trees on the eastern side of the glade; sturdy oak trunks were severed, lopped boughs sailed through a storm of leaves. The devil was flying east.

As the forest tempest receded into the east he noticed, out of the corner of his eye, a green luminosity emanating from the eastward-gazing face of the monolith. He also saw the masked and mantled figures converging on the mouth-door at the base of the burial mound.

He wheeled round to the unnerving sight of the silver-masked shape on the slopes above. The grey mantle slithered and the long grey hair rustled as the tall figure started its descent, the strap of the leather pack gripped firmly in its gauntleted hand.

Hua Shan trembled, every muscle in his bulky physique urging him to run, and keep running, but how could he leave the precious message to Chia, marked with Teacher Sung's seal, in the hand of this uncanny stranger? He winced at the smell seeping from the grey woollen folds – it reminded him of rancid pork and sour milk. And as for the silver mask, its details clearer with each descending step, it made his heart dither like an erratic drum.

The beaten silver visage bore a close resemblance to the stone faces on the monolith. A moon, an owl, a toad – all and none of these – it approached him from the dark, a perplexing union of the bestial and geometric with a luminous green sign glowing from the brow. Gazing into the bewildering patterns in the silver face, Hua Shan felt that the mask would scramble his wits if he stared at it too long.

And he wondered what sort of face would wear such a mask.

The tall figure in grey halted less than a pace away.

A penetrating whisper blew from the rounded orifice of the metal mouth. 'Who are you?'

The whisper was as paradoxical as the mask. It was louder than a shout. Eager not to antagonize the stranger, he stammered a passably coherent response.

'I'm – a hermit of the T'ao. From Melodious Temple in Silver Music Bay. I'm searching' – the echoes of the whisper wrung the truth out of him – 'for Chia Black Dragon.'

'You seek our enemy,' whispered the mask. 'Seek no longer. Join us.'

The imperative forced him to turn and confront the round, green-glowing face on the east side of the monolith. He meant to say no to the green moon face surveying the eastern stretch of forest. His lips struggled to say no to the green moon.

'Fly to the moon,' whispered a voice at his back. 'Share the loving flesh. Give up your face.'

Hua Shan sighed a docile 'Yes.'

His avid soul flew out into the night.

And he tumbled, head over heels, into a bright green moon.


Deep under the Five Faces burial mound, wall torches were relit in the domed vault.

Flame by flame, the torches threw ruddy glances across the dank chamber.

In reverential silence the Silver Brethren congregated in a wide circle around the stone sarcophagus of their shattered Master, the dance of torchlight shimmering on their silver masks.

A Silver Brother with a red sign on his metal brow signalled twelve of the Brethren to gather the scattered remains of the Master. The twelve laid devotional hands on the devasted flesh and spilt blood.

They carried the moist remains to an ornate silver coffin placed nearby, and positioned the bones, organs and skin in a crude approximation of human form. Then, in silver bowls, they scooped up what blood was left in the sarcophagus and poured it over the collected remnants of the Master.

As a final act, the silver mask was lowered on to the cracked shell of the Master's head.

A Silver Brother with a luminous green sign on his brow stepped up to the head of the coffin, bowed devoutly to the clumped relics, then whispered a single word:

'Resurrection.'


'*I live,*' exulted the Wind Flesh, blasting east through the Forest of the Ancestors.

'*I live.*'

The truth should have killed it, but now it lived with the truth. It lived. And it was stronger.

'*I am mortal, but I endure.*'

What drew it east, over shocked earth and topsy-turvy trees, was raw instinct; an instinct buried for perhaps thousands of years. It was drawn by obscure origins, by tenuous beginnings, by what might pass for Paradise.

It was summoned by the distant sea, and by a solitary tree on the shore. It was summoned by bells. A Tree of Bells.

'*I live.*'

The sea and the tree and the bells were a memory – and a promise. Paradise.

Paradise for the Wind Flesh.

Hell for Chia.

Year 166 of the House of Eastern
Han: 191AD
Also known as the Year of
Resurrection

Witness, by the Great Sea
All the white bones long forsaken on the shore.
Hear, in the lament of a stormcloud day,
The new dead singing in chorus with the old.

Tu Fu: *Ping ch'e hsing*

A briny conch, the size of a skull, spun on the pine floorboards.

A booted foot recoiled from its accidental striking of the bleached seashell.

A final spin and the conch rattled to rest against the torso of a wicker and straw cage the size and shape of a child.

The creak of new leather and the croak of old wood drew a wince from the intruder as his booted feet retreated a couple of paces over the uneven floorboards. For a dozen deep breaths he kept his gaze fixed on the seashell and the wicker effigy, half fearing that the open mouth of the conch might whisper to him once more.

When the thump-thump in Ming-kai's chest subsided he gave vent to a low sigh, exhaling a little fear.

'I must have imagined it,' he murmured. 'Must have. It couldn't have spoken. Couldn't have.'

Ming-kai's burly shoulders, still strained from carrying his unlucky burden so far, relaxed an inch or two as his foot slid almost a pace towards the wicker cage. Imagination, he told himself as he took another tentative step. Just imagination.

He stood over the prone wicker figure, gradually

marshalling his scattered wits as he quietly recited a passage from the *T'ao te ching*:

Hiding himself, he is seen everywhere.
Being many, he is one.
Foreseeing no success, he succeeds.
Contending against none, none under heaven can stand against him.

They were the words of Lao Tzu, revered founder of T'aoism, and should have fortified the spirit of a T'aoist hermit such as Ming-kai. They were words hallowed by centuries of use since Lao Tzu penned them as he sat before the Jade Gate to the West. They were words to the spirit within.

But Ming-kai's spirit was diminished to a feeble flame in this quiet, one-roomed house with its silent occupants. He tried not to look at the far wall. Tried not to think of the blind judgment of all the blank eyes. And – his vision alighted for a moment on the conch – he told himself to forget the name he had heard. *That* name, of all names.

'No' he exhaled harshly. 'I couldn't have heard her name. Imagination.'

He transferred his attention to the figure at his feet, a wicker and straw shape that concealed its relic of mortality. Inside the hollow wicker doll was fitted the headless body of a small girl, her flaccid arms and legs filling the rigid limbs of the effigy as snugly as the corpse of a Chinese princess in her green jade burial suit.

Ming-kai had discovered the girl's remains on the beach near Forest Bell Village at the northern end of Silver Music Bay. A large conch lay close to the beheaded corpse, as if nature had chosen to supply what the hand of man had removed. Nobody in the village knew of her. Nobody cared. Silver Music Bay had its own way with the dead, and outsiders were excluded from its singular ways, in life or death. So the unknown girl was forbidden a place in the Ancestral Gallery. Such was the custom, the propriety.

18

But Ming-kai didn't care about custom and propriety. He hadn't spared the silent villagers a backward glance as he headed south along Silver Music Bay to the makeshift houses of the Ancestral Gallery, the wicker corpse-suit strapped firmly to his shoulders. The corpse had been a light burden then – fourteen li and several hours ago – but by the end of the journey it felt like a granite statue bumping his bent spine. But he would have travelled twice the distance if necessary; all the way to his room in Melodious Temple at the bay's southern edge.

He shrugged off his long, dark green cloak and knelt beside the encased corpse. His wide face, heavy with the weight of forty years, kneaded from the mauling of thirteen years of war, betrayed nothing of the anger and sorrow that raged inside.

'How old were you?' he asked softly as he lifted the small form. 'Five? Six?' His long, matted hair swayed as he shook his bowed head. 'No more than six.'

Anger. Sorrow. At first more anger than sorrow. Now more sorrow than anger.

Anger when he'd first stumbled on her, at daybreak by the sea. Wherever her head was now – under the waves, or mounted like a hunting trophy in some locked room – anger, raw anger at the wielder of the axe.

But now, sorrow. This day was declining like a habitual regret outside the open window. Time was on its downward slope. And he held a small, lost life between his scarred hands. Anger at dawn. Sorrow at dusk.

And memory. His daughter had been about the same age as this girl when the woman called Chia Black Dragon had –

'Ah,' he sighed, gazing thirteen years into the distance. 'My poor daughter – my poor wife.'

For a stark moment he saw their eviscerated bodies. Saw their red lives splashed all over the walls.

Then he blinked the red memory to the back of his eyes and resumed his duty to the beheaded girl.

19

*Would have been about my daughter's age.*

A square of mellow light framed the shoulders and neck stump of the wicker and straw figure as Ming-kai propped the corpse in front of the window. He could still feel the blind eyes at his back, but he couldn't face them, not yet. Not until the task was done. No need to tempt fear. Fear – lightfoot fear – was all too easily summoned in this hushed room.

The girl was nameless: she must be given a name. She was headless – he suppressed an urge to glance at the conch behind him – she must be given a head. According to the mythologies of heaven and hell, those who went nameless into death would find no refuge with the ancestors, no haven in the Blue Palaces of the August of Jade. And those whose heads were taken in life were condemned to a headless afterlife. It was common practice for relatives of a beheaded criminal to bribe the executioner to sew the head back on after the fall of the axe. As in life, so in death: such was the belief. And Ming-kai accepted that the belief might, just might, be true.

He'd been given a name for the girl. The head – or what he thought of as the head – had given him a name before it fell from his shocked fingers and spun on the floor. But it was a name he hated more than any in all of wide China.

And, surely, fear must have tricked his hearing. Fear of what he'd seen back in the village and in the mansion that overlooked it. Fear of the Ancestral Gallery. Surely he hadn't actually heard that name?

'Imagination. Must have been imagination,' he snorted, straightening his back.

He turned and faced the silent occupants of the tiny house where they were lined up along the far wall.

The dead stood rigid against the pinewood wall, smiling their painted smiles, staring their blind stare. Like puppets hung up between performances, the dead, in their wicker body-cages, hung from rusty hooks in the

20

wall. Tattered robes of green and blue silk mantled their awkward outlines. Wide, conical hats crowned the wooden masks which served as faces for the skulls beneath. Inlaid eyes of malachite and lapis lazuli kept a stony blue and green gaze fixed on the sea beyond the window. Smiles had been painted in dark blue on the mask faces, and between the dark blue lips were seashell slivers for teeth. The smiles were meant for joy, the green and blue eyes intended for ocean visions. But, to Ming-kai, the dead dangled in a row like life's cast-offs, gathering dust and exuding a musty smell.

For centuries the dead had been installed in small, imitation houses, facing the sea and the rising sun with green and blue eyes imbued with the power of the ocean, awaiting the summons of Tung Wang Kung, god of the Eastern Paradise of Mount P'eng-lai. Paradise. Immortality. Beguiling prospects. But now – here in the ramshackle house with its fusty odour of dangling cadavers – Ming-kai found it easier to believe in sad ghosts rather than radiant spirits. The dead looked like decrepit dolls, unlikely candidates for paradisiacal splendour.

Unlikely or not, Ming-kai owed the beheaded girl a chance of gaining paradise. A slim chance was better than none. He cleared his nervous throat and addressed the row of pendant corpses.

'Last in the line of the family Tsin, having no more descendants to carry on your name, and having space in this third resting house of your illustrious name, accept, I beg you, this orphan into your family so that she may bear your name in the after-life. Accept this girl under your roof, and welcome her into the afterworld.'

It might have been an illusion, but he thought he perceived a slight rustle and stir amongst the bundled members of the family Tsin.

Muffling his resurgent unease, Ming-kai busied his hands with the duty he had set himself. He extracted a wooden mask from his leather pack, its surface inlaid

21

with lapis lazuli eyes and seashell teeth; reached for the briny conch –

– and stayed his hand. He couldn't touch the huge shell – not yet. The mask could be bound on to the conch later. He would have recovered from that first shock then. Yes, later.

Drawing a green silk mantle from the roomy interior of the pack, he fixed it round the tiny wicker figure. The body was pathetically small in the voluminous folds of the mantle, and the silken hem trailed over the floorboards as he slotted the body-cage on to one of the two hooks under the window. From this vantage point, the girl, if she had eyes, could view not only the multitude of islands crowding the sea from north to south, but also the Tree of Bells on Sea Rock near Forest Bell Village, and – Ming-kai's gaze veered from the northern end of the bay to the southern fringe – the flamboyant profile of Melodious Temple, some sixteen or so li distant. He had instated her where she could see, with spirit vision, the temple that served as his home, from her window in the resting house of the family Tsin. Deprived of a station in life, he had given her a station in death.

Only one task was left to finish. He must fix the mask to the conch and bind the conch to her neck stump. The lapis lazuli eyes would gaze east, to mythical P'eng-lai. He would give the girl a sea head to look over the sea.

As he crossed to the conch, he had to force his reluctant fingers to touch the salt-encrusted surface. Childish, he admonished his trembling hand. Childish fear. Why be frightened of a seashell? What he thought had happened earlier was the product of overwrought imagination. Imagination. That was all.

The shell didn't burn his hand or freeze it as he picked it up. It didn't shriek or turn into an incandescent astonishment. It was just a shell, like the ones he used to play with as a child. A few minutes ago he had held it to his ear, listening to the echoes within, seeking inspiration for naming the girl. Then he'd heard, or *thought* he'd heard, a sound flow from the conch. It had filled his head with fear.

It would be a kind of exorcism to repeat the exercise. Why let an infantile fear get the better of him?

He glanced for an instant at the spiny ridges running back from the wide mouth of the conch, then peered into the opalescent aperture. His brows knitted as he thought he glimpsed a flash of silver from deep within the seashell. He stared for some time, but the silver flicker wasn't repeated. Finally he drew a deep breath, telling himself not to be fear's fool.

Then he cupped the shell to his ear.

Counting ten breaths as he listened to the whorled interior of the conch, he heard nothing but the familiar sigh that resembled the sough of the sea. A small smile tweaked the corners of his heavy lips. Nothing to fear. Just a sigh.

Then a whisper grew out of the sigh, as if born of the sea. It had a remote note, cold, pristine and inhuman. It streamed into Ming-kai's ear and echoed a name inside his skull.

'CHHHIIIAAA . . .'

The conch dropped from his nerveless fingers.

'Chia,' Ming-kai mouthed, that hated name sharp as brine on his lips. That hated name. That evil woman.

'CHHHIIIAAA . . .' whispered the shell as it struck the floor.

'CHHHIIIAAA . . .'

The briny conch, the size of a skull, spun on the pine floorboards.


Almond eyes watched the fleeing figure of Ming-kai. A young mouth curved into a crescent smile.

The smiling youth gathered his colourful silk robe tight to his tall, willowy body and leaned against the creaking wall of funeral house Su.

'Ah yes,' he exhaled softly, peering down the Ancestral Gallery from under the curled brim of his conical hat. 'It's amazing what a little word in your ear will do.'

Then his smile acquired a wistful slant as he glanced at the girl who kept him company. 'It was just a word from the moon, my sweet – the silver-tongued moon. Ming-kai really shouldn't go picking up other people's conches and sticking them on the bodies of perfect strangers. He totally ruined my little joke, didn't he, dear heart?'

The youth heaved a sigh and glided from the wall as he resumed his stalking of the Melodious Temple hermit. 'The joke's on you now, Ming-kai.'

He flicked a glance northwards to where the Tree of Bells was hidden in distance and the rumpled folds of Sea Rock promontory. 'Play a song for me,' he commanded in a whisper. 'A merry tune for me – and a funeral dirge for Ming-kai.'

With the passing of a few seconds the youth caught the first silver tones from the bells on the distant willow tree. They blew past him on the breeze, their percussion swiftly mounting in strength.

'Ah,' he breathed gently. 'Ah yes. A suitable accompaniment for my little joke.'

He winked at the girl who travelled with him. 'Ming-kai shouldn't have stuck his nose into my affairs, should he, peach blossom? After all, they're *family* affairs. And as for strolling into my house uninvited – well, he really was asking for the worst.'

The stalker's long, effortless strides soon took him within a hundred paces of the apprehensive Ming-kai, whom he knew was utterly unaware his steps were being tracked, pace for pace. He was the Holy Man, and no one saw or heard the Holy Man unless he wished to be seen and heard. 'Here comes the worst, plodding hermit. Here it comes – lightfoot as a cat.'

The Holy Man unfurled his left hand. Nails sharp as needles started to sprout from the tips of the long fingers.

His right hand retained a firm grasp of the little girl's

24

braided hair. He hummed a song to himself as he twirled the girl's lopped head like a ball on a cord.

'Here comes the worst.'

He tried to keep from running.

When you ran you invited pursuit, be it from dog or nightmare.

Just walk. Keep walking.

The distant music of the Tree of Bells that followed his steps seemed to strike responsive notes from the metal talismans dangling from the doors, windows and eaves of the little houses flanking his path.

Ming-kai threaded his way along the Ancestral Gallery in the fading light, ducking occasionally as a vine trailed from the cliff edge some ten or twelve feet overhead. The forest that crowned the cliff was thick at this point and cast the gallery houses into deep shadow. At times, he had to tread carefully where the boards of the walkway were rotted or absent. Between the gaps in the boards he intermittently glimpsed the scree of the upper beach some three hundred feet below. Plenty of time for a long scream if you missed your footing. Concentrating on that danger was an almost welcome relief from the long line of little houses.

He had covered four li since he'd run out of House Tsin and almost toppled over the railing of the Ancestral Gallery. Before his hasty exit he had forced his shaky fingers to tie the mask to the conch and fix the masked shell to the girl's neck stump. He had performed his duty, and, duty performed, he couldn't get out of House Tsin fast enough.

And now he couldn't wait to reach the central stair and descend from this lofty lane of funeral houses. The dead were bad company.

Also – he couldn't resist another glance over his shoulder – he couldn't shake off the uneasy feeling that he was being followed. But, as with previous backward looks, the wooden lane was empty behind him.

25

Another two li, and he would leave these tiny, winged-roofed dwellings behind. Just two more li, and the galleries, terraces and balconies of the Ancestral Gallery would be at his back.

Ming-kai would have sacrificed a week's supply of wine to be free of this long, narrow street of the dead perched high above the sea. His toes itched to feel the sand and scree of the beach under his feet again.

It was easy, in this dimming light, to imagine a masked head leaning in your direction as you passed its window. Easy to imagine a door creaking open in invitation . . .

'Imagination,' he snapped. 'Get a hold of yourself.'

But it was the Ancestral Gallery that had a hold of his imagination. To the front and back of him were three thousand seashell smiles in the windows of four hundred imitation houses. And the omnipresent tingling of the Tree of Bells seemed to strike a faint resonance in the funeral lane. Bells to make the quiet dead a little less quiet.

Panic started to thrum in his chest.

*Outnumbered by the dead, three thousand to one.*

Sweat beading his forehead, he sought escape from the onset of panic. And almost immediately an avenue of escape opened wide and true, invoked by a talismanic word:

'Chia.'

That name, flooding from the conch in House Tsin, had chilled his heart, but now it warmed him with the glow of hate.

'Chia.'

The hate helped him ignore the eerie spell of the shabby houses with their gaudy wall paintings and bell-hung eaves. The hate was exorcism; he indulged it to the full.

Chia. Chia Black Dragon.

Chia the Vampire. Chia the Damned.

Ageless Chia, whose crimes ranged down through the

26

centuries: treason, mass murder, sexual depravity, torture. All men (and women) who met her were so smitten with her beauty that they couldn't believe it hid such evil. Beauty blinded. And her beauty-blinded devotees were always eager to give Chia the benefit of the doubt. They pleaded her case. They made excuses.

Teacher Sung, the head of Melodious Temple, had met Chia long ago and been blinded by adoration. Two and a half years ago Sung had persuaded Hua Shan – Ming-kai's old comrade-in-arms – to search for Black Dragon Mountain in the far northwest of China and induce Chia to come and save Silver Music Bay's inhabitants from the strange cult that was enslaving their minds.

Hua Shan had set out on his mission with eager eyes, assuring everyone that he would be back within four months.

Nothing was heard of Hua Shan for nine months.

In the end it was Ming-kai who tracked down his missing friend. He found him a thousand li inland, in a village that fringed the Forest of the Ancestors south of Celestial Buddha Temple. The villagers had tended Hua Shan for months, regarding him as a holy man.

The villagers regarded all madmen as holy men.

And the Wind Forest Man, as the village folk called Hua Shan, was especially blessed. He had stumbled out of the Forest of the Ancestors in the dawn succeeding a prodigious gale. Some villagers even believed that Hua Shan had created the awesome hurricane, wielding the power of Fu Hsi, god-emperor of wood and wind.

All Ming-kai could see when he laid eyes on his one-time comrade was human wreckage.

Hua Shan, once a brave warrior of the Yellow Headband army in the wars against the Imperial battalions, had degenerated into a shrivelled husk with the vacant eyes of the senile and the dribbling mouth of an infant. It was as if the forest had stolen his soul.

Ming-kai might still have blamed the ill-famed Forest

27

of the Ancestors for Hua Shan's spiritual destruction if he hadn't ridden to Celestial Buddha Temple to purchase a wagon to carry his friend on the long journey back to Melodious Temple.

Celestial Buddha Temple was locked and barred and surrounded by armed guards. And its tall walls were plastered with Wanted posters of Chia Black Dragon.

The temple, a guard had informed him, was deserted, its community of Indian Buddhist monks having fled north after the twelfth night of the fourth moon. Chia had been in the temple that night. Witnesses reported that she had cut the abbot's throat with her silver dagger. That was before she unleashed a living nightmare inside the monastic walls – a nightmare that didn't die with daylight, a nightmare that might never die, but only be contained, trapped inside the temple walls. The nightmare had been given a name in the following months: the Shadow of Chia.

With each disclosure from the guard, Ming-kai became more certain that Chia – the Woman in Black – was responsible for Hua Shan's devastation. A spirit-wind had soared out of Celestial Buddha Temple on the night that Chia had cursed its hitherto sacred precincts. The gale had torn a path through the Forest of the Ancestors, beneath whose trees Hua Shan was making his way – easy prey for the wind born from the Shadow of Chia.

When Ming-kai rode back to the village he gained further proof of Chia's guilt. He was told that Hua Shan had muttered a few coherent words when he first staggered out of the forest. After that, he had lapsed into unbroken silence. But those few words, recounted by the head of the village, told Ming-kai a great deal. Hua Shan had spoken of a 'wind devil', saying also that 'the devil had green eyes'. There were other, more puzzling phrases about a green moon and silver faces. But the wind devil with green eyes could only apply to Chia. Chia had launched a spirit gale on to the forest. And Chia, uniquely among Chinese women, had green eyes.

Beautiful green eyes, it was said by those who beheld them.

Devil's eyes.

Some of their green had been borne on the wind, and blown Hua Shan's wits away.

Safe now back in Melodious Temple, Ming-kai's old friend was still a witless shell. After a few months he had begun to speak, but only to repeat the same three phrases over and over: 'Mountains of the moon . . . plains of the moon . . . valleys of the moon . . .'

All the hermits in Melodious Temple had long since given up trying to derive any significance from the repetitious chant. Hua Shan was a lost soul. He was the last entry in Ming-kai's personal list of Chia's victims.

The first two names were Ming-kai's wife and daughter, murdered thirteen years ago.

He hadn't witnessed the act, but others had. Reliable witnesses. Witnesses who had seen Chia wielding her infamous silver dagger.

And after the slaying she had nailed her victims' viscera to the walls of their house.

Undying Chia, the plague of China since the daybreak of the Dragon Empire's history.

'I wish that bitch was interred in one of these little house replicas,' he growled softly, his eyes roving the worm-eaten masks that bared splintered grins to the passer-by, 'her innards ripped out by my knife and her corpse hung up like a doll in a doll's house.'

A frown furrowed his broad forehead. If Chia was hung up on the Ancestral Gallery she might come back to life . . . Anything was possible on this strange shore-line. Even in the provinces far to the south, beyond the Yangtze Valley, this curve of coast was known as 'Ghost Bay'.

'Ghost Bay,' he mouthed softly, his mind returning to the village twenty li at his back.

He bit back a yell as a dank vine brushed his face, its ragged length looping over the winged eaves of a tiny pinewood house, its crooked walls festooned with bronze talismans. An instinctive flick of the hand swept the vine aside but also dislodged an array of dangling talismans.

The pendant charms fell in a bunch and slipped through a gap in the gallery's boards. Ringing a raucous alarm as they tumbled down the cliff face, their din echoed in his skull as he glanced nervously up and down the Ancestral Gallery.

When the talismans met sand their tuneless music ceased.

But the Tree of Bells played on, its distant peals carried on the breeze.

And the multitudinous hanging metals of the Ancestral Gallery resonated with that remote jangle. Even the vast crescent of trees overlooking the bay bounced back the silver chimes as though the boughs had metallic leaves.

A man would be forgiven for thinking that the whole bay was conspiring against him in the speech of bells.

Step for step, the Holy Man kept pace with his prey.

He was in no hurry to slice into Ming-kai with his long needle-nails. Let the clumsy oaf shamble on for a while in his evident fear of the dead. Let the fool sweat.

The tall youth slanted a smile at the girl's head, which he swung by the hair. 'The temple clod certainly spoilt our little joke, didn't he, peach blossom? A shell as a head for your body, and your head on a body of shells. A little family joke. A joke on Chia.' He flicked a petulant look at Ming-kai, some forty paces ahead. 'Not much of a joke now, is it, my sweet?' He flexed his inches-long needle-nails. 'The hermit deserves an imaginative punishment for spoiling my game. And I have *such* imagination, don't I, darling?' He raised the girl's head and kissed the slack lips. 'You know the heights and depths of my imagination, don't you? Ah yes. How you squealed!'

He kissed the lips again. 'Nothing personal,' he said.

'Your mother aided Chia Black Dragon once, and that is quite definitely not allowed. Mother and daughter were both made to pay for that – ah – indiscretion. Unfair on you, perhaps, but' – his voice sank to a confidential whisper – 'I have a friend – an intimate friend – who's most put out if anyone gets close to Chia.' He winked at the dead eyes. 'You know, I think my friend is jealous.'

His gaze slid from the waxen face to the sweep of the bay. 'Mind you,' he remarked, 'I'm jealous too. Jealous of my bay. My domain. Aklo's kingdom. It's the most sacred spot in the big, big world.'

The youth called Aklo threw a look at the trees hanging overhead. 'And when fish swim in the forest, the big, big, world will learn just how sacred this spot is.'

Aklo's eyes angled back to the bay. Memory flooded his gaze. A faint tremor parted his lips as he mouthed the ancient name for Silver Music Bay:

'The Wound.'

Emerging from his reverie, the youth fixed his stare on the hermit. Aklo's smile went a crooked path. He was ready to let loose his needle-nails on Ming-kai. He owed the man a double dose of terminal pain. Not only had the hermit spoiled his game, but worse, he had invaded Aklo's privacy.

Last night Ming-kai had stridden across Aklo's threshold and blundered about the halls and stairways of the House of Heaven. Aklo had taken strong exception to the trespass.

The House of Heaven wasn't open to visitors.

Aklo would have obliterated the intruder there and then if he hadn't been vaguely amused by the man who plodded around inside the most haunted house in China. Instead of letting the old mansion have its way, Aklo had held back the power of the house, satisfying himself with giving the clumsy fool a couple of mild scares.

'But you don't amuse me any more,' the youth muttered. He swung the girl's head by its hair. 'Let's do some inventive killing, shall we, darling?'

31

The dead head shook on its braids, as if conveying disagreement.

'We demur?' he queried, arching a painted eyebrow.

Then a grin split his handsome features. 'Ah yes, yes. A game! A game! That's what you want, isn't it, little peach?' He jerked his elbow so that the head bobbed its agreement. 'How clever you are, dear head. A game. We'll play a game for Ming-kai's life. I know just the thing . . .'

Aklo tossed the girl's head high in the air. 'Heads face upwards – he lives,' chuckled the youth. 'Heads any other way – goodbye Ming-kai.'

He knew perfectly well that the human head wasn't constructed to land face upwards. It always tilted left or right.

Goodbye Ming-kai.

The head thudded on the planks.

It rolled to Aklo's feet.


The incessant chimes of the Tree of Bells resounded in Ming-kai's skull. The silvery tones were fragile but penetrating, playing havoc with his nerves. Even his heart seemed to beat out of tempo.

'Two years,' he whispered, treading gingerly over a gap in the boards. 'Two years of a singing tree, setting the bay on edge.'

Two years ago – the twelfth night of the fourth moon. That was when the convoluted willow known as the Tree of Bells first sang in earnest. The moon had been green that night, and huge – a green head peering closely at the earth. And a thunder-wind had roared out of the west and shaken hell out of the eerie willow on Sea Rock promontory.

The Tree of Bells had often rung its silver-laden boughs since then, regardless of wind or breeze. And, nine times out of ten, the willow's carillons preluded a thunder-wind that blasted up and down the bay.

The twelfth night of the fourth moon, two years ago.

That was the start of the uneasy time called the 'bad music' by the hermits of Melodious Temple. The villagers had another name for it: 'the time of the green moon'.

Twelfth night of the fourth moon: something had invaded the bay that night. And after two years' slumber the invader on the wild wind seemed to be awakening.

And on waking, perhaps it was making its dreams come true.

He shivered at the memory of his arrival in Forest Bell Village. Was it only yesterday morning? Most of the villagers had been standing in the narrow lanes of the tiered village. It was raining heavily, and they were drenched. But they just stood in the downpour, un-speaking, unmoving. And all wearing garments of green that clung wetly to sharp ribs and stick arms.

When the rain finally stopped, they went indoors.

The regimentation of the villagers was reflected in their homes, as though the houses had adopted the uniformity of their owners.

Forest Bell Village had always had the look of the barracks about it: near-identical houses all in straight rows. But now the houses shared a single mood, the villagers' faces a single identity.

'Full Pearl,' Ming-kai murmured as his eyes moved from the winding Ancestral Gallery to the dimming eastern sky behind the serrated outlines of the Ten Thousand Islands. The half-moon was an uncertain presence above the rounded peak of Fragrant Orchid Island.

He shook his head, then glanced at a nearby window. The grinning burial mask had two green eyes of malachite, blindly fixed on sea and moon.

Ming-kai's mind jumped back to yesterday morn-ing . . .

. . . The majority of the villagers stood out in the rain. One of the few indoors was Chien-long, an old sailor and long-standing friend of Ming-kai.

Chien-long's eyes constantly streamed with tears – tears that spilled from green eyes.

'The sea came into my eyes,' the wrinkled sailor sighed. 'My eyes turned green a month ago. You can't stop crying when the sea's in your eyes. It's the brine, you see – it burns so. Every day and every night, eyes of fire and water. I'm being punished. Justly punished. The Holy Man said so.'

Ming-kai had looked into the flooded green eyes – and yes, the sea looked back at him. But behind the swirling green, he thought he glimpsed a hint of silvery light that disturbed him more than even the miraculous green of the sailor's stare. That cold light behind the sea-eyes reminded him of something he couldn't quite place.

'I was punished for rejecting the Holy Man's new religion,' Chien-long muttered. 'But everything's all right. My suffering will save me. The Holy Man told me so . . .'

. . . The ominous crack of a board under his foot snapped Ming-kai back to the present. He hurriedly stepped over the splintered timber and, for a time, watched his step.

A hundred paces on he passed a window in which two of the dead had tilted on their perches, masked heads touching. And an image sprang from the back of his skull to the front of his eyes . . .

. . . His boots had splashed through the puddles of the village, his shoulders warmed a little by the afternoon sun. He had glanced into an open door. What he saw inside rooted him to the door's threshold for uncounted beats of the heart.

Two dead infants, a boy and a girl, lay on the floor, fused together at the crown of their heads. He recognized the infants. They came from two separate mothers.

The two mothers, smiling happily, set about encasing the linked infants in a bifurcate burial cage of wicker and straw. 'It's a natural union,' crooned one. 'My little boy with your little girl.'

34

'Yes,' smiled the other mother. 'They'll be joined forever in Mount P'eng-lai's paradise. The Holy Man said so.'

The two women appeared utterly unaware of Ming-kai's existence. He wanted to scream at them: 'Why has this happened? *How* has this happened?'

But the women wouldn't have heard him. They were in another world – lost in a terrible bliss.

The dark miracle of the linked infants stirred an insight within him. There was little logic behind it, but there was intuitive conviction:

'Something has woken in this bay,' he heard himself breathe. 'And it's making its dreams come true. Flesh dreams. Fused heads.'

Exhaling a dreamy content, the two mothers looked up from their funeral preparations. And behind their eyes he discerned the same remote, silvery light he'd seen behind Chien-long's sea gaze.

'Full Pearl,' exhaled the boy's mother. 'The Holy Man's blessed our little ones with Full Pearl.'

'Ah,' sighed the girl's mother. 'All honour be upon the Holy Man's head. All honour be upon the head of holy Aklo.'

Head whirling with grief, rage, disgust, Ming-kai lurched away from the door and stormed towards the central stair that led to the upper tiers of the village. Above the upper lane of houses, beyond the willow woods, was the dark, four-storey mansion where Aklo the Holy Man was said to live. The House of Heaven. The Old House. Despite Aklo's supposed residence in the House of Heaven, it was said that no mortal had ever lived, or died, there.

But then, there was some ground for the belief that Aklo, the founder of the new religion he called the way of Full Pearl, was someone either more or less than mortal. If he was to be found, the most likely course was to search the House of Heaven.

'Full Pearl,' Ming-kai had intoned softly as he neared

the huge mansion that reared against the cliff high above Forest Bell Village. 'It was behind the sailor's eyes, behind the mothers' eyes. A cold, distant light.'

A moment before entering the willow woods that enwrapped the grim House of Heaven, he turned and stared at the half moon rising in the fading east. Half-moon. Halfway to Full Moon. Halfway to Full Pearl.

A remote, silvery shine . . .

. . . Ming-kai slanted his gaze from the touching mask heads in the death house and cast a swift look over the Ancestral Gallery's rickety railing to the sliced moon above Fragrant Orchid Island.

Teacher Sung had asked him to report on Forest Bell Village. But what was he to report? That the village was haunted by – moonlight?

Last night he had sought answers in the House of Heaven. He had sought the eerie youth known as Aklo, the Holy Man of the Way of Full Pearl . . .

. . . Somehow, Ming-kai had endured a full night in that dour house with its bare rooms and restless dust.

Some time after midnight he thought he'd glimpsed the swirl of Aklo's Rainbow Robe flitting like a butterfly through a shudder of candlelight at the end of a long corridor. That was the only sign of Aklo all night. Ming-kai seemed to be alone in the old house.

Alone, that is, except for the voices that you could never quite catch, the footfalls that you could never quite hear. And the overwhelming sense of a bad soul in the very timbers of the house. A bad soul that was old past counting.

Even the air that lay on room and stair was heavy with age. Thick with the centuries, it was hard to breathe. That weight of antiquity shrivelled the intruder into a small, creeping thing.

As time wore on, the halls and chambers began to play tricks on his mind. He started to imagine that the house had a secret face, a face it kept hidden from his prying eyes.

36

What frightened him most was the thought that the house might show its face. As a child, Ming-kai had dreamed of a figure with a cloaked face, and he had known, with the clarity of fear, that if that face was uncloaked the mere sight of it would damn him in spirit and flesh. There was something about the House of Heaven that reminded him of that cloaked face of childhood nightmare.

Ming-kai, veteran of the wars against the imperial Han armies, had never considered himself a coward until last night. An hour or so before dawn he panicked at the thought of the hidden face. He tried to escape the Old House. He fled down passages that led to passages and still more passages. Rooms opened to rooms that opened to more rooms, like unfolding boxes.

The longer he ran the more he felt that a face was peering over his shoulder. He began to think of the mansion as a huge head in which he was trapped. A head that wouldn't open its mouth to let him out. And he wanted to get out before the head showed its face.

It was during that frenzied flight that illusions dazzled his eyes. The old timbers seemed to radiate moonlight. Bright pictures jumped on to the walls for a brief spirit carnival. Then moonlight-of-wood glowed once more, like silver phantoms.

He tripped and slammed his head on the floorboards. The blow shook fear's delusions from his brain. When he regained his feet his surroundings were free of wild colours and impossible moonlight. All he was faced with was an angled interior of dark wood and age, age, and more age.

When he finally caught his breath he resumed his stealthy search for Aklo. As he climbed steps, traversed corridors and halls, the dark of the wood and the air slowly seeped into his skin, filtered into his soul. He almost believed that his flesh and spirit were merging into ghostly substance. In the end, he wondered whether the house was haunting him or he was haunting the house.

37

And he learned what a few other foolhardy trespassers had learned of the essential terror of the ancient mansion. The edifice posed the simplest of threats. The house wanted you to become the house.

But he forced himself to continue exploring the innumerable rooms until the first hint of dawn blinked through a window.

He leaned against a wall, rubbed his raw eyes, then slanted his gaze up a steep flight of stairs.

It was then that he saw, at the top of the stairs, a tall, black-garbed woman with green eyes glowing in the dark.

He had never set sight on her before, but only one woman in the whole of China looked like the figure on the stairs. Chia Black Dragon, murderer of his family.

Chia's image disappeared before he could draw his knife, and he was left with the frustration of empty air.

After a long, fruitless search for the Woman in Black through the halls and chambers of the old house he had finally admitted defeat. Chia wasn't in the House of Heaven. He could explore for years and never find her there.

But at least he'd discovered something. The image of Chia lived in the memory of the house.

There had to be a link between Chia and the House of Heaven, however tenuous. Somewhere, there had to be a link . . .

. . . Ming-kai peered at the flamboyant profile of Melodious Temple some ten li to the south. Teacher Sung would be waiting there, in his room on top of East Tower, for Ming-kai's report on Forest Bell Village.

Let him wait. News of the village and Old House would only prompt Teacher Sung to send more men in search of Chia's supposed aid. Silver Music Bay had troubles enough without Chia. True, Ming-kai yearned to separate her head from her body, but that was a task he'd perform in his own time. He'd deal with the threat here first, then seek out Chia and send her back to the hell she came from.

38

As for Teacher Sung, he'd be told that nothing was wrong in the village. Nothing more than usual. Sung had met Chia almost thirty years ago and had fallen in love with the ageless sorceress. Any excuse to send for Chia – no, the teacher just couldn't be trusted.

'Beauty blinds,' Ming-kai hissed softly. 'Beauty blinds.'

Again he tried to lose himself in his hatred of Chia to escape the blank-faced menace of the Ancestral Gallery and the fear-by-moonlight twenty li behind him.

But the hate began to falter in the face of the unrelenting procession of stone eyes and seashell smiles. The omnipresent chimes dinned out his warm anger. He glanced up at the long crest of branches overhanging the cliff. There was no escape in the forest. Even in the trees, the sound of silver bells.

'Enough to wake the dead,' he snapped, then tried and failed to smile at his remark.

He peered ahead, in the dying light, down the dismal lane of miniature houses strung along the upper reaches of the undulating cliff. Rigid faces watched from every window.

Although it was spring, the Ancestral Gallery, with its wistful, melancholy air, seemed trapped in a perennial autumn. The litter of decayed wood and broken tile was heaped round each flimsy house like clusters of autumnal red and gold leaves.

The breeze played a disconsolate tune on ridge, rafter and beam.

Somewhere at his back an open door tapped an erratic pulse.

The decayed, bumpy boards creaked under his feet.

He wanted to run, but he kept on walking.

The Holy Man sat and stared at the head in glum silence.

The head had thudded to the planks and rolled to his

39

feet – and become wedged in a gap in the Ancestral Gallery's rotted boards. Face upwards.

He'd been tempted for a while to break the rules of the game and kill the hermit anyway, but without rules there were no games, and Aklo loved his games. Besides, his friend – his intimate friend – cast a cold eye on the breaking of rules. His intimate friend was a very religious man.

At length, Aklo shrugged his shoulders. Never mind. Win or lose, what was one small game? In a few moons would come the great game – a game he and his intimate friend would win.

He stroked his cheek with the gossamer caress of his silk robe, his gaze idly following the rainbow patterns which interlaced a thousand embroidered scenes of spirit festivities.

Heaving a deep sigh, he got to his feet and swerved his eyes northward to the tip of Sea Rock promontory, from where the ancient willow played its silver music.

His thoughts roved back to the age when the bay was known as the Wound.

His eyes swam in dreams and memories.

'Born in the sea,' he murmured. 'Reborn in the sea.'

Then, softer still: 'They were wounds in nature.'

He felt the bells ring in his lithe body. Felt the attraction of like to like. Summoning chimes. His mouth stirred in response.

'It's time for my devotions.'

Aklo knelt in silence with slumped posture on Sea Rock promontory, the silk Robe of Rainbows draping his crouched shape, his back to the sea and the moon.

The Tree of Bells, an ancient willow, reached above him with slender trunk and shapely branches, graceful as a dancer in arrested pirouette.

Its song was sung. All was quiet.

Aklo knelt as he had knelt almost two years ago, on

that twelfth night of the fourth moon. And he remembered . . .

. . . It had come from the west, on that twelfth night, a
sudden west wind that shook the willow's silver fruit in
the tones of percussive heralds.

Almond eyes snapping open, Aklo jerked up his head
and shoulders as the black ink and milk-froth of a wave
reared behind him and crashed in an exuberance of foam
and spray on to the jutting ledge on which he knelt.

'Yes,' he sighed, lips curved in greeting to the
harbinger wind. 'Ah yes.'

He spread out his wide-sleeved arms as if to embrace
the entire bay, or the whole world. The host of delicate
bells on the willow tree played its jingle-jangle music
with mounting fervour as the west wind blew with
increasing vigour, carrying the scent of a remote forest
on its breath – the Forest of the Ancestors.

'Ah yes,' Aklo breathed. 'Yes.'

The scent of distant forest became the scent of Wind
Flesh, torn in five. A dangerous nonsense in the night.

Aklo flexed his long fingers, sinuously weaving the
needle-nails.

A whirling wind roared down like thunder on the
frantic Tree of Bells.

'He's coming,' Aklo had whispered, scratching the
wind with sharp nails. 'Ah yes. He's coming.' . . .

. . . 'Ah yes,' Aklo sighed, opening his eyes to the quiet
present. 'He came.'

The youth's dreamy vision skipped over the bumpy
length of Sea Rock, ascended the terraced rows of Forest
Bell Village, and came to rest on the House of Heaven.

'He's *here*. Ah yes. He's in the house. He never leaves
the house. Never. Ah no.'

Aklo hugged his graceful body, shapely as the willow
tree. He smiled wide at the secret he kept deep inside.

His eyes fondly traced the angular silhouette of the
wing-roofed mansion.

'He's in the house, but he's not in the house.'

41

Laughter tingled out of his mouth like fragile bells. 'Ghosts and moonlight,' he chuckled. 'Ghosts and moonlight.'

I went the way of wind and wave, drifting to
 nowhere,
A voyager on a forever voyage, and no way back.

Chiu chang: *Ai Ying*

Xanthippe pushed the last morsel of millet cake into
Hua Shan's slack mouth. He swallowed with a mechani-
cal action. His vacant eyes meandered over the Ten
Thousand Islands that receded to the sea's horizon, but
they didn't see the ocean or the islands.

Ming-kai, still tight-lipped since arriving back from
Forest Bell Village last night, had carried his old friend
down to the beach below Melodious Temple in the late
morning. But it had been left to Xanthippe to take care
of Hua Shan for the rest of the day. Nothing new in that.

'Mountains of the moon,' Hua Shan intoned for the
hundredth and more time.

Between Hua Shan's interminable chanting and the
unlovely music that flew down Silver Music Bay,
Xanthippe the Egyptian was ready to bite off her lower
lip.

The willow known as the Tree of Bells, out of sight at
the far northern end of the bay, made its presence felt in
discordant music, for the second time in as many days.
The strange tree, which seemed to play of its own accord,
had been sounding its bell tones for the best part of an
hour. And when the willow sang, Hua Shan invariably
commenced his chanting. There had been a period when
Xanthippe tried to puzzle out the link between bell-
music and chant. That time was long past.

Ever since that day over two years ago when Ming-kai had found Hua Shan lost and witless near the Forest of the Ancestors, the addled hermit had mumbled of the moon. Nor did he always require the Tree of Bells' prompting to launch into his incantation.

Xanthippe pressed the milky fur of her robe to the rich brown of her skin and walked a few paces up the beach. Her nerves were tangled from the remote jangling of the willow tree and, despite her compassion for poor Hua Shan, she needed a break from his lunar obsession. She peered up the cliff face to the clump of wing-roofed dwellings that sprouted from a huge ledge, some linked by corridors, others by rickety flights of stairs open to the sky's vagaries. The Melodious Temple of the Five Fragrant Peaks had the appearance of a warped fir tree, magnified to titan size.

The lower structures were the oldest – two hundred years, it was said – and the upper chambers and halls had been added in a haphazard fashion, culminating in the Teacher's tilted room perched atop the spindling edifice. The temple had not so much been constructed as grown over the years: it gave an impression of organic proliferation. And it looked as precarious as a tree with shallow roots. The uneven tiers of the temple proclaimed its insecurity. But that insecurity was embraced by the T'aoists as a basic ingredient in their philosophy. Teacher Sung never tired of remarking, with quiet satisfaction, that his room was the most unstable in the whole temple, crowning as it did an already unsteady mass of dwellings.

She glimpsed Teacher Sung's silhouette in the candle-lit square of his window, and lifted her arm in greeting. Sung's failure to respond was no surprise. His ailing eyesight, to which he would never admit, would reduce her to a mere blur – if that. And perhaps his insight was fading too.

As a child she had respected the Teacher almost as much as her father, but now she was nearing twenty she

44

saw Sung with clearer vision: an ineffectual leader of a community of self-styled hermits, brimming with regrets and prone to melancholy, seeking solace in rice wine and magic mushrooms. But if she had lost her awe of him she had found a deeper affection, inspired by his bemused vulnerability. Indeed, the dwindling community shared in its leader's confusion and despondency. She suspected that the brethren were descending into spiritual degeneration rather than dissolving into the harmonies of the T'ao.

'But then,' she murmured softly, 'who can stay sane for long in a haunted place?'

Haunted.

She could have bitten her lip in remorse. She had spoken that word she'd intended to avoid.

Haunted.

She had said it out loud.

Now that she'd voiced the word, the irregular face of the temple seemed to assume an aspect of malicious glee. Behind the yellow eyes of the candlelit windows glowed a baleful invitation. The blue roofs spread their winged gables in a grandiose gesture of acceptance. She could almost hear the wooden visage creaking its eerie welcome, underscored by the distant percussion of the Tree of Bells like the beat of a metallic heart:

*Be-with-us . . . Be-in-us . . . Be-us . . .*

It was what the Melodious Temple hermits called the 'bad music'. It had started in earnest some two years ago: a disharmony, a discord in the bay that emanated, according to some, from the Tree of Bells, and according to others, from the grim House of Heaven that towered over Forest Bell Village.

Whatever the source, it disturbed the harmony that held stone, soil, tree, soul and sea in rhythmic accord. All life, according to many Chinese, was music. The sea was music. A stream was music. Laughter, weeping, the hurry of a mouse, a hill, a house: music was in and under everything.

45

But a major disruption in nature was bad music, a disharmony that violated what the Chinese called the T'ao: the harmonic unity, the natural balance of yang and yin, light and dark.

And had the bad music, those off-key notes in nature, given the temple a malign aspect?

'No!' she laughed, and the phantasm fled in the flicker of an eyelid. The temple regained its customary wistful appearance: red paint peeling from weathered timbers, ramshackle stairways with rickety balustrades. Picturesque neglect.

Xanthippe's gaze moved down the zigzag trail from the temple to a two-storeyed, conical-roofed house where cliff met sand and shingle. The House of the Temple Servitors. Ostensibly a sanctuary for female T'ao seekers, but in fact a straightforward whorehouse: what the Chinese called a 'blue house'. Each hermit in the temple above had been born in that house, and each night at least one of the hermits shared a bed with a woman from the house.

Half of her twenty years of life had been spent there, strictly as guest, not employee. Perhaps, if her Nubian mother and Greek stepfather were still living, they would have taken her back to her birthplace by now – Alexandria, the glory of Egypt and the boast of Rome. But her parents were gone, and wishing wouldn't bring them back. She was stranded, an Egyptian exile on Chinese shores; probably the only Egyptian in the entire Empire of the Dragon Throne. A dubious honour . . .

'Mountains of the moon . . . Plains of the moon . . . Valleys of the moon . . .'

Her gaze swerved to the shrivelled shape of the hermit, swaddled in a thick grey blanket where he sat on a low rock ten paces from the tide. He looked lost in the sea mist.

A pang of guilt twitched her face. Who was she to feel sorry for herself? Compared with Hua Shan she was lucky. His skin was so deathly pale that the curved scar

46

on his brow stood out like a bright crescent moon. And his devastated mind . . . His mind was on the moon, unreachable.

Ever since Ming-kai had brought back his old friend to the comfort and care of their temple, she had been happy to take her turn at nursing the unfortunate hermit. But sometimes, with the best of will, she found his monotonous chanting throbbing so relentlessly in her brain that she wanted to scream long and loud.

It's not his fault, she kept telling herself when taxed to her limit, not his fault. It was the fault, most agreed, of the Forest of the Ancestors a thousand li to the west. That forest, it was said, took men's souls. Confronted with the mental ruin of Hua Shan, she could well believe it.

Xanthippe's ebony hand slid nervously over her close-cropped curls. She felt as if the bay was closing in on her, trapping her in China forever. Her troubled gaze drifted out to sea. Her thoughts began to drift also. Back home, to Alexandria, to Egypt.

She had come to accept that she might never again see Egypt with waking eyes. But she dreamed, each night. She dreamed of Egypt.

Xanthippe clung to her Egyptian dream as tightly as she sometimes clasped her white fur robe.

It was a strange dream, the one that visited her every night.

In sleep, she lived in Egypt of the ancient times, when the Land of the Nile was known as the Black Land of Khemet. She sat on her throne, head adorned with the double crown of the Upper and Lower Kingdoms, incarnate Daughter of the Nile. By her side sat the Pharaoh Akhenaten. But her royal husband was not the one she loved.

She loved a young woman from a far eastern land. A woman with deeply slanted eyes of vivid green. A woman who always dressed in black, and called herself Chia. For Xanthippe, Chia was a wild lover, a living goddess, a mischievous sister.

47

Most of all, Chia was Chia – the soul of beauty.

Each night, in dreams, Chia and Xanthippe made love.

Each morning, Xanthippe would wake up to a country a thousand years and thousands of miles from the Egypt of antiquity.

Often, during the day, she would try to remember Chia's face. But the fabled Woman in Black belonged to the night, and her exquisite features eluded recall.

But the Woman in Black, she had discovered in the last two years, wasn't simply her personal night-time vision.

Chia Black Dragon was a notorious Chinese sorceress, born, according to legend, some three thousand years ago, and virtually ageless. Teacher Sung had met her, and swore that she looked no more than twenty years old. He had taken delight in enumerating her long list of crimes.

Chia, it was generally agreed, was the most evil woman that had ever lived.

But if her nightly lover in sleep and the most feared woman in China were truly the same person, Xanthippe refused to believe any ill of Chia.

Evil couldn't wear such a face of grace. Could it?

'Mountains of the moon. Plains of the moon. Valleys of the moon.'

The raucous celebration of the Tree of Bells, ringing over thirty li from Sea Rock promontory to the north of the bay, failed to drown out the mystery face of Chia swimming up behind Xanthippe's eyes. Hua Shan's incantation became a peripheral event, a repetitious scribble in the margin. Moon-mutters and jingle-jangle.

Chia. Chia Black Dragon in the Egypt of the Pharaohs.

Chia's face. Evocative of twilight mystery, Eden innocence, magic made flesh.

It couldn't be a mask.

Could it?

'Chia,' murmured Xanthippe. Then, more softly: 'Nefertiti.'

'Chia, Chia, Chia, Chia, Chia,' intoned Teacher Sung, gazing adoringly at a painted image of a woman.

'Sex, sex, sex, sex, sex,' drawled Kang, his sleek physique, clad in a red Kang-i robe emblazoned with erotic symbols, reclining on a heap of silk cushions in the corner of the Teacher's room.

'That's all you ever think about, isn't it?' snapped Teacher Sung, dragging his eyes from the female image that he'd painted on his wall. 'Sex, sex, sex.'

'Chia, Chia, Chia,' Kang echoed mockingly.

'That's different. We need her. Really need her.'

Kang the Lascivious pursed his full lips. 'Well, I wouldn't say no. She must get bored with her female lovers. Now a man like me might – '

'Oh, eat your mouth, Kang,' groaned Sung, nervously brushing his fingers over the embroidered cloud patterns and slender spirals of his Kang-i robe. 'I asked you here to help me deal with this new problem, not indulge in lusting after a woman no man can ever have.'

Kang took a swig of wine from a leather flask. 'I don't know how I can help you. What about Ming-kai?'

'Don't talk to me about Ming-kai. He got back from the village yesterday. He did, I know he did. And he still hasn't reported to me. I wonder where he's hiding himself.'

Kang waved a lazy arm. 'It's a big temple, and less than a dozen hermits left in it. He could be anywhere.'

'All right, all right,' Sung sighed, glancing at the letter in his thin hand. It was from a Buddhist monk who occasionally supplied news of the major events in the Dragon Empire. The news was all bad. China had become a giant battleground since the massacre of the Imperial Family in Loyang. Now three generals waged ceaseless, bloody battles over the spoils of the Han Empire.

49

Here, in the northeast, General Tsao was forging his own kingdom. In other people's blood. Especially the blood of the straggling remnants of the T'aoist Yellow Headband armies. One report put the casualties for the last year at well over half a million.

Sung struggled to temporarily clear his head from the dreamy magic of the ling-chih mushroom that he chewed between worn teeth.

He slanted a pleading look at Kang. 'You'd stand a good chance out there,' he began tentatively. 'You can use a sword. You could make it to Black Dragon Mountain. And – and if you *really* want to, you know, try your luck with Chia . . .'

'Four thousand li is a long way to travel for a refusal,' Kang grimaced.

'But we need her,' the older man protested. 'And no one else will go. Not – not after what happened to Hua Shan.'

Kang stood up and sauntered to the door. 'Well, *I'm* not going. So nobody's going.'

He slammed the door shut with a force that shook its warped timbers. Left alone, Sung found himself glancing around the candlelit room. The flickering flames of a dozen bronze candelabra made shadows dance on the painted wood of the walls. Paintings ranging from the whimsical to the grotesque covered the entire pinewood surfaces of walls and ceiling. Sage immortals sat cross-legged on swirling clouds or in ornamental gardens perched on mountain peaks. Sinuous dragons undulated from turbulent skies or soared from stormy oceans, sparkling with all the colours of the rainbow. The Jade Emperor looked down from the parks and pavilions of his Celestial Palace on the ceiling. Demons and kwai ghosts thronged the lower regions of the walls, tumbling into a notional netherworld under the floorboards. Each brushstroke that traced the diabolic or divine had issued from Sung's own hand, a visible manifestation of the dark and light of his spirit.

A strong gust from the window made the candles flare wildly and eerie shadows pranced like angry shades of the living across the faces of bearded dragons and blue-skinned demons. The shadow play tricked Sung's eyes into perceiving the pictures as moving, ready and willing to jump off the wood and populate the room with their devilries and benisons.

As if seeking salvation, the Teacher's gaze flew to a painting of an angular mountain on whose slopes reclined a green-eyed woman dressed in black.

Where are you? he wondered silently. Where are you, Chia?

Exhaling swiftly, Sung turned and moved to the window, pushing open the ornamental grille of the shutters. The sea breathed its briny breath into the Teacher's face, leaving the taste of salt on his raw lips.

He glanced at the camphor-wood figurine of Lao Tzu in its ornamental shrine by the window. 'Can you help me, ancient sage?'

Lao Tzu grinned back in amiable reticence, as if to remind him that 'those who know do not speak'.

'Thanks a lot,' Sung sniffed wryly.

As dusk congealed and the tide ebbed, mist meandered in from the sea. Grey vapours slid up the sandy beach some two hundred feet below the jutting ledge on which the Melodious Temple of the Five Fragrant Peaks was precariously perched.

Sung, self-styled Teacher of Melodious Temple, squinted down to where sand met stone at the bottom of the sheer drop. Perhaps if he jumped he'd float down like the soul of a feather, he idly mused, taking a bite of what was left of the ling-chih mushroom in his unwashed hand. Munching the vision-inducing mushroom, his hazy gaze glided north to become lost in the majestic sweep of Silver Music Bay, its colours and contours subdued and softened by the encroaching fog.

There was a damp gust from the vastness beyond the small window; a low groan of complaint from the pine

51

floorboards under Sung's slippered feet. He felt that someone else was in the room, watching him.

All the Melodious Temple hermits had that sensation of being watched. The sensation had heightened over the last two years.

Sung shuddered and pulled his red Kang-i garment tight about his emaciated frame, his bony fingers brushing the embroidery of stylized dragons and clouds, symbols of ch'i – the breath of life – that surged through heaven and earth.

'Ch'i,' he muttered, reeling a little from the giddiness induced by the ling-chih mushroom. 'Breathe the dragon breath into me. Show me P'eng-lai.'

'Chia,' he said, trying to break the soft spell of watching eyes.

Shifting to one side of the window, he scanned his latest Wanted poster of Chia. If anything could blow away intangible fears, it was that wild storm of a woman. He had met her only once, a long time ago, and then he had collected her Wanted posters and read them avidly. It was the closest he could get to her. Her list of crimes, was, of course, exaggerated:

*By order of the Emperor Ling, Fragrant Son of Heaven*:

*Wanted*: preferably dead, Chia Black Dragon, also known as Black Dragon Sorceress, the Woman in Black, the Dragon Vampire, Green Eyes, Death-bringer, The Castrator.
*Reward*: Forty million coins.
*Residence*: Somewhere on Black Dragon Mountain, T'ien Lung Shan Region.
*Characteristics*: Female. Tall. Exact age unknown, but youthful in appearance. Distinguishing mark: green eyes.
*Crimes*: Mass murder, major theft, arson, grave-robbing, arms smuggling, desecration of shrines, unauthorized torture, unauthorized castration,

52

incitement to riot, writing obscene comments on the Imperial Palace walls, incitement to rebellion of the lower orders, vampirism, necromancy, wilful destruction of public and private property, insulting behaviour during religious and civil ceremonies, cannibalism, seduction of nine ladies of the Imperial harem, conspiracy with foreign powers to overthrow the Dragon Throne of the House of Han, conspiracy within the court to overthrow the Dragon Throne of the House of Han, bestiality, dressing in a manner likely to cause a major breach of the peace, conspiracy in the Yellow Headband uprisings, attempted assassination of General Tsao (foiled solely by the general's superior fighting skill), and three hundred and seventy-five cases of minor misdemeanours.

Signed: *General Tsao, Commander of the Northern Armies*

The Teacher's thin lips spread in a wide smile.

'What a woman,' he sighed. 'She who never obeys.'

What he wouldn't give to set her loose on Aklo. That Holy Youth, with his crooked smile, always bubbled with good humour, and never did good humour feel so bad.

There was trouble, big trouble, in the bay. And Aklo was surely part of it.

Less than two months ago Aklo had stood below the temple and shouted out the shortest and oddest of messages:

'You are all living inside the head of a madman.'

The Teacher felt his heart start to sink again. 'Chia,' he whispered.

His gaze, ascending the far wall, came to rest on the painted image of a woman in black reclining on the cloud-swaddled heights of an angular peak, silver ankh dangling at her breast, silver dagger jutting from her hand. A flutter of flame brightened the green-eyed visage of the graceful figure.

It was no good. Viewing her image only made it

worse. Chia wouldn't come. There was no one brave enough to fetch her. He would never meet her again. Never.

His mood darkened. His fears deepened.

He stared out of the window to the phantasmal shapes of the Ten Thousand Islands in the sea mist, hoping to escape intangible fears in dramatic visions, aided by the sacred fungus. With the rising fog and the descending dark, the profiles of the islands were indistinct, offering boundless possibilities to the imagination. And he stretched his imagination to the obscure horizon, trying to conjure up an image, an apparition, of paradisiacal P'eng-lai.

But Paradise, as always, was elusive. The island of Mount P'eng-lai, the Paradise of the East, radiant throne of the god Tung Wang Kung, lay beyond the reach of imagination.

'Beyond *my* present imagination, that's for sure,' he admitted ruefully, studying the various shades of grey that comprised the horizon.

There had been a time, years ago, when a gulp of ling-chih and a jump of the mind would magic a vision of Paradise. But the saturation of drugs and the passage of years had banished the Land of Light from the edge of the sea to the back of the stars. Nothing remained. No holy light.

*You are all living inside the head of a madman.*

'The world's a phantom,' he murmured.


'I live!' exulted the Holy Man. 'I was never born. I will never die. I live!'

'Hail, Aklo!' roared the congregation.

'Rejoice!' enjoined the tall youth from the crown of a rocky column rising from the sandy beach. 'Rejoice in the body of Paradise!'

The green-clad congregation on the wet, seaweed-ribboned sand crossed their arms and chorused in unison: 'We rejoice!'

54

The speaker atop the granite pinnacle flung out his wide-sleeved arms as if to embrace the crowd of upturned faces below. All – old, young, men, women – all – from prune faces to peach faces – found acceptance in the joyous bosom of Aklo. None were turned away. All were deemed worthy.

The incoming tide nibbled at the seaward base of the rearing pillar of rock, then withdrew, gathering its resources for the next foray. From its energetic depths, between shore and horizon, loomed the peaks of the Ten Thousand Islands in the roseate radiance of late afternoon. But the resplendent vista meant nothing to the animated congregation of Forest Bell Village. All they saw was the slender shape of Aklo, avatar of Tung Wang Kung, sovereign of the Eastern Paradise, Lord of P'eng-lai.

And Aklo's exhortations lifted the villagers to the heights of jubilation. With a word – a flick of the hand – he summoned up their souls to mingle with his spirit. They shared the rugged crown on which he stood. In imagination, they looked down on themselves.

He had raised them up with a word. He cast them down with another.

'Traitors,' he sighed, his deep exhalation carrying over the beach and the erstwhile fishing village that nestled in the small bay.

The villagers came back to earth with a bump. Their spirits sank down to their shoes.

'I offer you so much,' the languid youth gently reproached, brushing back his long, silky hair from his dreamy face. 'Purity, love, immortality. Ah yes. And all I ask in return is your purity of body – little food, no sex.'

He paused for a moment, his long, honed fingernails stroking a sinuous path along the emblematic labyrinth of his robe.

Aklo's silk Robe of Rainbows, florid and whimsical, rustled in the indecisive breeze from the sea, its whispering surface decorated with an extravagant menagerie of fabulous beasts cavorting in flamboyant palaces whose roofs were swaddled in silver clouds and bedevilled with golden lightning. Each of the numerous scenes was interlaced with a rainbow band winding around the imagery in a serpentine pattern without end or beginning.

'Ah yes, faithless followers,' he resumed softly in that eerie tone that floated as far as the crescent of pines overlooking the village. 'If your belief was true then all would believe as you do. But, my children, many are not yet converted to the Way of Full Pearl.'

He stretched his left hand south to point along the sweeping shoreline of Silver Music Bay. 'Why do the hypocrites of Melodious Temple still fumble into the darkness of the false T'ao? And why are the whores in their house of shame beneath the temple still plying their trade? Sex, my children, leads to hell.'

The smooth voice became more insistent as he swung his needle-finger towards Forest Bell Village. 'And – ah yes – what saddens my heart most of all . . . why are there still lost souls in the village who reject my gifts?'

The congregation drooped their heads in shame. Yes, it was true. There were those who skulked in the houses and huts behind them, those who spurned Aklo's love, those who turned their impious backs on the Paradise of P'eng-lai.

Aklo's tone shifted to a more consoling note. 'But the patience of a god is boundless, my chosen children. Your faith in me will strengthen – ah yes, I know it will strengthen. And when you truly believe, all others will believe. And I will lead you all into Paradise on the night of Full Pearl when fish swim in the forest. On that night there will be sex in abundance for the faithful. Sacred sex. Sex without end.'

The enthralled congregation fell to its knees and bowed to its silken-robed god on the high pinnacle. Tears of mingled remorse and gratitude spilled down hundreds of cheeks. Hundreds of mouths murmured their devotion.

And Aklo smiled at the silver twinkle in their eyes.

Inhaling the scent of adoration, Aklo stretched luxuriously, allowing his gaze to slide up the tiered slope of the decaying village until it came to rest on the huge, four-storeyed mansion of dark timber built on the landward cliff. The peak-roofed, wing-gabled crest of the mansion was on a level with the pines that fringed the curving brink of the crescent cliff. The mansion was old before the first hut was erected in the scalloped bay. The original huts had come and gone. The mansion remained. The House of Heaven remained. Its weathered timbers were bent and cracked and patched with mould. Rank weeds luxuriated on the ramshackle verandah. Broken shutters clapped in tempo with the whistling wind. But the House of Heaven endured.

With a slanted grin, Aklo surveyed his congregation.

'Follow me, and I will lead you into the glories of Heaven,' he declared in the thought-whisper that could be heard for over a li.

The congregation blessed him from below.

He glanced back at the gloomy House of Heaven, and a secretive smile crossed his lips. He unfolded his needle-fingers like cat's claws.

'Oppose me,' he said in a private murmur, 'and I'll give you Hell.'

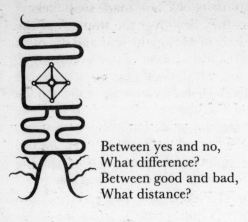

## 3

Between yes and no,
What difference?
Between good and bad,
What distance?

Lao Tzu: *T'ao te ching*

'Sometimes the dead don't lie down.'

Her green eyes glared into an abstract distance.

'Might he come back?' Chia wondered aloud, lifting the flute to her lips, then slowly letting it sink back to her lap. 'No. Nyak won't come back. I killed him.'

Chia leant with her back on the curved sandstone rim of her cavern, and gazed at the sunlit steeps and hollows of her small valley in the heart of Black Dragon Mountain, her mind straying two years into the past and three thousand li to the east. She raised the hsiao flute to her mouth, then lowered it again.

'If the dead don't lie down,' she murmured, 'they come back stronger.'

And, she reflected, he was always stronger than me. He hid from my approach, he sent his servants to fight for him. But for all that, he was stronger than me.

Chia glanced at the bamboo flute in her hands, an instrument fashioned thousands of li to the south in the bamboo groves beyond the Yangtze River. With a sigh she tried to banish all thoughts of that two-year-old battle with Nyak as she raised the hsiao flute to her parted lips for the third time.

*Let the bamboo speak with its own voice. Let the flute make music of me. Let the way be tzu-jan.*

Tzu-jan – the spontaneity of T'ao – made swift flickers of her long fingers as they flew over the stops. And the flute warbled the melody of spring, the soar and dip of its notes flying through the fresh leaves of the moist valley. In response to the lively air, a flock of swallows winged from their nests and wheeled above the treetops. Chia's spirits took wing and flew wild.

Her flute blew a false note as a dog's bark abruptly terminated her spell of music. A bulky black hound rushed out of the dark cave and into the light of the valley.

'Hello, Fire,' she greeted the he-dog as it sped from the cave. Fire, his nose full of spring smells, ignored her. As did Water, the she-dog, who tore after her mate. The three half-grown pups, Wood, Earth and Metal, were similarly oblivious as they followed in their parents' wake, bounding with energy and devilment. Chia laid the flute aside and smiled at the unruly pack. The five dogs were her only companions in Black Dragon Valley, cross-breeds of nearly extinct strains. She had bred them into her image of the ideal dog: big, black, and bloody-minded.

The soft curve of her smiling mouth broadened as her long, slanted green eyes tracked the hounds on their erratic course. The five beasts gambolled through the fern, gorse and wild flowers of the wide crescent glade fronting the cavern. Reaching the bottom of the mild incline, the dogs splashed about for a time in the gurgling stream that was born from a waterfall on a southern precipice then wound to its rest in the deep pools at the foot of a northern wall of rock. Then the pack sprang on to the opposite bank of the stream and raced up the gradually steepening ascent, their sleek black shapes blinking out of sight with increasing frequency as copses of elm, larch, oak and willow closed in to form a single wood which blanked out the dogs entirely.

At the arrowed head of the valley, where the cliffs almost touched, the dogs came back into sight – five black dots on the green glade sweeping up to the narrow gap that led out of the valley. The gap was so slender that it was all but blocked by a solitary weeping willow. Behind the weeping willow hung a young sun in a vivid blue sky, spearing the foliage with golden shafts and transforming the bronze and silver and gold talismans bedecking the branches of the lonely tree into a dance of sparkling light. Even at this distance the miniature bells and chimes, engraved with pictograms and t'ao-tieh masks, sent a faint jingling down the valley to the cavern mouth, carried on the easterly breeze: the music of the Sentinel Tree.

It was a veritable barricade of wooden and metallic sorcery, the Sentinel Tree. It had a deadly liquid silver for sap, a small residue of an ancient secretion – moon-silver, the most dangerous substance under the sky. There was just enough moon-silver in the tree to preserve the wood through centuries as it worked in concert with wood and metal magic to protect Chia's valley from invasion. But even a dash more moon-silver in trunk and bough might prove more lethal to her home than a score of invaders. As it was, the tree repelled the unwelcome by twisting their minds and turning them away from the valley. And for those who strayed too near, it gave the mind an extra twist – into oblivion.

The dogs, like all animals, had the good sense to steer clear of the tree. They swerved round and plunged back down the slopes. Although the Sentinel Tree did no harm to anything leaving Black Dragon Valley, its aura was sufficient to intimidate the hounds.

A stab of sunlight teased a drop of water from her eye. She smiled wryly at the mild eyeache brought on by the sun. Aversion to sunlight was the legacy of a mode of existence she had experimented with for a few decades some two centuries ago. The after-effects were slow in fading, even by Chia's long-term view of passing time.

'Don't ever become a vampire,' she advised the empty air. 'It's not worth the headaches.'

Still, she admitted, being a vampire had its compensations. It was a quiet life, lazing about in coffins all day, strolling through the forest at night. True, you had to drink blood occasionally, but she had always left her prey with enough red life in their veins to run speedily on their way once she had finished with them. Apart from the blood, there was nothing of note that she recalled from her vampire days. Quite dull, really.

The mild ache behind her eyes intensified to a remorseless pounding. She reached into a pouch at her side and extracted one of her proudest possessions: two small discs of black glass, framed by copper wire with a copper nose-bridge and copper earpieces. She fixed the black glasses on to her nose, adjusting one slightly askew earpiece so that it rested as securely on her ear as the opposite partner.

The black glasses were an idea inspired by the scientist Claudius Ptolemy on her last visit to Alexandria, greatest city of the Roman Empire, on the far side of the world, and they served not only as a disguise for her green eyes – a clear mark for bounty-hunters in China – but also as protection against such a bright sun as hung in this morning's sky.

The relief was immediate. The harsh glare of brash sun was softened to a lambent glow. The morning valley took on the soft hues of twilight. *Twilight*. The word drew a wistful smile from her lips. Twilight was her favourite time. Her father must have known something when he named her Twilight: Chia was the name for twilight in the pre-Chinese Ko dialect of the upper Yellow River. Now, three thousand years later, the same sound signified wood, the living wood. Had her near-omniscient father foreseen that, too?

The wistful curve of her mouth re-formed into a hard line.

Her father.

A screaming mouth.

A tumbling head.

61

She shook her mind free of troubling images.

For most of her immense lifespan, she had wallowed in a mixture of ignorance and delusion about her origins and nature. Two years ago, near the Forest of the Ancestors, on the twelfth night of the fourth moon, her ignorance and delusion were mercilessly shattered. She had discovered who her real father was – *what* he was. He was the last survivor of the race called Thzan-tzai – the Nothing Masters. The last of a bad breed, a wound in nature.

And she was of his blood, although her mother was human.

Chia was a wound in nature.

All her life she had abhorred the memory of the Thzan-tzai, and the terrible legacy they had left on earth. For her, they were the supreme enemy.

Now she knew that she was one of them.

'I am the enemy,' she quietly stated.

Then she drew a deep breath and expelled it sharply.

'But I'm also, in part, what I think myself to be. I think of myself as human. I even look human. And that's more than can be said for some people. As for emotions – I can love and hate as well as the next woman. So what is it to be human? What's left?'

Her fingers stroked the silver ankh at her breast. 'Mortality?'

Chia's mouth formed a pensive line. 'I grew as normal in my childhood. Even the legends say that about me. After childhood, I only aged some three years in every thousand. But I *do* age. All that ages is mortal. I age. Therefore I am mortal. A sound syllogism.'

She slowly nodded her head. 'I'm mortal. Human.'

The nodding stopped abruptly. 'But what sort of creature can renew her flesh and bone every few years? A creature with bad blood?'

Her head lowered. Bad blood; that was it. It always came down to what was bred into her blood. Thzan-tzai breeding.

Chia had always considered the primordial Thzan-tzai as a kind of conscious disease. She had inherited that disease. It made you live a long, long time.

Her father had given her a latent legacy: wild flesh. After three or four years of normal aging, her hidden Thzan-tzai lineage rebelled and assumed command of brain and body. Her mind was obliterated, her body kneaded like dough. When the regeneration was complete, her human side resumed control. Her body became human in shape, her thoughts human in pattern. Emerging from the rejuvenation she was only a day older for each year since the previous eruption of time-rejecting wild flesh.

'Until I age as others do, I'll always be a pretty monster,' she muttered. 'I'll always be the enemy.'

A moist nudge of her hand startled her out of incipient gloom.

She grinned at the sight of Wood, the she-pup, nuzzling her palm, and laughed at the tickle of whiskers. Wood wagged a tail of frenzied delight when Chia rubbed the sleek black back.

'There's nothing quite like a dog,' she winked, lifting her black glasses for an instant. 'Nature's comedians.'

The pup leapt on to her lap, licked her face, then tried to pull her glasses off. Saving them from possible damage, she replaced the glasses in the pouch.

Chia jiggled her head from side to side, swaying her long, untidy hair as she scratched the animal behind its pert ears.

'I used to be a hero, you know,' she confided in mock solemnity. 'I could unleash the flow of ch'i in my body and charge about at ten times normal speed. With that same wild ch'i I could shatter stone, snap metal, break bone. I could lower my weight and float to ground like a feather. I've defeated small armies single-handed. I've dethroned a dozen or so emperors. I've fought my way to Britannia and back. I've numbered queens and princesses amongst my lovers. Oh yes, I used to be a hero . . .'

Wood was obviously unimpressed by Chia's exploits. She hopped off Chia's lap and raced to join her frolicsome family.

'Yes,' Chia continued, well used to talking to herself, 'I used to be a hero. I used to have amazing powers. Just like in the old legends of Yi the Archer and Cheng-o the Immortality Thief. I used to think I was so special, revelling in my superior powers.'

Her tone became introspective and subdued.

'Two years ago, I saw my father's ghost. He told me where my powers came from. Bad blood. Bad flesh. A wound in nature.'

Lines formed in her brow. 'Once I learned the source of my powers, I couldn't use them any more. Knowing their source shouldn't have robbed me of the choice to wield them. But that's what happened. I suppose they're like the symptoms of a disease to me now. It's not that I *won't* use them – I *can't* use them.'

She sighed as she roused herself out of her sinking mood. 'I *am* special – that's what's wrong with me.'

Her hand gripped the silver ankh at her breast. 'I'm bad flesh. But I can live with it. I'll survive. In a thousand – two thousand – years I'll still be young. I'll still roam the world. But I won't be a hero.'

She slapped herself on the face. 'Stop mooning, Chia. You've finally killed Nyak, after three thousand years of trying. Why not lean back and enjoy a little peace for a while?'

The sun had dimmed slightly, and her eyes no longer pained her.

Her vision skimmed round the ring of tall cliffs, the dour ramparts of her tiny kingdom, and came to rest on the pools beneath the northern wall. The sight of water made her skin itch. She hadn't bathed in days, not since the first day of the fourth moon, and that was – what? ten? eleven? days ago. Her smooth brow suddenly creased with a frown. The final battle with Nyak had ended on the twelfth day of the fourth moon, a battle that had hurled his spirit from Celestial Buddha Temple.

*But was it the final battle? I never saw his body . . .*

'To hell with it,' she snorted, jumping to her feet. 'Nyak's dead. Dead as dirt.'

*But I never saw his body . . .*

Ignoring the nagging doubt, Chia strode to the shadowed pools, loosening her body-hugging black silk gown as she walked.

'He's dead,' she insisted under her breath. 'Dead and done with. His spirit took the truth back to his body. And Nyak isn't one who could live with the truth. The truth killed him.'

She reached the largest of the pools and stared at its inky surface. Her image stared back at her, tall and slim and – so she was told – graceful and beautiful as a young goddess. The thought teased a small smile from the corners of her wide mouth.

'Well *I* don't fancy you,' she informed her reflection, then pulled off her silver ankh pendant on its silver chain and dropped it on the loamy ground. Drawing the long silver dagger from the crimson sash girdling her waist, she felt two-year-old memories resurrecting at its metallic touch.

'Not again,' she groaned, shutting her eyes. 'Not *again.*'

Two years ago. Twelfth night of the fourth moon.

Celestial Buddha Temple, north of the Forest of the Ancestors.

Nyak had soared from the temple in a spiral of confusion, a mad spirit, an invisible terror. She had sensed his terrified flight from Celestial Buddha Temple, had felt his turmoiling presence hovering over the Forest of the Ancestors. After that –

After that his spirit would have fled to his unbreathing body. Wherever the hell that was.

Chia's wide mouth bent into a crooked smile.

'Hell, indeed. You were the expert on hell, Nyak.'

65

Nyak had given hell to the folk of Celestial Buddha Temple. He had almost sent her to hell. But she had a secret he knew nothing about. A secret told her by her father's ghost. A last trick to play in her deadly game with Nyak.

That secret was a kind of truth, a killing truth. When she learned it from her father's spectre, its impact had almost killed her.

Even now, that killing truth was hard for her to live with. She had wailed when her father's ghost told her of her first and worst crime, performed when the world was young. For almost three thousand years she had blotted that crime from her memory, until her father's phantom voice had forced the truth of it back on her. Truth was cold comfort. Like sleeping with a corpse . . .

She flinched as a stark memory blazed in her skull. A memory of a night, three thousand years ago: her father's screaming mouth . . . her father's head, tumbling from his shoulders . . . hot red dancing in a fountain from the neck stump. And the knife in her hand, more red than silver.

'Why?' he had pleaded the moment her knife slashed into his throat. 'Why?'

The instant the slaying was done, her heart rebelled. She remembered screaming. She remembered aiming the dagger at her heart. But her brother had caught her hand. After that all she could recall was running into the night. Running, running, running.

She'd been running in circles ever since.

Every few years she would undergo a partial death, a physical transformation, from which she would rise rejuvenated. But the regenerations – a Thzan-tzai inheritance from her father – although they vastly extended her lifespan, also blotted out much of her memory. It was no small matter to jump in and out of oblivion every few years.

Chia let the silver dagger fall to the soil, alongside the

ankh. She untied the crimson sash and let it slide to the earth.

She hoisted the black silk gown over her head and stood naked, garment in hand. The fabric was torn, stained, and worn through in places. The embroidery of silver spirals on the hem and wide cuffs was becoming disentangled.

'It's like me,' she observed wryly.

The observation gave birth to an idea. Perhaps she could live with the cold truth if she gave up some of her old ways. Maybe she could warm to the truth.

With a slight twinge of regret, she threw the gown into the pool. It took its time in sinking.

'Off with the old,' she muttered.

Then she jumped into the pool, enjoying the shock of cold water on her skin as she slid into the depths. She felt her bramble-bush hair change into floating seaweed as the surface closed over her head. Slowly, she drifted down, the weight of the earth lifted from her buoyant body. Gradually, the tension eased from her muscles. Sinking lower into the blackness, she stretched languidly as her anxieties dissolved. The sensation of cold evaporated as she merged with the element of water.

*This is so easy. Not fighting, but accepting. The T'ao has its rhythms, and I will flow with them. The rhythms of the pool. The rhythms of –*

It hit her with such force that her body convulsed. Memory. Water memory. Sea memory.

*A mask in the mists from the sea . . . a mask summoning her with the voice of the tide: 'Chhhiiiaaa . . .'*

She swallowed mouthful after mouthful of water as she flailed about in the wet dark. She didn't know where to go. Then she didn't know where she was. She became a simple fact of drowning.

*Born in the sea. Reborn in the sea.*

Suddenly there was a surge of light and a commotion in her ears as her head broke the surface of the pool. Daylight dashed into her eyes and she gulped a small lungful of air before she sank underwater again, her panic releasing the precious air in a stream of bubbles. Fighting to subdue the panic, she flippered her limbs and arched upwards.

Chia erupted from the pool in a brawl of spray and launched herself on to the muddy bank. Her hooked fingers scrabbled in the wet mud as she heaved her supple body clear of the agitated water.

She pulled herself into a seated position, drew her knees up to her chest, rested her arms on her knees, and let her head sink to rest on her arms.

The rising sun soon dried her skin as she sat hunched by the pool, but from time to time icy trickles from her drenched hair ran down her smooth back. After a while, she wrapped her arms round her waist and rocked back and forth, playing mother and daughter to herself, self-consoling.

She was afraid of the memories that the pool had resurrected. And the fear was all the sharper because she didn't fully understand its cause. Sea mist – a mask calling her name with the surge of the tide – why were the memories tinged with dread, and what did they mean?

'Born in the sea. Reborn in the sea,' she mumbled, slowly raising her head to stare abstractedly at the swollen rock and drapery of vines on the surface of the northern cliffs.

But why should she be afraid of the sea? There was nothing left to fear now Nyak was gone.

She had witnessed his destruction with her own eyes. With her own mouth she had revealed to him the truth of his nature, a truth that had blasted his spirit.

That spirit had possessed the body of a monk in Celestial Buddha Temple. It was through the monk's ears that Nyak heard the destructive secret. And he had blown the monk's body to fragments as he fled howling into the night, his soul tearing itself in two. He would have flown back to his own body. There was nowhere else to go.

When that self-destroying spirit entered Nyak's true body, it would have blasted that to pieces too. His devastated soul would have devastated his body.

But was there something, perhaps, that she'd overlooked? Had Nyak made preparations, foreseeing the possible wreckage of his body?

At length she shook her head in resignation and rose to her muddied feet. She turned her back on the dark ring of water and made her way back up the slope to the arched mouth of her cavern, halting only to scoop up the ankh and the dagger.

No more, she told herself. No more brooding on the past. No more riddles from the hidden years. No more subtle ghosts. Let them lie with a discarded gown at the bottom of a pool. I'll find new paths to walk, new thoughts to think. Somehow, I'll live with the truth.

Her gaze alighted on the crumpled folds of a black cloak near the entrance to the cavern. For a moment she pondered whether she should throw that away too as part of a scheme to jettison the past, then rejected the idea.

'No point going overboard,' she declared. 'One step at a time.'

A thoughtful look stole into her expression as she studied the ankh in her left hand and the dagger in her right. Although the two objects had the appearance and weight of silver, and she always thought of and referred to them as silver, they were of another mineral entirely. As to what that mineral was she hadn't a notion, except that there was a legend which spoke of a rock that had fallen from the moon thousands of years ago. But whatever the truth of the matter, the element from which the ankh and dagger were formed was impervious to acids, fire, or the stroke of a hammer. And the dagger cut sharper and surer than the finest steel blade.

Could I ever give these up? she asked herself. The answer was instantaneous: never.

Chia drew the two silver objects closer together. When

they were a hand's breadth apart the ankh jumped from the palm and clung to the long blade. The force of magnetism had long been understood in China, but the familiar behaviour of her two silver relics was more like sundered twins seeking reunion. And just as they clung to each other, Chia clung to them.

As for apparel, she had adhered to the same garb for – how long now? Two centuries? She flicked a glance at the folded black cloak. Yes, it was at least two centuries since she had first designed the cloak and the gown, making exact copies as each garment wore out.

The Woman in Black.

Chia swivelled on her toes and studied the wooded valley brimming with mild sunlight. The five dogs scampered between a clump of willows on the slope that curved up from the far side of the stream.

'I'd happily go out naked on my next journey,' she declared. 'But I'd shock China speechless.'

A smile sprang to her wide mouth, and lingered there awhile. At least now she was free to travel out of Black Dragon Valley without constantly scanning the horizon for Nyak and his diseased servants. Now that the Master was dead, his servants would decay with him. Let them rot together, unmourned.

She shut her eyes and heaved a satisfied sigh, luxuriating in the caress of the mild breeze. Minutes blew by.

In the distance there was a low rumble. In seconds, it rolled louder, closer. Then it exploded over her valley like the emperor of all thunderclaps.

Her eyelids sprang open. Her vision darted around the sky as her hearing registered the rapidly receding roll. The last echo of thunder bounced back.

And something was happening to the valley.

The leafy slopes were being drained of their green radiance. Minute by minute, the spring trees shed a little of their colour, as if the earth was absorbing the light of the leaves. Sunlight bled from the air with the advance of murky clouds in the rising wind. A feeble yellow ray struggled through the stormcloud, bringing a touch of transitory life to the metal-adorned willow tree, then was obliterated, leaving the solitary Sentinel Tree a black silhouette against the gloomy slate of the thundercloud.

And the Sentinel Tree jangled its alarm, its metallic echoes resounding from the stone ramparts of Black Dragon Valley.

Shivering in the cold wind, Chia wrenched the ankh from the dagger and looped it round her neck as her right hand tightened on the silver hilt.

*Something has invaded my valley, and drained its colour. The pale colour has the look of – moonlight.*

'Fire! Water! Earth! Wood! Metal!' She summoned the five hounds on the near bank.

But the dogs were as immobile as the stones littering the edges of the stream. Not a flicker of a tail. Not a twitch of a whisker. Frozen black images on the muted green of the glade.

A muscle tremored in Chia's right cheek.

*Something has possessed the hounds. They can't hear, can't see.*

'What are you?' she asked the dimming air. 'Who are you?'

She was about to start down the ferny slope when the dogs went berserk in an eruption of snarls and flashing fangs.

Wood, the she-pup, sprang at Earth, her sister, a moment before Metal, the he-pup, made a dash for Wood. Wood's fangs ripped a chunk from Earth's belly. Metal tore into Wood, cracking a foreleg. Metal, in his turn, was savaged by Fire, his father. And Water, Fire's mate, buried her teeth in his flank.

Stunned by the slaughter of her beloved animals, Chia's voice was as shaken as her heart. 'And now Earth will devour Water, completing the circle of the Five Elements,' she breathed hoarsely. She was witnessing a canine re-enactment of Chinese cosmology.

As if on cue, the she-pup Earth, with Wood gnawing

71

her spilling intestines, dragged herself to her mother Water and sank sharp teeth in her mother's neck. The last link was complete in the chain of savagery. The five maddened hounds were joined in a ring of death.

Almost in unison, five crimson, frothy jaws delivered the final stroke. Almost as one, five ripped throats gushed red floods.

Chia, her steps unsteady, walked down to the circle of dead dogs, tears adding a lustre to the green of her eyes. What had been her brave companions were now wretched, lifeless lumps; cast-offs of whoever had used them as puppets in a symbolic performance. And who was perverse and powerful enough to be the puppeteer in such a vicious display?

'No,' Chia protested with a vigorous shake of the head. 'No.' *Nyak's dead. The truth must have destroyed him.*

That truth was the killing secret her father's spirit had disclosed to her two years ago, on the night that the so-called Shadow of Chia fell on Celestial Buddha Temple.

It was the truth of a murder carried out three thousand years ago.

Chia had murdered her father because of what he once was, and might be again. Thzan-tzai. Wild flesh. That was the truth she had to live with.

Nyak had murdered his father because he'd renounced the almost limitless power of the Thzan-tzai, thus depriving Nyak of much of that power. That was the truth he couldn't endure.

Like Chia, Nyak had blanked the crime from his memory. And, in his deranged mind, he had constructed a fictional father who was pure Thzan-tzai, untainted by humanity.

The truth that Nyak couldn't bear was the fact of his own humanity.

Chia had also fashioned a fictional father in her mind: an exalted, godlike being who battled against the Thzan-tzai in ancient times. She was just as mad as Nyak.

The two of them had committed parricide for opposite reasons. And, for opposite reasons, the crime had driven them insane.

'I killed what I thought was a monster. He killed what he thought was a man. Now I'm afraid that I might be a monster. And he's afraid that he might be a man.'

A mounting intensity in the rattle of the talismans on the Sentinel Tree roused her from sombre speculations.

Chia's eyes tightened with anger as they focused on the remote weeping willow. Whoever was standing at the head of her valley, shaking an alarm from the tree, she wouldn't shrink from them. Whatever power had killed her dogs, she would make it pay.

Tigerish, she leapt over the torn bodies and splashed through the stream. Her naked body warming with rage in the teeth of the icy wind, she raced up the slopes, darting like quicksilver in the shadows beneath the boughs. Dipping and dodging the jutting spokes of branches, she soon reached the crowded trees of the upper inclines. The chill slap of leaves on her skin reawoke her sense of caution. And with caution there returned apprehension. By the time she broke out of the woods and confronted the thin grass and thick gorse of the topmost glade, her spirit had changed from wrathful tiger to wary wolf, heeding the rowdy alarm of the Sentinel Tree talismans.

'If there's any way back from death,' she whispered, 'Nyak will find it. I should know. After all – he is my brother.'

She stole up the wild glade, crouched and stealthy, silver dagger pointed unerringly at the pass. Her pace slowed almost to a halt when she arrived at the agitated tree. The percussion of gold, silver and bronze was all but deafening. There was a frenzied note to the talismanic din that made Chia feel she was being warned to go no further, to run, run and hide. But she ignored the presentiment and crept under the tree which crowned the humped path between the crags.

Beyond the Sentinel Tree the trail fanned out from a gap barely wide enough to admit an ox-cart into two broad arms that spread out as if to embrace all of China with its ancestral forests, fertile plains and clouded peaks. But Chia halted in the precincts of the talisman-hung boughs, her muddy feet frozen to the spot. There was a sick smell in the air: sour milk.

Bad memories stood solid in the daylight.

Ten paces beyond the protective barrier of the Sentinel Tree reared three tall figures in ragged grey mantles and silver masks adorned with long, grey drapes of hair. The hue of their garments blended with the drab shades of approaching thunderclouds. The central figure had a luminous red sign on his mask brow, denoting his status as a priest of the Thzan-tzai cult. The others bore the plain metal brows of acolytes.

'The Silver Brethren,' she exhaled.

The priest lifted a mail-gauntleted hand and voiced the ancient salutation of the Thzan-tzai followers: 'We bring you the sharing love.'

The wind that carried the words also wafted the stench – like sour milk and rancid pork – of the flesh hidden under the grey cloaks. It seeped into the shrinking pores of her bared skin, as if eager for intimacy.

'Brotherly love,' she winced.

Trying to keep the blade from trembling in her knife hand, Chia steadily backed away from the three intruders, not daring to take her eyes off the cloaked shapes despite the protection of the Sentinel Tree.

*Sour milk: Nyak's scent. Nyak's servants have come for me . . .*

The corner of her mouth twitched in angry spasms. 'How did you kill my dogs? Did you whisper a death command at a distance? Is that how you killed my dogs, you bastards?'

'We didn't kill your animals,' declared the central Silver Brother. 'It was the Master who made play with their flesh.'

74

She shook her head, refusing to believe. 'No.'
Once more, the masked figure raised its hand.
'Your brother sends his love.'

## 4

From bad luck, good luck.
From good luck, bad luck.
At the same threshold, the happy and
    unhappy assemble.
Under the same roof, the lucky and
    unlucky mingle.

Chia Yi: *Fu niao fu*

The Tree of Bells sang in Silver Music Bay.

It sang from the seaward tip of Sea Rock, a narrow promontory that pointed like a stony finger into the ocean. The bell-laden weeping willow, celebrating its lonely eminence, tripped peals of metallic laughter over pebbles and stones to the landward root of the dour promontory. Its agitated glee struck a resonance in the littered boulders and loose scree of the upper beach.

On the grey cliffs, high above the long, bending bay, overhanging the Ancestral Gallery, the hilly pine forest was mute, as if maintaining silence in numbers.

On the beach twenty li south of the Tree of Bells, Ming-kai glowered at the distant silhouette of Sea Rock in the mellow saffron light of the setting sun. Although the sea breeze was sufficiently strong to lift aloft his tiger-emblazoned white paper kite and tug at the scarred hand that gripped the kite's cord, it should have stirred the Tree of Bells to no more than a subdued tintinnabulation instead of manic jubilation. But then the strange tree had a way of playing its jangly music regardless of the way of the wind. Like Aklo, who often knelt before it, the tree was its own law, and its carillons issued from within, from root and trunk and branch.

Ming-kai grimaced as he squinted up at the tiger-kite sailing a hundred feet above his tousled head. In the last two years he had lost three good kites in the thunder-wind, the paper ripped to ragged shreds. And the wooden frames rotted. A wind that could instantly rot wood must be a wind born bad.

He shrugged off the unease with a shake of his stocky shoulders. Let Teacher Sung tremble before the air-cracking wind like the timorous fool he was. Ming-kai had stridden over the extruded insides of men on the slippery battlegrounds of the Yellow Headband Wars; he wasn't ready to cower under a fey gale and pray for the coming of the deadly Chia Black Dragon.

'Unwise to invite the dragonstorm to quell a mere gale,' he growled, glancing at the fanciful outlines of Melodious Temple at the southern arm of Silver Music Bay.

'I wonder if they're still arguing.' He half-smiled, thinking of his exasperated departure from the 'conference' in Sung's room two hours ago.

Teacher Sung had called a conference to discuss a haunting. All of five hermits had made an appearance.

The meeting had speedily degenerated into the usual squabble that ignited when the remaining temple hermits were in each other's company for more than a hundred breaths. It had proved fortunate that only five of the temple occupants had responded to Sung's request to gather in the crown of East Tower: Ming-kai could imagine what violence might have been sparked by their mutual loathing if all of the loose community had answered the Teacher's invitation.

It had been folly to call that gathering; folly to attempt to forge a unity of purpose in so disparate a group; more folly to expect any of them to be capable of distinguishing a haunting from the drug visions that visited all their eyes with spirit carnivals; and – the supreme folly – to hope that the absurd anomaly of a brotherhood of

77

hermits could ever agree on anything, anywhere, at any time.

Within minutes of entering his chamber, Sung's guests had become embroiled in their customary bandying of insults concerning Lung-ch'i's cooking, and how only Lung-ch'i could stomach enough of the muck he dished up to grow fat as a palace eunuch. The cook, as usual, had glared his detestation of his companions and snarled his own vituperation between shoving substantial chunks of congealed rice, fish slices and onions into his capacious mouth. He called Lao, the Mad Hermit, here on one of his rare appearances, a giggling skeleton. He called grizzled Fen-chou a slimy toad. *And* – Lung-ch'i had bellowed, rounding on the sleek curve of Kang lounging indolently on Sung's unmade bed – Kang the Lascivious, Kang the sex-worshipper, should take his permanently aroused member and ram it into a rabbit hole. Kang had responded to Lung-ch'i with an obscene gesture of the fingers and a sneering remark.

'Sour milk,' Kang drawled. 'That's what you are, Fatgut. We've all smelt it lately. A barbarian drink that would make any Chinese vomit. Sour milk, Fatgut.'

Hsiang – grey-haired, empty-eyed, bumbling Hsiang – sat through it all, smiling vacantly at the wall and mumbling, 'Seek wisdom, seek wisdom, seek wisdom, seek . . .'

And so it went on. Each time Sung had pleaded with them to pool their ideas on ghosts, the Tree of Bells, and the thunder-wind, they had shrugged their shoulders in manifest indifference. So what? they had said. Who cares about a few miserable ghosts? Maybe the temple's haunted. Maybe it isn't. What of it?

Eventually the Teacher had admitted defeat when even the sudden, eerie music of the Tree of Bells had left the hermits unmoved. Disgruntled, he left them to their arguments about erotica, bad food, sour milk and the true way to the cosmic harmony of the T'ao, preferring to squint out of the window and mutter to himself: 'I'm not mad. I know I'm not. It's the Watchers. They're here. I know they are.'

Ming-kai had laid a hand on Sung's shoulder. 'Why don't you leave?' he gently suggested. 'We all have a strong feeling of being watched. Nobody's saying you're mad. But you're worn thin with fear. Why not go to Tung An for a while?'

Sung shook his head. 'There's no way through the forest. Ask Kang. He tried to find one.'

'He couldn't have looked very hard.'

The Teacher's eyes dithered. 'The trees won't let us out. We're locked in with the Watchers.'

Somewhere at Ming-kai's back, senile Hsiang mumbled on. 'Seek wisdom, seek wisdom . . .'

'No way out,' whined Teacher Sung.

At that point Ming-kai decided he'd had enough. He pushed past the considerable bulk of Lung-ch'i. 'I'll be flying my kite if anybody wants me.'

He glared up the beach to the temple, tightening his grip on the kite's cord. 'And if I had any sense I wouldn't go back.'

Thanks to Sung's obsession with summoning Chia, the temple had lost a good man in Hua Shan, and he had lost a friend. The withered shell that mumbled of the moon wasn't Hua Shan: the man's spirit had fled from his face. What a waste. What stupidity.

Another victim to lay at Chia's feet. Sung's too, perhaps?

He shook his head. The unease in the bay was addling Sung's wits. It was time the Teacher left.

Ming-kai's attention was suddenly caught by the bobbing tiger-kite, its streamer flicking like a tail. Deep lines formed in the hermit's wide forehead as he observed the errant aerobatics of the flimsy kite. The paper tiger was dancing on air. There was a distinct rhythm, a regular tempo, to its antics. Puzzlement changed to apprehension when he realized that the kite was dancing to the tune of the singing tree.

79

Perhaps we're all dancing to the tune of the tree,' he speculated glumly. His gaze flicked down to his tapping foot: it was beating in time with the percussive boughs.

'Maybe it's time *I* left the bay.'

He glanced across the waves to where a small, square-sailed junk with a Green East Dragon figurehead on its snub prow was scudding over the surges. No other ocean-going craft had set sail from the nearly derelict wharf of Forest Bell Village in over a year. Ah – could the cargo be the dwindling minority of sane souls in the village, seeking escape from Aklo's inhuman cult? He hoped so. Escape was the best option for them. And he hoped that his friend Chien-long, the old sailor with the streaming green eyes, was aboard. There might be balm for his eyes outside the bay's influence.

'Perhaps it's time we *all* left the bay,' he concluded.

He recalled Sung's dithery eyes, his frightened glances. *There's no way through the forest.*

Turning west, Ming-kai studied the unbroken ranks of clifftop trees that hemmed the bay from north to south.

Coming to a decision, he started to wind in his kite. 'No way through the forest,' he repeated slowly. 'I'll prove that wrong. Right now.'

Memory was the sea. Xanthippe was immersed in memory.

The sight of the junk heading out of the bay had drawn her to the sea's edge.

Lingering on the beach in the prelude to dusk, seduced by tidal rhythms, she thought of Egypt, and of her parents.

Melodious Temple and its whorehouse had lost most of their hermits and whores in the last two years. They seemed destined to become empty relics, wooden follies facing the sea.

Her mother, Fulvia, and stepfather, Didymus, wouldn't have been too sorry to witness such a bleak fate for the House of the Temple Servitors, although they would have viewed the demise of the temple with regret.

Xanthippe ran slender fingers over her close-cropped hair. As the tide ebbed the memories advanced.

'Mother, Father – why did you walk into the sea?' she questioned in a faint breath. 'Why did you leave me alone in a half-strange land?'

Six years she had lived in China, and two years before that in most of the major ports between Egypt and her present haven, but the Land of the Nile was the land of her birth, and the rest of her twenty years had been spent there. The colour and bustle of Alexandria were still fresh in her memory. She recalled the animated harbour with its monumental concourse – the Heptastadion – that linked Pharos Island and its renowned lighthouse with the mainland. And the colonnaded facades of the Serapeum and Athenaeum.

'But there were colonnades everywhere,' she whispered to the rising mist from the dusk sea. 'Ah, the colonnaded streets of Alexandria.'

Porticoed walkways surrounded the Royal Palace that had long ago housed the dynasty of the Ptolemies, concluding with the glorious disaster of Cleopatra. And she remembered rank on rank of soaring pillars, marble statues of gods and heroes, luxuriant gardens, shaded swimming pools, and cosmopolitan Alexandrians lounging on cushioned benches, rare spices teasing the tongues in their heads, exotic perfumes charming the air in their spacious, elegant villas.

Her father's villa, to the best of her memory, hadn't been notably elegant; he was only a moderately success-ful playwright and could boast of no strong connection with any of the noble Greek houses. But their modest villa was situated in the magnificent Brucheion quarter, north of the four-mile Canopic Way that stretched from the western Moon Gate to the eastern Sun Gate. In all, they had lived like nobility compared to most of Alexandria's citizens.

81

Although Xanthippe had known, from the age of five, that Didymus wasn't her natural father, he had treated her as if she was flesh of his flesh. Her natural father was as much an ebony-skinned Nubian as Fulvia, her mother, but he had died within a year of Xanthippe's birth, and Didymus had married the widow shortly before her daughter's second birthday. And he had proved a loving husband and father.

As for her mother – she adored her new husband. Too much, perhaps. A shrewder eye might have discouraged his obsession with the Gnostic writings of Thomas the Apostle. Didymus was a Gnostic Christian, adherent of a sect whose sources of inspiration were the Gospel of Thomas and other works ascribed to the apostle. One of those works – the Apocryphon of Eastern Paradise – had inspired her father's obsession with the story of Thomas's journey to the east in search of the Island of Paradise, a journey undertaken a hundred and fifty years ago. He resolved to follow in the apostle's wake. And he had no intention of travelling alone. A few days before her twelfth birthday she was holding her mother's and father's hands and staring over the stern as the ship slipped out of the port of Clysma and into the Red Sea.

There followed two years of sailing and strange coastal cities, always heading for the sunrise, searching for lost Eden. The search finally brought them to the northern shores of China, and Silver Music Bay.

It was from this bay, according to Chinese legend, that the Island of Paradise could be glimpsed on rare occasions. But although Didymus sometimes caught a glimpse of Paradise – which the Chinese called P'eng-lai – it always vanished when he set sail for its beguiling shores. Then he would rage and storm at elusive Edens and visions that peek and hide like coy courtesans behind unfolded fans.

But they had no cause for complaint in their reception from the hermits and the whores. They had been treated as honoured guests, particularly Fulvia and herself, because of their dark skin. Dark skin, it transpired, was regarded as the stuff of magic by the bay's inhabitants. And the family lived like nobility in three rooms of the House of the Temple Servitors. Although she and her mother often pined for the glittering air of Egypt and the resplendent streets of Alexandria, they were glad of this friendly haven after the hazards and deprivations of the long, long journey. All in all, they were content enough.

And then, one cold dawn two years ago, her mother and father had walked into the sea. She had watched them from her top-floor window, smiling at first, assuming that the walk into the ebbing tide was some sportive diversion or romantic frolic. Then the waves started to wash over their heads . . .

She remembered seeing a figure far up the beach, apparently watching. It looked like Aklo.

Xanthippe hugged the pale furs to the rich brown of her flesh, shivering in the chill surges of fog. The tears that trickled over her high cheekbones and into her ripe mouth held the harsh salt bite of the sea. She tasted the bitterness on her lips.

'Why did you leave me? I'm so lonely . . .'

Loneliness, vaster than China, vaster than the ocean, opened out to engulf her orphan heart. But this was a battle in which she was a two-year-old veteran, and she had learned the hard lessons of survival.

Behind her dark eyes, she summoned a familiar face. A face of the night.

Every night, the dream came. It was a dream of a long-vanished Egypt, before the rule of the Caesars, before the dynasty of the Ptolemies. In the dream she bore another name: Nefertiti. And she loved a woman from an unknown kingdom in the far Orient. A woman in black, her slanted green eyes almost luminous. A woman who made her ache with pleasure in the bed they came to share. And with each exquisite shudder she called out the woman's name . . .

'Chia,' whispered Xanthippe. 'Chia Black Dragon.'

Love between women, of which Sappho the poetess had once sung so evocatively on the Aegean isle of Lesbos, had been something of a sexual fashion in Alexandria when she was a child. But Xanthippe had never experienced Sapphic emotions as a child or woman. They belonged solely to the dream. To Chia.

And when, over a year ago, she described the dream to Teacher Sung, he took her to his room and pointed out a figure he'd painted on his wall a few weeks before. It was the figure of the girl-woman in her nightly dream. As she stared in awe, Sung informed her that Chia had lived for three thousand years, according to legend and her own testimony. Her physical age, he insisted, was that of a woman of twenty. Did he know if she had loved an Egyptian queen named Nefertiti? No, he didn't. But he knew that she loved only women. Her sexual preference was something of a scandal in the lore of China.

'Chia,' Xanthippe murmured as she turned her back on the dank vapours that ghosted in from the sea and headed for the lamplit door of the conical-roofed whorehouse, her doeskin-booted legs pacing in a steady tempo, brushing tangled seaweed, splashing salty puddles.

Who was Chia? The legends were numerous, and in most she was a figure of evil. She was the Death-bringer. The vampire. The feaster on flesh. She was Chia the Nightmare. Chinese children who misbehaved were warned that Bad Chia would come and get them.

Chinese history condemned Chia. How did Chia's evil reputation square with Xanthippe's dream vision of the sorceress? The dream-Chia inspired awe, but never terror. But how much faith could be put in a dream? One hundred million Chinese couldn't be wrong.

But then, she reminded herself, Teacher Sung – the only person she knew who had met the sorceress – had worshipped her at first sight. Ming-kai hated her, for an undisclosed reason, but he had never met her.

Perhaps it wasn't so foolish to trust a dream. And she so wanted to trust that dream of old Egypt. Chia was her only link with her homeland. The sorceress knew Egypt, knew it better than Xanthippe. Perhaps – perhaps the green-eyed woman in black intended to visit the Land of the Nile again. Perhaps soon. Perhaps she might take Xanthippe . . .

The small, square-sailed junk was halfway out of the bay . . .

All speculation dispersed when Wu-li's dainty profile showed in the open doorway of the whorehouse, still thirty paces distant. 'Xan!' she called out, her summons a fragile plaint in the restless fog and the omnipresent jingle of the Tree of Bells.

'Coming.'

'I was worried,' Wu-li complained as Xanthippe strode up to the door.

The Egyptian smiled down fondly at the small, chignon-crowned face with its delicate features frowning anxiously under a mask of chalk-powder and garish paint. She slid a bare, compactly muscled arm around the tiny, quaking shoulders.

'Don't tell me. Your son's afraid to go to sleep again.'

'You know how he gets when the tree sings,' fretted Wu-li. 'Little Chai-san is so afraid of the thunder-wind bringing the Shadow Man. And I'm so, so tired . . .'

'Say no more,' Xanthippe laughed, waving her long hands in a silencing gesture. 'You're looking at a fool, a volunteer – someone without enough sense to say no. Go ahead and catch up on your sleep.'

Wu-li stood on tiptoe and gave her friend a grateful peck on the cheek. 'I don't know what we'd do without you, Xan,' she declared.

'Oh, forget it.' Xanthippe chuckled shyly. 'I know some stories that'll bore the little devil to sleep in no time.'

'I wish you luck,' grimaced the smaller woman, leading Xanthippe into the mellow lamplight of the Room of Hospitality.

After removing her boots and leaving them in the

company of a small congregation of other discarded footwear on the inner threshold, she followed in Wu-li's mincing steps up the narrow, creaking stairways to the top floor. Grunting and moaning sounds from behind one of the red-painted doors indicated that one of the women was busy about her sacred work of earning more money for the temple from some client in lusty quest for the Jewel in the Lotus, the lingam in the yoni.

Wu-li jerked her head in the direction of the noise. 'That's the magistrate's clerk in there with Nu-chou. Third time this week. I don't know where he gets all the money from.' Arriving at her son's door she gingerly unlatched it and slowly pushed it ajar.

'Bribes,' said Xanthippe. 'That's where the money comes from. Remember how often the old magistrate used to call?'

'Chai-san?' his mother called out softly, peering into the room.

No response. Nothing but the jingle of wind-chimes near the seaward window.

Carefully closing the door, Wu-li flashed a smile at the Egyptian. 'We're in luck, Xan. He's buried in sleep. Let's go back downstairs and empty a jar of wine. Don't worry – he'll be all right. Bad dreams never killed anyone.'

As the tiny woman brushed past her, Xanthippe threw a quick, thoughtful look at Chai-san's door.

'Bad dreams,' she whispered. Her skin tingled in accord with the jingle of the chimes. 'Bad dreams.'


Ming-kai plodded south along the beach, tiger-kite slung over his broad back.

Tramping over the wet sand below the tide-line, he tried to fix his gaze on Melodious Temple just five li ahead, but his eyes were sometimes tempted to stray up to the forest, or dart a quick look back along the northern stretch of shore.

After climbing back down to the beach, he had started

on his trek back to the temple at the time the Tree of Bells lapsed into silence. That silence had tracked every step of his southward journey, evoking the occasional backward glance in the thickening twilight.

*Nothing is following, of course. Nothing is there. Just the silence. Never mind that the silence is like a quiet lute with too-taut strings, ready to leap into life with a snap and a crack. Never mind that it has an unlucky air. Just keep heading for the temple – only five li to go – and try not to keep looking over your shoulder.*

*And don't dwell too much on the forest that fences the bay. Don't let imagination run riot amongst the trees overhead, seeing impeding arms in branches and hindering hands in twigs.*

Ming-kai had spent the best part of daylight in the forest above, looking for trails through the trees. He couldn't find a single one. He was even unable to trace the path he'd taken less than a month ago.

Giving up on the trails, he had plunged into the shadows under the leafy canopy, judging his direction by the moss on the north side of the tree trunks. He had headed due west – so he thought.

But each time he found himself back on the clifftop overlooking the beach. He had lost count of the times he'd aimed west and discovered that his steps had taken him east.

And he had never known the forest to be so quiet: no scuttle of squirrels or trill of birdsong, no sign of any animal.

Just a profoundly disturbing sense of being watched. He had experienced that sensation in the temple: they all had. But in the forest it was as though there were *more* watching eyes. More Watchers.

*Watchers.* He was starting to think like Sung. And he was beginning to sympathize with the aging Teacher.

And there had been one moment, one very specific moment, during his final attempt to breach the barrier of trees, when his heart had hopped a beat.

He had halted under the spreading eaves of a pine, suddenly convinced that someone stood in his path, unseen. The feeling of being stared at by invisible eyes intimidated him, made him almost step back. Then he summoned his resolve and prepared to march straight through the invisible presence.

That was when he heard a soft crunch that drew his attention to the ground in front of him.

A pine cone was folding inwards, crunching as it folded. It closed up and splintered as it pressed itself into the soil.

His fear had been out of all proportion; he had witnessed stranger sights in Forest Bell Village.

Nevertheless, he retreated quietly from the crushed cone and headed back to the bay – not that there was anywhere else to head for . . .

'No,' he exclaimed. 'I won't give in. I'll find a way through the forest. Tomorrow, or another day – I'll find a way through.'

He surveyed the sandy beach ahead, acutely aware of the enfolding silence.

When the Tree of Bells lapsed into stillness, the thunder-wind usually followed. The jangly music of the weeping willow was, frequently, a prelude to the uncanny wind.

He could almost imagine this dense silence as the bay holding its breath, ready to blow down the beach.

The frail cries of seabirds served only to emphasize the unnatural quiet.

Ming-kai's gaze travelled out to sea. The departing junk had kindled its torches. It was visible as a little flame near the southern arm of the bay. The craft would soon be free of the dangerous rocks and shoals, and could speed over clear ocean. He wished it well.

A chorus of forlorn cries overhead made him peer up into the darkening air to a lament of gulls circling overhead. A thin smile creased Ming-kai's lips as he winked at the gulls; any company was welcome this evening. And all birds, it was said, were souls descending from the fields of Heaven to visit the lands of flesh and breath . . .

The thunder-wind exploded from the north, reverberating in the forest, sending echoes flying out to sea.

Ming-kai spun round and squinted northward as though commanded by the voice of the gale. Even at this distance he discerned the first visible manifestation of the thunder-wind: the wet sand and clumped pebbles of the beach erupted in a lightning-snake trail of wild energy headed directly south.

Less than a li from Ming-kai the wind sprang off the sand and hurtled over his head with a tiger roar, launching itself into the middle airs above the waves. He covered his ears against the deafening bellow as the purposive gale stormed overhead.

The gulls flapped and screeched, panic beating in storm-blasted wings.

Then they dropped like stones.

A white brawl of spray sliced across the dark waves as if the sea had suffered a slash-wound and bled boiling milk.

The path of frenzied foam raced south in an unerring line, straight as an unloosed arrow, and almost as fast.

And aimed directly at the torchlit junk, its roar swiftly receding as it approached the ship that rested like a firefly on the waves.

Before the hermit had drawn ten breaths, the little flame on the sea was quenched. No more firefly.

A second or so passed before the distant sound of exploding timber reached his ears.

By that time the roar was returning. The black sea bled white blood as the thunder-wind sped back to the shore, this time aimed straight at Melodious Temple.

As it neared the temple its progress slowed, its white path subsided to a faint silver line. Reaching the shore, its roar lowered to a sullen growl, then sinking below Ming-kai's hearing, its progress now invisible to his sight.

'It springs like a tiger,' he whispered, 'but it stalks like a fox.'

89

After-shock set his limbs trembling. His legs folded and he fell to his knees.

Slumping forward, he spied an object on the sand almost within reach of his trembling fingers. It was the head of a bird, its neck stump resting in the thick sauce of its blood.

It took Ming-kai a few moments to identify the head as that of a gull, for the front part had been freshly ripped off and the eyes were missing from their sockets. The bared bones of the frontal skull, hooded with sleek feathers, faced him like a delicate ivory puzzle.

Chai-san woke with a start, sweat hot on his seven-year-old brow. A Man of Bones, his naked ribs writhing, striking each other, beating a skeletal percussion, chased the boy out of sleep. He could still hear the rat-at-at of jiggling rib-bones in the murky room.

Heart thumping, he sat up in his disordered cot, the pulse of blood in his ears tricking his hearing for a brief spell. As the drumbeat of his heart eased, the clatter of bones changed to a metallic jangle.

It was the jangle of a cluster of bronze wind-chimes dangling near the window that he'd heard, not the clatter of ribs.

His agitated gaze darted about his bedroom. Where was his mother? She'd promised to watch over him tonight. She'd *promised*. And if not his mother, then Xan should be here with her friendly black face smiling at him. He was about to reach for the woollen comfort of the Green Dragon doll that Xan had made for him when his ears picked up the dying noise behind the racket of the chimes. It was the fading sound of the thunder-wind as it approached the house. Other things became louder as they came nearer: the thunder-wind was quieter and quieter the closer it came. And now – he listened intently – now it was as quiet as a ghost's footstep.

But the figures of the chimes made up for the stilling of the thunder-wind. Trembling, Chai-san peered at the wind-chimes that dangled in front of the locked wooden shutters. The bronze shapes seemed to shiver from some strong draught, their rattle resonating in the boy's skull. The noise rose to a din. The din mounted in a raucous crescendo. Gulping back a sob, Chai-san shut his eyes and covered his ears, praying for the Noise Demon to go away. Discord clanged inside his head, rebounded from the pine walls.

And abruptly ceased. A heavy spell of silence descended on the room. Chai-san's eyelids flicked open in surprise, and he surveyed the room with a wary stare. The fitful flow of the yellow paper lantern filled the walls with flickering shadows that were as animated as the silenced chimes were frozen.

The calm of the room didn't fool him. He knew what was coming. He knew what the thunder-wind brought. The Shadow Man. When the thunder-wind blew, the Shadow Man came, each time a little nearer the bed, always quiet, never speaking.

The boy struggled to shout for his mother, but his tongue was like a rock in his mouth. If Mother came in the Shadow Man would stay away because Mother didn't believe in the Shadow Man. If you didn't believe in the Shadow Man then you wouldn't see him, that was what Mother said. But he couldn't stop believing in the Shadow Man no matter how hard he tried. All he knew was that if Mother was here the Shadow Man wouldn't show his face.

That's because he's clever, thought Chai-san. He only comes when you're alone.

Tears filling his eyes, the boy grabbed his Green Dragon doll and hugged it to his chest. Maybe Green Dragon would protect him from the Shadow Man. He buried his face in the woollen doll, mutely pleading for his mother to come and keep him safe.

A gentle creak came from the window. He looked up, startled. Green Dragon dropped from his grasp.

The shutters had swung wide open, displaying a grey evening sky sliced with pink.

Chai-san shrank under the coverlet. The room seemed to expand as the dark in the corners thickened.

It ascended like smoke, wafting from the foot of the bed. It grew a head, arms and legs as it drifted around the straw mattress. The boy fought desperately to convince himself that the Shadow Man wasn't real; that he was dreaming; that he would wake up, and it would be a fine sunny morning, and Mother would ruffle his hair and tell him it was time to get up, and Xan would poke her head round the door and flash one of her lovely smiles as she told him that she'd be taking him on another long walk up the bay to collect more seashells.

He woke up. It was morning. Mother and Xan were with him. He willed it to be so.

But it wasn't so. It was grey and pink evening outside the window. It was dark inside the room. And he was alone with the Shadow Man.

The smoky figure slowly congealed into a shape of flowing silvery-grey, and loomed over the quaking boy.

Who are you? Chai-san screamed in his mind.

And, for the first time, the Shadow Man spoke, in a voice like the sigh of the sea or the whisper of silk:

'I am Quicksilver.'

The so-soft voice lulled some of the boy's fears to sleep. This time was different. This time was special. This time the Shadow Man had spoken his name: Quicksilver.

'I mean you no harm,' soothed the silky tones of Quicksilver. 'Not to worry, little one. You'll never see me again.'

The soporific voice banished Chai-san's lingering qualms, and he regained his speech as a somnolent smile parted his lips.

'What do you want?' the boy heard himself murmuring.

Quicksilver's hand stretched down to the boy's head,

92

his fingers hooking into sharp barbs as they touched the small, smiling features.

'Give me your face,' said the voice of silk.

## 5

When will there be an end of old times and new
    times?
In the wind, a thousand years are plucked and
    scattered.

Li Ho

Black Dragon Valley resounded to the warning peals of
the Sentinel Tree.

Chia, standing fifty paces from the agitated boughs,
glowered at the narrow pass to her mountain valley. The
lonely weeping willow with its talisman-hung branches
had been sounding its alarm for an hour. That meant the
Silver Brethren had been standing on the other side of
the willow for the past hour.

It was fifteen days since the first appearance of the
Silver Brethren. Their presence signalled by the Sentinel
Tree, Nyak's diseased servants had visited the threshold
of her home every day since then, and sometimes three or
four times a day.

Blocked by the tree, they couldn't get in.

Trapped by the Silver Brethren, she couldn't get out.

Impasse.

She expelled a sharp breath and wheeled round from
the pass to scan the tainted slopes of her valley.

As with the first appearance of the Silver Masks, the
soil and trees had been bled white in the last hour. A
pale, silver light glowed from the dipping inclines and
soaring cliffs.

It was a valley brimming with moonlight at noon.

'Tricks,' she muttered, absently drawing her silver dagger. 'Tricks of the light.'

Once every two or three days, they would play this trick of the light on her, as if to show that the silver shine of their masks could invade her home even if they themselves were forbidden access. How and why it was done she couldn't fathom. To threaten her? Rattle her nerves? Convince her that Nyak was alive, playing games with moonlight? Too many options. She had given up trying to choose between them.

Raising the sharp point of her silver dagger, she stared pensively at its gleaming length clasped in a hand made white by eerie moon-glow. The blade was the strongest of her talismans, and at times she sought inspiration from its cold metal, thinking nothing of talking to it as if it were a person.

'What should I do, my little silver killing thing?' she murmured. 'Hide deep in my caverns and stuff my ears until the Silver Bastards decide to go for good?'

She threw a quick glance back at the pass. 'Or should I charge out, dagger in hand, and decorate the day with a little red?'

A frown creased her brow.

*My dogs. My poor dogs. I should make someone pay in blood for them.*

Her green eyes blazed like a forest fire. Perhaps their killing was just the same old message from Nyak's servants. No lovers for Chia. No friends for Chia. No animal company for Chia. The same old message: *You-will-live-alone.*

'Is Nyak back?' she caught herself whispering. She bit her lip at the thought she'd let slip.

No, he wasn't back. Her brother was dead and done with. The Silver Bastards were trying to fool her into thinking he'd returned, or was returning, from the dead. She struggled to expel the thought from her mind. But the thought, like a rabid hound, wasn't easily driven away.

Chia recalled the thunder that had echoed in her valley on that first day, heralding the Sentinel Tree's warning and the moonlight-by-day. Its curious rumble reminded her of the thunder-wind of Nyak's passing as his spirit roared out of Celestial Buddha Temple and over the Forest of the Ancestors.

'No!' she snapped, shaking her head free of speculation. 'I'm falling for the Silver Masks' tricks. They want me to think he's back. They like me to be afraid.'

And, she reasoned, there was one man who might have taken over leadership of Nyak's leaderless flock: a man called House.

She had never set eyes on the oddly named House. But she had seen the results of his handiwork all over China.

First he eviscerated his victims, then he nailed their five wu-hsing organs to the walls of their homes.

He wasn't one of the Silver Brethren, that was evident in the manner of his murders, but he was closely connected with Nyak's followers. One of the few facts known about House was that a Silver Brother named Providence often accompanied him on his travels and killings. Otherwise, House was dark mystery. Origins, unknown. Description, unknown. Residence, unknown.

The only real scrap of information she had, based on rumour, was that House was a T'aoist hermit.

Chia sighed and shook her head. What was the point in speculating? Without her Thzan-tzai powers she hadn't a chance against more than a few of the Silver Brethren, let alone the formidable House.

Without her powers she was all but helpless.

Without her powers —

She glanced at a small boulder near her feet.

Before the Silver Brethren's arrival, she wouldn't have dreamed of releasing the powers she'd locked in a dungeon deep inside her body. Even now, she was sure she was incapable of turning the key. Her mind would rebel against the Thzan-tzai power of thought made flesh.

96

But – she studied the boulder – if she could free just a little power. The tiniest amount. It might not corrupt her, and it would supply a sharp edge over the Silver Bastards.

Perhaps a small test. After all, she could halt the experiment the instant it threatened to get out of hand.

She picked up the boulder, the fingers of her right hand barely managing to sustain a purchase on its smooth surface, and closed her eyes.

Chia went within, into the dark behind her eyes; into the deeper dark of her soul. The descent was surprisingly effortless.

A dungeon. A door. A key.

*Don't open it. Don't even touch the key.*

Her right hand, pale as the moon, touched the key. And turned it a fraction – a mere fraction . . .

Eyes springing open at the crack of shattering stone, Chia saw the boulder explode in her hand. Sharp shards flew through the long fingers like flint knives. As though her entire flesh had petrified, the shards bounced harmlessly off her face and torso.

Adamantine though her body had become, her mind was in turmoil. Lunatic notions of power, power and more power whirled her wits.

Vaguely, she was aware that the unnatural moonlight had intensified in the valley, plunging her into a world of black and white.

It was a long fight back to what passed for sanity in Chia's brain. But she fought it, every step of the way.

And finally, she won. Her vision cleared. Her surroundings swam back into focus. The mad power conceded defeat and slunk back to its dungeon. Inside her, she sensed a key snap a lock tight shut.

As if to crown her success, the moonlight faded from the valley, and the colours of nature returned, all the brighter for their hour-long absence. At her back, she heard the Sentinel Tree lapse into silence. Her unwelcome visitors had departed – for a while.

97

The thud of her heart receded to a steady pulse, and she heaved a sigh of relief. It had been an insane test to attempt. But she had survived it.

'Never again,' Chia said. 'Never, never again.'

Her eyes strayed to her right hand, palm filled with flakes of stone from the massive contraction of her fingers.

'Never again. Never – '

There was a small lump at the base of forefinger and thumb. It throbbed rhythmically. Its surface rippled like wind on water. And it grew. It grew very fast. Something resembling a mouth unfolded from the bulging lump, and formed pouting lips . . .

Chia's face was moist with sudden sweat.

*My hand – wild flesh.*

But almost as swiftly as the lump had expanded, it started to shrink. The pouting mouth sank into smooth skin. The flesh-ripples died out.

Before she had expelled a dozen breaths, the lump had faded into oblivion. But Chia kept her hand under close scrutiny for a long time until she was thoroughly convinced that no more bad miracles still lay in waiting.

Dropping her hand to her side, her gaze slid down the wooded slopes of Black Dragon Valley until they alighted on the distant mouth of her cavern.

Much of the past was hidden in the dark of that cavern mouth. The loving past.

Right now, she needed to live in that past for a little while.

With each step into the past, it grew a little lighter.

'Lu t'ai-fong, dead for thirty years,' murmured Chia as she passed a mound of stones erected against the cavern wall. The name on the wooden marker, barely visible in the blue radiance of the Night-Shining Jewel in Chia's hand, bore a dedication at its base: 'I, Chia, loved you.'

'Wu-kai,' she read out, passing the next tomb, 'dead

for seventy years.' And below the woman's name: 'I, Chia, loved you.'

The same dedication was on the next woman's tomb, as it was on all the tombs. 'Chan-li,' said Chia, 'dead for over a century.'

Step by step, she walked further into the past. And the older the shrines of her dead loves became, the nearer she drew to the bright arch of daylight at the end of the tunnel. One by one, she called to memory all the women she had loved in her life.

Dead for over a hundred and fifty years. Dead for almost two hundred years. Dead for two hundred and thirty years. Dead for over three hundred years.

Each name brought forth a memory, no matter how fragmentary, and the fragments of memory ranged back through the centuries. The deeper into the centuries she moved, the more easily discernible the names became with the increasing light, and the more hazy the remembered face, as if daylight was the enemy of memory.

Ten centuries . . . eleven . . . twelve . . .

The tunnel widened as it neared its mouth. Sunlight picked out the details of mounds of clumped stones, and the lustre of the Night-Shining Jewel faded in the light of the sun.

Thirteen centuries . . . fourteen . . .

She halted at the last tomb. Like the rest, it was a mound of stones. Unlike the rest, it was empty. It had always been empty. It was a token tomb, a memorial for a woman buried in a distant land. It was raised in homage to the first woman she had loved and the one whom, after all these centuries, she loved more deeply than all others.

In this one shrine, bright light and bright memory were in accord.

Fifteen centuries ago . . .

Chia's voice was barely louder than the mild breeze blowing into the cavern: 'Nefertiti, Queen of Egypt, Daughter of the Nile.'

She stood for a time, head bowed, suffering her recollections of past happiness. Then, eyes misting, she turned her back on the shrine and walked over to her handiwork near the cave mouth.

'Almost finished,' she muttered as she lifted up the black serge garment she had been working on for the last fifteen days. Chia had a dual purpose in mind when she commenced fashioning the garment: it was firstly an experiment, an attempt to create a novelty; it was secondly an effort to doff her cloaked, hooded image which had become a virtual second skin, a constricting skin. If she shed it, perhaps a new character might grow.

She had fulfilled her first purpose, or very nearly. She had adapted the long, almost ankle-length robe favoured by the courtiers in the Imperial Palace of Loyang, adding a waist-belt secured by loops, a wide, flexible collar that could be turned down as well as up, and patch pockets. And she had replaced metal peg-and-loop fasteners with a row of silver moon coins that slotted into a corresponding row of holes. All in all, the result was fairly inventive and appealingly outlandish. There was probably a law against it.

But as for the second purpose – changing her character by altering her attire, changing the contents by changing the wrapping . . .

'Foolishness.' She exhaled heavily. 'Utter foolishness. Put a monkey in a red Kang-i robe, by all means, but don't expect it to start writing poems about the T'ao.'

Her wide mouth stretched into a wry smile. She gazed up at the valley until her vision came to rest on the Sentinel Tree. The smile faltered. The talisman-bedecked weeping willow was mute for the time being, which meant that Nyak's servants had departed. But they wouldn't be gone for long. They had come and gone many times since their first appearance fifteen days ago, their alternating presence and absence marked by the jangle and silence of the magical metal on the weeping willow. She glowered at the narrow gap beyond the Sentinel Tree.

'They'll be back, the bastards.'

*What do they want?*

Casting the black serge overcoat aside, she picked up the long, lacquered box of the ch'in lute, and idly improvised a melody, twanging its seven silken strings with her fingernails.

Her thoughts meandered into the past . . .

Golden fingers plucking an Egyptian lute behind beaded curtains. The golden fingers of Nefertiti, fingernails painted silver. The warm brown eyes of Nefertiti. The full, moist mouth. Mouth parted, whispering – 'Forgive me, Chia.'

A discordant twang issued from the ch'in lute in sympathy with a jolt of disharmony in her spirit. Chia frowned in puzzlement as she placed the lacquered instrument on the ground. *Forgive me, Chia?* What had Nefertiti ever done that required her forgiveness? Had Nefertiti ever hurt Chia in any way?

'Nonsense,' she snorted. Nonsense. False memory. Treacherous memory. 'She would never – '

The alarm of the Sentinel Tree jangled into her thoughts. She stabbed a sharp glance at the narrow head of the valley.

'The dung-heads are back,' she growled, seething with resentment at their incessant coming and going.

*What do they want? To keep me prisoner in my own valley? They can't get in, but they're making sure that I can't get out. But why? What the hell do they want?*

For stretched minutes she sat, eyes fixed on the Sentinel Tree, ears assailed by the metallic din of the talismans. Then a flare of rage swept her to her feet.

'To hell with this!' she exclaimed. 'I've had as much as I can stand.'

Chia tightened the cord on her black cotton trousers and was on the verge of racing up to confront her tormentors when she realized that her black silk tunic was wide open at the front, exposing her compact breasts.

101

'They're not going to ogle my nipples again,' she muttered, wrapping the tunic tightly around the upper body and securing it at the waist with a crimson sash. Thrusting the silver dagger inside the crimson sash, Chia strode purposefully down the mild incline to the shallow stream. As her feet splashed through the muddy waters, her green eyes flashed a look at the five small mounds containing the remains of her dogs. The line of her mouth hardened.

'Wood, Earth, Metal, Fire and Water,' she said in a sad breath. 'They used to kill the women I loved – now they're killing the animals as well.'

*What do they want? Has Nyak returned, fresh from the dead? Does the battle go on?*

The trees closed in as she ascended the trail to the narrow pass in the circle of cliffs, the alarm of the Sentinel Tree ringing ever louder in her ears. Emerging into the wild glade fronting the weeping willow with its clattering talismans, she drew the magical blade from the sash, her expression grim.

Sometimes there were three Silver Brethren on the other side of the Sentinel Tree. Sometimes there were as many as seven. If, this time, there were three – or even four – she would take them on. The loss of her Thzantzai powers reduced her chances against Nyak's masked servants, but she still believed that she had the edge on her enemies if they were fewer than five. And it was time she made some move to dissuade the Brethren from lurking at her threshold.

'Here comes trouble, you masked morons,' Chia hissed as she rounded the jangling tree.

In the pass beyond the Sentinel Tree the Silver Brethren waited. Scores of them. Rank after rank of silver-masked, grey-mantled figures, all mounted on skittish horses.

A hundred arms were raised in salutation.

A hundred voices were lifted in greeting.

'Share in our loving flesh.'

Chia shrank back until her spine was pressed against the scaly bole of the weeping willow. Tremors ran up her knife-hand.

'Who sent you, you pack of vermin?' she called out, unable to keep a shake of fear from trembling in her tone. 'It couldn't be Nyak – he's dead and damned.'

The foremost of the Brethren edged his steed forward a few paces, halting less than five strides from where Chia shivered under the agitated branches. A red sign glowed from his silver brow, blazing his cult-name for all the world to read: *Reproach* shone luridly from the wrinkled metal.

'We bring you love,' proclaimed the hoarse tone of Reproach. 'Protective love. Love that will keep you safe from the world.'

'Who sent you?' persisted Chia, fighting to subdue the monster fright rearing up inside her breast. 'Not my brother. He's in hell. I sent him there.'

'The Master is returning,' wheezed Reproach from the small, rounded mouth of his monstrous t'ao-tieh mask. 'He returns in power. The truth has made him strong.'

'He returns from death?'

'Disease is the flesh at play,' intoned Reproach, his mask sparkling in the noon sun. 'There is no death for the playful flesh.'

'Then where is he, or are you afraid to tell me?'

Chia almost imagined that a mocking smile touched the silver lips for an instant. His answer served to heighten the hint of mockery. 'The Master has many faces. The Master is where you will never look.'

The sorceress gradually eased round the trunk of the tree to place it well and truly between herself and the mounted host.

'What in the names of the hells do you want?' she whispered.

The Silver Brethren could pick up the faintest whisper – or even a thought, if it was strong enough.

'We offer you the playful flesh,' replied Reproach. 'But we know you of old, Black Dragon. Your mind is as dark as your attire. You always refuse the love of the infinite flesh. So what you will not receive gladly, we must force upon you.'

Chia's sweating hand clasped the ankh hanging at her breast. 'Keep your sacred diseases to yourselves. That's one game my flesh isn't going to play. The Sentinel Tree blocks your way into my valley. None of your kind has got within two paces of it and lived – not in three thousand years.' In an upsurge of confidence, she squared her shoulders and tilted her chin at a haughty angle. 'But perhaps you think the barrier has weakened, or that you've grown stronger.' She bowed and flourished her hand in invitation. 'Why not ride into my valley, Reproach? Urge that nervous steed of yours past the Sentinel Tree. See if you survive.'

To her surprise, Reproach shook the reins, and his horse, ears flicking, mouth champing at the bit, obeyed the signal. As the horse stepped forward, Chia stepped back, pace for pace.

Her vision of horse and rider misted briefly as she experienced a sharp, disconcerting tug in her brain. By the time her gaze had cleared, Reproach was riding under the jangling boughs of the Sentinel Tree.

Thinking that a mixture of fear and bright sunlight had tricked her eyesight, she rubbed her eyes. When she looked again, the Silver Brother had already steered his mount past the weeping willow.

And the gold and bronze and silver talismans on the tree became suddenly mute, as if in shock from the violation of her valley. Chia was stunned: what kind of creature had Nyak bred in this Silver Brother called Reproach? Nyak himself would have been ripped asunder if he had dared to breach the protective barrier, but here was one of Nyak's servants riding in as if she had lifted it to admit a friend. Nothing in the set of

Reproach's body suggested that he was even suffering discomfort as he invaded her home.

Instinctively, Chia crouched into a fighting stance, silver dagger weaving to and fro, her left hand hooked in the action of the tiger claw. A Silver Brother who had the power to breach her invisible wall was a formidable foe to confront, especially in her present enfeebled state. It would take all her remaining skills, fused in concentration, to overcome this advancing menace. But it took all the strength she could muster to keep the dagger steady in her perspiring palm.

Reproach reined in his grey mare and dismounted from the bulky saddle. With slow strides, he came almost within range of her dagger. With exaggerated emphasis, he commenced drawing the mail gauntlet from his right hand.

Chia exulted inwardly, hardly believing her luck. The deadliness of the Silver Brethren resided in their hands – their naked hands. Her adversary should have removed the gauntlets while still on horseback. His brief delay was an error. A fatal error. Chia unleashed her deep hate . . .

. . . and leapt with a roar at the mantled figure, her bare feet slamming into the narrow chest, cracking ribs and lifting him into the air to flop on his back beside the nervous mare. As he landed she pounced on to his flailing arms, pinning them with the downward thrust of her knees. In a derisory gesture, she waved the glittering blade a nail's breadth from the eye-holes in the t'ao-tieh mask.

'Try planting your hands of loving flesh on me now,' she taunted.

A noxious odour wafted from the silver mouth-aperture as Reproach exhaled his response: 'As you wish, Woman of Darkness.'

Tiny reverberations in the outspread arms made Chia glance from gauntlet to gauntlet. Beneath the musty bandages enfolding the arms, lumps were burgeoning in

105

the upper wrists. As the swelling blossomed the bandages stretched to near ripping, and the glove fingers flopped, emptied of their contents.

Watching the performance with dismay, Chia recalled what she should never have forgotten: that the Brethren had an impressive repertoire of flesh-play. And one of the flesh-games was the retraction of hands into wrists.

The engorged lumps of the wrists now came free of the gauntlets. Barely in time, Chia spread her knees wider, shifting her weight from the opponent's elbows to his lower arms. The bloated wrists sprouted the root of a hand, the hand-root sprouted fingers, the fingers sprouted long, metallic nails. The sprouting flesh was blood-red and palpitant, like hand-shaped hearts.

The Silver Brethren rarely held weapons in their hands, for their hands were their weapons, throbbing with the diseases of the playful flesh. And this Silver Brother wielded the Red Plague in his palms and fingers. A single touch of that red hand on her exposed skin would kill her unless quickly scoured by fire – and a scratch from the sharp fingernails would spread scarlet corruption through her body in seconds, leading to a swift death, fire or no fire.

But the squirming hands couldn't reach her skin. The prone Reproach was helpless. It seemed she'd greatly overestimated his prowess, assuming his invulnerability to the Sentinel Tree was evidence of deep power. But here he lay, innocuous as a trapped bat.

Chia's smile had all the curved glee of a scimitar. Positioning the point of the dagger above the right eye of the unearthly mask, she spoke in a tone of mock-regret. 'Look your last on the world, Reproach.'

'You too, Black Dragon,' breezed a carious breath from the silver mouth.

His words were underscored by the rhythmic thump of hooves from above . . .

Heart slamming, she looked up to witness a sight that nearly stopped her heart.

Silver Brethren were galloping around the silent Sentinel Tree and down into her glade.

In that one, awful sight was revealed why the Silver Brother beneath her had proved so easy to vanquish. It wasn't any inherent power in Reproach: it was the Sentinel Tree itself. It had lost its efficacy. It was no longer a barrier. Black Dragon Valley was open to her enemies.

And in they stormed, mask-helmets glinting in the sun, grey mask-hair swirling in the wind, the vanguard of a hundred invaders.

Chia bowed her head in despair, her bleak, defeated gaze resting on the silver dagger.

What was one blade against two hundred killing hands?

'Nothing,' she groaned. Nothing. Her days under the sky were done.

'Nefertiti,' she sighed, closing her eyes, visualizing her dead lover's face. It was the last image she wanted to see before true death offered her nothing.

'Nefertiti, I love you.'

## 6

> The dead leaves, don't you see them?
> They are restless on floors and stairs.
> Will the leaves that are brown turn to green?
>
> Pao Chao: *Hsing lu nan*

The bloated body went the way of the tide, toing and froing with the streaming seaweed. As though in league with the sea, it offered ponderous resistance to the two pairs of brawny arms that struggled to wrest it from the waves.

At length, the two fishermen succeeded in hauling the corpse on to the shore of Silver Music Bay, where they let it drop, face down, into the suction of the soaked sand.

'Do you think he'll still have those sea-green eyes?' pondered Wen-fen, the younger of the two men.

From the tattered tunic they had already identified the dead body as that of Chien-long, who had once been a skilled sailor in the distant days when Forest Bell Village had been a small but thriving port-of-call on the India route.

'Poor old Chien-long, he taught me a handy trick or two when I was a lad,' reminisced Fo-tong, the elder of the two fishermen. 'He said he was going to desert the Full Pearl cult – swim free of the bay. The only way out, he said, after what happened to the ships.' He sucked in a deep breath. 'Come on, turn him over. Let's take a proper look.'

The inflated body emitted a silty squelch as they tipped it over. It flopped face upwards.

Except there wasn't a face.

There was a rough circle of puckered skin around the front of the head, but all that gleamed from within the ragged circle was bone, polished bone.

Chien-long's entire face – eyes and all – had been lifted off. His head looked like a skull wrapped in a hood of skin.

'Mother of the West,' invoked Wen-fen, making the sign against evil as he sprang back from the body.

'Just a few of us left now,' reflected the other. 'How long do you think we're going to last outside Aklo's cult?'

Wen-fen shook his head, bulging eyes staring into empty sockets. 'Not long.' He gestured to the faceless head. 'What – what could have done that?'

'Do you think it could be the work of a man?'

'Perhaps,' came the tentative reply, along with a slight shudder. 'But what sort of man collects faces?'

Clouds of midges, summoned by dusk, pestered Xanthippe's face as she headed for the main door of the whorehouse.

'Get away, you little devils,' she snapped as she waved her hand and slapped the insects on her brow and cheeks. Once indoors, the midges dispersed and she mounted the stairs, free of their attentions. Her skin still smarted, but the trouble in her mind gained precedence.

These days, there was nothing but trouble . . .

*Chia – when will you come to us?*

Tears formed in the corners of her eyes as she opened the door of Chai-san's room and gently closed it behind her. Wu-li was in her usual place, squatting on a velvet cushion plumped close by her son's bed. Sung, Ming-kai and Hua Shan sat on a heap of cushions in the far corner, their expressions sombre in the dusk. Lighting an orchid-scented candle, Xanthippe stole softly to the dainty figure of Wu-li.

'Any change?' enquired the Egyptian as she knelt beside her friend.

Wu-li didn't respond. Her once pretty, delicate

features were lined and haggard, as if a harsh decade had seeped into her face. Smeared paint framed her glassy eyes. Hanks of hair hung about her shoulders, like frayed rope. For all Xanthippe could tell, Wu-li wasn't even aware of her presence.

The Egyptian switched her attention to Chai-san, tucked up in his cot.

If what was in the cot could be called Chai-san.

No matter how much Xanthippe fought the idea, she couldn't help wishing that the boy had died two months ago on that twelfth night of the fourth moon. Surely he was better off dead.

Chai-san's mother commenced her sing-song lament. 'The Shadow Man came for him. I should have believed. The Shadow Man came for him. I should have —'

'Hush,' soothed Xanthippe, sliding an arm round Wu-li's shoulder. 'No one's to blame.' *But I blame myself.* 'He'll get better.' *He'll never recover.*

'No, no, no,' wailed the distraught Chinese. 'I've lost him. I've lost my boy.'

Biting back her own remorse, Xanthippe comforted the grief-stricken woman as best she could, sparing the occasional icy glance over Wu-li's head at Sung munching his magic mushrooms and minding his own selfish business.

But time and again, her attention was pulled back to the small figure in the cot.

There was nothing missing from Chai-san's face. No gouges marred the plum cheeks. No chunks had been cut from his lips. Everything was intact: skin, eyes, nose, mouth, ears. Nothing out of place, nothing blemished. As far as physical appearance counted, the boy's visage was whole and healthy.

But the human face is more than an assemblage of parts, Xanthippe bleakly observed. It's more than skin and tissue. Every human face has an expression, however vacuous. Each face has a character, albeit the

110

shallowest. Even in sleep, personality shines through the skin. And in death – even in death – character is imprinted in the rigid features. The seal of the soul is in all facial flesh.

But Chai-san's face was – not a face. It was devoid of either humanity or inhumanity. It was nothing. Moulded meat, robbed of individuality. Breathing meat – that was all that was left of Chai-san. The wavering light of the candle revealed a nothing face.

For two months he'd just lain there, breathing. He – it – didn't speak, or eat, or sleep, or even blink his open eyes. And he smelt as if his body was saturated with sour milk.

Between the waxen face, pallid yellow in the small, hot room, and the curdled stench, she shook as she fought a bout of nausea.

'He's on the moon. He's on the moon,' Hua Shan rambled. 'Looking at moon stars.'

The sour-milk stench thickened, curdling the air she breathed. Her stomach staged another rebellion. Hand over mouth, she sprang to her feet.

'I'm just going – I won't be – '

She flung open the door, then slammed it behind her.

A few deep breaths and her stomach steadied. She made her groggy way down the stairs and out on to the shingle of the upper beach.

Her stomach continually threatening to heave, she yearned, with every fibre and muscle, to be free of China. She wanted to stand by the quiet shore of Alexandria's Lake Mareotis, not by this alien, turbulent sea.

She glanced at the wide energy of the ocean with its multitude of islands, then darted a fierce look at the crescent of tree-clad cliffs. She was locked in. Locked into a nightmare. The thunder-wind destroyed the craft that sought freedom by way of waves. The trees were a secret society that drove you back from the forest.

Locked into a Chinese nightmare

'*No!*' she screamed out. She had nothing to do with Chinese ghosts. In the well of her soul, she rejected them.

Then she saw a Chinese ghost, as if her rejection had prompted its appearance.

It appeared thirty paces in front of her. It was clad in a long, ragged grey mantle. It had a silver mask, and from its crown flowed a mane of grey hair almost as long as the mantle, grey on grey. A Chinese character glowed from its brow in luminous red.

She felt the intensity of its masked gaze beating upon her. It was the same feeling of being watched that she'd experienced a thousand times in this bay. And she suddenly realized that she'd seen such silver-masked men many times over the past years – and forgotten that she'd seen them.

The masked figure raised a gauntleted hand. 'We bring you the sharing love.'

Numbly, she shook her head, trying to back away. But it was impossible to deny the eerie whisper that flowed out of the metal mouth and swam round in her skull.

'You can't really see me,' the whisper thundered in her head.

The figure faded quickly from her sight.

'I'm not really here.'

She had a strong feeling that someone stood some thirty paces in front of her, but the feeling dispersed in moments.

*I don't exist.*

Xanthippe hugged the white robe tight to her skin, and stared bleakly out to sea. 'I wish I was by Lake Mareotis,' she murmured.

She stirred uneasily, pulling the robe still tighter.

That feeling is back again, she observed ruefully, that feeling of being watched. The Watchers: Sung's 'subtle ghosts'.

For a moment it struck her that she had forgotten something, but the thought quickly passed.

Eventually she retraced her steps to the whorehouse. If some power had locked them into the bay, then she would lock *herself* into her own room. She would climb into her own bed, then climb into her own dream. The Chia dream. The Egypt dream.

'Nefertiti . . .'

'Mmm – yes,' the sleeper mumbled.

'You are Nefertiti, Queen of Egypt, Daughter of the Nile . . .'

'I'm Nefertiti,' she muttered, deep in sleep.

'You are in the North Palace of the City of the Horizon of Aten. And Chia Black Dragon is making love to you . . .'

'*Yes,*' Xanthippe sighed contentedly, curling up under the woollen covers.

'You must love Chia Black Dragon,' whispered the metal mouth.

Xanthippe's answering smile was a wide, curved yes.

'The more you love Chia,' the Silver Brother whispered, 'the more she will love you.'

'I know,' sighed Xanthippe, sealed eyelids flickering.

'If you are willing to die for Chia, then she will be willing to die for you,' whispered the Silver Brother, whose name 'Devotion' glowed red on his silver brow.

Xanthippe's smile softened in response to the sibilant suggestion.

'Sleep on,' Devotion commanded, moving back from the Egyptian's rumpled bed. 'Dream of Egypt. Dream of Chia.'

Xanthippe snuggled deeper into the mess of blankets with a low, happy whimper like a satisfied pup.

And Devotion stepped out of her room, trod softly down the stairs, and joined the white-sign Silver Brother named Providence by the edge of the sea.

'She saw again,' Devotion exhaled softly.

'She sees too often,' Providence wheezed through the rounded lips of his mask.

'What is your command?'

Providence turned his metal face towards the whore-house. 'Follow her at all times. Whisper to her always.

113

When she has served her purpose, the living wood will want her intact and obedient. Keep her safe and bend her to our will. Bend her to our will, Devotion.'

Devotion bowed. 'I hear, Providence.'

Aklo, a solitary rambler, covered the beach in lazy strides, his gaze straying left to the high stretch of the Ancestral Gallery, and right to the high, high moon.

'Beautiful,' he sighed. 'Beautiful.'

His pace slowed almost to a halt as he neared the landward end of Sea Rock. Lunar lustre enchanted the promontory, the glittering waves, the crescent bay, uniting heaven and earth in silver communion.

Aklo's Rainbow Robe, all the shades of silver and grey in the eye of the moon, susurrated as the silken folds were drawn off his body by needle-nailed fingers. And the willowy youth stood naked on the beach, arms uplifted to the moon.

'White Lady,' he crooned. 'You are in the moon, lonely Cheng-o. You *are* the moon, lovely White Lady. Night's pearl. And the world' – he gave a shrill titter – 'the world is your oyster.'

His mirth subsided as a gauze of cloud veiled the gleaming sphere. He tilted his head and bent his lips in a wistful slant. 'Oh, *Lady*, why so coy? I'm naked before you, yet you hide. Why so demure? How can you resist my beautiful, beautiful body, Miss Prim?'

In moments, the moon was unveiled, irradiating the earth with the splendour of her nudity.

'Yes,' Aklo moaned softly. 'Oh yeeesss . . .'

He felt the moonlight sift into his pores, tingling his smooth skin. Moonbeams played night games with his flesh. He swayed, languorous as a deep sea frond, in a liquid trance.

Sighing gently, Aklo bathed in the moonlight.

At length, banners of cloud were raised over the moon, the earth darkened, and Aklo slumped to the sand.

'Oh – oh – ' he exhaled. 'I feel so – so *different*.'

114

Lurching to his feet he donned the Rainbow Robe and resumed his progress towards the weeping willow at the tip of the promontory.

His nimble steps negotiated the jagged spine of Sea Rock with the easy grace of an acrobat.

'I feel so – special.'

Entering the waste garden surrounding the weeping willow, he gazed fondly at the bell-crowded branches.

'Male and female in perfect accord.' He smiled benignly, his eyes roving the involute configuration of the Tree of Bells. It was, despite its name, two trees, but two trees so interfused and interwoven, male willow and female willow, that the two willows grew and lived as one.

Aklo's attention glided from the tree to the long sweep of cliffs to the south, his eye-line tracing the full twenty-li length of the Ancestral Gallery. He could envisage the dead in their shabby little houses, eyes of malachite and lapis lazuli glinting in moonglow. Inside their wicker effigies, the dead stood so quiet and patient in front of the tiny windows. So quiet. So patient.

He reached out a comforting hand to the dead. 'Soon, my children. A little more patience. Soon.'

Aklo knelt before the Tree of Bells, his back to the sea and the moon. Eyes closed tight, he murmured his supplication: 'Come back, you male-females, you female-males, come back to the Wound.' His needle-glinting hand swept across the curve of the bay.

'Come back to the Wound you left behind.'

As the moon floated across the sky, he closed his eyes and swayed from side to side, listening to the voice in his skull.

From time to time he touched the ten needle-nails to his temples. 'It's all in the head,' he chuckled quietly. 'All in the head.'

Finally he opened his eyes and turned south, stretching his needle-nails to the whorehouse hidden in dark and distance.

'Beautiful Black Skin of Egypt,' he sighed. 'Beautiful Dark Woman. I'd love to become familiar with that unfamiliar Black Skin.'

He sucked in a deep draught of night, visualizing the exact hues and textures of the Black Skin . . .

. . . and sent out a piercing thought-whisper south down the bay. It carried his invitation thirty li over sand and sea. For dark ears only:

'Come live with me in the moonlight.'

## 7

Night's ink floods the falling road at my back.
The tiger's roar descends from the rising road
    ahead.
Such times as these, the traveller's heart
Is a lofted flag in a high wind.

Meng Chiao

Silver dagger . . .

The sleeper stirred for a moment, unsettled by her dream, then quietened under the covers and dropped back into sleep.

Chia –

Chia, in her valley, straddled the prone figure of the Silver Brother called Reproach.

She stared at her silver dagger in despair as the Silver Brethren, mounted on their horses, charged round the impotent Sentinel Tree.

'Nefertiti,' whispered Chia, eyes fixed on the Silver blade. 'I love you.'

Her head sank in defeat.

Then her whole body tensed. She glanced back at the dagger. Then gave a swift look at the tree, with its mute talismans: wood and metal.

'Talismans,' she declared. Another glance at the blade. 'Talisman,' she whispered.

Her arm was rising even as the last syllable parted her lips. Grip tight on the point of the blade, she bent her arm . . .

. . . and launched the dagger at the bole of the weeping willow. It hurtled through the air, a flash of quicksilver in the sun. And buried its point deep in the wood.

The effect was instant. The Sentinel Tree came alive, thrilling to the energy of the greatest of her talismans. It beat its metal music with gusto. Its jubilant peals rebounded from the walls of Black Dragon Valley.

And the metallic percussion beat into the masked heads of the Silver Brethren, hammering death, stroke by stroke, into the skulls inside the silver helmets. Only three riders were far enough into her glade to resist the sorcerous battering; they steered their mounts as best they could, spurring the horses to gallop at full stretch down into the valley and away from the maddening tree. In front of the weeping willow, the bodies of six Silver Brethren sprawled on the ground. As she watched, with dark glee, one of the bodies was trampled by a bolting horse.

Chia laughed with pure joy. Six dead Brethren in the glade, and at least that number on the far side of the tree. And the Sentinel Tree a mighty barrier once more, as long as the dagger rested in its wood. And inside the valley, four Brethren, three of them already half-crazed from the jingle-jangle music.

She looked down at Reproach, her cruel smile touched with a hint of the sensual. 'This is going to be such a pleasure,' she murmured. 'Don't spoil it by dying too soon.'

Reproach began to thresh wildly under her. She felt her body rocking . . .

The sleeper twisted beneath the covers as the dream evaporated.

Shifting to and fro, the valley disappearing . . .

The dreamer's eyes flickered open.

Stretching, yawning under the rustling covers . . .

No Black Dragon Valley. No Silver Brethren. No Sentinel Tree.

'Just a dream,' she yawned, sitting up and rubbing her eyes.

'Except,' she smiled, 'the dream really happened.'

The smile broadened. Yes, indeed. It really happened.

She reached inside her overcoat and drew out the silver dagger, holding it with point upraised.

'Yes, indeed, my little silver killing thing,' Chia sighed fondly, her green gaze fixed on the gleaming metal. 'It really happened.'

In her dreams, she had often relived that day, three months ago, when she had risen into triumph from despair. Occasionally her dream extended to the slow justice meted to the silver Brethren trapped in the valley. And twice – as she recalled – she dreamed of her escape from the valley on Reproach's horse, although it wasn't much of an escape as there were no Brethren confronting her when she plucked the dagger from the tree and rode into the pass. A lucky happenstance, for she had sensed in her bones that the Sentinel Tree had lost its potency the instant the blade was withdrawn.

'Shame I had to leave, though,' Chia muttered. 'The Brethren must have poured in after I left. They've probably stained all my belongings with their festering hands by now.'

Her mouth slid into a wistful slant. Yes, it was a pity to leave her ancient refuge wide open to her enemies. But there was no choice. The Silver Brethren were incapable of acting of their own volition, and who else but Nyak could order them? She hadn't destroyed Nyak that night, over two years ago, in Celestial Buddha Temple. Doubtless he'd been maimed, his power briefly diminished, but now he was back. And he was stronger. She had to find him, and quickly, before he grew beyond all opposing.

'The battle goes on,' she declared to the torchlit air as she slipped the dagger back into the leather sheath sewn inside her coat.

Chia turned up the collar of the black serge overcoat to muffle her numb ears and, pushing the covers aside, tightened her belt with a double knot. Her movements caused the covers to slide off her body. The covers were paper sheets: Wanted posters – eleven of them, all of her. A smile flickered her lips as she lifted one of the posters into the uncertain illumination of the torchlight. It was the first she had collected in her three-thousand-li journey to the east. When she had sufficient sheets to wrap herself in and conserve warmth during sleep, she left the forty or so other wanted posters in place. If any bounty-hunters were insane enough to stalk her, they would deserve whatever inventive form of death she would concoct for them . . .

'I think I'll use the needles next time,' she mused, momentarily forgetting the poster in her hands.

Her nostrils twitched from the scent of sour milk as her sleepy senses grew wide awake. Like any Chinese, she loathed the smell of milk. Sour milk was ten times worse. And this particular scent, redolent of an old, old acquaintance, was singularly nauseous.

But – she glanced round – in this particular location, the stench would have been more remarkable for its absence.

Sour milk: she'd never get used to that smell.

'But it's part of the territory,' she shrugged, returning her attention to her Wanted poster.

The list of her crimes filled the sheet from top to bottom. She read at random.

*Mass murder.* 'It was fifty men against one woman, and I won,' she shrugged. *Seduction of nine persons of the Imperial Court.* 'It was three,' she contradicted, regretfully. *Incitement to rebellion.* 'I'd do it again.'

There were a few other charges she ruefully acknowledged. *Cannibalism.* 'I was starving,' she muttered. *Unauthorized castration.* 'I loved her. He raped her. End of subject.'

Most of the listed crimes were beyond belief: *flaying babies alive, roasting pregnant mothers over a slow fire.* It wasn't that such vicious acts weren't performed by a few demented lords, it was the notion that she was capable of them which was so ridiculous. 'I'm bad, but I'm not that bad.'

The signature at the corner of the paper explained a great deal: *General Tsao*.

Chia slowly released her breath as she lowered the poster and deposited it with the rest of the sheets. She had already calculated that the authorities would have to execute her more than three thousand times if every supposed case of murder, theft, and so on was to be justly punished.

Who drew up this absurd list of charges? she wondered. General Tsao himself? Did he think that she had tried to kill him the last time their paths crossed? Was that the reason for his vindictive attitude? She sniffed her disdain.

'If I'd wanted to kill you, General, you would have been cold meat these past eight summers.'

But no need to worry, she reminded herself as she unbuttoned the moon coins on her overcoat and stuffed the Wanted posters into two capacious inner pockets, no need to worry about pompous generals. Nyak could literally eat them alive, if he so chose.

'And Nyak,' she observed, eyes roving the narrow confines of the stone sarcophagus in which she lay, 'was here.'

This was where Nyak's body had been kept while his spirit roamed free, over two years ago. Here, in this sarcophagus where she had slept the night. Right here, in this vault far below the Five Faces monolith in the Forest of the Ancestors. And it was here that his tormented spirit had returned, playing havoc with his body.

'But not enough havoc,' she sighed as she rose up inside the stone sarcophagus and glanced down at the rusty residue of old blood around her booted feet. 'Not enough to destroy him. Damn.'

She stepped out of the sarcophagus and glared around the vault.

121

Chia had roved through northern China, exploring seven out of the forty or more sanctums in which Nyak's body might have been kept, before she had investigated this underground vault. It was, in many respects, the most likely chamber in which to house Nyak's body, but she had thought it too close to Celestial Buddha Temple for comfort, from her enemy's viewpoint.

But here it was. Here was where he had lain. The dried blood in the basin of the sarcophagus emitted a faint silver glow. It was Nyak's blood. But where had the body been taken? For two nights she had sat in the vault, absorbing its atmosphere of spiritual slush, but no drops of memory could be wrung from the gelid air. No trace, no clue remained of Nyak the necromancer and his diseased flock. No hint of where the body, living or dead, had gone. And last night's sleep in the sarcophagus had ushered in no dreams of revelation. There wasn't a whiff of the necromancer's after-scent in her dreams, just the usual mixture of lucid recollections and riotous phantasmagoria.

Defeated, she shouldered her leather pack, thrust her chilled hands deep into her overcoat pockets, and headed for the stairs that led up to the base of the mound.

'Where are you?' she kept repeating as she ascended the dank stone steps. 'Where are you?'

By the time she emerged into daylight, pushing open the bronze doors and stepping out into the Glade of the Five Faces, she was dithering between a number of decisions.

'What the hell am I supposed to do now?' she muttered, scanning the ring of forest around the barren glade.

A breach in the northern wall of trees suddenly caught her attention. She had arrived at night, so the gap in the forest had been hidden from her when she entered the glade. Withered, uprooted tree trunks littered the slope that lurched up to the breach.

*The trees were flung into the glade. That was the path by which his tortured spirit had entered.*

Her right hand started to clench and unclench as a spark of hope ignited. Her hopeful gaze surveyed the circle of forest . . .

'There!' she exclaimed, her tight fist thrusting towards the east. *There.*

There – due east of the mound – was another breach in the forest wall. And the trees had toppled *away* from the eastern face of the monolith.

*That was the path by which his spirit fled the body. East. Due east.*

Chia pulled out her round, black glasses and slipped them on. Now she was ready for anything.

All she had as a clue to Nyak's location was the way his spirit had taken. But there was a good chance his servants had carried his body in the same direction. Somewhere to the east, she suspected, his body was slowly re-forming, linking once more with his spirit. She doubted that the resurrection was complete. If Nyak were fully resurrected she wouldn't have been able to ride out of her valley and through China with no opposition from her brother and his cohorts.

Yes, the chances were that he was still resurrecting, powerful, but still vulnerable. And whatever weakness her dear brother possessed, his sister would exploit it to the full.

Fired by enthusiasm, she beat a direct trail to the cleft in the trees, scything through gorse and starved, tall grass. Pushing fingers between pasted lips, she whistled for the horse that Reproach had unintentionally supplied. By the time she had scaled the eastern slope of the desolate glade, the grey mare was galloping across the weed-choked circle, whinnying a welcome to its new rider.

'Had a pleasant wander in the woods, Tumult?' Chia called out as the frisky beast heaved up the slope.

She had named her steed Tumult in memory of the horse's tumultuous response to her first approach. Tumultuous hooves, mostly; she still wore some of the

123

head grazes. But, for all her failings with people, she had a gift for dealing with animals. People could easily be corrupted by the Silver Brethren. Animals were made of sterner stuff and responded more readily to firmness and kindness.

'And anything's an improvement after bearing a Silver Brother on your back, isn't it, Tumult?' she grinned, stroking the light saddle on the mare's back. The saddle included stirrups, an invention she'd thought up during an idle hour, but one she had so far kept secret from the military. The simple innovation gave her the edge in combat, an advantage she intended to keep.

'Glad to see the mad goddess again, are you?' Chia winked as she swung up into the saddle.

Tumult stamped her hooves and whisked her tail. The beast was clearly glad to see the mad goddess again, its previous rider nothing but a bad memory.

Her spirits raised further by the mare's companionship, Chia stared at the eastern face of the monolith rearing from the crown of the burial mound, and smiled with amused contempt.

On each side of the massive rectangular slab, erected in the remote Chou dynasty, mad moon faces had been carved. Their sculpted expressions of inimical mirth stirred a sludge of dread in most souls. But the giant visage that gazed back at her, with its circular head and pouting lips, left her unmoved.

'You're as blind as the moon,' she derided, leaning on the pommel of the saddle. Her shoulder brushed a broken branch that dangled by a slender strip of bark from a tilted beech.

'I wonder,' she mused, eyeing the branch and the moon visage, and the intervening distance – about a hundred and fifty paces.

A hundred and fifty paces was a long way to throw a branch, especially from horseback. But still . . .

'I wonder,' she grinned, pulling the branch free and

standing up in the stirrups, reins firmly in her left hand. With a violent swing, she unleashed the projectile in a spinning arc aimed at the broad, flat nose of the easterly facing visage.

'Take that, five-ways-facing Five Faces Stone,' she laughed, noting that the dipping trajectory was right on target.

As if plucked in mid-flight, the trajectory altered. The branch swooped down to the pouting mouth-aperture. It vanished into the blackness between the ringed lips, for all the world as if the mouth had inhaled the wood.

'Fluke of the wind,' she murmured, sinking back into the saddle. Lines furrowed her brow. *The eastward face, had it swallowed the wood?*

The visage faced east, and wood was the symbol of the East. East was Wood. West was Metal. North was Water. South was Fire. And the Centre was Earth.

Her mouth a wistful curve, she wheeled Tumult round to confront the easterly path of devastated trees.

'Wood, Earth, Water, Fire and Metal,' she breathed to the roaming wind and the woodwind of the boughs. 'My dogs. My poor dogs.'

Surveying the littered aisle between the trees, she attempted to forget the moon face peering at the back of her head.

'Let's go, Tumult,' she urged quietly, twitching the reins. 'There's a two-year-old trail of destruction to follow.'

*And at the end of it, what? Family reunion.*

The mare made slow progress over the shattered boughs, its hooves picking a careful path.

When the nape of her neck prickled too much for comfort, she relieved the cause by glancing over her shoulder at the pouting moon face. It didn't seem to get any smaller the further she travelled.

*The moon is following me, drifting through the trees . . .*

'Oh, Chia!' she exclaimed, furious at herself. 'Sometimes you really get on my nerves.'

She was still grumbling at herself when Tumult whinnied and drew to a halt, foreleg pawing the ground, ears flicking.

'What is it, girl?' Chia leaned forward in the saddle, frowning.

'Easy now,' she soothed, stroking the horse as she dismounted. 'Not to worry. Not to worry.'

She peered down the trail, saw nothing, then looked to the right and saw what had apparently startled the horse: a headless human corpse, half-hidden by a jumble of boughs.

She raised a quizzical eyebrow at the mare. 'You were the steed of a Silver Brother in a China torn apart by three generals squabbling over the ruins of the Han empire, and you're frightened by the sight of a corpse?'

Then her nostrils dilated at the stench from the body. It wasn't the sight that had frightened the horse; it was the scent. It was no natural smell of decay. The sour-milk odour in Five Faces Tomb was Damascene perfume in comparison with this curdled smell.

With a pensive air, she slipped off her dark glasses and slid them into a pocket.

'Brings back bad memories, does it, girl?' she said quietly, wrinkling her nose as she knelt by the corpse.

It was a scent that should have died out ten thousand years ago, the scent that was called either moon-milk or moon-silver. As humans secreted sweat, the Thzan-tzai secreted moon-milk. For humans, moon-milk was lethal acid – to body and soul. And the transformations it wrought were best not remembered on a full stomach.

The Thzan-tzai had long since been expelled from the earth, but they had left their secretion behind. The smell lingered on. And in no person was that moon-milk secretion more concentrated than in Nyak.

The stench hanging in a cloud above the corpse might as well have been mist-characters written on air: *Nyak was here*.

A quick glance showed her that the rib-cage had burst

126

from within – another clear sign of Nyak's prior presence.

Her brother's tormented spirit must have sought habitation in this unlucky traveller two years ago. He would have entered the flesh easily enough. It was perhaps his most vaunted skill – body invasion, spirit possession. Yes, he would have got inside without difficulty.

Staying inside was another matter. Nature turned a blind eye to violations against it – for a time. Then Nature had its own way. In Nyak's case, he was probably allowed only a matter of minutes, or even seconds. The T'ao of the traveller's body would have reasserted the natural balance and flung Nyak's spirit out into the night it dropped from.

And when Nyak was expelled from a body he had stolen, he blew it to pieces from the sheer ferocity of his departure. And left his smell on the remains. Sometimes he left more than that sick scent – sometimes he left a trace of the secretion that was the original source of the smell: moon-milk.

'You were the first to be caught in his path out of Five Faces Mound,' she told the cadaver. 'But you won't be the last. There'll be a line of exploded bodies all the way from here to the Great Sea, or the Great Wall – or wherever.'

She caught sight of the victim's head in a thicket, only visible by its hair, and within reach of her hand – just. She grasped the tangled locks and wrenched the head free of the thorns.

'Call me superstitious, but I wouldn't let you go into the after-life with an incomplete body.'

She held the head between her hands. And her hands froze.

The head was wrapped in fresh, vibrant skin. And for an old, dead head to be in such lively condition, with such a silver twinkle in its eyes, there was only one possibility.

127

The head became a bad miracle in a single breath.

The skin glowed with a pale silver light, forming pits and puckers like the surface of the moon. Then, as if the moon had become a mollusc, it began to grow a shell. There were no eyes to speak of – just two deep folds. The mouth, however, was formed into a rounded pout like the face on the monolith behind her.

The pouting lips blew her a kiss. And spoke.

'Brotherly love.'

A prehensile tongue slid between the lips. It was followed by a flood of frothy moon-milk that coated the sensually probing tongue.

'It's a family affair,' said the milky mouth.

Chia, released from the paralysis of shock, flung her arms wide as she sprang back and vaulted on to the skittish mare.

The head tumbled to the ground and spun for a moment.

When it came to rest, its creased eyes faced east – and watched Chia's flight with quiet amusement.

## 8

I grieve that I was not born in better times,
But have been plunged instead into this mad, fear-ridden age.

*The Songs of Ch'u:* 'Chiu pien'

The tall youth, his florid Robe of Rainbows swishing about him, paced about a bare room of age-darkened willow, uneasy dust swirling from its floor.

In one corner, two lovers cowered. In another, a pregnant young mother quaked in fear.

Aklo, sporting a wide-brimmed hat that mimicked a conical, blue-tiled roof, finally halted his pacing to face a window that let in spears of morning light through its broken shutters.

'Welcome,' murmured Aklo, 'to the House of Heaven.'

Left hand gripped tight, he wheeled round to slant reproachful eyes on his shivering guests. 'Although,' he sighed wistfully, 'it saddens my heart to have to summon you here. Ah yes. Sad. So sad.'

The two lovers, Feng and Wua, exchanged glances but knew better than to speak.

Left hand still bunched into a fist, the Holy Youth uncurled the fingers of his right hand. Three pairs of wide eyes stared at the tips of those fingers, waiting for needle-nails to sprout.

Aklo kept them waiting.

Finally he lowered his right hand and smiled at the lovers with a light, fluttering laugh. 'Oh, I had you worried for a moment there. Go on, admit it.'

Feng nervously nodded his head. Wua, after an uncertain look, bobbed her head in concert.

Aklo's smile thinned. 'What,' he demanded, 'was your great transgression against my religion of love? Do feel free to speak freely.'

'We – ' began Feng, knowing full well that to speak freely was suicide. 'We – me and Wua – fell in love. We –we loved each other instead of loving you above and beyond all things.'

The Holy Youth arched a painted eyebrow. 'Ah yes. This is true. And what do you have to say for yourself, girl?'

'We – we've re-realized our error,' Wua stammered. 'We love you now, more than anything.'

'More than anything,' echoed Feng, sweat flooding his temples.

Aklo ran fingers through his long hair and tilted his dreamy head. 'Hmm,' he mused. 'Has there – how shall I put it? – been any act of what one might call physical congress between you?'

'Oh no,' Feng answered instantly, the truth of his denial evident in his expression. 'We always obeyed you in that.'

Time stretched painfully in the grim, draughty room as Aklo pensively studied the fingertips of his right hand. The lovers bowed their heads, ready to accept whatever terrible punishment was in store.

Aklo's lips suddenly broadened into an indulgent smile. His graceful hand waved them to the door.

'Go, young lovers, and love no more. Your transgressions are forgiven.'

Mouths gaping in gratitude, the two stumbled to their feet, darted a brief glance at the pregnant mother, and headed for the door, tears of relief starting in their eyes.

Still nodding in thanks, they made to step through the open door.

'Just one thing,' Aklo remarked, halting their exit.

They stood at the door, happy to oblige the Holy Man in anything.

130

Aklo smiled benignly at Wua. 'Kneel for a moment, would you, my child?'

She instantly complied, discreetly adjusting the folds of the green cult gown.

The cult master turned his smile on the young man. 'You truly love me above all others, do you, Feng?'

'Oh yes, Master,' came the fervent reply.

'That gladdens my heart,' Aklo sighed. 'Kick Wua in the face.'

Feng's mouth moved but no sound escaped. Wua shuddered at his feet, but managed a shaky whisper. 'Do it. Please do it. *Please.*'

A hurt look showed in Aklo's face. 'Perhaps you don't love me, either of you,' he murmured sadly. He studied his fingertips. 'I really couldn't bear to think that you were lying to me. I really couldn't.'

'*Please,*' Wua begged Feng. 'You must.'

Feng's expression contorted in anguish. There was no appeal against the judgment of Aklo, avatar of Tung Wang Kung. And there could be no delay in obeying his commands.

A sob of pain was forced out of him as he kicked Wua lightly on the cheek. Wua winced but made no sound.

'Oh, Feng, Feng, Feng,' chided the Holy Youth. 'Look how you betray my faith in you.' He flung back his head, as if cut to the soul. 'What half-hearted obedience is this? What demi-loyalty?' He laid reproachful eyes on the tormented young man. 'One last chance, Feng. For both of you.'

Blood trickled from where Feng's teeth ground into his lip. He groaned out loud as he kicked his beloved hard on the jaw. Wua reeled but forced back a cry.

'Again,' ordered Aklo.

Feng bawled like an infant and kicked her on the cheek-bone. Wua gasped in pain.

'Again,' commanded the Holy Youth. 'Break a few teeth.'

The lovers screamed in unison at the crack of enamel.

'Again. The nose this time.'

Screams and the snap of bone.

'Again, wherever you choose.'

Noises of anguish and hurt.

'Again.'

Anguish and hurt.

'Again.'

Anguish. Hurt.

'Again.

'Again

'Again

'Again.'

The Holy Youth lifted his hand. His voice rang out in the empty spaces of the room. 'You may stop now. You have justified my faith in you.' He waved an airy hand. 'I won't bother to show you out. The house itself will do that. Take whichever turns you want, and you'll find yourself at the front door. Go on. Go back to your homes. You're forgiven.'

Racked with remorse, Feng assisted the swaying Wua to her feet. She raised a battered face to her lover and wheezed out a request between broken teeth to her sobbing lover.

'Say thank you to the Holy Man, Feng.'

Shoulders heaving, Feng succeeded in blurting out something that resembled a thank-you.

'Now *that's* what I like to hear,' beamed the languid youth as the lovers stumbled out of sight. 'Unprompted appreciation.' He stroked his smooth chin. 'I might even let them live.'

His good humour subsided as he slowly approached the pregnant young woman huddled in the corner.

'Now *you*,' he spoke softly, 'are a different case. You've broken the fundamental law of the Way of Full Pearl.'

He glanced down at the distended womb, observed the contraction of her muscles. 'Not long now, I think, before you birth your brat.'

Her pained face lit up with a sudden defiance. 'Why do you hate sex so much, Aklo? Does it frighten you?'

The youth chuckled amiably. 'Hate sex? I *love* sex, dear heart. More than you can begin to imagine.'

'You've condemned me to death for having sex,' she snapped, the onset of birth-pangs twisting her features.

'Ah, but you should have waited,' he murmured. 'A little patience, and you'd have known sex such has not been experienced for ten thousand years. The sex of the gods.'

Aklo's expression became rapt. His gaze tilted heavenward. 'Ah, you have traded a transient, feeble pleasure for an ecstasy higher and deeper than your dreams. What's copulation? A brief, meaningless touching of flesh. And birth is nothing more than an admission of death. Mortals must give birth because all mortals must die, yet their race must continue. Immortals have no need of birth. Mortals should wear death masks when they make what they like to call love.'

The woman yelled out loud at the first true stab of birth pain. Aklo barely noticed, lost in his reverie.

'Ah yes,' he sighed. 'Primal sex. The sex of the gods. The true union of male and female. One being. Mother of itself. Father of itself. Child of itself. Immortal sex.'

She was starting to convulse, but Aklo was loth to step out of his dream domain. 'This bay is where they were thrust from the world, those ancient gods, those male-females,' he whispered. 'This is the Wound they left behind. The world thinks them dead. But sometimes the dead don't lie down. They're coming back, dear heart. All of them. This is the Year of Resurrection. An ancient tide will wash this shore. Fish will swim in the forest. And a green moon will smile on the earth. Oh yes, by the next full moon the gods will return, and all those who have followed the Way of Full Pearl will be fit food for the gods. That's the only immortality open to mortals – to become a cell in the anatomy of a god.'

Shifting out of his trance, he stroked his right hand

133

over his brow. 'And how do I know all this? I have a friend – an intimate friend – who speaks to me in prophecies.' The youth flashed a quick smile at his clenched left fist. 'And my friend has a friend who'll make all the prophecies come true.'

Finally noting the woman's condition, he sniffed disdainfully. 'A messy business.'

As she pushed down with all her might, she forced words between tight teeth. 'My death, but my baby's life – you promised.'

'And I always keep my promises, my sweet,' he assured, patting her head. 'It's part of the game. I swear that your child will grow, mature, and reach old age. You have my word.'

Wrinkling his nose at the smells of birth, he made a polite withdrawal.

His long, easy strides took him speedily up the shadowed stairways of the House of Heaven. Passages ran to everywhere and nowhere on all sides. Small rooms and voluminous halls echoed with ancestral laughter, ancestral mourning.

Eventually he stepped out on one of the upper balconies, and surveyed Forest Bell Village some two hundred feet below. A quiet satisfaction curved his lips. His task was almost done. Soon he would be free to merge with the woman he had chosen as his own – the Black Skin called Xanthippe.

He sighed contentedly. The birthing woman below was the last of the obstinate souls who opposed his will. And she wouldn't see the sunset.

Forest Bell Village was ready for the Great Resurrection. '*He's* coming back, stronger than before,' he whispered to the roaming wind. 'They're *all* coming back.'

Aklo glanced at his left fist. Smiled a crooked smile. And slowly uncurled the fingers of his hand. 'And of course,' he crooned to what lay in his palm. 'We mustn't forget *you*, must we, dear heart?'

134

'Rats and bones. Rats and bones. Milk of Paradise. Rats and bones.'

The Mad Hermit voiced a throaty chant as he poured corpse dust into a small bronze jar, then licked the remaining particles from the palm of his hand.

He needed the dust today. There was bad magic in Melodious Temple, and he required a little dark sorcery to protect himself from it.

Chia's painted image had disappeared from Teacher Sung's room in East Tower. The paint around and under it was intact. The painting of Black Dragon Mountain was untouched.

But the figure of Chia had vanished as if she had jumped off the wall. Bad magic. He needed stronger magic.

Corpse dust was strong magic, especially from the fresh dead. A corpse usually required decades for its flesh to acquire the friable texture of earth. But Silver Music Bay had unusual properties. In dealing with the dead, those properties were invaluable. All along the Ancestral Gallery some bodies were preserved for centuries, while a few rotted like slugs in salt. One clutch at the patch over the heart was enough – it came away like mould – if the secret work of decay had carried on apace.

'You' – he addressed the crumbling body inside its wicker shell – 'were perfect.' Bowing his gratitude, the Mad Hermit made his exit from the rickety funeral house of the family Chang and sauntered up to the balustrade. Propping his bony elbows on the creaking wood, he scanned the beach far below before surveying the clumped dwellings of Melodious Temple ten li to the south.

'Hope you're not missing me,' he chuckled.

Lao, dubbed 'the Mad Hermit' by his fellow hermits, wasn't likely to be missed. Of the dwindling number of Melodious Temple hermits, he was the only one who lived like a hermit. He lived alone in West Tower, shunned by his fellow T'ao Seekers, and that's how Lao wanted it. He was well aware of the effect he had on others, with his shaven, tattooed head, his teeth filed to points, his necklace of rats' skulls.

Lao's skull-like face split into a spiky grin. The more revolting you were, the more privacy you enjoyed. The more privacy you enjoyed, the more revolting things you could do.

Now that he had his corpse dust, he would mix it with rat's blood and human semen when he got back to West Tower. It would make a potent drink. He anticipated its taste with relish.

'Rats and bones. Rats and bones. Milk of Paradise. Rats and bones.'

His lean lips tightened for a moment. The weird disappearance of Chia's image bothered him more than he would have expected. A little portrait, hopping off a wall, shouldn't have impressed the great Mad Hermit. But then, Chia Black Dragon was his supreme hero, and even the mystical theft of her portrait seemed an affront to that gloriously bad, bad woman.

'Oh well,' he sighed. 'It's a strange world.'

The eyes in his cadaverous head swung north and south along the crescent of Silver Music Bay.

'The Wound,' he intoned, using the ancient name for the bay. 'The Wound in the shore.'

He sucked in a deep draught of morning air as he stepped back from the railing and ambled up to the next funeral house. The House Su. Lao ducked under the low lintel, batting flies from his face as he squinted in the semi-darkness. As the interior details grew clearer a frown creased his narrow forehead.

There should have been only two corpses in House Su, as the husband and wife had died without issue over ten years ago.

But there was a small shape hung on hooks between husband and wife. As he approached the dangling shape, his vision and scent simultaneously detected two anomalies – a small body composed of seashells, and the scent of blood.

The figure between husband and wife had a torso, arms and legs of netted shells bound to sticks. And a human head had been jammed on to the sharpened stick that served as a neck.

His eyes jumped to the writing on the pine wall above the small corpse. Red words. A message scrawled in blood:

BROTHERLY LOVE

For an instant he wondered if the blood might jump off the wall, like Chia's portrait.

The small girl's head jammed on the seashell body also had words on her brow, words carved deep into the blanched flesh:

*It's a family affair.*

The Mad Hermit was suddenly not quite so mad. A touch of cold sanity pulled his steps back from the pitiful little girl with her body of shell.

How old was she? Five? Six? Whoever had done this to her was someone who considered himself above the human race. He had taken and used the girl's head as a kind of game – a puzzle. Perhaps he had forgotten all about his little game once it was played, had moved on to more challenging pastimes.

'Whoever did this might look like a man, but inside he's another species.'

Lao halted his retreat and forced his feet towards the girl with a body of shells. He couldn't leave her like this. He had to do something. Remove the head and search for the body? He reached out his hand.

There was a faint rustle from the wife's suspended corpse, a stir of straw hair, a creak of a wicker body-cage. Startled, he shot a glance at the face mask. Behind the green stone eyes there was a light at the furthest edge of sight. A pale, silver shine. Moonlight.

137

He heard his bronze jar clatter from hand to floor-boards and roll to the wicker feet.

If he stayed a moment longer, he would never leave. That he knew, in his pumping heart and shrinking flesh. He had to run – run and go gently mad.

Lao wrenched his stare away from the green eyes – and was sprinting out of the door in a streak of panic.

As he raced over the bumpy boards of the Ancestral Gallery, too terrified lest he glimpse moony eyes peering over his shoulder, he thought he heard a whisper fly down the gallery.

The huge whisper was paradoxical. It was louder than a shout; yet it was barely heard at all.

The whisper echoed in his skull, gradually shaping a word in his mind:

*Resurrection.*


The baby was slipping from the mother's womb as Aklo strolled back into the room.

'Ah!' he exclaimed. 'I missed most of the unpleasantness. I'm so pleased.'

He leaned down and studied the little shape lying in its liquids on the floor. The little shape started to cry and wiggle its limbs.

'Congratulations,' he smiled. 'It's a boy.'

'You promised,' the mother muttered hoarsely. 'You promised to let him live. I don't mind dying if you let him live.'

'Oh – he'll live,' beamed the youth. 'To a ripe old age.' The smile hardened as he pointed to the baby. 'Look.'

The baby was growing. In ten seconds it gained as many inches in length. The odd ripping sound of accelerated growth in bone and tissue resonated in the room, almost drowning the infant's wailing and the mother's screams.

The child went on stretching and blooming until a young man writhed on the floor, howling.

His skin gradually coarsened. Wrinkles formed like

the creases on a deflating bladder. Grey mixed into the black of the waist-length hair.

The woman, horrified past all reason and reality, gazed vacantly at the grotesque spectacle.

Her contorting son, screeching like a soul in hell, was an old man now. White snaked through his grey mane of hair. Folds of thinning skin flopped over each other. The screech rose to a reedy warble.

When the thin whistle of complaint piped its last, what lay on the floor, still attached to its mother by the cord of life, was an ancient crust of a man.

Aklo took a bow. 'Just as I promised. A ripe old age.'

But the mother was too far gone in shock to provide him with amusement. A little later perhaps.

He sauntered over to the broken shutters of the window, glancing occasionally at the tight fist of his left hand. Peering at broken daylight through the shutters, he murmured softly, partly to himself, partly to another.

'Youth stolen is youth acquired. Youth is strength. Grow strong, my intimate friend. Grow strong.'

His left hand gradually unfolded.

'You'll need your strength, my intimate friend. An old friend of yours will soon come calling.'

The hand opened wide, revealing a rare sight.

A tiny, painted image, vibrant with life, glowed on his palm. A miniature portrait of Chia, touched by a magic light of the moon, seemed to tremble on the skin.

'Pulled it straight off the wall I did. Ah yes. Amazing what a dash of moon-silver will do.'

He tossed Chia's animated portrait into the air and caught it with an open hand.

A smile angled up the side of his face.

'I've got you in the palm of my hand.'

139

## 9

Without moving, I have come,
Without haste, I have sped.

Chang Heng: *K'u lou fu*

The thump of metal on wood brought a smile to her face.

'They don't bury them deep in Lang-yeh Province,' muttered Chia as she scraped the friable soil from the coffin with broad strokes of the spade.

Before completing the exhumation, Chia glanced around the cemetery, its gravestones barely visible in the faint illumination from the new moon. The three men who had attempted to stop her act of desecration were sprawled in the long grass nearby, sleeping off the effects of the hand-blows she had dealt to their necks. No one else was in sight. No lanterns bobbed in her direction from the small town one li to the west.

Beyond the town were nine unearthed coffins in nine different cemeteries stretching back six hundred li to the Forest of the Ancestors.

Her mood suddenly darkened as she recalled that moon-silver head. She paused briefly, leaning on the spade.

'Brotherly love,' she grimly recited.

She lifted a sardonic eyebrow. 'It's a family affair.'

Then, forcing herself to the task in hand, she shovelled the remaining clods of earth aside and slipped into the narrow gap between coffin and soil. Inserting the point of the silver dagger into a slim crack under the elmwood lid, she speedily prised the wood loose.

According to the inscription on the gravestone, the

man inside the casket had died two and a half years ago, on the twelfth day of the fourth moon. And if the rumours in the nearby town were accurate, Chia knew what had killed him.

Flinging the lid to one side, she extracted the Night-Shining from an inside pocket of her overcoat and held it over the corpse. The blue luminescence made the dough-faced figure in its white burial suit an icy apparition instead of the simple cold clay of mortality. But the feeble light of the blue stone was sufficient to reveal what she sought.

The man's corpse had been expertly reassembled, but no knack of the mortician's art could hide the fact that the body had burst from within. The lumpy head was almost a maze of stitched cracks, covered in cosmetic wax. There was no need to check the rest of the body. It would be like all the others she'd dug up since the Forest of the Ancestors – bits and pieces slotted back into place.

Nor did she need to check the map in one of her numerous overcoat pockets to trace her path to the east. This tenth exhumation merely confirmed the trail she already pursued. She had hoped it would prove otherwise, but hadn't seriously expected it. Seven of the restructured corpses she'd unearthed had lain virtually in a straight line from the Glade of Five Faces to these low mountains in central Lang-yeh Province, east of the Great Plain of the Yellow River. And the line pointed directly to one region – Silver Music Bay. The sea was the end of the line.

'Silver Music Bay – I don't think I've ever been there,' she mumbled, replacing the lid on the coffin. 'What gives me the feeling that I had good reason to steer well clear of it?'

*A mask in the mists from the sea . . . Born in the sea. Reborn in the sea.*

'Whoever's chattering in my head, shut up,' she groaned as she sprang out of the grave.

*It's a family affair.* 'Oh, be quiet,' she sighed, starting to shovel the first spadeful of soil on to the coffin. The inner voice lapsed into silence, leaving her to fill in the grave in peace. She wanted to finish the task quickly so that she could get back to where Tumult was stabled in the town, and ride well clear before the three men she'd knocked senseless came to and stirred up trouble. The soil mounted up at a brisk rate, rising almost to the level of the surrounding ground. A few more spadefuls and –

A wrench at the base of her right thumb sent spasms running up and down her hand. The spade thudded to the earth as she tightened her left hand over the trembling right knuckles.

The pain slowly receded but the flesh tremors persisted. She held up her right hand to the moonlight and saw what she had witnessed months before when she shattered that small boulder in Black Dragon Valley.

There was a swelling at the base of thumb and forefinger, a swelling that expanded and contracted rhythmically. A throbbing lump. The longer she looked, the larger the pulsing lump grew.

Her mouth a wistful slant, she stared at the errant flesh.

'It's starting again,' she murmured.

Chia's image slip-slid like quicksilver across Aklo's palm as he mounted the crest of the cliff overhanging the House of Heaven.

'Ah, Chia,' he exhaled. 'Lovely, treacherous Chia. If only you knew. If only.'

With a slanted grin he popped Chia's lively portrait into his mouth and gulped it down.

He halted by a weeping willow that trailed its long hair over the brink of the cliff. This was one of the special willows, with rich silver liquid for sap. He shrugged off his Rainbow Robe and, naked to wind and wood, moaned softly as he rubbed his body up and down the tree.

Aklo's great work was almost complete. Forest Bell

Village was prepared for the Great Resurrection that would come with the next full moon. The trees of the forest, linked root to root, and touched by the moon, spread wide, welcoming arms around the bay to receive the Thzan-tzai when they returned from their long exile.

All that remained was to complete the welcoming crescent. The only task left was to absorb Melodious Temple in the coming radiance of Full Pearl. And that was the easiest of tasks.

Melodious Temple had been constructed, long ago, to draw the ancient male-female wonders back from exile. Its wood was soaked in the juice of the moon. Its architecture was a direct violation of the T'aoist principle of feng-shui – wind-and-water harmony. It produced what the hermits called 'bad music', although the fools had no notion that their own temple was partly the cause of the supposed hauntings in 'Ghost Bay'. Melodious Temple inspired bad melodies in the T'ao of nature.

All thanks to the temple's founder: Master Willow.

Master Willow had conceived the unmelodious Melodious Temple two centuries ago. He had made it a temple fit to welcome ancient gods.

'Clever Master Willow,' chuckled Aklo.

Then he closed his eyes as he rubbed his body harder against the willow tree. It was time. Time to spread a silver communion through the root and branch of the forest. Time to bring the temple fully into the fold.

Aklo's body started to tingle like delicate bells. The tingle resonated in the trees, travelling south. No other ears but his would catch this faintest, most gentle of sounds. But the trees would hear. The wood of the temple would listen. And understand.

As he transmitted the silver music from his body to the trees, he briefly permitted himself a personal wish, a special desire:

*Be mine, Black Skin Girl. Come live with me in the house by the sea.*

143

Then he lost himself amongst the trees and the subtle music, voicing a huge whisper that bent south to the temple . . .

*Come live with me in the moonlight.*

Xanthippe raised her eyes from the rough-hewn steps she ascended on the crooked path to Melodious Temple. She stared at the leaning, ramshackle gates in the palisaded wall slung between cliff wall and cliff edge. Tier on tier of blue, winged roofs rose behind it, drab in the light morning mist.

She tried not to listen to the faint footsteps following her.

A bronze banner dangling by the gate tapped in the wind. She peered at the embossed dragons and thunder-clouds on the old metal, but the patina of age had smothered the images in shades of green.

The old gates creaked alarmingly as she pushed them open. Her nervousness converted the screech of timber into speech: *Come-and-stay*. And when they creaked shut: *No-way-back*.

Don't start imagining voices in wood, she told herself. If you set imagination loose in a place like this it will go wild.

She hugged the warm fur of her white robe tight to her skin. The wind was playing a lonely tune this morning. No one in sight. The only company she had was the barely audible footfalls a pace behind her booted heel, and that was the only company she didn't want. Lowering her gaze to the ground, she sought solace in the mundane trails of footprints in the mud.

'Sung, tell me about these half-heard footsteps. You should know. You're the Teacher.' The wind plucked the words from her mouth as she rounded the looming Hall of Invitation. She darted a look at the long, low building, its pine surface almost bare of paint from the scouring of salt sea wind.

'Where are you, Sung? I want you to tell me all the answers, like you used to do when I was little.'

144

Her upward path took her through the doorless derelicts of the Lower Temple precincts. It was a dreary sight. The houses, once homes for a hive of hermits, long ago, in the time of Master Willow, were now abandoned to fate and weather. She soon arrived at an upward lurch in the rock, spanned by a flight of oak steps bordered by frayed rope-rails which looked ready to snap at the next firm tug. But the ropes held as she scaled the uneven steps and emerged into the Upper Temple area.

*I can't hear any steps following. I really can't this time.*

The wind from the sea was stronger in this more exposed region. It whooped up from the waves and agitated the creamy fur of her robe.

Shivering a little, she strode up a mild incline to the main structure – the Temple of the Five Fragrant Peaks.

Viewed from the beach, Five Peak Temple had the appearance of a single structure, but up close it was revealed as five separate edifices, clumped close together as if huddling against the cold.

To the north and south of the cluster reared two sturdy *tai* towers, glorying in spreading 'cloud roofs' on each of their three storeys. To east and west loomed two *chueh* towers, slender, precarious spires fit to fall if a cloud should puff its cheeks and blow too hard on bracket and beam. The four towers had their own, elaborate names: the eastward tower, perched at the rim of the ledge, from whose topmost room Sung often gazed soulfully at the ocean with its Ten Thousand Islands, rejoiced in the title of Esteemed Fragrant Peak of Contemplation of the Glorious Paradise of P'eng-lai. But everybody called it East Tower.

Xanthippe glanced up to where the pinnacle of East Tower speared the leaden canopy of clouds. Cresting it was a bronze dragon, its metal dull in the glum light, giving it a melancholy air.

It reminded her of the Teacher.

Her gaze swung away to the central building, a squat, two-storey *lou* pavilion, whose top floor – the Hall of the

Immortals – gave the entire edifice its name: Pavilion of the Immortals.

Her eyes scanned the spidery network of bridges that linked the pavilion to the four towers. They resembled flimsy stairs rather than bridges – flights of fancy realized in wood.

How the temple didn't reel and topple in the buffets of coastal gales was a mystery she would never solve.

'Talking of mysteries . . .'

She looked over her shoulder.

No one there.

For an instant she'd thought there was softest of sounds, the pad of a foot.

She shook her head swiftly. Judging between the real and the imagined was becoming difficult.

'You should know, Sung. You're the Teacher.'

Her attention switched to the topmost tier of the Pavilion of the Immortals, its winged roof like a giant eagle poised to soar into a sombre heaven. 'The Hall of the Immortals,' she whispered.

She stepped into the open portal of the pavilion and ascended the angled stairs of its dark interior, sneezing occasionally in the dusty swirl of roving draughts. As she scaled each step, she tried not to listen for following footfalls.

But she should have told Sung. For all his faults, Sung was ever ready to listen to her troubles. Whether his mind was sufficiently free of drugs and rice wine was another matter.

The red door, at a push of her hand, opened with a long croak. She stepped in, and the door groaned shut behind her. She squinted in the eternal dusk of the windowless, candlelit hall.

Row after row of tall bronze statues, each holding a lighted candle in their metal hands, formed five narrow aisles between the ranks of immobile expressions. In all, two hundred bronze images, barely visible in the shadow dance of flickering flames.

When she was younger, she used to have nightmares about this place. Statues slowly turning to face her . . . Sliding soundlessly towards her . . .

Not until she was eighteen did she summon the courage to walk here alone, listening to the special silence of the Hall of the Immortals. That awesome silence was so much a part of the devotional shrine that she could well believe it emanated from the wood of the walls and the bronze of the statues, its aura thickened by the musky odour of sandalwood figurines and the cloying scent of flowers clustered at the brazen feet of the more favoured Immortals.

In that silence, the creak of a floorboard was clearly audible about a pace behind her feet.

Someone, she thought, is watching over me.

Providence, white sign glowing from his silver mask, stood over the couple talking quietly in a corner of the Hall of Transformations. He had no need to whisper the command that made Kang and Wu-li blind to his presence. Like all in the temple except Xanthippe, the blindness command was planted deep in their minds.

Providence waited to deliver another command passed on by the Holy Man. A command of death sex. The Silver Brother had already carried out one wish of Aklo by ordering the two to meet in the Hall of Transformations. It was a symbolic joke, apparently. Providence was unsure whether the Master would approve of the command, but for now the Holy Man spoke for the Master. And a Silver Brother always obeyed.

Confronted by Wu-li's anguish over her son's soulless face, Kang the Lascivious felt anything but lascivious. He felt nothing but simple human concern.

Wu-li's small, stricken features evoked all the compassion in him, which was more than he would ever have guessed.

147

'Have you seen the separation devices at work?' he enquired, determined to discuss anything and everything except Chai-san. 'They make quite a sight at full steam.'

'No,' she murmured, just above a breath. 'No – I – I don't think so.'

'Oh, you should – ' He halted as he saw Ming-kai stride into the alchemical murk of the hall. He didn't like Ming-kai, and Ming-kai didn't like him. It would make sense to take Wu-li somewhere else, but – now that he thought of it – he experienced a curious reluctance to leave. Almost as though he had no will in the matter.

He continued to describe the intricacies of separation devices. And Wu-li continued to half-listen.

The glow and bubble of alchemy went on apace in the Hall of Transformations at Ming-kai's broad back. He paid it – and Kang – scant regard.

Other considerations filled Ming-kai's mind.

He had finally concluded that he didn't trust anyone in the temple. Not even Xanthippe. His distrust had proved useful. It had led him to investigate Sung's room while the Teacher was walking on the beach.

Ignoring Chia's missing portrait, which was plainly some chemical trick played by one of the hermits, he had studied a wu-hsing circle painted on the floor, presumably by Sung. It was a schematic representation of the Five Elements: Wood, Earth, Metal, Fire and Water. Earth, symbolized by a yellow square at the centre of the mandala circle, was surrounded by the Black Serpent of the North, the Green Dragon of the East, the Red Phoenix of the South and the White Tiger of the West. There was nothing strange in that – a simple wu-hsing circle. What was puzzling was the words scrawled across the circle: *the gods had five faces*.

And inside the yellow square of Earth, representing the central point of the cosmos – and also the crown of the head – had been written: *it's all in the head*.

Where had the Teacher gleaned the information? An exhaustive search of Sung's room revealed the source.

It was the Book of Master Willow.

It was Master Willow, that ill-famed founder of Melodious Temple, who had spoken of gods with five faces and – intriguingly – the coming of a green moon.

The book confirmed all his unease about the temple. The eccentric construction of the temple was, it transpired, chiefly conceived by Master Willow. Which spoke ill of that Temple Master of two centuries ago.

Melodious Temple was steeped in bad feng-shui. Feng-shui, the wind-and-water-fashioning of the earth, was the art of the geomancer. He would identify lucky sites for buildings, lucky ways to construct them, lucky shapes, lucky colours.

But the temple's buildings were set at all the wrong angles. The pools were wrongly sited – no fish, not even carp, had survived more than a week in them. Even the colours were wrong. Black doors faced south. Red doors faced north.

Bad feng-shui. A temple that was designed to bring bad luck.

Master Willow had contrived to build a haunted temple.

It seemed he had succeeded.

Two buildings were cited again and again in Master Willow's Book – the Hall of the Immortals and the Hall of Transformations.

And of the Hall of Transformations the same words were used repeatedly: *Sexual alchemy is immortality.*

Immortality, the supreme goal of T'aoist magic, was supposedly achieved by uniting the quicksilver tiger and the sulphur dragon, giving birth to the crystal child of immortality in the head.

As far as Ming-kai was concerned, the hard fact of mortality was too hard a pill for most men to swallow. They preferred the 'immortality pills' so arduously concocted in the tan-t'ien, each of which was supposed to add ten days to your life.

It was the tan-t'ien that he had come to the Hall of Transformations to study. According to the book, Master Willow himself had constructed this tan-t'ien – for the purpose of sexual transformation.

The tiers of crucibles, three in all, connected by pipes from top to bottom, were fashioned in a crude approximation of androgynous human form. A fresh chunk of cinnabar rested in the top crucible, ready for heating and separation into quicksilver and sulphur on the middle and lower tiers, leading, in magical terms, to the 'inner copulation of the tiger and the dragon' which would give birth to the immortal crystal child.

That was the intention of Hsiang, the aging alchemist hermit, but all the old man was rewarded with was a lot of missing immortality pills, filched and gulped down by Lung-ch'i the cook when Hsiang wasn't looking.

Lung-ch'i's greediness, however, was of no concern to Ming-kai. What engaged his interest was Master Willow's use of the tan-t'ien.

Master Willow had experimented with techniques designed, not to gain immortality for the living, but to raise the dead. And to raise them in a bizarre manner. He would arrange the body parts of a man and woman in the tan-t'ien, and raise up a man-woman from the dead.

Resurrection by sexual transformation.

Master Willow also boasted of his skill in cutting off the faces of the dead and preserving them in what he called moon-silver solution. He would sometimes take one of those preserved faces and wear it over his own. More often he would take a skull or a conch and fix a male and female face to each side. Then he proceeded to merge the two faces in the tan-t'ien.

A resurrected head, male-female, would rest on the top tier of the tan-t'ien. And it would speak to Master Willow of a Paradise called Full Pearl Home.

To his followers, the Master, as they called him, was a kind of god, above all moral codes.

'Too many similarities,' Ming-kai murmured.

Too many similarities between then and now.

Had someone decided to emulate Master Willow?

Ming-kai stroked his heavy jowl, disturbed by a sudden suspicion. 'I wonder if the enemy is one of our own.'

Abruptly, he turned on his heel and walked out of the hall.

'Go,' Providence had commanded Ming-kai in a thought-whisper. The hermit had instantly obeyed.

The Silver Brother wanted to be alone in the hall with Kang and Wu-li. He had sensed a power flowing from the north, a power that had Aklo's scent about it. He had been told that it was a form of subtle music communicated through the trees. He couldn't hear it, but he could feel its influence falling on the temple.

It was the signal for him to deliver the death sex command to Kang and Wu-li.

Inclining his masked head, Providence began to whisper.

The Hall of the Immortals.

For Xanthippe, it was dark childhood, with motionless figures even bigger than adults.

Listening once more for the tread of a foot behind her, hearing nothing, she expelled a sharp breath and forced her legs to move along the wall so that she could peer down the aisles. The intermittent squeak of a board under the tread of her booted feet made her wince. It seemed a sacrilege to disturb the sanctity of the hall.

*If I anger them, the statues might come alive . . .*

The sight of the Teacher at the far end of the fourth aisle brought a sigh of relief. When she hadn't seen him in front of his favourite image of Hsi Wang Mu, Mother of the West, in the second aisle, she'd begun to think she stood alone under the scrutiny of two hundred metallic stares.

Twenty brisk strides took her to Sung's side.

He twitched a smile at the Egyptian. 'What do you want, Xan?'

'To talk. To talk about – ' Now her fears seemed absurd, merely overwrought fancy. But still, he'd never laughed at her anxieties before. 'Do you ever hear things?' she began tentatively. 'Footsteps. Footsteps – very faint. So faint they're almost not heard at all. Faint footfalls that follow you wherever you go.'

No sooner were the words out than all traces of mirth evaporated. She became aware once more of the dense silence, a silence accentuated by the spluttering of the greasy candles. And the aroma of sandalwood became all the more pungent, mingling with the various perfumes hanging in the murk and glow of the air.

The Teacher's thin lips quivered as he glanced about the hall. The vacant look in his eyes unsettled her. Sung was even more frightened than she.

He raised a shaky finger to his lips. 'Shh . . . Those who know don't speak. Shh . . . Mustn't let them know you know. They watch. They listen.' His unsettled gaze probed the shadows in the hall, the shades inside his soul.

He leaned his mouth close to Xanthippe's ear. 'When you walk, don't look round. Don't let him know that you can hear his oh-so-soft footfall. I know who's watching me. Oh yes – I know. Do you want to know who it is? Do you?'

The Teacher's demented tone set her nerves a-jangle. She had come for his advice, his support. But now Teacher Sung wanted to lean on her. Childhood was truly over. 'Yes,' she nodded, forcing a smile to her lips. 'I'd like to know who's watching you.'

After a wary glance round the hall, he breathed a name in her ear. 'Mister House.'

'Mister House,' she repeated slowly, remembering to keep her voice quiet.

152

'Yes,' he nodded furiously. 'He's got bright yellow boots and bells and he walks upside-down.'

'Upside-down.'

His confidential lips were now touching her ear. 'Yes. And – I think I know who's following you.'

Intrigued, despite Sung's evident madness, she whispered 'Who?'

'It's Jesus. He's coming to get you. That Christos of yours. He's coming to take you to Paradise. And – and there's something I've got to tell you: I don't think you're going to like Paradise.'

Kang found himself studying the tan-t'ien.

Its shape and function started to remind him of the sacred quest, the quest for the Jewel in the Lotus, the lingam in the yoni.

Sex, after all, was high alchemy in the achievement of the ultimate: the tai-ch'i. Semen in place of dragon sulphur. Womb-juice in place of tiger quicksilver. 'Oh, Wu-li,' Kang sighed, avid to perform the sacred act of flesh, burning to rejoice in the lingam in the yoni.

Through his bleary vision, he found it difficult to distinguish Wu-li's features. All he could clearly comprehend was that she was laying herself down on the floor.

His wits were more hazy than his vision, but a remaining scrap of intellect intimated that something was wrong about all this. What *was* wrong? Something –something about her little boy. Something wrong with his face. But what had that got to do with indulging in a bit of the old wind-and-rain with a woman?

He fell to his knees beside the prone Wu-li.

'Love me,' she breathed softly.

'Oh – yes, I'll love you.'

'Love me to death.'

'Jesus? Paradise?' Xanthippe frowned. 'What are you talking about? What's happened to you?'

Sung gave a knowing tap to the side of his nose. 'Answers. I've come close to answers.' His addled stare tilted up to a statue. 'Faces,' he mumbled. 'Five Faces. I'm so near the answer. So close. He talks to me, you know.'

Shocked by the Teacher's crazed wits, moved by his skeletal condition, she touched his stick-like arm. 'We could try leaving through the forest,' she suggested gently. 'We could at least *try*.'

He wasn't listening. His mind was with the dark.

'It's here,' he mumbled, a string of saliva swinging from his lower lip. 'Can't you feel it?' His eyes darted around the ranks of glimmering bronze images.

She shuddered, feeling as if her heart had been licked by a cat's tongue.

'Listen, Sung,' she said hesitantly. 'Here's a straight-forward, simple fact: you're starved, and a starved body is a starved mind. Don't let fear eat you up. Listen – I'm going to look after you. You need feeding. I'm going to move into East Tower and make sure you're taken good care – '

The glacial look in his eyes froze the speech on her lips.

'Can't you feel the fear, my once-upon-a-time little Xan?' The cutting edge of his tone was metal scraping glass. 'It's here. Right here in Melodious Temple. And it wants you.'

As he spoke, his cold stare wheeled back to the lofty statue. Her eyes followed his, and came to rest on the head of the tall bronze. The image he'd been studying on her arrival was, to her mind, the most disturbing of all the two hundred Immortals.

It was the wu-hsing Immortal, head composed entirely of faces – five faces bulging out of one head. Five faces, each identical, their sleep-sealed visages remi-niscent of a Buddha drowsy with bliss. But the serene countenances, protruding from the front, sides, back and crown, instilled no bliss or serenity in Xanthippe. The darkness in her knew that what was bliss to Five Faces was bane to all others.

'Why should it want me?'

'Because you're different.'

On the verge of responding, she suddenly caught the faintest of whispers. It tingled bone-deep:

*Come live with me in the moonlight.*

She sensed a metallic excitement in the hall. Like silvery bells.

And she heard, quite distinctly, the steps of an unseen intruder approaching down the aisle.

Then she saw that Five Faces was starting to rock on its pedestal.

Each of the five faces glowed like a moon and sang with silver tongue.

*Come live with me in the moonlight.*

Then a blast of thunder and blinding silver lightning hurled Xanthippe off her feet.


Wu-li tore off Kang's red silk robe.

Then she started to tear off the skin from his chest.

Wu-li, for brief moments, was vaguely aware of what she was doing, but as the wildness grew in her flesh those moments became more infrequent.

In the receding instants of clarity, she would shout inside her threshing head:

*I'm not doing this. Who's making me do this? Why can't I stop?*

But those semi-lucid moments were rare. Mostly she thought of nothing. She was flesh; flesh with infinite possibilities.

Her clothes were ripped apart by Kang's frenzied fingers. Then her breasts parted company as Kang's fingernails ripped a rent over her breastbone.

A final clear thought blazed in her skull:

*We're not doing this. It's doing this to us. It's playing a flesh game with us. Why – Chai-san . . . Chai –*

Their kiss was a bloody affair.

Lip rending lip. Bright red lips.

They went wild with love.

An all-consuming passion that sought to consume all.

Consume mouth, nose, ears, eyes.

Desire for each other's faces drove them to devour every morsel.

For Wu-li and Kang, it all ended too soon.

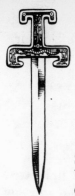

## 10

Stars and Spectres, come and feast.
Your ghostly hunger
Chills mortal flesh.

Li Ho

Xanthippe's fingers caressed the fur robe that hugged her body. The fur was presumed to have magical properties, being the hide of that rarest of beasts – a white lion. Imported from the little-known lands south of Nubia and put on display in the market near Alexandria's Athenaeum, it had caught her father's eye and he had bought it as her birthday present. Her mother had added a touch of her own, designing a robe from the hide and investing it with Nubian hand-spells, albeit with a twinkle in her maternal eye. Xanthippe liked to imagine that the spirit of the lion inhered in its fur, wrapping her in a friendly embrace.

And if ever she needed a friend, it was now.

Kang and Wu-li – their faces had been unrecognizable. Face had devoured face.

Wu-li – gentle little Wu-li, her closest friend. She would miss Wu-li so much. The woman's absence was a crack in the heart. And the way she had died . . .

Xanthippe shuddered.

Never had she felt so acutely orphaned as at this moment. This room, which she had moved into six days ago, immediately below the Teacher's room in East Tower, was unbearably strange. Architecture, furniture, decoration – everything was alien. The years of gradual familiarity with Chinese imagery and customs had been stripped away. She felt doubly exiled in this strange country at the edge of the world.

That whisper she had heard in the Hall of the Immortals: *Come live with me in the moonlight.*

She sensed that it was, in part, addressed to her. An icy invitation followed by a stab of silvery light.

And a frightened girl, stranded alone on a foreign coast, was easy game, easy meat . . .

*Come and stay. Be with us.*

Determination tightened her mouth and narrowed her eyes as she walked barefoot to the shuttered window facing the Pavilion of the Immortals. 'I won't stay. I won't be with you.'

Flicking the bronze latches, she opened the shutters. The midnight air was thick with sea fog. From the hidden forest high above descended a melancholy sign of autumn in the shape of a withered oak leaf twirling a few feet from her window. It vanished in the mist long before it found the ground.

An eddy of fog swirled into the room, wafting a hint of the ocean and a breath of moist leaves.

'After tonight,' she declared, 'I'm going.'

When dawn came she would try to make her way through the forest, no matter what dark dryads twisted and turned the trails.

The only way was the lonely way – through the forest.

As for tonight, it was her turn to keep vigil over Chai-san. When day dawned and her duty was done, she would pack a few belongings and go. But tonight she would watch over that empty face that had once been full of mischief and fun.

Teacher Sung had ordered the boy to be brought to the temple three days ago, so that the hermits could watch over him as well as casting spells aimed at restoring his face-soul.

Chai-san had been laid out in a room directly below her own, and in a few minutes she would go down and relieve Lao the Mad Hermit from his watch over the boy.

Tugging on her doeskin boots, she glanced at the multi-coloured Candle of Hours. The black Hour of the Rat had almost melted into the yellow wax of the Hour of the Ox. 'Later than I thought,' she frowned, making for the door.

Lighting a tallow taper, she slipped out on to the landing and carefully picked her way down the narrow, angled stairs. Melodious Temple wasn't so liberal with lanterns as the whorehouse, and the enfolding darkness closed in tight so that all she could see was the tiny taper flame and the hand that held it.

Playing the taper along the left wall, she dimly discerned the red door of what was previously Kang's chamber. She entered quietly, gently closing the door behind her.

The long room was crowded with candles. The air was ablaze with their radiance. In a cleared square at the centre of the bared floor a straw-padded pallet had been unrolled, and on it was placed the naked body of the boy. To the head and foot of the pallet, and to each side, reared four waist-high sacred candles engraved with Ssu-ling talismanic signs and t'ao-tieh visages, orientated north, south, east and west. The protective candles were black, red, green and white, symbols of four of the five directions and the five elements. A yellow square painted on Chai-san's midriff, emblem of earth and the centre of all things, completed the pattern of the Five Elements.

All had been arranged according to Chinese conceptions of cosmic order. The one discordant element was the man who sat cross-legged under the green candle of the east. It wasn't the bald and bony Lao, grinning above his necklace of rat skulls. It was the shorter and even bonier figure of Teacher Sung, a ponderous iron neck chain slung over his puny shoulders. He bent a wan smile of greeting.

'Where's Lao?' she asked.

Sung waved his hand in a gesture of contempt. 'The

159

Mad Hermit failed to turn up, so I've done a double watch. Doubtless that tattooed moon-fool is performing some stomach-churning wonder-working with his rats and toads and vials of blood and semen, and can't spare the time for a simple duty.'

He heaved himself to his feet, the weighty links of the rusty iron chain clinking as he rose. 'I'm off to bed,' he yawned, trudging to the door.

'How long are you going to keep wearing that thing around your neck?' she enquired. 'Is it your way of mourning Kang's death?'

'Of course not,' he snorted. 'It's to rebuild my strength. I told you that.'

'Seems a strange way to do it.'

'There's no pleasing you, is there?' he complained as he unlatched the door. 'You scolded me for being a sack of bones, and now I'm strengthening my muscles you still manage to find fault. *And* I'm eating well these days, aren't I? Why don't you shower me with praise?'

Before she could respond, he shut the door and left her staring at its red-painted surface. She listened to his tread, made heavy by the cumbersome iron, as he scaled the stairs.

Resisting the impulse to run after him, she sat down by the head of the pallet. She would have told him of her intention to leave if he hadn't vacated the room so quickly. She would have told him. But all in all, it was better left unsaid. Sung would only waste his breath in trying to stop her. Better to say nothing.

She forced herself to look at the unresponsive shape of Chai-san. He's a boy, she told herself. A little boy in trouble. That blank face is a trick of imagination – or fear. Ignore it. He's just a small boy with an unknown illness.

But that face – that not-face – seemed of a piece with the haunted wood and metal of the temple. Had it been emptied of every vestige of soul in order to be filled with another soul, a soul sprung of creaking wood and groaning metal? Xanthippe bit her lip and forced back the tears. Poor Chai-san. Poor Wu-li. Victims of some god's whim or demon's pastime. The moulded flesh on the front of the boy's head, its skin as waxen as the surrounding candles, was a mask utterly unlike any mask hitherto conveived, a mask devoid of all character. A mask perhaps waiting to be invested with malicious zest?

'Oh, no,' she groaned. Imagination ran riot again, she thought. The shared madness. This must be how it feels to go mad, starting with a small anomaly leading to larger anomalies, branching crooked limbs in all directions. In the end, nothing's right. Everything's against you.

Unable to bear looking at the empty face one moment more, she swivelled round and scanned the paintings that smothered the pine expanses of walls and ceiling. She felt she was living inside a sex-frenzied mind, thought made paint, in a welter of colourful abandon.

Men with women, in every conceivable posture. Men with men. Women with women. Men and women with animals. Animals with animals. And some strange relations she didn't attempt to identify. It was all there, in bold, lurid strokes; a jungle of intertwining limbs and torsos, tongues and tails, tentacles and genitalia, so lasciviously rich and steamily sensuous that it cloyed the atmosphere of the candlelit room. And the shades cast by the fluttering flames were up to their customary trickery, conjuring the illusion of motion in slick thigh and prehensile tongue.

Tasting bile on her palate, Xanthippe lowered her eyes to the undecorated grain of the pinewood floor, then closed her eyelids.

With absence of sight there came, stealthily, a heightened acuity of hearing.

Behind the sputtering of pungent candles, there was the creak of wood. The more she listened, the more pronounced was the groan and croak of timber. Board grated against board, like clenching jaws grinding towards the rudiments of speech. And as time shortened with the shrinking candles, she thought that the flexing wooden tower was starting to mumble its first words . . .

*Come-and-stay. No-way-back. Be-with-us. Be-in-us.*

'Go away,' she pleaded. But it didn't oblige.

The tempo of her pounding heart underscored the incantations of timber. And the thump-thump of coursing blood echoed the final invitation: *Be-us . . . Be-us . . . Be-us . . .*

The thudding ascended and descended from foot to crown and crown to foot. Thudding in her veins. Thudding in the tower.

Thudding in the stairways of the tower . . .

Her eyelids sprang wide and she wheeled to face the red door. Both door and frame were shivering from the blows that buffeted the tower from top to bottom. Conspiratorial floorboards under her feet twitched in time with the rhythmic percussion. Although the seaward window was tightly shuttered, small gusts soughed into the room, smelling of sea and forest, and extinguished the light of a score of tallow candles.

Xanthippe felt her skin contract as she wove her way through an agitated congregation of candles, her unsteady fingers reaching to slide the bolt into its catch. If anything was out there, outside her head, she doubted that a bolt would keep it out, but a bolted door was a token reassurance. More candles spluttered and gasped their last as her fingertips contacted the cold metal.

It comes again, she reflected dourly. A ghost. Or my madness, magnifying wind-shaken walls into a demon's palsy. It comes again.

She snapped the brass bolt into place and retreated a step, gaze still fixed on the shuddering door.

The resonance reverberated up and down her spine.

Be-us . . . Be-us . . . invited the thud-thud voice, ascending and descending the angled stairs.

Wrapping arms around her chest, she discovered she

162

was shaking in accord with the tower. The booming receded into the upper storey, its tone subtly changing, and the tremors were less severe in the door's timbers. But apprehension shook her with unremitting force.

*It's looking for me. It's up near the roof. And if it finds me – I will never be Xanthippe again. When you see a ghost, it doesn't matter if it's really there. Seeing is being. That's what it means to be a ghost.*

The thudding mounted in volume once more, its altering tone now resembling the thunk of metal on wood, like bronze feet, heavier than the tread of oxen, descending the steps of the tower.

*It's searching for me. Five Faces. Wu-hsing. But it can't find me if I keep very quiet.*

A fragile tingling mingled with the booming footsteps. She glanced at the silver wind-chimes suspended near the window. In seconds, it swelled to a manic jangle, shrill with metallic laughter.

And then stopped abruptly, frozen into immobility and silence.

Her gaze swerved back to the red door. It shuddered violently from the boom of the brazen footsteps and the rhythmic battering of the walls.

'Be us,' invited a voice from within the room. A voice like ripping meat.

She whirled round, throat pulsing with the quick blood of alarm.

In the weaving shine and shadow of guttering tapers, Chai-san's moulded meat face was a deceptive interplay of glow and shade. But the unfolding slit of the mouth was clearly visible. And the gristle voice was distinct as it repeated the invitation.

'Be us.'

A hand smothering her gaping mouth before a scream escaped, Xanthippe backed away from the shocking sight of the boy rising – no – *slamming* up, like a loose floorboard stamped on one end. He rose on the backs of his heels, rigid as wood. The wet slit on the front of his head, hard to envision as a mouth in a face, delivered a second invitation:

'Come live with me in the moonlight.'

Then the boy's mouth, its message delivered, fell slack. And the stiff body, mission fulfilled, crashed back to the floor.

Something had used the boy's corpse as though it were a toy, an object to play on her fears. It told her more than all the banging on walls about the kind of being that stood outside the room. Shivering, she backed slowly from the door.

*It's heard me. It knows I'm here.*

The brazen intonation from the far side of the door rattled into her bones.

'Xanthippe,' it grated. 'Come and stay.'

The door creaked and cracked as a massive pressure was exerted at its centre, bulging the wood into the room.

'You're not real,' she gasped. *It doesn't matter. Ghosts don't need to be real.*

A loud report rebounded from the walls as a vertical split appeared in the door. She heard the ominous screak of strained hinges.

'Xanthippe . . . Come and stay.'

She flung her hands over her ears to muffle the grinding voice. A hinge snapped free.

'Xanthippe . . .'

Then, to her surprise, the door snapped back into place, and the bronze tone was silent for a space. Then it returned with the screech of tortured metal.

'DARK WOMAN!' it bellowed.

The din was so loud that she was deaf for some moments, but she kept her hands cupped over her ears in readiness for the next onslaught. She counted the passing seconds, praying mutely for deliverance. As the seconds accumulated, there was an upsurge of hope . . .

It was instantly dashed by a crash that nearly split the door in half.

'Christos, help me,' she moaned.

The panels thundered and cracked under another blow.

'Help me. Save me.'

The red door burst asunder, its shattered timbers smashing into the room, scattering candles in a wide sprawl.

A tall, dark figure strode into the room. Xanthippe shrank back in terror, then paused as the invader entered the aura of candlelight.

The newcomer lifted a friendly hand. 'I thought I heard all hell breaking loose up here – somebody was trying to smash your door in,' declared an amiable, mellow voice. A woman's voice. 'They almost got through. It didn't take much effort for me to kick in what was left of it.'

The woman took another step into the illumination of the candles, her face and form becoming clear. Her hair was long and wild. Her deeply slanted eyes were an almost luminous green. Her smile was wide and quirky in her young, exquisite face.

Unbuttoning the neck of her long, black overcoat, the woman took a couple more paces towards Xanthippe.

The Egyptian felt as if she had just vaulted from Hell to Heaven.

'My name's Chia,' announced the green-eyed woman. 'Chia Black Dragon. I don't suppose you've heard of me . . .'

## 11

Not to look out of the window
Is the way to see the T'ao of Heaven
Those who travel the furthest
Are those who know the least.

Lao Tzu: *T'ao te ching*

Chia threw the elmwood chopsticks on to the cluster of emptied food bowls and leaned back with a satisfied sigh, resting her head on the golden wing of a dragon painted on the east wall of Sung's room.

'You finished off that food as if you hadn't eaten in a week,' grinned Sung, casting a sideways wink at Xanthippe, who sat beside him on a high cushion.

'Maybe I haven't eaten in a week,' Chia responded drily. 'Can't remember. I always did have a terrible memory.'

'A terrible memory for everything except the women who catch your eye,' smirked the Teacher, slanting a roguish glance in the direction of Xanthippe. The Egyptian girl shifted uncomfortably at the remark, nervously averting her gaze from Chia's brief, ambiguous look.

Less than an hour had elapsed since the sorceress strode into the room below and lifted Xanthippe from dead despair to living hope. She must have pinched herself a dozen times since then to see if she was dreaming. Now that Chia – the real, breathing Chia – sat in front of her, the Egyptian realized she'd hoped but never truly believed that this woman of legend was actually alive. But alive she was, and the reality of her

166

presence, hitherto only experienced in her nocturnal spirit-journey to long-ago Egypt, was almost overwhelming in its impact.

Even as she struggled to come to terms with the astonishing fact that the woman in her dreams was within touching distance, Xanthippe couldn't help but notice the newcomer's outlandish apparel. Not once in all her travels had she encountered such bizarre garb. The black cotton trousers and the mid-calf-length boots they were tucked into were unremarkable – it was commonplace for Chinese women, especially those in the lower classes, to wear trousers and boots – but the long coat which draped her slender form would have raised eyebrows from Loyang to Rome . . .

'Admiring my overcoat?'

Startled by Chia's sudden question but reassured by the flicker of a smile playing along the woman's lips, she nodded hesitantly. 'Yes – it's – it's most unusual.'

Can this really be happening? she asked herself incredulously. A small hour ago Chia transported me from Hades to Elysium. And now I'm discussing clothing styles with my deliverer as if we were a couple of girls readying themselves for their first party.

Chia's hand strayed vaguely over the black serge. 'This is just a practical garment that I made up in a spare moment,' she stated with thinly disguised satisfaction. 'Chinese nobility use ornamental buttons as a sign of rank, but it struck me that I could use them to fasten my overcoat. Good idea, don't you think? And these patch pockets – why carry bags and pouches around when you can stuff anything you want into your own coat?'

'It's certainly – different,' commented Sung, his lips pursed.

Chia arched an amused eyebrow. 'Go on – you shifty old T'ao Seeker – admit it. You think I look a disgrace.'

He stirred uncomfortably. 'Not a disgrace. Just – different. Out of the ordinary . . .' He threw up his hands in defeat. 'All right, all right – you look *bizarre*.'

167

'That's more like it,' she smiled.

'*Grotesque.*'

'I think you've made your point, Sung,' she said through tight teeth and a forced smile.

'I thought you wanted my honest opinion,' he pouted, fingering the links of the iron chain that weighed on his shoulders. The gesture was presumably calculated to emphasize his newfound strength of character. 'Correct me if I'm wrong, sorceress, but your words suggested that you required a candid statement of my views.'

Xanthippe listened to the exchange with a growing sense of estrangement. It was difficult to accept the reality of the scene she was witnessing. Chia belonged in dreams. Even the small smear of orange sauce at the corner of those wide lips was like a disfigurement: a scab on the mouth of ethereal Aphrodite. When Chia spoke, her words should be pearls, radiant with enlightenment; the idle banter she indulged in had several discordant notes. Xanthippe recognized the foolishness of her reaction, which doubtless would pass in a day or so, but for the present she was left floundering between dream and reality. Only the green gaze formed a bridge linking the dream and the real. They were young eyes – with ancient deeps. Those eyes had seen everything. And – she recalled a remark of Sung's – it was hard to look into Chia's eyes, and much harder not to look.

Suddenly conscious of Chia's pensive scrutiny, Xanthippe smiled nervously at the woman's hooded gaze. She hoped that the uncertain smile masked her dismay at yet another revelation: Chia was frightening.

The woman's voice underscored the intuition; it resonated in a tone as dark and deep as midnight: 'I make you feel mortal.'

Chilled in heart and head, the Egyptian nodded numbly. The sorceress had expressed it exactly.

Mortal.

Chia's immensity of centuries dwindled Xanthippe.

She was made ephemeral, her life a brief butterfly existence.

'Mortal,' she heard herself whisper.

'Mortal because you face the immortal?' Chia's melodic tone was lighter, kindlier. 'Don't be so easily impressed, Xanthippe. I'm not immortal. I'm just well-preserved.'

The incongruity of the statement drew a chuckle from deep inside: it bent Xanthippe's lips and broke the thick spell in the room. She warmed to Chia – the breathing, sauce-smeared, fallible Chia. When it occurred to her that she'd been behaving like a lover who's suddenly discovered that the adored one is only human, after all, she chuckled all the more loudly.

Chia, sauntering across the room, looked askance at the spluttering Egyptian. 'A creature of extremes, aren't you, my svelte Alexandrian?'

'Like recognizes like,' observed Sung, scratching his flaky scalp.

Ignoring the comment, Chia stopped in front of a painting of an angular mountain. 'This the one?'

Sung nodded.

She licked a forefinger, stroked the finger down the painted edges of the slopes, then sniffed the moist finger. 'No mystery here,' she concluded, giving a dismissive lift of her shoulders. 'Huang-lung preparation – acids in solution. Rubbed gently, it lifts paint off paint, without a mark. That's why my image disappeared off the mountain. No magic.'

Recovered from her fit of mirth, the Egyptian frowned her puzzlement. 'But why should anyone do that?'

'It was probably a threat aimed at me.'

'Why not write "Chia is dead" in letters of blood?' queried the Teacher. 'Much more striking.'

'And much less subtle. The subtlety – and the timing – might just as well be a signature.'

The Teacher leaned forwards, brow creased in curiosity. 'Whose signature?'

169

The green gaze grew inward. 'Someone old. Someone subtle.'

'Who?'

'That's my affair.'

A touch of craftiness showed in Sung's milky eyes. 'Let me guess. This "someone old and subtle" is connected to what happened in the Forest of the Ancestors over two years ago.'

Whatever the sorceress was thinking, her stern, refined features were impassive, betraying nothing. Her tone was equally noncommital. 'I know at least six Forests of the Ancestors in the Dragon Empire. And what do you mean by "over two years ago"?'

'I'm referring to the Forest of the Ancestors in San Lung. On the twelfth day of the fourth moon. It has something to do with Five Faces.'

Chia's face refused the slightest reaction. 'Everyone's heard of the trouble I had in San Lung, on the twelfth day of the fourth moon. As for Five Faces' – with a toss of her head, she indicated the wu-hsing circle painted on the floor – 'you obviously have an obsession with the Five Elements, an obsession shared by everyone in China. Five Elements. Five Faces. Any Chinese would connect *anything* with the number five. You are transparent, Sung. You are bluffing.'

'Am I?' he challenged. 'And would any Chinese know about the Nothing Man?'

The change in Chia was not immediate; nor was it dramatic. A slight tremble in the jaw. A suggestion of green flame in the wavering stare. And a strained edge to her speech.

'No. They wouldn't know about him,' she conceded.

Sung gasped as she swerved a wild glance at him, cracking her finger-bones as the hand spasmed into a fist.

Xanthippe's eyes widened. *She looks deadly. And I like it.*

'Tell me about the Nothing Man,' Chia commanded. 'And don't hold back – I have a bagful of chen-chiu needles in one of my pockets.'

'Chen-chiu needles are intended for healing!' Teacher Sung protested in a shrill pitch.

'They can be used in other ways.' If coagulated blood had a sound, Chia's low growl would have been thick with it.

Sung acquiesced on the spot. 'I've told you about Aklo, remember?' he began, wiping a sheen of perspiration from his upper lip. 'I – I talked about Aklo, you recall . . .'

'You've hardly stopped talking about Aklo from the moment I arrived.' She frowned, folding her arms and leaning against the image of Black Dragon Mountain. 'Tell me about the Nothing Man.'

'I-it w-was Aklo who men-mentioned the Nothing M-Man,' he quavered. 'He said something about the Nothing Man in the moon, and that the Nothing Man must be protected from the – what was it? – oh yes, the moon-silver . . .'

Studying Chia's austere expression, Xanthippe noticed a flick of the eyelids – a tiny surface tremor faintly echoing the inner storm. The sorceress's glance had been directed to the ankh dangling at her breast. The silver ankh – moon-silver?

' . . . and there was something about the Nothing Man needing new flesh,' the Teacher was saying, looking furtively at Xanthippe. 'Dark flesh. Black skin. And he talked of an old soul inside a Dark Woman – no, *the* Dark Woman. An old soul with a strange, foreign name – Nefertiti. Oh, one last thing – quite important, I imagine – according to Aklo, the Nothing Man has a message for the Green-Eyes . . . Just two words . . .'

'Yes?' prompted Chia, suddenly subdued.

' "I live." '

Chia nodded slowly, her gaze lost in abstract distance. Her echo was hollow: ' "I live." '

With a stiff, deliberate motion she drew a long silver dagger from inside her black overcoat and aimed the sharp point at the ankh. The silver pendant jerked and clung to the blade: stuck fast, the magnetic metals seemed all of a piece. 'Moon-silver,' she whispered. 'The Nothing Man. He lives. I *knew* it. The dead don't lie down.'

'Has everyone forgotten me?' exclaimed Xanthippe, alternating an accusatory glare between Sung and Chia. 'He wants *me*, this Nothing Man – isn't that right? He wants new flesh – black skin. And *I'm* the one who dreams of being Nefertiti . . .'

Visibly shaken, the sorceress flashed a dubious glance at the girl. 'I haven't forgotten you. I know you're in danger, and I'll help. But don't tell me that you dream of being Nefertiti – not if you think that it means reincarnation.'

'I never said it did. Sung suggested that – just now.' The Egyptian rounded on the Teacher. 'Why didn't you tell me about the Nothing Man before? If he wants new, dark flesh, a Dark Woman who he claims has Nefertiti's soul, don't you think I should have been told?'

'I was trying to keep you from worry,' he muttered, fingering the embroidered hem of his sleeve. 'Trying to protect you.'

'Not a very good idea,' said Chia, pulling the ankh from the dagger. 'What we don't know can easily hurt us.'

Xanthippe threw a shy look at Chia, and her anxiety dissolved in the unexpected warmth of the woman's expression.

There was a genuine note of compassion in Chia's reassurance: 'It's easy to be hurt when you've lost all the childhood faces; easy to be hurt when you're different from everyone else, an outsider looking in. It's hard to be alone amongst strangers. It's hard to keep your footing in a world that's strange to you and familiar to everybody else. I know. Believe me, I know.'

Xanthippe nodded her appreciation. Chia's wistful face and voice conveyed evident understanding. Understanding of everything – with one, crucial exception: 'You're not an exile,' she stated quietly.

Chia's low sigh was barely audible. 'You can journey back thousands of li. You can't journey back thousands of years . . . Now I think you shouldn't be alone. Are there two beds in your room?'

Xanthippe's mouth fell open. 'No, just the one.' She shifted uncomfortably on the high cushion, fishing for the right approach, the right phrases. 'It – it would be very cramped, the two of us in one bed.'

'I can live with it,' said Chia.

'I – I'm very flattered,' Xanthippe stammered. 'You're very beautiful. Very – special. And I'm so grateful to you for saving me from that unseen thing downstairs. But I'd like us to be – you know, just *friends*.'

Chia lifted an imperious eyebrow. 'I don't swoon with rapture at every pretty face I see, despite what you may have heard. I usually have to fight them off, you know.'

'Sorry,' Xanthippe apologized out of the awkward slant of her mouth.

'Don't worry,' the sorceress laughed quietly. She angled her head towards the disgruntled Teacher. 'Another bed required in Xanthippe's room. Arrange it, will you?'

Nervously plucking and pulling at his red Kang-i robe, the Teacher stood up and stomped a heavy path to the door, each step accompanied by the clink of the ponderous iron neck chain. 'I'm not a servant!' He muttered into his dangling beard. 'I'll get Ming-kai to make up a bed for you. He's downstairs keeping vigil over Chai-san.'

The red door slammed shut with a ferocity that rattled the latch. Chia sniffed contemptuously as she slipped the dagger back inside the overcoat. Her head inclined in a pensive air as she studied a riotously coloured picture on the upper reach of the east wall. The shuddering lanterns and candelabra brought the festive imagery to the brink of prancing life. Golden-skinned Tung Wang Kung sat enthroned on the glowing peak of P'eng-lai, the rising sun a halo behind the orange swirl of the god's

173

hair. Stately ladies in butterfly- and blossom-emblazoned gowns paraded through elegant parks, dainty parasols in fragile hands. Nymphs cavorted in streams of liquid crystal, releasing an uprush of joyous bubbles. Incense-wisped, enfolded in rare perfumes, the blessed took their ease beneath trees with stars for leaves or on towers shaped from high dreams.

'Paradise,' Chia said softly. Then, more softly still: 'The golden time.'

Xanthippe didn't need to glimpse the hint of moisture on the woman's long eyelashes to catch an echo of Chia's loss and longing. The infamous Woman in Black had the melancholy face of an orphaned child, the forlorn gaze of an exile.

The Egyptian was about to speak when the door swung open and Sung entered, trailed by a sombre Ming-kai. Chia was instantly transformed from lonely child to impassive sorceress, wearing her legend like armour. She regarded the two men with bland indifference as she donned an extraordinary pair of round black glasses, masking her eyes.

'This is Ming-kai,' announced the Teacher, seemingly unimpressed by the glasses. 'He wished to meet you before making up your bed.'

'So long as he doesn't want to climb into it with me,' she yawned ostenatiously.

'I just want you to answer a single question,' said Ming-kai, standing foursquare by the door, his face as unresponsive as granite.

Chia exhaled sharply. 'Questions, questions, questions . . .'

'Just one. Why did you betray Chang Chiao and the other leaders of the Yellow Headband armies?'

Momentarily taken off guard, she arched a quizzical eyebrow at the scarred veteran. 'I took no side in the war. I am my own commander.'

Ming-kai's features remained as unyielding as granite. 'Chang Chiao told me that you'd promised to

174

join the T'aoist army before the year of T'ai-p'ing. You never joined. We were butchered in our thousands, with General Tsao dishonouring the corpses in each of his victories. With you on our side, we might have won. Now Chang Chiao is dead. And one of my brothers lies in a mass grave.'

Chia ran long fingers through her brambly hair. 'I honour your dead,' she said quietly. 'I regret that you lost the war.'

The granite was starting to crack. 'Save your regrets, Black Dragon. The Yellow Headbands died for a noble cause. They gave their lives in a glorious war.'

'Is there such a thing?' she asked gently, her forefinger stroking the silver ankh.

'A war fought with heart and fortitude is always glorious,' he declared.

A little sadly, she shook her head. 'If you've fought in a war you should know better.'

Ming-kai advanced a few paces, nails digging blood from his palms. 'You've lived three thousand years, so it's said – you must have seen a thousand great battles, heard a thousand battle-songs. The glory of the battles is in the songs. Do you know what we sang as we marched to the western border of Lang-yeh? A song of the ancient Chou dynasty. We sang the Kuo shang, from the Songs of Ch'u. It's a thousand years since its words first resounded, but you – you of all people, who lived in the time that the Kuo shang was written, who saw those antique battle-chariots on the plains of Ch'u – how could your blood not race rich and strong with the glory of battle? Who are you to stand so aloof? Is your soul dead? Can't you hear the battle-glory in the songs?'

'I know the Kuo shang' she said. 'I know all the Songs of Ch'u. Somehow, I think you don't know the Kuo shang.'

The veteran stood as taut as a bowstring, his mouth muscles working in spasms. 'Do I not? Then I'll recite it for you . . .'

175

She sighed heavily. 'Ming-kai – don't – don't . . .'

He straightened his spine, squared his broad shoulders, and recited the Kuo shang in a ringing tone, evoking the bright swords, the clashing blades:

'With our heavy shields and hide armour,
Chariot wheels locked in battle, we fight hand to hand.
Our banners cloud the sky and the enemy swarms like clouds.
The warriors brave a hail of arrows.
Our ranks are struck, the enemy beats us down
To the left a horse is down, to the right a steed is maimed.
Dig the chariots in and round up the horses!
Grasp the jade drumstick and sound the drum!'

His intensity fierce, he glared at the sorceress. 'I know the Kuo shang, Black Dragon. It's a true battle-song that envisages defeat as calmly as victory.'

Chia's head sank forward. Her long, uncombed hair shadowed her features. In stark contrast with Ming-kai's triumphant delivery, she spoke in a thoughtful murmur, the words slightly slurred. 'You've omitted the second half of the song.' Her hand tightened on the ankh as her recital progressed:

'The times are our enemy: the gods are our foes.
Now the battlefield is full of the dead.
Those who marched forth did not return.
They are spread out on the distant plain,
Long swords at their sides, gripping their elmwood bows.
Heads lopped from bodies, but their hearts unconquered.
Mighty in courage, great in nobility,
Stout-hearted to the end, worthy of all honour.
Dead in the body, but alive in the spirit,

Heroes in the midst of ghosts these brave souls will be forever.'

The sputter of candles and Ming-kai's stertorous breathing were all that could be heard for a brief space. Everyone in the room was aware that Chia wasn't imagining a thousand-year-old battle and its mournful aftermath. She was remembering.

At length Ming-kai's gritty voice splintered the silence. 'All you've said is that the greatest glory has the greatest price, and that the brave find victory in defeat. That I knew.' He turned on his heel and left the room with a parting shot: 'And to a man who's witnessed true glory, beauty doesn't blind.'

Xanthippe, ignoring the war veteran's departure, kept her attention fixed on the bone-white hand that Chia clasped around the ankh. A trickle of bright blood issued from the tight fist, staining the silver metal.

In a chamber of dark willow, its timbers damp with the soul of the sea, the Rainbow-Robed youth arched back in his kneeling position, arms outflung, fingers flexing, needle nails glittering in the excited dance of candlelight.

'Ah yes,' he sighed sensuously, tongue gliding over his lips. 'She's here.'

A low moan escaped the moist cavern of his mouth. 'She's *here*.'

A lazy hand caressed a wooden sculpture. The wood was from a weeping willow, and it was carved into a tiny replica of the tree from which it was taken: a miniature weeping willow adorned with tiny bells.

'She's here. The Dark Woman. The beautiful traitor.'

Aklo's smile was silk-smooth, his whisper gossamer: 'Sweet dreams, Chia.'

## 12

My shadow clings to forests where
  gibbons screech,
But my spirit spirals up towers of sea
  dragonbreath.
Next year I will rise as the rivers
And quest for you until the final white
  cloud of the east.

Tu Fu

Another spasm hit Chia as she stepped over the brink of
sleep, only to be flung back with the slam of her heart
and the lurch of her sprawled body. Eyes flickering open
to the shadowed ceiling, she listened to the blood-thud
receding in her ears. As her pulse quietened, she caught
the heavy sound of Sung's tread creaking the floorboards
as he paced to and fro in the room above. What was he
doing – exercising with that massive chain weighing on
his small shoulders?

Chia rolled over on her makeshift bed and peered at
the curvy contour of Xanthippe on the other side of the
room, her form curled up under the thin woollen
blanket. Her soft, regular breath was evidence of sound
sleep.

The sorceress wished that she could achieve such swift
forgetfulness.

But it wasn't easy, surrounded by cloying scent,
curdled air. The stench of sour milk wasn't so strong in
this room, unless she was starting to get used to it. *No. I'll
never get used to it.* It seemed that the temple occupants
were partially conditioned to the odour: they showed no

signs of discomfort although Melodious Temple was steeped in a malodorous aura.

That scent had drawn her to the rumpled clifftop overlooking the temple. Two nights ago, she had settled down by the cliff edge to keep watch on the flamboyant towers and pavilion. The creaking wooden edifices reminded her of flimsy containers straining under an internal pressure. Tonight, during the Hour of the Rat, they looked ready to blow apart –

' – like one of Nyak's victims,' she murmured under her breath.

An inner urgency had impelled her to scale the cliff and run round North Tower and the Pavilion of the Immortals as the first muffled boom echoed from East Tower. Intuition had again been her ally. A few seconds' delay and she wouldn't have reached Xanthippe in time: a disaster for the Egyptian and, also, a setback for Chia. Xanthippe was the only one in Silver Music Bay who could be trusted – in part, at least. The dark-skinned girl was an outsider, and Nyak had great difficulty in controlling outsiders. What was happening in the bay was a uniquely Chinese phantasm. A family affair.

A family affair.

A family.

And a lover, long ago.

'Nefertiti.'

Someone was using Xanthippe, and they were trying to use Chia's feelings for a woman fifteen centuries dead. They knew where to press the flesh for pain. They knew what drew blood. Chia wanted nothing more than to believe that Nefertiti was reborn in Xanthippe, and that want was a constant temptation, a lure to entangle her in Nyak's mesh. She must resist. She must.

*I refuse love. It is not in me. It is not of me. It is not around me. Where I am, it is not. Where it is, I am not. I remain within myself.*

Unbidden and hurtful, the memories came . . .

Yellow distance, hot and hushed. Blue distance above. Sphinx Face, linking sand and sky . . .

The golden body of Nefertiti swimming in the deep, vibrant Nile . . . the golden limbs of Nefertiti flashing through the earth-brown ripples of the Nile shallows . . .

Golden fingers plucking an Egyptian lute behind beaded curtains . . . the golden fingers of Nefertiti, fingernails painted silver . . . Full, moist mouth parted, whispering – 'Forgive me, Chia . . .'

'No,' she groaned, rolling on to her back to stare absently at the now silent ceiling, 'No.'

Sleep came, as was its way, quite unexpectedly.

A nowhere blackness, lasting a moment or a kalpa.

Then, a little light. Night light.

Lanternlit faces in Celestial Buddha Temple wheeled around her. The dome of the stupa, blanched by moonlight, swung by her sliding vision. The wing-roofed Buddha Hall swerved past – and tilted up to the moon . . .

A strand of hair brushed across her eyes as she toppled. The silver dagger, bright with blood, glinted on the stamped clay. The ankh spiralled down to the dagger in her slow tumble to the ground.

*Nyak is dead. Nyak is dead.*

*But sometimes the dead don't lie down.*

The ankh dangling from her neck struck the discarded dagger.

Tears filled her eyes, a memory springing from the salty trickle. A moist memory. A memory of mist. Sea mist. Mist from the sea facing Silver Music Bay. And a mask in the mists from the sea.

The mask summoned her with the sough of the tide: 'Chhhiiiaaa . . .'

For a short space, she was under the impression that she was in Silver Music Bay, listening to the sonorous music of its tide. That she was in a creaking wooden room with a dim blue lantern, and somewhere, a hundred li away in the distance, a nutbrown Nefertiti slept beneath a cloud of red dragons. And there was someone near: a male presence, kneeling by her overcoat.

180

Then she realized the room by the sea wasn't real. The brown Nefertiti wasn't real. The kneeling man wasn't real. She was dreaming.

She woke up.

And she was –

– a wound in nature. She ripped the night air with the keen wind of her flight. She was ghost flesh, spectre blood, spiritual paradox.

A whirlwind within a whirlwind, she soared from Celestial Buddha Temple in a spiral of confusion as she sought to spin a body from the winds and weave a cloak of air.

She was a dangerous nonsense in the night: Wind-Flesh – with killing intent.

Forest of the Ancestors above.

Moon and stars below.

She set sail between sky and earth. The further she flew, the faster she flew.

She dived into the forest: was up and about in the forest, shaking the life out of the trees.

Anomaly.

Earth above.

Moon below.

She tilted – tilted again – and the moon was above and the earth below.

Boughs shattered in her wrathful wake. Soil erupted.

An ancestral shrine on a hillock – she burst it asunder. Wooden figurines, wilted flowers, broken statues and delicate bronze bells rained down on the forest.

Man in brown cloak running . . .

Devour him.

But the love of her flesh, the attraction of her flesh, was too strong. The breath must be with the body.

She whirled above Five Faces. Skyward-looking Earth Face yawned his mouth to swallow her. Glad to be gulped down, she plunged under the earth.

Zigzagging wildly down stair after stair, she burst into a vault.

My flesh, she exulted. My flesh . . .

In the sarcophagus was another's flesh. Rancid pork soaked in curdled liquid. Another's flesh. *His* flesh . . .

She struggled to whirl away, to spiral into the sky –

His flesh unfolded to her with a voice like ripping meat . . .

'Be with me. Be in me. Be me.'

He sucked her in through the Five Ways – Sight, Hearing, Taste, Smell, Touch. Trapped in the turmoil of his flesh, she ceased to distinguish who was Chia and who the enemy.

He was Twilight. She was the Owl.

She was the enemy.

Chia was Nyak's rebellious flesh, insurgent to the sour juice with which it was awash. And the rebellion in blood, skin and organs was all too successful.

The flesh burst asunder, the Five Viscera – liver, heart, spleen, lungs, kidneys – flying apart in the Five Directions of the wu-hsing.

And Chia's spirit, that integral ghost flesh, was torn in five.

Torn in five, Chia invoked the magnetic cohesion of the spirit. To be a spirit in five phantom shreds was a paradox of the psyche, a nonsense soul. The T'ao of nature ordained that the ch'i circulating in the human couldn't be divided, any more than the wind could be sliced into five equal portions. And the T'ao of nature couldn't be opposed.

Except –

She was a wound in nature.

She was a mortal immortal. Enfleshed paradox. She could be an impossibility.

Leaving the vault to its sarcophagus and red ruin, she fell asleep for a moment . . .

. . . and dreamed that she lived inside a picture painted on a wall. A picture of a pinewood room in a tower by the sea. She walked out of the room, leaving it to its two rumpled beds and ebony sleeper . . .

. . . she awoke as she blasted east through the Forest of the Ancestors.

'I live,' she exulted.

'I'm Nothing. But I live.'

Fen-chou rubbed drowsy eyes as he finally responded to the gentle but persistent knock at his door. As he heaved his aged bones from the enticing comfort of a deep, soft mattress and thick blankets, he shuddered in the dawn chill. A drab foretaste of gloomy day filtered through the gaps in the shutters, robbing the yellow night-lantern of its lustre but adding little of its own.

The old hermit winced at the cricks and cracks in his brittle joints as he pulled a warm woollen shawl over his green silk gown. Dull day today, he glumly reflected. Better to stay in bed.

The shutters rattled from a vigorous gust.

Rough, raw wind too . . .

Thoughts of the wind instantly brightened the day's prospects. It was the ninth day of the ninth moon. It was the Festival of Ch'ung Yang: the festival of flying kites from clifftops, and later, the customary feasting on a whole roast pig.

Fen-chou's thin face, etched with nearly seven decades of living, smoothed out a wrinkle or two as he fondly recalled the Ch'ung Yang festivals of his youth. The kites were all of silk back in the old days. Marquis Tsai hadn't yet invented that remarkable, magical stuff he called paper. Where would Ming-kai be without his paper kites? But the old silk kites were good enough for Fen-chou: he'd owned his first kite when he was six. A gift from his father, on Never-Grieve Flower Ridge, that Ch'ung Yang morning long, long ago.

The knock at the door was more insistent.

'Coming as fast as I can,' he grumbled. 'I'm not sixty any more, you know.'

As he trudged up to the door and slid back the bolts, he remembered something the Mad Hermit had told

183

him – how long ago? – a month? No – more than a month. That bald ghoul hardly ever set foot outside his locked and bolted fastness in West Tower, the last time he'd seen Lao's spiky grin was a good seven weeks ago. Come to think of it, he hadn't seen much of Teacher Sung, either.

'And Ming-kai doesn't come to see me much these days,' he murmured quietly, raising a hand to the latch. 'Taught him all I knew about kites when he was a young lad.'

He had already lifted the latch when it struck him who the early caller might well be. Now *there* was someone he hadn't seen in a very long time. Someone who'd promised to visit old Fen-chou within hours of her arrival.

The open door revealed the slate sky of dawn behind the dark bulk of the Pavilion of the Immortals. And, framed by the dark pavilion, the unexpected guest.

'Ah,' smiled Fen-chou. 'I was just thinking about you.'

The other's mouth split in a wide grin. 'Were you really.'

'Cold morning,' remarked the old man, hugging arms to his sides.

'I hadn't noticed.'

'Oh well,' shrugged Fen-chou. 'Getting old, I suppose.' He peered at the courtyard. 'You've not spotted my cats, by any chance?'

'I've spotted nothing. There's no one about.'

'Ah – ah – ' dithered Fen-chou, suddenly uneasy.

'No one to see.'

'See what?'

The figure brandished a handful of metal, its sheen dull in the glum light of dawn. 'These.'

Fen-chou squinted at the clumped metal in the rigid fist. 'What are those?'

'Needles.'

*

'I live.' She was drawn east, over shocked earth and topsy-turvy trees, by an inner response to a call of obscure origins, the tree of life, the bells of Paradise.

In sight of the Tree of Bells by the shore, she dreamed on the wind . . .

. . . she walked into a dark, wooden pavilion and mounted its creaking stairs. She had someone to meet. He was not her friend . . .

. . . toying with wood and wind, she fashioned woodwind, and made melody on a flute. *Let the way be tzu-jan. Let the music play me.* To the percussion of bells, the flute song thrilled to the birds. The birds of the trees ascended. The birds of heaven descended.

Hovering over the Tree of Bells, a scent arose. An old scent. A scent from an Old House. There was a sea in the Old House. A curdled sea.

Born in the sea. Reborn in the sea.

Inside the Old House there was milk of the moon gone sour. And there was Paradise inside its walls. Bad Paradise . . .

. . . she dreamed she walked past ranks of bronze statues in the Hall of the Immortals . . .

There was someone waiting for her inside the house. He was not her friend.

. . . she walked past statues . . .

In the Old House, no one was her friend . . .

*This is not a dream.*

. . . the visages of the wu-hsing, Five Faces, tricky in the jumpy candlelight . . .

*This is not a dream.*

We are wounds in nature.

*This is not –*

Chia's cry was strangled in her throat as she seemed to come fully awake. She was on her knees, her spine arched back like an overstretched bow a creak away from cracking. Her hair was tied tight to her ankles, forcing the crown of her head to the floor, inverting her view of the murky surrounds. The floor was the ceiling;

185

the ceiling, the floor. She tried to move her head, but the slightest movement came near to breaking her neck. Naked as a supplicant slave or blood-criminal, her skin was flayed from neck to ankle. And her hands and feet were nailed to the floor.

It was many centuries ago, in the early time of the Shang rulers. And she was inside the Old House of dark wood. And everything in it looked upside-down.

The figure standing before her appeared to dangle down from the floor. The long figure inclined its head. It wore her father's face, the cold milk of the moon in its pale silver skin, its gash of a mouth gaping in a frozen scream. But the soft voice that sighed from the wound of a mouth was the voice of her brother.

'Why do you come back to the Old House, prodigal sister?'

Chia choked out the answer. 'To give birth to my dead love, Nefertiti.'

Her father's moony head tilted on her brother's neck. 'Rebirth, sister? Ah yes, that would take the two of us. Flesh alchemy: the thought appeals.'

'I suspected it might,' she managed to croak. 'If we succeed in mating, you'll become truly immortal. If we fail, it means my death. Either way, you win.'

'Ahh, Chhhiiiaaa . . .' exhaled her brother from her father's contorted mouth. 'Lovely, guilty, treacherous Chhhiiiaaa. I love you more than all worlds. And trust you less than all hells. You'd never give me anything that wasn't death to my heart and head. If you offer me your sex, then you must have a poisoned womb. Love and death. Is that it, sister? Ah yes, I think so. Resurrect Nefertiti on your own, beloved Chia. I'll not risk your touch on my flesh.'

'I can't bring her back on my own. It can only be done by combining our power.' She could barely force out the words from her straining throat. 'I'm not trying to trick you. Can't you see I'm telling you the truth?'

There was a wistful note in his reply. 'Ah, once I knew

186

what was in your head – long ago, when we were young and I was the Owl and you were the Twilight; before we became enemies. Once you were clear as sunlight. Now you're dark as night.'

'If you won't help me,' she wheezed, 'then kill me. Set me free.'

The silver head shook slowly. 'I'll not unite with you. And I'll not kill you. Killing Father was enough – we're both still paying for that. But one day' – the silver head suddenly became a wu-hsing, growing faces – 'we will reunite . . .'

Chia struggled to escape from the bulging wu-hsing faces. And the dream broke.

She was kneeling with her spine arched back and the crown of her head touching the floor, her vision inverted. An upside-down Five Faces confronted her defiant glare. But Five Faces had inextricably metamorphosed to bronze. Her brother had become a statue with eyes shut in baleful beatitude. Her hair wasn't tied to her ankles. Her hands and feet weren't nailed to the floor. And she was fully clothed: trousers, boots, tunic, overcoat. The wu-hsing-Nyak, and her pain, were gone.

Chia lurched forward on to her knees, then stood upright, flexing her muscles to restore the circulation to her legs. Thrusting cold hands into deep patch pockets, she studied her environs.

She was in the Hall of the Immortals, judging from Sung's sketchy description. Ranks of revered Immortals surrounded her, their contours an inconstant shimmer in the sparse candlelight.

She glared at the wu-hsing statue towering above her. Its closed eyes and sealed expressions were supremely aloof.

'Be like that,' she muttered, turning up the collar of her overcoat. 'You gave me a hell of a nightmare, you tall, bronze bastard.'

She winced as the memory whiplashed in her face. The dream of the Fivefold in the Old House hadn't seemed like a dream at the time. She'd been sure it was a relived memory from the beginning of the Shang dynasty. Its edge of reality was sharp as flint.

But it couldn't have happened. Couldn't have.

'Not the sort of thing you'd forget if it had,' she observed grimly.

Then she remembered Chuang Tzu's famous story of the butterfly. Chuang Tzu had once dreamed he was a butterfly, then woken to find he was a man. Then he wondered if he was a man who once dreamed he was a butterfly, or a butterfly who was now dreaming that he was a man.

She dismissed the recollection with a contemptuous twist of the lips. The wu-hsing dream was a dream, and this – she gave the Five Faces statue a hefty kick – is *not* a dream. Damn Chuang Tzu and his butterfly.

How did I get here anyway? she pondered. I haven't sleep-walked in years. She threw Five Faces another hostile glance, then her brow wrinkled at the same time as her nose.

The curdled scent was so pungent that it was one sniff away from becoming a visible aura around the statue. The scent was present, in widely varying degrees, throughout the temple, but here – by the wu-hsing – it was stomach-churning.

She was already heading for the end of the hall, hand cupped over her nose, when she heard Ming-kai's voice calling from its dense shadows.

'Black Dragon! Are you here?'

'Yes, I'm here.'

She rounded the last Immortal in the line and confronted the war veteran's impassive gaze.

'Fen-chou's dead,' he stated in a tone as impassive as his steady stare.

Chia concluded her examination of Fen-chou's throat and chest, with Sung and Ming-kai the only observers.

The upper chest area was covered in minuscule

pinpricks. A certain amount of delicate probing disclosed that sharp metallic tips were embedded under the skin. A surreptitious slip of her hand into one of her inside pockets confirmed her suspicion. Her bag of chen-chiu needles was gone.

She didn't know where the bag was. But she knew where her needles were. Inside Fen-chou.

Someone had treated the old man like a pin-cushion.

She dimly recalled dreaming that a man knelt by her bed last night. If so, that was when the bag was stolen. The thief and murderer had displayed contempt for her by using her own needles to kill the old man. A wistful reminiscence slanted her mouth. Gentle old Fen-chou. She'd known him as a young lad. Mad about kites, he was. It must be at least ten years since she last met him in Tung An.

'I promised I'd call on him first if I was in the vicinity,' she said quietly. Then she ruffled the brindled hair and winked affectionately at the gaunt features. 'Come back as your favourite animal.'

'He's full of needles, isn't he?' cut in Ming-kai.

*Damn*, thought Chia. 'That's right,' she said, rising to her feet. 'Most observant.'

'Where are your needles?' queried Sung, his seamed face a mask of innocence.

'Where I can't get them back without gross impropriety,' she muttered, pushing past the two men.

## 13

My heart is not a stone
To be rolled away.
My heart is not a mat
To be folded up.

Shih ching

Chia looked at Silver Music Bay through black glass.

There was scant sunlight, but she felt exposed in front of so many villagers celebrating Ch'ung Yang, flying their kites along the beach. So she hid behind her dark glasses. Crowds, no matter how scattered, made her uneasy. She always felt that they were staring at her.

Which, in fact, they usually were.

The Forest Bell Villagers, however, were singularly oblivious of her presence. They appeared to be totally absorbed in the kite festival.

Chia's eye traced the rumpled curve of the bay. 'The Wound,' she said. 'That's what the bay was called, long ago. The Wound. No wonder they changed the name to Silver Music.'

A sky-happy kite escaped its cord and soared over the cliffs.

In ancient time, according to a popular Chinese legend, a mighty tidal wave had engulfed those cliffs and fish had swum in the forest. A sage had escaped the flood by fleeing to a high place. To celebrate his escape, kites were flown from high places on Ch'ung Yang. But the inhabitants of Silver Music Bay had no high, open spaces to which they could escape. They were locked in.

Did Aklo hold the key?

She was intrigued by what she had heard of the mysterious Aklo.

Apparently, he had first been sighted ten years ago. And he hadn't aged in those ten years. Stranger still, there were reports that went back centuries of a similar youth making sporadic appearances.

Aklo was a youth she was eager to meet: if anyone could point the way to Nyak, it was him.

Her thoughtful gaze skimmed up and down the bay.

Ch'ung Yang was in full swing. Colourful paper dragons and tigers fought half-hearted battles under the grim, grey canopy of clouds that continually threatened a downpour, but never made good the threat.

The population of Forest Bell Village had stormed south down the bay at mid-morning, making the most of a strong wind from the sea. The dragon and tiger kites tugged the cords held in tight fists in eagerness to ride high in the rising gale.

Chia, standing on the beach near Melodious Temple, regarded the approach of the villagers with a wary eye, remembering Sung's mistrust of the Forest Bell people and the infamous Aklo's hold over them. And at closer look – some two li for the nearest of the festive groups – although they appeared a happy enough crowd, there was an element of performance in their actions, a theatricality. Ming-kai had few good things to say about them. And Fen-chou –

*Poor, lonely old man. Should have got married.*

– had made some damning comments about the village, with particular condemnation of Aklo. According to Sung, it was Fen-chou who had overheard Aklo's references to the moon-silver, the Dark Woman and the Nothing Man. Chia wished she could have discussed Aklo's words with Fen-chou himself. She might have learned much to help her in her preparations. The old man might have shed some light where none was now forthcoming.

'Aklo,' she hissed softly, scanning the darting figures

191

and dancing kites on the vast sweep of the bay, 'where are you?' Her lips twitched in a quirky smile.

Nowhere, under the shadow of the cliffs or by the frothing lip of the sea, could she spot his reputedly unmistakable Rainbow Robe. Green and blue predominated as the favourite colours of Silver Music Bay. They wore green smocks, mostly. Nothing elaborate; the villagers had simple tastes. Aklo's variegated attire should stand out like a major eccentricity, even through dark glass.

'Where are you, Aklo?'

The groups of animated children shrieked their excitement like seagull plaints: distance lent a hue of sadness to the scenes of merriment. Her gaze wandered from shore to sea. The thresh of a swimmer could be glimpsed here and there in the tumbling waves.

'Where are you – '

'Chia?'

She swung round, startled by the intrusion into her meandering thoughts. Xanthippe stood behind her, weaving garlands of seaweed.

'Ah,' Chia sighed. 'Didn't hear you coming.'

Xanthippe shifted her foot on the wet sand, curling and uncurling her toes. 'I wondered if you intended to revisit Egypt sometime soon.'

Chia discerned the lorn look in the girl's lustrous eyes. And she guessed that her arrival had accentuated the Egyptian's sense of loss: first of country, then of parents.

Before she could open her mouth to reply, Xanthippe pressed the point home. 'Teacher Sung once told me that you have a particular attachment to Egypt.'

Chia's rueful stare wandered over the beach scene, perceiving little of what it had to offer. 'The Egypt that was once my home isn't the Egypt you know. Your Egypt has Greek names for Egyptian cities. Even the name Egypt is Greek – in the time of the Pharaohs, Egypt was called the Black Land of Khemet.' Behind black glass, her green eyes were deep with distance and memory.

'I remember the great city of Akhetaten,' she murmured. 'The whole vast city was built in less than three years. I remember. I was there. I was there when Akhenaten ruled, with Queen Nefertiti at his side. Now Akhetaten is a brown ruin and Akhenaten and Nefertiti are lost dust.'

'They live in your memory,' said Xanthippe, gazing out to sea.

'My memory's a shattered jar. The fragments defy reconstruction.'

'Perhaps you're afraid of the pattern,' the Egyptian suggested with a sideways glance.

Chia's regard for the gentle young woman rose several notches, but she kept her admiration hidden behind a nonchalant expression. She scanned the beach, ready to take note of the first hint of abnormality from the kite-flying villagers. As the nearest group drew closer she was able to distinguish the faces. Each had an individual physiognomy, but the expressions – not so individual.

'Ming-kai's been talking about you,' Xanthippe stated quietly. 'He suggested that Fen-chou's death – those needles . . .'

'I can imagine.' Chia smiled grimly, her attention straying to the long, undulating Ancestral Gallery. 'I've been accused of a lot worse.'

The Egyptian's lip trembled. 'Why would anybody want to stick your needles into that kind old man?'

'Lots of reasons, none of which interest me.' The sorceress shrugged, still eyeing the Ancestral Gallery. 'Have they concluded the funeral rites yet?'

'Yes, just now. Why weren't you there?'

'I don't like funerals. Mind you, I'm making one small exception this time – taking care of one last detail.'

'I heard.' Xanthippe exhaled softly. 'You're taking the body to House Feng. Fen-chou always said he wanted to be interred with his parents on the Ancestral Gallery. But Ming-kai insists *he's* going to place Fen-chou with the ancestors.'

'He can say what he likes. I'm taking the corpse to House Feng. Alone.' She assessed the position of the smudged sun. 'In about an hour.'

'Tell me about Egypt.'

The sudden, earnest request took Chia unawares. On the verge of delivering a blunt refusal, she caught the look of profound loneliness in Xanthippe's gaze. Her homeland was on the other side of the world. Her parents were dead. There was alien land under her feet, a desolation of the heart inside her lithe, dark body.

Orphan. Exile.

'Tell me about Egypt,' the gentle voice repeated. 'Tell me about Nefertiti. Is it such a secret? After all, you must have told Liu Chun.'

'What do you mean?' frowned Chia.

'Well – Teacher Sung told me that Liu Chun, Master of Luminous Cloud Mountain, assisted you during the haunting of San Lung. And – and that you confided your deepest secrets to the Master of Luminous Cloud Mountain.'

'Sung told you wrong.' Chia snorted. 'Sung's an even bigger fool than Liu Chun.'

Puzzled, Xanthippe scratched her tight crop of curls. 'But it's said that Abbot Nagarjuna of Celestial Buddha Temple regarded Liu Chun as your invaluable ally.'

'And look what befell Nagarjuna,' the sorceress muttered, memories crowding behind black circles of glass. 'In San Lung, when all hell was breaking loose, Liu Chun was about as much use as a solitary chopstick.' She glanced at her companion, her heart touched by the girl's quiet, inner battle with loneliness. Chia understood such battles. 'I'll tell you about Egypt,' she found herself answering. Then, in an attempt to make light of the heavy tone in her response, she gave an airy flick of her hand. 'After all, it's obvious you can be trusted with a secret. I'd trust you above a hundred Liu Chuns.'

Abashed by the compliment, the Egyptian had to force the words out: 'So – about Egypt, and Nefertiti.'

Chia threw a last look at the Ch'ung Yang kite-battles. 'All right,' she said, sitting on a broad, flat rock beside a small sea-shrine of massed conches and cowrie shells. 'Sit down. I'll tell you a little of what happened in Egypt long ago. After you've listened, you may never want to be near me again.'

Xanthippe shivered at the warning, disturbed by the notion that Chia – her idol – would have feet of clay, or brimstone. 'I'll *always* want to be near – ' A hand flew to her gaping mouth. 'Oh, I'm sorry – all I meant was . . .' The speech faltered in mid-air. She wasn't sure what she meant.

Chia lowered her gaze. *Is Xanthippe falling in love with me? Too soon to tell. What's certain is that I'm falling in love with her.*

And – was it possible that this girl received echoes from Nefertiti's spirit each night? Xanthippe wasn't Nefertiti reborn. But still . . .

'Egypt,' Chia murmured. 'The Black Land of Khemet, fifteen centuries ago. I first went there when Akhenaten was co-regent with Amenophis. At the beginning, Amenophis believed me a Hittite spy, but I finally persuaded him otherwise. Then I was paid generous sums to become an Egyptian spy and assassin, infiltrating Hittite strongholds north of the land of Canaan. A fair number of Hittites have green eyes, so my appearance passed without remark, although my height was always a drawback in a spy's line of work.'

A smile brightened the Egyptian's full mouth. 'I can imagine. I thought *I* was tall, here in China, three fingers' breadth short of six feet. I was a giantess. But you – you must be . . .'

'Six feet, by Greek reckoning,' she said in the flat tone of one who had held similar conversations a million times. 'Anyway, I sometimes disguised myself as a man when insinuating myself into the enemy's camps. I survived. I got by. I did good work for Amenophis – that fat, declining Pharaoh. Two years' good work. When I returned to the city you now know as Memphis, I was rewarded with a small villa near Heliopolis. That's when I first met Akhenaten's wife, Nefertiti. She was fifteen.'

Soft remembrance flooded into Chia's musing face.

'She changed my life. Not in a moment, as I sometimes like to fool myself. No, not in a moment. Nor in a day. But not in a year, either. It was two weeks – three at the most. I was in her chambers, ostensibly serving as a tutor, but secretly appointed by Amenophis to spy on his co-regent's wife. I studied her every expression, sifted her every word, looking for signs of treachery. Then – I remember she picked up a lute. And she sang to me from behind a glass-beaded curtain that rustled like spring rain. Her hands were golden, I recall, and her silver-painted fingernails plucked rippling chords from the strings. The more I was entranced by her music, the effervescence of her soul, the more I was enthralled by her face, her mannerisms, her very being. My maze of nerves were hers – she plucked music from them. When she'd finished playing, she looked at me. And, suddenly, I wasn't Chia any more.'

Lost in her narrative, Chia was unaware of Xanthippe's absorption in the account. Her deep voice became faint and slightly slurred, as if she was talking to herself.

'We made love, in that chamber. Afterwards, she told me that she played and sang to me because she had already fallen in love with me. The idea staggered me. I had never believed in gods – or goddesses. Now I had found my own goddess. She wasn't a sacred statue for me, nor an inviolate shrine. I smelt her sweat, saw the small blemishes on her skin, and loved them because they were part of her. I realized then that there was divinity in the human shape, the human spirit. For me, making love was the only religion I had, or wanted to have. Of course, I knew it wouldn't last – '

Sorrow suffused Chia's features. At last, Xanthippe discerned what others had noised abroad: the tragedy in Chia's face.

'– I knew she had to die, in a year, a decade, or five decades. She had to die. And I had to go on living for thousands upon thousands of years, remembering. Sometimes, when I think back to that brief time with Nefertiti, it seems to have passed like summer lightning or the span of a dragonfly – a flicker of time's eyelid. Human lives always seem so pathetically short to me. But there are moments, now and again, when I recall my years with Nefertiti as a world-age, or a long sojourn outside time. Yes, occasionally I recollect it so. I call it the golden time.'

Her head lowered. She seemed to be folding inwards as her arms clutched the overcoat tight to her sides.

The rising sea breeze ruffled her long, tangled hair. The tide was drawing in, frothing a few paces from the rock on which Chia sat, hunched and oblivious of silver sea, dark islands and grey sky. Her wistful face, from Xanthippe's line of sight, was framed by a shrine of seashells.

'Akhenaten eventually turned against Nefertiti. After Akhetaten was constructed – the City of the Horizon of Aten – on the boundary of the Upper and Lower Kingdoms, the Pharaoh imprisoned Nefertiti in the North Palace. I was allowed to stay with her. She was approaching forty then, and I was forced to explain my agelessness to the Pharaoh's ministers. At least, I gave them a story that satisfied them for a time. We were left in peace. Life was good for a while. That was the golden time – golden, like the colour of her body.

'When it ended, it ended in a rush. Akhenaten was obsessed with his new religion of the Aten, the Sun Disc, and threw all his energies into fostering the cult and supplanting the ancient gods. He neglected everyday affairs and affairs of state. He forgot that he was ruler of an empire. When the Hittites attacked the eastern border, Egypt's war-machine was rotted and rusty, its weapons outdated. General Horemheb made a brave show, but the Kingdom of the Nile was virtually open to any invader. I had no choice but to escape from the North Palace and head along the Nile for the scene of conflict. I promised Nefertiti that I'd return soon . . .'

A twinge of pain remembered troubled Chia's hidden gaze.

'I fought like a demon. And I fought alone. I stalked northern Sinai like a murderous phantom. I don't recall how many Hittites I killed – hundreds, perhaps thousands. I saw them as a threat to Nefertiti, you see. Each time I encountered a Hittite soldier, I said to myself, "If I let this man live, he might kill Nefertiti." I didn't care if they were young, or unwilling to fight – I didn't listen to their pleas for mercy. I just killed them. I killed them for love.'

Xanthippe placed a tentative hand on Chia's shoulder. 'It's a soldier's duty to kill.'

Chia gave a slow shake of the head. 'I didn't kill as a soldier. And the way I slew some of them – I didn't let them die as soldiers . . .'

'In your long life, you must have killed before,' said the Egyptian. 'In the legends, you're called the Death-bringer.'

The sorceress paused for a moment, weighing considerations in her mind. 'At the very beginning of my life, a thousand years before the Shang Kingdom gave birth to China, I killed a man. It was a crime that crushed my spirit, afflicted my conscience. I blotted it from my memory. When I visited Egypt, I thought that there was no blood on my hands. I considered myself incapable of taking life. After I fell in love with Nefertiti, I learned the slaying ways. I thought I waged my own war for the queen's sake, but later I discovered the true reason. Later – when I returned to Akhetaten – the Pharaoh had been murdered in an uprising, and Nefertiti was in fear for her life. I started to liquidate everyone who might prove a threat to my Egyptian love . . .'

She halted for a space, struggling to say the words, confess the crime. At last, she dragged the admission from herself. She lifted her black glasses and stared straight at Xanthippe.

'Nefertiti killed herself because of my actions. She thought that by ending her life she'd stop my slaughtering. At the time, I didn't realize that – I was under the illusion that she'd committed suicide to evade the pain and humiliation of execution.'

'Did her death halt your killings?'

Behind Chia's green eyes was the red of blood. Her voice was attuned to the lonely cadence of the wind from the waves. 'No. It didn't halt the killings. In a way, that's when they really started.'

She replaced the glasses, and her eyes became black moons again. Xanthippe shivered. Once more, the black figure of the sorceress was an image of menace. 'But why – what reason was there for continuing the slaughter?'

'Because she was dead.'

Perplexed, the Egyptian fingered the soft comfort of the white lion robe. 'I don't understand.'

Chia subjected her companion to a brief stare. There were long centuries in that brief stare. and a primal echo in the distant reply:

'I hated everyone in the world because they were alive and my love was dead.'

'You – you knew she had to die one day,' Xanthippe reminded hesitantly. 'You said so yourself.'

'I knew it as you know that tomorrow will come, without knowing how tomorrow will feel.'

'I see,' sighed Xanthippe, wishing that she didn't see. 'But you said there was a reason you made war on Nefertiti's behalf. A reason you didn't understand at the time. What was it?'

Chia turned from the question, skimmed her gaze along the Ancestral Gallery until it came to rest on the rocky spur that blanked out the village and the House of Heaven. The sharp edge of her voice cut into the Egyptian:

'I killed my father. I will kill my brother. And that's all you need to know.'

She stood up abruptly. 'I don't think Aklo's going to show up. No point waiting here. You can conduct me round the temple before I have to take Fen-chou to his ancestors.'

Xanthippe bit back the apology she was about to deliver. It was easy to draw blood from Chia's soul, even when your words were aimed with good intent.

'I'm not the only one who's easily hurt,' she observed, somewhere below a breath.

Faint as the whisper was, Chia heard it. She wanted to hug the girl and assure her that all was well between them, that she would die to defend Xanthippe. But she hid her feelings behind a stern facade. She was used to hiding her feelings. Those whom she loved, the Silver Brethren killed.

*You-will-live-alone*.

As the two walked up the beach towards the temple, Chia cast a backward look at the seashell shrine. Its clumped conches reminded her of skulls.

Why conches and skulls should stir a residue of dread from memory's sludge, she wasn't sure. But something told her that she'd soon be finding out.

'The Hall of Invitation,' announced Xanthippe, waving a brown arm at the shabby, ramshackle hall with its pine walls bleached from the rough salt lick of the sea wind.

At their backs, the temple gate rattled in the strengthening breeze.

'Uninviting,' commented Chia. She swung her gaze to the right and studied the outline of a long, low building. She sniffed the air that emanated from its round door. 'Alchemy.'

'Yes,' Xanthippe nodded. 'The Hall of Transformations. Old Hsiang works there with his assistant, Little Ko.'

'Then let's go in and speak to them.'

'They'll be at the funeral rites in the Pavilion of the Immortals.'

'Let's go in anyway.' She slipped off her glasses and pocketed them.

Chia was already entering the round mouth of the portal before Xanthippe could speak a word. She followed Chia's long strides into the murky interior, feeling like a little dog on a leash.

Lifting a crystal from one of her numerous pockets, the sorceress gripped it tight for a moment, focusing her thoughts on light. Before three breaths had steamed the chilly atmosphere, the crystal distilled a cold blue radiance. She held it aloft, casting a cold blue light on her immediate surroundings.

'How did you do that?' gaped Xanthippe. 'What is that stone?'

'It's a crystal. A luminescent crystal. The Chinese call them Night-Shining Jewels,' came the abstracted answer, as Chia's attention moved into the southern shadows at the end of the hall.

'I'm familiar with Night-Shining Jewels. What I can't understand is how you made the crystal shine so bright.'

'Slowing down of the ch'i activity within the crystal,' came the swift reply as Chia wound her way through jumbles of disused, arcane apparatus. 'Reduction of ch'i causes light-emission when subjected to a pre-dominance of yin modulated by the hand between head and crystal.'

'Oh – I see. That's how it's done,' she said blankly.

A half-smile flashed on Chia's wide lips as she threw a look back at the flummoxed Egyptian. 'When this is all over I'll give you all the lessons in alchemy that you desire' – she hesitated for a moment, the smile becoming pensive – 'in Egypt. In Alexandria.'

Xanthippe inhaled sharply, hope flooding her face. 'You mean it? You *mean* it?'

Chia's face, in blue light, was hieratic and remote: a contemplative priestess. 'I mean it. When I've destroyed what must be destroyed, we'll go to Egypt together. It's been fifty years since I last walked the colonnaded streets of Alexandria and pored over some of the volumes in the Great Library.'

'Almost a million different volumes,' the Alexandrian girl proudly declared. 'My father often described it to me: Eratosthenes, who proved the earth was round, and calculated its circumference. Claudius Ptolemy, who studied the night skies and explained the orbits of the planets – '

'So *that's* what Ptolemy was doing sitting on top of the Pharos lighthouse,' exclaimed Chia. 'I often wondered.'

A sudden thought crossed the Egyptian's mind – one that excited her heart to a rapid rhythm. 'You've been to Alexandria many times, yes?'

'Yes,' confirmed Chia, her attention straying back to the southern end of the hall. 'It's my favourite city.'

'Were you there about two centuries ago, during the reign of Augustus – at the time when Herod the Great died?'

Intrigued by the girl's eagerness, the sorceress gave a quick nod. 'I lived in Alexandria throughout Augustus's entire reign.'

'The Virgin Mother took her infant Christos to Alexandria near the time that Herod died,' Xanthippe said, her eyes shining. 'Did you meet them?'

'Virgin Mother?'

'Mary of Bethlehem, and her son Jesus the Christos.'

Chia reflected for a moment, then shook her head. 'Not as I recall. Why do you ask?'

'I'm a Christian.'

A slight tilt of an eyebrow betrayed Chia's misgivings. 'Christians – they're those people who go around in pairs and try to convince you that the world's about to end.'

'Not *those!*' snorted Xanthippe. 'They're Ecclesia Christians – followers of Peter's Church. I'm a Gnostic Christian – I was taught to respect other people's religions, and to seek the truth inside the heart instead of in scriptures.'

'Ah yes,' interrupted the sorceress, lifting a silencing

hand. 'Gnostics. I know about the Gnostics, but the only famous one I've met was Simon the Magus of Samaria. He would have been alive at the same time as your Christos.'

'Simon Magus? You met Simon Magus?' The actuality of Chia's longevity hit the girl with full force. It was so easy to treat the sorceress's immense life-span as an abstract hypothesis, but her casual mention of the long-dead founder of her father's school of Gnostics shattered the abstraction. Suddenly, the dream Chia and the living, breathing Chia coalesced for the Egyptian girl. Chia was neither ethereal divinity nor mundane mortal. She was the union of opposites: immortal and mortal, good and bad. She was both yes and no. She was Chia Black Dragon, a living miracle.

'Oh no,' groaned Chia, observing the Alexandrian's rapt expression. 'I appreciate the sentiment, Xanthippe. But your timing is terrible. Holding hands isn't going to defeat the Nothing Man.' She jerked her bramble-haired head in the direction of the hall's south wall. 'Come on, we'd better move our feet . . .'

Tracking the tall woman's steps, a crestfallen Xanthippe kept her eyes lowered to the ground in front of her booted feet. She felt gauche and belittled. Chia had seen right to the heart of her newborn love – and rejected it. Xanthippe felt very, very small.

Hardly able to keep the Night-Shining Jewel steady in her hand, Chia couldn't bear to look over her shoulder, couldn't trust herself to look back. She was falling in love with Xanthippe. But that was all right. She could live with it. Xanthippe was falling in love with her. That wasn't all right. The Egyptian couldn't live with it.

*And even if she can bear to share the life I live, she'll become a target. She'll be a target for Nyak and the Silver Brethren. A target. Like Wei. Like Chiu-su. Like Fu. Like a hundred others – all tortured to death. That's how to kill an immortal heart – by killing her mortal loves. I'll not add Xanthippe to the list. I'll kill her love with my hard face and hard words. The Silver Brethren aren't the only ones who need to wear a mask.*

Chia halted in front of a tall apparatus of polished bronze set close to the southern wall. She was about to play the blue light of the Night-Shining Jewel over its complex configurations when Xanthippe's small voice stayed her hand:

'Will you still be taking me back to Alexandria when your task here is finished?'

Chia bit her lip; she hoped the blood didn't show. 'That's where I'll be going, so you are free to come with me. Don't expect anything more.'

The girl's answer took her by surprise. 'What made you the way you are, Chia?'

The honesty of Xanthippe's tone deserved an honest response –

*I killed my father. I thought I killed my brother. But the dead don't lie down. And I, also, am the dead.*

– but she could supply merely a partial response, an Egyptian reply:

'After Nefertiti's death,' she began quietly, staring into the deathly blue light, 'I became what I am. Mad. Death-mad. I never fully understood mortality until I lost Nefertiti. Before Nefertiti, I had some vague notion that losing somebody meant that you might find them again, sometime, somewhere. After Nefertiti, I saw death in the rings of trees, the flight of birds, autumn chrysanthemums, the ripple of streams. I saw death in the rocks – earth's bones. And I hated everyone who walked above ground because their hearts beat and their mouths laughed while Nefertiti was still and mute as sand.' Her eyes lowered. 'The last words she said to me were "Forgive me". I've never been certain what she meant.'

Xanthippe's reaction was immediate and confident. 'She was mortal. She wanted you to forgive her for being mortal.'

Chia made sure that her profile was averted from the Egyptian. She wanted to scream at her, wanted to shout out the monster grief in her breast: *Don't you see what you're doing to me? I loved Nefertiti. I lost Nefertiti. Long ago. I live with it. But you, with your love-me eyes and your Nefertiti of the night – you're unearthing the buried golden time. The dead don't lie down. You're being used. Used by the enemy.*

She tried to keep a shake out of her voice. 'If I'm not sure of Nefertiti's meaning, how can you be so certain?'

'Because she speaks to me in dreams.'

'Dreams,' echoed Chia, grimly recollecting the wu-hsing dream. 'Dreams are liars. Dreams are tricksters.'

'Not *my* dream,' Xanthippe insisted. 'I feel what Nefertiti once felt. I share her thoughts.'

Chia's mouth formed a hard line. There was no point in arguing. She wanted to tell the Alexandrian that she was being used, that her family had been lured here by Nyak – or perhaps Aklo – for purposes far removed from Paradise. Was it reasonable, she wanted to yell, was it reasonable to believe that an Egyptian happened to be waiting for a sorceress at this particular time and place out of sheer good luck? And as for her nightly Nefertiti, seemingly biding Chia's arrival – also good luck? It was coincidence magnified to cosmic proportions. No. She was being used as a puppet. And when she ceased to be of use, the puppeteer would dispose of her.

'Ah, Xanthippe,' she sighed. 'You've no conception what's in store for us here.'

The girl inclined her head. 'I'm sorry. I shouldn't have spoken of Nefertiti. I should have realized how much it hurts you.'

The sorceress opened her mouth, then closed it again. Xanthippe continually displayed notable insight. Perhaps the deadly puppeteer wouldn't be able to make her dance too readily to his tune.

Chia squared her shoulders, expelled a sharp breath and put a smile on her mouth. 'Well, Miss Gnostic Christian, I expected you to show me all the fascinating features of this rickety temple. Not much of a show so far.'

Xanthippe gave her a knowing look. 'Somehow I don't think you need me to show you any features.'

205

'I'm not so sure.' She waved a hand at the bronze apparatus. 'I know what this is supposed to be, but tell me what you think it is.'

A shrug twitched Xanthippe's shapely shoulders. 'It's Hsiang's tan-t'ien: an alchemical separation device. I don't think the old man uses it much these days – he mostly stumbles around saying "Seek wisdom" all the time. Maybe Little Ko makes use of it. I'm not certain – I rarely come here.'

Chia pursed her lips as she surveyed the device. The three tiers of crucibles were constructed in a crude approximation of human shape. The alchemical texts varied, but it was clear that Hsiang had directed his efforts to the formation of a so-called 'immortality pill' in the top crucible, and that enterprise was one she'd never encountered in any text. Also, the tan-t'ien acquired something of a shape of dread the longer she looked at it. Male-female combinations, literal, not symbolic, were suggested in the form and functions of the apparatus.

'It'll never work,' she said, her lips crooked. 'It's too literally based on sexual alchemy – the Ceremony of the Deliverance from Guilt.'

'The Deliverance Ceremony,' Xanthippe chimed in. 'The hermits conduct that on the fifteenth day of every moon. I've not been allowed to witness it so far.'

'I'm not surprised.' Chia smiled. 'The Deliverance from Guilt is a no-holds-barred orgy. Sexual alchemy in the mating of men and women.'

She stepped back from the tan-t'ien, slowly shaking her head. 'If he was resurrected, it wasn't through this eccentric contrivance.'

'If *who* was resurrected?' asked a mystified Xanthippe.

'Nyak,' came the answer. 'The Nothing Man. My brother.'

There was a brief silence as Xanthippe digested the news, and the sorceress stared at the bronze device. The Egyptian broke the silence.

'Mercury.'

Chia tossed a questioning glance at her companion. 'Mercury? What do you – Oh, you mean the Latin name for quicksilver.'

'And the winged messenger of the gods,' Xanthippe added.

It hit Chia like a wild gust from the sea: a raw idea, too raw to be fully formed, but an idea that held a sound core. She struggled to give it shape.

'Quicksilver,' she said slowly, as if savouring the taste. She touched the ankh. 'Moon-silver. Quicksilver. Mercury. The god who rides on the wings of the wind. Quicksilver. Liquid metal . . .' It was near, tantalizingly near, but, like quicksilver itself, she couldn't grasp it. It ran gleaming through her fingers. Then, unbidden, a word rose from some wise inner dark, glistening droplets spilling from its sides: 'Protean.'

*Born in the sea. Reborn in the sea.*

Xanthippe, perplexed, was frowning at the sorceress, but Chia stuck to her zigzag line of thought. 'Protean,' she repeated. 'Proteus, servant of Poseidon, god of the sea. Proteus, with the gift of prophecy – and the power of shape-shifting. The shape-changer from the sea.'

*A mask in the mists from the sea.*

'Chia – ' Xanthippe tried to break in.

'Wait,' Chia silenced with a wave of her raised hand. 'Wait. Mercury. In Greek, Hermes, the messenger of Olympus. Hermes – and Aphrodite. Hermes and Aphrodite mated and gave birth to Hermaphroditus – the primal hermaphrodite, self-procreating, immortal.' Eyelids slid down, hooding her green gaze.

'Chia . . .'

*The idea – it's slipping and sliding . . . I can't quite grasp . . . Quicksilver and sulphur combine in the tan-t'ien to form the crystal child of immortality. And the crystal child, sprung of yin quicksilver and yang sulphur – is the primal hermaphrodite, female and male combining. The female – the Dark Woman; the male – the Nothing Man . . . Sexual alchemy . . .*

Xanthippe had gripped Chia's arm; she shook it with

207

the impatience of a jumpy dog. 'Chia! Are you all right? You look lost . . .'

Chia gently released the Egyptian's grasp, and assumed what she hoped was a reassuring smile. 'I'm fine. I took my thoughts for a ramble, that's all.'

The smile must have been convincing, as the Alexandrian relaxed visibly, jerking her head towards the grey daylight circle of the door. 'Shall I show you the rest of the temple?'

'Ah – no. Will Fen-chou's body still be in the Pavilion of the Immortals?'

Xanthippe pursed her full lips. 'They might have taken him to Kang's room by now. There was some talk of requesting Fen-chou's spirit to aid Chai-san's stolen spirit-face.'

'We'll go straight there,' came the immediate response as Chia headed for the door.

The sorceress fought to keep her emotions from her stern expression. It was a difficult fight. She felt as if someone was stroking her heart with the point of a nail.

Nyak wanted to ingest Xanthippe's flesh to achieve resurrection. The Nothing Man desired a dire mating with the Dark Woman . . . Sexual alchemy. Gentle-natured Xanthippe was Nyak's target, the chief object of his desire. All his hopes of rebirth were pinned on the Egyptian. Nyak was coming back through Xanthippe.

Chia threw an amiable look at her companion as they emerged into dull daylight and the first suggestion of autumn drizzle. And she hoped, once more, that her face didn't betray her dismay.

But Xanthippe was no fool. Worried lines formed in the dark brown forehead. 'There's something wrong. What is it? What's wrong?'

*Mustn't tell her. Mustn't nourish her fear. Nyak feeds on fear. Deflect her concern. Deflect it.*

The sorceress pulled a wry face as the two women ascended the steps to the upper temple area. 'Of course something's wrong. There's been something wrong in this bay for a long time. But – yes – I've just realized how much danger I'm in. I'm Nyak's target. He's not concerned with anyone except me.'

Xanthippe was dubious. 'But I've had this strong feeling that it's me they – or he – are after. I thought I was like a – like a magnet.'

Chia gave a dismissive shrug. 'Everybody feels like that when there's menace in the air. Everyone thinks "It's *me* they want. It's *me* they're looking for". It's a sense of persecution. Everybody feels that way.'

The Egyptian remained unconvinced. 'Everybody? Including yourself?'

'I'm different,' came the muttered reply after a moment's hesitation. 'I know what I'm talking about.'

'Was it you the haunter was hunting last night? Was it you that was trapped in Kang's room with Chai-san's body and some terrible power battering the door? Was it you that Chai-san's ripping meat voice invited to "Be us"? Was it you the brazen tongue outside the door summoned "Xanthippe – Come and stay"?' Shaking, the girl held out her nutbrown arm. 'And I must be the only Dark Woman in China, let alone the bay.'

'They're attempting to fool you – and me,' Chia lied smoothly. 'It's natural that you should wish to protect yourself first – that need is intrinsic to survival. But, believe me, I'm the one they want. It may surprise you, but *I'm* the one who needs *your* help.'

Xanthippe's uncertainty evaporated at the notion that she was failing Chia by becoming entangled in groundless fears for her own safety. A twinge of shame twitched her mouth. 'I'm sorry, Chia. I suppose I was thinking too much of myself – of my own importance. It stands to reason that *you* must be the target of the Nothing Man – you're his greatest foe. I'm sorry. I'll help you all I can.'

Chia gave the girl's hand a quick squeeze. 'Thanks, Xanthippe. I'm rarely offered help. And I need all I can get.'

Xanthippe's evident gratitude made Chia feel like the lowest form of life, the worst kind of traitor. She wished that the feeling was not so familiar.

Pushing open the red door to Kang's room, Chia entered without ceremony. Nine hermits, in the midst of their chanting, looked up as the two women came into the room.

The nine mourners were kneeling in a circle around the prone figures of Fen-chou and Chai-san. Encircling the nine men were hundreds of flickering candles. Chia's booted feet knocked three candles over as she strode towards the mourners. They continued the monotonous chant regardless of her brusque arrival:

'Tung-wang-kung-tung-wang-kung-tung-wang-kung-tung – '

'That's enough,' Chia declared, breaking through the chanting circle. 'You can leave now.'

'Wang . . . Kung . . .'

'I said that's enough!'

The bellow killed the chant stone dead.

'You can leave now,' Chia repeated in a quieter tone. 'If I don't instate Fen-chou in House Feng before sunset, the kwai ghosts will take his soul – isn't that what the Silver Music ritual sets forth?'

Ming-kai rose angrily to his feet, his voice large with rage. 'First you murder him, then you interrupt the mourning rites due to him. You belong in Hell, Black Dragon.'

But Teacher Sung, grasping Ming-kai by the elbow and signalling the others to leave, strove to pacify him. 'We've performed all the rites in the T'ao-tsang manual. And we've requested Fen-chou's soul to find Chai-san's lost spirit and guide it to the Blue Palaces. We've done all that can be done. Let's go – come on . . .'

After clear signs of an inner struggle, Ming-kai relented. But as he passed the sorceress he glared his loathing of her and hissed softly between tight teeth:

210

'Beauty blinds, Black Dragon. Beauty blinds. But it doesn't blind me. I know what's behind your face. And sooner or later I'll rip your mask off, Black Dragon. I want you to remember that.'

Chia shrugged her indifference. She studied the two bodies at her feet as the last of the hermits shuffled out of the door. Her finger stroked the ankh at her breast, then froze in mid-motion. Her nose twitched to a scent, a scent reminiscent of . . .

She swung round and saw a bald, gangling figure about to swing the door shut.

'*You!*' she snapped, thrusting a finger at the departing hermit. 'Come here.'

With a shrill chuckle, he stepped back into the room, shutting the door with a sharp click. His teeth, filed to points, formed a spiky grin in his cadaverous, tattooed features. A dangling necklace of rat-skulls rattled as he chuckled. He spread out his tattooed palms as he confronted the sorceress. His voice was high-pitched:

'I'm only the Mad Hermit.'

'Aren't they all,' she muttered, waving the man to approach.

Barefoot, he stepped through the crowd of candles, his gaunt hand straying to a bulge in the folds of the red Kang-i robe over his chest. The movement suggested a gesture of protection.

'Yes.' Chia nodded, casting a sideways glance at a mystified Xanthippe before subjecting the Mad Hermit to a penetrating stare. 'What I want is what you've got hidden, Mad Hermit. I don't like the smell of it.'

Pouting his displeasure, the hermit drew a pouch from his robe, letting it hang by its neck-cord. Then, at a glower from Chia, he extracted its contents.

'It's just a conch,' he said, holding the shell in his outstretched hand. 'Found it on the Ancestral Gallery. It's only a conch.'

Taking the shell in her hands, Chia shuddered at the momentary sensation of bone, old bone, touching her skin. Fleetingly, she saw a small skull in her grasp. Then she mastered her imagination – for imagination was all it was. The smell emanating from the conch merely resembled that old, hated scent, causing her to glimpse the contour of a skull – or mask-helmet – in a harmless shell. She sniffed at the open mouth of the conch, wincing her distaste. Chia's aversion was the hermit's delight.

'Ahhhh ... it disgusts you, Black Dragon. Lao's magic potion is too strong for the great sorceress.'

'Nonsense,' she snorted, tilting her chin at a haughty angle. '*Nothing's* too strong for my stomach, you Man of Bones.' She glanced at the viscous liquid in the shell. 'Your concoction is a feeble imitation of a certain recipe – the smell, however, is close to the original.'

The spiky grin was back. 'It *is* the original. It's moon-milk.'

She thrust the conch back into the hermit's waiting palm with a contemptuous air. 'It's not moon-milk.'

The grin was undisturbed. 'Oh yes, it's moon-milk, sure and certain.' The tip of his tongue circled his inner lip. 'Rat's blood, corpse dust, dissolved pearl at full moon, and human semen mixed in sea water.' The grin faded slightly. 'Mind you – it's not as efficacious as it might be ... I have to use my own semen. Can't get anybody else's.'

Chia lifted a disdainful eyebrow. She waved a hand at the door. 'Go on. Get out.'

Clutching the conch with its precious moon-milk, the Mad Hermit swept out of the room, leaving the two women to the splutter of the candles and the silence of the dead.

Chia knelt by the corpse of Fen-chou, his thin face like old ivory in contrast with the stark white of the funeral garment. With quick, nimble fingers she undid the neck-clasp and bared the bony expanse of the chest.

Briefly, she recalled the scent and sight of the Mad Hermit's potion. *If the crazed hermit had poured real moon-*

212

*milk into Fen-chou's dead throat, he wouldn't lie down for long.
Oh, no. He'd soon be up and about. But he wouldn't be Fen-chou
any more.*

'What are you doing?' questioned Xanthippe, evident
alarm in her tone.

Chia drew her silver dagger. 'I want my needles back.'

The Egyptian's mouth formed a perfect oval. 'But –
you *can't*, it's desecration.'

'He won't feel a thing.'

'Chia, don't do it,' she implored. 'You can't – '

'I'm doing it.'

Chia leaned over the body and held the silver blade a
nail's-width from the unbeating chest. Her brow furrowed in concentration as she slipped her spirit into a
path that circled gradually inwards. From under hooded
eyes, she had the illusion that the room was spinning.
Her thoughts, stray leaves, whirled in spiralling eddies.
She was transformed, in imagination, into a spiral spirit,
sucking in – sucking in . . .

. . . silver needles, through the magnetism of the ch'i-
enhanced silver dagger.

Behind the green fire of her eyes, she was flesh-of-
whirlwind, a ghost-gyre. The spiral spirit, like a magnet,
drew the needles into its suction. Drawing . . . attracting . . .

A hundred needles were ejected from Fen-chou's
chest. They clung to Chia's blade like children to a
mother.

Slowly, the sorceress reversed the inward spiral of her
spirit. The inner whirlwind subsided. She sat back on
her heels, expelling a sigh of relief. Seeing Xanthippe's
concerned expression, she gave a quick wink of reassurance.

'Not as bad as you thought, was it? The needles
departed the body by the same tiny holes of entrance.
Fen-chou is virtually unmarked.'

Xanthippe    shook    her    head    in    bemusement.
'Magnetism is still something of a mystery to me. I

didn't know it could work in that fashion – and not with silver.'

'It's not true magnetism,' Chia stated, depositing the needles into a small leather pouch. 'With the inward spiral, like attracts like. And this' – she held up the dagger – 'isn't true silver.'

'Then what manner of metal is it?' asked the girl, warily eyeing the blade.

A hint of tension showed around Chia's mouth. 'I don't know. It's said that it comes from the moon.'

'A gift from Cheng-o, goddess of the moon, sitting under her cassia tree?' Xanthippe's sardonic tone was a thin veneer for her unease.

' "In the moon, a toad and hare," ' the sorceress recited, quoting from Chinese legends of the moon and its strange goddess, Cheng-o, the White Lady. The green gaze became inward, the voice withdrawn. 'Cheng-o stole the herb of immortality and fled to the moon. And there, on the moon, she remains. Immortal. But the gods punished her for stealing what they regarded as their special privilege, their sole right. They turned Cheng-o's skin as white as dead flesh and spread her warped face across the moon.' Chia's abstracted stare moved to Chai-san's small face. ' "In the moon, a toad . . ." '

Catching Xanthippe's curious glance, she smiled awkwardly. 'Of course, that's just an old legend. A story for little children.'

'I know it,' said the Egyptian, lip trembling a fraction. 'I used to tell it to little Chai-san.' Moisture glistened in the dark brown eyes as they gazed at the boy's naked body – midriff painted with a yellow square – spread out on a straw mat. Her whisper was cobweb-soft: 'Can you help him?'

Chia shook her head as she retrieved sixteen of the hundred needles from the leather pouch. 'He's dead, Xanthippe. He died months ago.'

Although certain instinct informed her that Chia was

right, she felt obliged to pose the question: 'How can you be sure?'

'He has a nothing face,' Chia replied, pressing two needles into the temples of the moulded-meat visage. 'I've seen them before, many times.' She pushed two needles into the flesh near the outer corners of the eyes. 'You look at a nothing face and tell yourself that you're seeing human features, but there's nothing there. Nothing.' Two needles penetrated the upper cheeks. 'It's like looking at one of those scrawls Wu shamans produce under spirit trance. You peer at the scrawl and try to distinguish some shape, some form, from the chaos, but there's no design, no purpose. There's nothing.'

'But he breathes,' murmured the girl, close to tears. 'Very faintly, but he breathes.'

Chia paused in her chen-chiu ministration, gripping the silver and nickel needles tight in her right fist. 'The base element of the soul – the pho element – is present in the body, beating the heart, drawing breath into the lungs. But the soul's centre and seat of awareness – the hun – has long since ascended to the Blue Palaces.' A faint, wistful smile brushed her lips. 'Don't let that soft heart of yours get the better of you, Xanthippe. Chai-san's happy enough now, playing in the glowing halls and corridors of the Blue Palaces. And when I've completed the chen-chiu operation, his pho element will sink into the Yellow Springs and release his body from the nothing face.'

The room, dim in the drab light filtered through overcast clouds outside the unshuttered window, un-refreshed by the dull patter of rain on the sill, was haunted by the absence in the boy's face. The painted parade of tongues and genitalia on the walls of Kang's erstwhile chamber was devoid of the sensual and erotic, as if the celebrations of lust were being drained into the oval of spiritual emptiness in the front of the boy's head.

She almost jumped at the sudden sound of Chia's

215

voice. 'Hold on to yourself, Xanthippe. Don't let it suck you in. Keep hold of your mind. I'll soon be finished here.'

The sorceress placed two needles in the lower cheeks. 'There are lines of ch'i in the face,' she murmured. 'They're like the dragon's veins in the earth – the lung-mei. These needles will restore the proper flow of ch'i to Chai-san's face.' Two more needles were pressed under the nostrils. Two more above the corners of the mouth. One above the centre of the mouth.

Xanthippe averted her gaze, unable to view that terrible not-face sprouting needles. She couldn't believe that the chen-chiu operation had the potency to banish that nothing back to the nowhere it came from.

'Finished,' declared Chia, pushing in the last needle between chin and lower lip. 'You can look now.'

Xanthippe looked. Her eyes widened. A grin split her face. In other circumstances, the reaction would have been outrageous, but even a death-face was far preferable to the facial void that had haunted her for so long. Chai-san was dead, but at least he wasn't being treated as a puppet, spreading a hollow message from an empty world.

Chia stood up and moved to the wicker and straw shell that lay open and ready to receive Fen-chou's body. 'Chai-san's remains will decay in a matter of hours,' she stated quietly. 'The body has five months of death to catch up with. You can watch over him, if you wish.'

As she observed Chia place the old man's white-robed body slowly and surely inside the wicker body-cage, Xanthippe experienced the lightfoot return of unease. An insidious voice inside her head told her that she would never see Chia again. The more she ignored the voice, the more insistent it became.

She was about to give vent to the premonition when Chia hoisted the wicker-encased corpse on to her back, carefully adjusting the leather shoulder-straps. 'Time to go,' Chia announced, lifting her hand in farewell. 'I'll be back soon. Stay with someone you trust while I'm gone.'

216

'That would be Teacher Sung, I suppose,' Xanthippe heard herself mutter.

'You trust *him*?' Chia queried, eyebrow raised. 'Oh well – there's little to choose from.'

'Let me come with you,' the Egyptian entreated, the presentiment of dread growing. *She's going into danger. I'll never see her again.*

'No,' came the firm reply. 'It wouldn't be safe for you on the Ancestral Gallery. Not today. Not with me. You stay here, and stick close to Sung.'

'Chia – '

Chia touched Xanthippe's cheek with gentle fingers. Both women wanted that touch to last into the night. But Chia, shrugging off a lead weight of reluctance, forced her fingers from the softness of the Egyptian's cheek to the rough texture of the leather shoulder-strap.

'Must go,' she muttered.

Her feet refused to move.

'Don't go,' Xanthippe pleaded.

Chia's hand rested on the bronze latch of the red door. 'I must go. I promise I won't be long.'

'Then let me come with you.'

Chia stared long and hard at the girl who had come to mean so much in so short a time. She wanted to hold her, warm and close. She wished that they lived in a safe, secluded wood, or a secure, deserted valley. Just her and Xanthippe. But if there were such places, this was not the time to search them out. This was the time of stalking a nightmare.

And Chia wasn't ready to take Xanthippe with her on the nightmare-hunt. For all that her heart ached to be close to the Egyptian's pulse, Chia forced her reluctant hand to open the door. For all that she longed for Xanthippe's company on the lonely path of the Ancestral Gallery, Chia lifted her hand in a final farewell as she slipped out of the room.

'I'll be back soon,' she said with a feeble attempt at a smile. 'I promise.'

217

*And when Nyak's destroyed, we'll be free to live together.*

The door closed on the promise, leaving Xanthippe staring at the roughly reassembled red panels hastily pieced together after the supernatural onslaught of the previous night.

Last night, Chia had walked through the ruin of that door and saved her from the hidden enemy.

And now . . .

'I'll never see you again.'

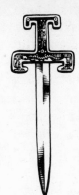

## 14

I thought to question the owl: when must I leave
    the world? '
If later, give me the good news: If sooner, give me
    the bad news.
Sooner or later, tell me the time of my going.

Chia Yi: *Fu niao fu*

The dead looked out of their windows, grinning their
seashell-splinter grins. The eyes of malachite and lapis
lazuli, in the swift light-shadow of scudding rainclouds,
did not appear quite so blind in the wooden faces
crowned with stiff drapes of straw for hair.

Chia had passed over forty of the small, imitation
houses. Another twenty or so and she should reach
House Feng and be rid of the burden on her back. The
rain, light drizzle when she left the temple, had intensified to a downpour, soaking the wicker and straw effigy
and adding extra weight. But the heaviness of the
burden didn't concern her – it was the way it slowed her
steps that rankled. She wanted to rush back to
Xanthippe. The Nothing Man wanted the Dark
Woman, and she wanted to be there to ensure he didn't
get what he wanted.

*The way she looked at me. It was as if to say goodbye forever.*

Glancing over the rickety rail to the beach some three
hundred feet below, she saw the last of the villagers
scurrying north with bowed heads and bedraggled kites.
The Ch'ung Yang kite-flyers had concluded their festivities, grace of the weather. She was curious to see them
in the company of Aklo. The young preacher's spell

apparently transformed ordinary village folk into silent fanatics.

Still, Forest Bell Village was for tomorrow. Xanthippe and the temple was for tonight. And the Ancestral Gallery – that was now.

Chia had no dread of the dead. Almost all of her best friends were dead. But ghosts were another matter. Ghosts – ghosts gossamer-light or ghosts lead-solid – were another matter. And if ever a structure was erected to depress the spirit and evoke the fear that spawned ghosts, the Ancestral Gallery was that structure.

If the death masks had been fashioned in the likeness of terrible demons, red eyes bulging, blue fangs snarling, the effect would have been too theatrical to inspire the subtle unease that the crude, inane wooden masks aroused. They made the dead look like large, puerile dolls. Adding to the impression, these doll-like dead had been hung up like puppets . . . waiting for the bells and drum that signalled the start of the performance?

She cursed under her breath as a wet vine, dangling from a curved blue roof, slapped her in the face. Thrusting the vine aside, her flailing hand struck a row of pendant bronze chimes. The little bronze dragons rattled their alarm. The jangle seemed to elicit a response from the long line of tiny houses. In front of her path, and at her back, a fragile jingling began, dispensing a sound like liquid silver. The soaked carpet of autumn leaves on the uneven boards of the gallery suddenly seemed like tenacious mulch, clinging to her booted feet as if it was eager that she stay for a few moments, linger a while.

How many houses to go before House Feng?

Twenty, at most.

'Nothing personal, Fen-chou,' she whispered over her shoulder. 'But the sooner I get rid of you the better.'

Her heart thudded, then missed a beat. In the window of a pink- and blue-painted house some twenty paces behind her, one of the wooden masks had turned in her direction.

She told herself that it was imagination's tricks, or that the wicker frame had tilted in its position through a mundane shift of weight. She told herself that she should walk right back and stare the malachite eyes out, defying them to display the merest hint of life.

But, under the faint jingling of chimes and bells, was the long, lonely silence of the funeral gallery. And the dead were so quietly watchful with their blue and green eyes inside their dolls' houses.

Chia walked forward with lengthened step, telling herself that she wasn't going to start running.

'I'll never see her again.'

Xanthippe bit her lip, swearing never to repeat those words. With a deliberate effort, she cleared her mind of speculations on Chia's fate and focused her attention on Chai-san's decaying shape.

'It's the wu-hsing,' Sung muttered, slumped against a wall. 'That's the clue.'

Xanthippe tried to blot his babble out. She kept her eyes on Chai-san. The rapid decay was astonishing. Nature was claiming its own with a vengeance; already one liquefying eye had dropped back into an emptying skull.

'Yes,' he persisted. 'Think of all that's happened here. Faces – it's about faces. So Five Faces statue must be the source of the haunting. Don't you see, Xan?'

'What?' she sighed. He'd been chattering about the wu-hsing since he walked in. 'Oh, yes,' she said distantly. 'I see.'

'The statue must be studied closely. The answer must lie in the statue. You see?'

'Oh, yes. I see.'

'Well,' he declared, standing up. 'Might as well get on with it – study the statue. I can't do any good here.'

'Yes,' she responded dully. 'You might as well.'

221

*Chia . . . Chia . . . Hurry back.*

As she heard the door close behind her, that grim intuition returned: *You'll never see her again.*

She thumped her forehead with her palm. 'Be quiet, be quiet, be quiet.'

Time stretched in the dimming room. The shape on the floor no longer resembled the boy she'd known.

'Oh, Chia,' she finally groaned. 'Where are you?'

The sudden rattle of the latch made her skin jump. She whirled round and sighed with relief at the sight of Ming-kai standing in the doorway.

'Teacher Sung wants us all to meet in the Hall of the Immortals,' he said.

'What – now?'

'Straightaway. He said that it's very urgent. And he's called for everyone to attend – even the Mad Hermit.'

'It *must* be urgent.' She smiled thinly, springing to her feet. 'Are you going there now?'

'No.' He grimaced. 'I've been told to fetch his wu-hsing charts from his room, *and* be quick about it. Have you seen the stacks of jumble in his oak chests? You'll be able to walk to the hall and back ten times before I get all his charts together.'

'I'll make my own way there,' she said, slipping past the hermit's bulky figure.

Only when she was out in the muddy courtyard did she realize that she'd not spared Chai-san a farewell glance. Still, she consoled herself, Chia said that the boy had been dead for months. But when she gazed more deeply into her regret, the consolation rang hollow.

'Goodbye, Chai-san,' she whispered. 'I hope you find some boys your own age to play with in the Blue Palaces.'

Skirting a stagnant fish-pool that fronted the south entrance to the Pavilion of the Immortals, she shook her head at the neglect, chiding the hermits on the grounds of their own T'ao philosophy. It was bad feng-shui for a temple to lack fish in a pool. The temple abounded in bad feng-shui.

As she ascended the lower stairs of the pavilion, squinting in the dense shadows, she listened for the sound of the temple hermits from above. But all she heard was the thud of her feet on the old boards of the stairs. Trust the lackadaisical hermits to be slow in responding to their Teacher's summons.

'And trust me to be first,' she muttered as she came to the red door that led to the Hall of the Immortals.

When the door creaked shut behind her she almost turned round to leave. Apart from the low crackle of the two hundred candles shimmering on the two hundred bronze images, there was silence. A silence heavy with devotional perfumes and incense. A silence of sleeping gods.

But Sung had sent out an urgent summons. Surely *he* must be here, at least?

As always, each groan of wood under her booted feet sounded like a protest against sacrilege. She was the alien treading on hallowed ground. She was the intruder in the forbidden sanctum. She was the Dark Woman.

Xanthippe walked softly through sacrosanct silence, trying to avoid the bronze faces as she moved along the aisles until she arrived at the fourth rank of impassive immortals. Peering down the aisle, she discerned nothing but congregated shadows at the far end.

She tried to call out Sung's name, but it caught in her pulsing throat. The aura of deadly sanctity intimidated her into silence. It seemed a blasphemy to speak out loud when the bronze immortals were so still and silent.

The thump of her heart sounded in her ears as she stole down the aisle, her vision fixed on the floor in front of her. She could feel the malign scrutiny of jewelled eyes beating down on her every step of the way.

*When I was a child, this place terrified me. Why don't I grow up? I used to have nightmares about this hall. Why do I still dread it so much? Nightmares . . . Bronze statues sliding soundlessly towards me. . .*

Her eyes started to ache from peering into the dark at

the end of the aisle. Teacher Sung had mentioned the wu-hsing, the Five Faces, before leaving her to keep vigil on Chai-san. Had he found the answer he sought in the Five Faces statue near the end of the aisle?

*Where is everyone?*

At last she could make out the tall shape of Five Faces, his visages sullen embers in the flickering candlelight.

But where was Sung?

Her pace slowed almost to a halt as she neared Five Faces.

*I'm not going any further. I daren't. Where is everyone? Something's wrong. Everything's wrong. I'm not going any further.*

A candle flared and sputtered in front of the wu-hsing statue, enlivening its faces with frantic shadow-play.

*Why don't I turn round? Why can't I turn round? Where is everyone? What's happening to me?*

She winced at the groan of a floorboard under her feet.

A voice greeted her – a metallic voice. A brazen tone invited her onwards. 'Xanthippe,' it grated. 'Come-and-stay.'

The Ancestral Gallery was, at last, silent of its jingling chimes. Chia wasn't sure if that was a good sign or not.

'Just keep going,' she muttered, keeping her attention straight ahead. 'Can't be more than a few houses ahead.'

In the dimming light of approaching dusk, some of the faded house-signs were virtually indecipherable. She prayed that she hadn't missed House Feng. More and more, an obscure misgiving was making heavy weather of her heart. She glanced up at the outstretching boughs of the forest some twenty feet above her head. The pines were thick at this stretch of the funeral gallery, casting an even deeper gloom on broken roof-tile and peeling paint.

Chia was convinced that she'd been right to leave Xanthippe in the temple. There *were* ghosts on the Ancestral Gallery – ghosts of the worst kind. Ghosts you could never quite see, never quite hear. Ghosts that got inside your head so that when you ran from the haunted place, you carried the haunting with you.

'Right to leave her behind,' she told herself. 'Right to leave her behind.'

*So why this stirring of unease for Xanthippe? What makes me feel I'm in the wrong place?*

House Feng.

'At last,' she said.

She ducked under the low door, ignoring the line of wooden-masked, silk-mantled ancestors suspended from the wall by rusty iron hooks. The shadows were dense in this comparatively large ancestral house, and the figures on the far side of the room were tall, sooty silhouettes in the thickening gloom.

Wrinkling her nose at the musty odour, she dropped the encased Fen-chou unceremoniously on the floor, eager to finish her task and rush back to Xanthippe. The House Feng masks were in a small chest by the door, and she soon had one fixed to the front of Fen-Chou's wicker helmet. To her mind, the malachite eyes, seashell teeth and straw hair were a gross insult to the kindly old man, but, after all, she was only fulfilling his wishes.

The far side of the room seemed to be crowded with stiff, dark figures facing the low growl of the sea and the soft whisper of rain. But there was a space left for Fen-Chou near the door and she speedily hoisted him on to the body-hooks.

The physical task completed, she stepped back and delivered a brief threnody drawn from Chia Yi's *Fu niao fu*, a poem dedicated to the owl of omen:

'I thought to question the owl: when must I leave the
    world?
If later, give me the good news: if sooner, give me the
    bad news.
Sooner or later, tell me the time of my going.
Exhaling, the owl lifted its head and shook its wings,
Bereft of speech.

\*

225

I shall speak for the owl:
All is change, unending change,
Round about and up and down and to and fro.
Beyond grasp, beyond expression.'

Valediction concluded, she turned to go, then pursed
her lips and shook her head. Keen as she was to run back
to the temple, such brief words of parting were sorry
tribute to seven decades of a man's life. She searched her
memory for an appropriate poem, half-listening to the
patter of rain on the roof and the faint rustle of straw hair
on the masks, touched by sea breeze.

The rain reminded her of one of her own poems,
dedicated to all the women she had loved and lost to
death in her overlong life. It would be a fitting valediction for Fen-chou, although she was incapable of love
for men. As the opening words of her poem stirred her
lips, her thoughts gravitated to all the women she had
loved. All the women of the past . . .

'Glass-beaded curtains of autumn rain
Fluttering with a breath that blows from the pines.
Water-filled footprints lead to the river.
Strangers speak of the siting of tombs.

Pine-cones fall with the windy downpour:
A damp cone drops into the open hand.
Earth is thirsty, draining the footprints.
What are the hands that sculpted the buried
        figurines?

Swollen flood of the river sweeps away pine-cones;
A torn branch plunges into the foam-fanged surge.
Heaven overflows, the footprints are swamped.
Others speak of graves that lie under the waves.'

For a short, silent space Chia stood with bowed head,
remembering lost voices, lost laughter, lost smiles.

Then she heaved a long breath and raised her head to the silent occupants of House Feng. The line of rigid dead, stretching from the dim light of the doorway to the thick shade at the far end of the room, retained their intrinsic quiet, their silent pathos.

'I wish you well,' she whispered to the row of figures.

At the end of the room, in the dense murk, there was a stirring.

Three shades detached themselves from the dark.

Three dark figures approached, their feet making soft creaks in the floorboards.

Entering the dim light of window and door, the three tall figures acquired hue and definition.

Long, grey hair swirled down from their silver t'ao-tieh mask helmets. Long grey mantles rustled about their tall frames.

The foremost of the three, his metal brow adorned with a green sign, raised a gauntleted hand.

'We bring you love,' his hoarse voice grated from the rounded metal lips. 'We bring you the love of the Master.'

For a stretched, painful moment she was rooted to the spot, heart drumming in her chest. Then panic sent her lurching at the door.

She fled from House Feng so quickly that she almost stumbled over the treacherous railing. A swift vision of the beach, a long death-drop below, blurred past her eyes. Then she swung round to escape the three Silver Brethren.

It was then that she saw figures emerging from funeral houses all around her. Tall, grey clad figures in silver masks were gliding out of every door.

The Silver Brethren had waited for her on the Ancestral Gallery, ready to give her the blessing of their virulent hands. They advanced, reaching out hands to bring her Nyak's terrible love.

*Now*, rejoiced Quicksilver, erupting out of Paradise.

Now, now, now, chanted Quicksilver, bursting into the House of Heaven.

Quicksilver exulted as it raced its jagged course down the stairs of the House of Heaven.

*Now is the time*, it roared, as it blasted through the doors and soared over Forest Bell Village, the speed of its passing cracking the air in a thunderclap that made the villagers quail and pray to their rainbow-robed god.

*If only they knew to whom they prayed*, laughed Quicksilver, veering sharply round the headland as it emitted peals of jingling merriment. If only they knew.

Aiming south across the crescent bay, the straight path of Quicksilver took it from sand to sea. Huge fans of white water sprayed in its wake – a long, luminous trail in the dark swell of the ocean.

For the cloddish feet of hermit or villager, the crescent bay presented a long, plodding progress. For Quicksilver, the journey was a swift thought.

The speed was Quicksilver.

Quicksilver was the speed.

Quicksilver streamed like airborne liquid as it hurtled south, from sea back to sand.

*Ah, Dark Woman*, sighed Quicksilver. *Dark Woman. Soon, now. Yes, soon.*

*Soon* . . .

*Very soon* . . .


'Xanthippe . . . Come-and-stay . . .'

The metallic voice was relentless in its welcome.

'Xanthippe . . . Come-and-stay . . .'

Fighting against the summons from the shadowy visages of Five Faces, Xanthippe tried to turn from the crowded shadows at the end of the aisle, tried to escape the baleful attraction of the wu-hsing statue.

But her feet were caught like tree roots. And her gaze was in thrall to the multiple eyes of Five Faces.

Again she struggled to wrest her feet free of the floor. But they were caught tight.

228

The pitch of her terror shrilled higher when she realized that her feet were no longer stuck to the floorboards. They were moving . . . Sliding soundlessly along the floor . . . Sliding towards the looming bronze image of Five Faces.

'Xanthippe . . . Come-and-stay . . .'

The nightmare . . . I'm dreaming . . . it's a nightmare . . . I'm sliding towards the statue, or the statue is sliding soundlessly towards me. . .a nightmare . . . wake up . . . wake up . . .

The aisle seemed to be on a downward slant. She slid between impassive bronze immortals, her slide gathering speed.

Five Faces was at the bottom of the slide, waiting to catch her.

'Not a dream!' she screamed in despair as she was wrenched from her feet and hurled on to the haunted metal of wu-hsing's East Face.

The entire statue was a magnet of immense power, binding her close with unseen tentacles. Her body clung like a limpet to the tall image, unable to break free from its loathsome embrace.

Her quivering, human face was pressed tight to the glowing bronze of the statue's eastward face. She stared directly into the malignant mirth that radiated from its sentient eyes.

'Be with us.'

A scream turned to a rattle in her throat as she felt her soul pouring out of her face and into the metal visage.

'Be in us.'

The rattle in her throat grew weaker.

'Be us.'

The rattle faded.

A hunger yawned in the eastern face of wu-hsing. It yawned wide . . .

'Give me your face.'

Her face was wrenched off, and her soul fled with it.

Xanthippe's body thudded to the floor.

229

In the dusk was a burst of speed.

The speed was Quicksilver.

Quicksilver was the speed.

It hurtled, invisible, over sand and sea.

It swept, unseen, over Forest Bell Village.

It soared to the House of Heaven.

Quicksilver blasted open the sturdy oak doors of the House of Heaven and stormed up the antique stairs, the magic of acceleration in its astonishing bone and inventive flesh.

*Ahhh* . . . sighed Quicksilver. *Dark Woman* . . .

*Yesss* . . . sang Quicksilver. *Dark Woman is ours to cherish* . . .

*Flesh to flesh* . . . *Flesh of flesh* . . .

*Flesh Alchemy.*

Quicksilver zigzagged up the stairs of the Old House; halls, chambers and corridors dark, transient smears to the liquid velocity of its eyes.

As it reached the upper floor it slowed to the pace of a racing hound.

By the time it approached the golden doors of Paradise, it glided through the murky air like a rare and remarkable fish.

And the rare fish swam into Paradise – dire Paradise.

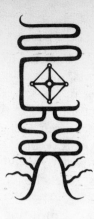

## 15

Heaven is darkened.
Earth is hidden.

Li Ho

The bastards were everywhere.

The Ancestral Gallery was swarming with them; they were coming out of funeral houses as far as she could see.

She glanced over the railing. Three hundred feet down – forget it.

Chia flicked a look upwards. No sign of the silver bastards on the cliff-edge, but the forest was at least thirty feet above her head at this spot, and sheer as a blade.

To the right – no. The cliff was as high and sheer for quite a distance.

To the left –

– to the left there was a small cleft in the cliff, not forty feet away.

But in that forty feet were more than a dozen masked figures waiting for her.

She looked at the signs on their brows . . . and saw a little hope. All the signs were the same. All glowed luminous white.

To the right was a Red Sign Brother, his gauntlets cast off, his hands ready to enfold her in the loving embrace of the Red Plague.

The two red hands, like fingered hearts, pulsed as they reached for her face.

'We love you, Chia,' wheezed the metal mouth.

'That's nice,' she responded, then sliced her silver

dagger clean through the red wrist. A violent kick sent the Red Brother sprawling. The lopped hand tumbled to the rim of the gallery.

She trapped it with her foot, and almost in the same instant thrust the dagger into the oozing stump.

Chia had reacted so swiftly that the Brethren were taken by surprise. They hesitated for almost a second.

In that portion of a second Chia had already hurled herself to the left, and into the company of exclusive White Signs.

The sorceress had a hand of Red Death sprouting from the little arm of her silver dagger. Red Death and White Death did not get along.

Her crooked smile would have frightened the Lord of Fourth Hell.

The White Signs backed away from the Red Plague that was deadly to their flesh. To each his own disease.

'Disease is the flesh at play!' snarled Chia, waving the red hand in front of her as she travelled in a low, spinning crouch through the agitated ranks. 'So let's play!'

Each White Sign flinched as she jabbed the hand at their white fingers bared for killing.

'Come on!' she screamed, now halfway to the cleft. 'Tasty red meat – come and get it!'

Between Chia's crazed eyes and the deadly hand, the White Signs' nerves broke. They cleared a path, knowing that the Red Signs were already rushing her from behind.

She took the chance the instant it showed itself. Sprinting the few paces to the cleft and swerving into its relative safety moments before a horde of Black Signs could interpose, she streaked up the narrow opening.

To her amazed delight, there were no Silver Brethren waiting at the top of the cleft.

*But don't trust to luck. You've had too much already. There must be scores of them in the forest. Don't pause. Duck and dodge. And run, run, run . . .*

She swiped the blade against a branch, dislodging the

232

hand of plague. No point keeping it, she decided. Never use the same trick twice on the same day.

As she ran, her mad exaltation subsided. She realized the stark danger of her situation.

Reaction set in, and she began to shake. It was getting dark. And the forest must be full by now with Silver Brethren hunting their arch-enemy. They might be behind any of these trees.

Panic was rising. She sensed her control slipping.

'So let it slip,' she gasped. 'Become an animal. Become raw survival.' She forgot her name. She became an animal, a running animal.

Fear was a forest.

She ran through fear.

Weaving and ducking, she avoided the branches stretched out to stun, the briar ready to rip, the tree-roots arched to trip. Bobbing to and fro, she traced an erratic path through the forest. Terror transformed the trees into gaunt, many-limbed monsters, the bushes into crouched grotesques.

Her breath was heaving in laboured gasps when a series of thunderclaps resounded beyond the trees.

*The thunder-wind . . . it roars from the north . . .*

A low branch, hidden in shadow, sent her hurtling down a steep slope, thumping into mossy boles, tearing through the sting of bramble. By the time the incline levelled out, her dazed head could barely recall how she came to be in the forest, or what she was running from.

She sat up and slowly regained her breath. Her head gradually cleared with the murmur of her lips:

'My name is Chia. I killed my father. I will kill my brother. I remain within myself.'

Exhaling painfully, she leaned her back against the patchy bark of an old pine and scanned the surrounding trees.

The spaces between the pines were filled up with dark. Her narrowed eyes probed that dark, seeking hints of silver. She attuned her hearing to the slightest whisper

233

from a metal mouth, the smallest crack of a twig or pine-cone under a booted foot.

She saw nothing; heard nothing.

Just the trees and the dark. And the last echoes of the thunder-wind flying back to its source.

A long sigh of relief escaped her lips.

When the panic had first hit her, she had run on pure instinct – a wild animal whose name was survival.

And she had survived.

'Until next time,' she muttered, brushing the leaves and lichen of the forest from the torn black serge of her overcoat. She glanced at her hands: a few cuts and a lot of dirt. Touched her hands to her face: just scratches, and stings from nettles. Not worth thinking about.

What mattered now was the next move. Making her way back to the Ancestral Gallery was out of the question. That left her one option – the forest. She gazed down the aisles of trees, their silhouettes smudged in the thickening twilight. What faint shadow there was lay to the left, which meant that she was facing south. If she traced a fairly straight path she should be back at the temple long before the end of the Hour of the Hound.

But pursuing a straight path was no easy matter in this stretch of trees. As she'd discovered in the two days spent surveying Melodious Temple from the cliff that loured over its clumped edifices, the trees had treacherous ways: try to walk a hundred paces due west in the forest, and some trick of perspective and twist of direction led you in a curving path back to the bay. Her horse had shown a marked aversion to entering the far side of the forest three days ago, and she had secured a stable for the nervous beast, fully appreciating the harrowing effect that the curdled scent of Nyak's minions would have on the sensitive nature of an animal. She had enough difficulty coping with that pervasive odour herself. Although –

– the scent shouldn't be so readily detectible by the sense of smell. It was usually very faint, or masked by the

pungent odour of the flayed human skins that the Silver
Brethren wore as clothing under their mantles. In Sang
Lung, during the Spirit Mirror haunting, the Thzan-tzai
scent had been below the level of what could be sensed.
That was the peculiar property of the lingering odour of
the Thzan-tzai: it was normally manifested in bad
dreams, bad ghosts, bad memories. The Thzan-tzai,
meaning, in the ancient Ko language, the Unshaped
Masters – or the Nothing Masters – had ceased to plague
the world many thousands of years before even Chia was
born, but their scent remained, a pungent memory. And
Nyak and the Silver Brethren were steeped in that
pungent memory.

But the Thzan-tzai scent – a living memory from more
than ten thousand years ago – had been all too rank in
her nostrils since confronting the three Brethren in the
narrow gap leading out of Black Dragon Valley. When
that sour-milk smell was at its strongest it meant only
one thing – Nyak was at his most powerful, his most
confident.

And that old scent had led her a false scent in the forest
– it always drew her back to its source, somewhere in the
bay. She had to watch her step if she wanted to avoid
bending back to the Ancestral Gallery.

'The scent,' she growled softly, brushing aside a
springy branch that jumped back and showered her with
rain drops. 'Moon-milk . . . moon-silver . . . quicksilver
. . . the Dark Woman . . . the Nothing Man . . . sexual
alchemy . . . The pieces are coming together in the
rudiments of a pattern, a threat. Resurrection.'

*Resurrection through the Dark Woman.*

'Xanthippe,' she whispered.

Xanthippe. Oh, Xanthippe – be *alive*. Don't let them
take you as they've taken all my other loves. Don't be the
latest name on that long, long list.

That long list:

Nua-chi – acid poured down her throat. Wu-kai –
flayed and rolled in salt, taking days to die. Fan-tu –

buried alive. Yi – hung from hooks like butcher's meat. And so many others. So many.

Nyak and his servants were meticulous in tracking, isolating and killing all she loved. There was nothing too small for their deadly attention. If she had a dog, they would kill it. A cat – kill it. A squirrel – kill it.

With each killing they spelled out the same message: 'You-will-live-alone.'

And now – Xanthippe?

'No,' she protested. 'Not Xanthippe. Don't touch her. Don't *dare* touch her.'

*After Yi, I swore I'd never fall in love again. My love is death. Why did I fall in love with you, Xanthippe? I should have remained within myself.*

Heedless of the keen ears of the enemy, Chia broke into a run, desperate to reach Melodious Temple before any harm befell her dark, mild-eyed Egyptian. As she raced between the darkening profiles of pines, elms and oaks, the moon was beginning to make its presence known in the forest. A resolve strengthened in her coursing veins: a resolve to let the world go to hell.

If Xanthippe was alive and well, she would take her away from Silver Music Bay. Tonight. She would take her back to Alexandria and the two of them would live there together. Friends or lovers – it didn't matter. Together – that's what mattered. Together – and half a world away from Nyak. If Nyak sought resurrection, let him take on life – and welcome to it. If he desired Silver Music Bay, let him have his desire. She wouldn't lift an eyebrow to stop him. Silver Music Bay could go to hell. The whole of China could go to hell.

'The whole of China – for one woman,' she breathed hoarsely. 'But if you've touched her . . .'

*Not to worry. Xanthippe's safe. Xanthippe's well. I'll soon be with her. Soon be throwing a few belongings into shoulder-bags. Soon be forcing a way out of the forest. Soon . . .*

The trees on her right leaned towards her like unwelcome friends urging unsolicited advice: *bear left, bear left*. The Thzan-tzai scent was strong in the trees, the sap was sick with it, and the leaning boughs offered an unwholesome embrace if she should stray too near.

*Keep away*, the leaves whispered, otherworldly in lunar light, *you wouldn't want us to cling to your face . . . bear left, bear left.*

She thought she glimpsed faces of wrinkled bark on some of the mossy boles, faces with mouths open in unvented screams. And several branches suggested knobbly arms with twig fingers grabbing moonlight.

*Run away . . .* rippled the leaves in waves *. . . or sleep and grow rings in the tree . . .*

There was a time, before she confronted her father's ghost and was forced to face the bad blood in her, the Thzan-tzai blood, that she would have smashed the boughs like sticks.

She wasn't a hero any more. In all but a few ways, she was as helpless as any villager or hermit. The feeling resembled being naked, with hands tied behind her back.

Seething with resentment, she veered from the inclining trees and headed left, following the only trail that seemed open to her.

*So this is how it feels to be mortal. To flinch at every provocation. To have red fear pumping in your veins.*

*This is how it feels to be you, Xanthippe.*

Kicking her way through a tall, tenacious bush, she suddenly felt her right foot contacting nothing – felt her body tilting forwards . . .

A quick clutch at the foliage and she pulled back from the sharp lip of the cliff. A scatter of stones rattled down to clatter on the peaked roof of a tower of Melodious Temple. West Tower – home, if she remembered aright, of Lao, the Mad Hermit.

Chia gave a derisive backward glance. The trees hadn't got the better of her. She had reached the place she wished to reach. The place where her love waited.

The black-ink silhouettes of Melodious Temple on the

broad grey wash of the ledge were a glad sight to her eyes after the multitudes of trees that stood between her and Xanthippe. And yet, looking down on the temple hunched like a dark beast facing a yellow moon and a wrinkled sea, there was a cold stir of unease in her soul.

*If you've touched her. If you've* dared . . .

She descended by the same way as the previous night. A ragged cable of vines and creepers hung down from the forest and took a tight grip of the wood at the top of West Tower, one of the many strands that established communion between temple and forest. Catching hold of the tangled cable, she slid down its length and dropped on to an upper balcony. From the balcony to the Pavilion bridge was a small jump that she accomplished with ease.

*We'll soon be out of here, Xanthippe. Soon* . . .

Walking over the stepped arch bridge linking West Tower and the Pavilion of the Immortals, she felt a resurgence of the unease. She tried to dismiss it as the dark of the buildings, the yellow of the moon, the silence of the night; but the unease persisted.

The black door, stiff from disuse, groaned in its joints as Chia pushed it open and slipped through the candlelit rectangle. Vast companies of candles, reflecting from two hundred bronze images, made a soft golden radiance of the Hall of the Immortals. Even the crisscrossed rafters simmered a sullen bronze. Most of the candlelight seemed to emanate from the southern end of the hall, from where she heard a murmur of voices.

A few paces took her to the fifth aisle, where she saw the source of the light and the quiet talk. At first, she didn't want to move. Her eyes slowly discerned four figures standing around something stretched on the floor. Something in her wanted to turn away and leave the scene.

But she walked between the tall bronze statues, her gaze fixed on the shape at the hermits' feet. *Don't let it be her. Not her. Never her.*

The four men – Teacher Sung, Ming-kai, and two she didn't recognize – stepped back at her approach.

'It's nobody's fault, nobody's fault,' she heard the Teacher say.

'What's nobody's fault?' she heard herself respond.

The bony hand waved in the direction of the shape on the floor. 'This – nobody's fault.'

Chia knelt down by the body, sprawled under the watchful gazes of Five Faces statue.

'Nobody's fault,' a reedy voice said, somewhere on the other side of China.

Xanthippe's lithe body, snug in its white fur robe, lay face up on the floor. Face up – except there wasn't a face.

There was a high forehead under the close-cropped hair. There were brow-ridges. There were eyes, half-hidden under motionless eyelids. There was a nose, a mouth, cheek-bones and a jaw-bone. All wrapped in dark brown skin, unblemished, intact.

But there wasn't a face. There was neither life-character nor death-character. Neither humanity nor inhumanity. There was an oval of soul emptiness on the front of her head. A nothing face. Xanthippe's face had been ripped from under her skin.

A black sun ignited inside Chia's head. Monster grief stormed up from heart to throat. Her fingers curled into barbs.

Her wits reeled at the sight of this not-face – this not-Xanthippe. She swayed to and fro, barely hearing the sound of anguish pouring from her mouth.

Chia's streaming vision swam to the smiling faces of the wu-hsing image. The bronze mouths held a secret satisfaction. The multiple eyes had a glint of victory. She could almost hear the metal resonating its triumph:

*Xanthippe has come to stay . . .*

## 16

Behind the Chung-nan Mountains,
the sun sets
And the unseen spirits are glimpsed in
the witch's face.
Her face shows
Ghostly rage and ghostly delight.

Li Ho

Cold autumn rain thrashed Ming-kai's upturned face as he glared at the crown of South Tower, its topmost room hidden behind locked shutters. This was the fourth morning since Chia Black Dragon had taken soul-dead Xanthippe into that upper room.

Chia – mad, arrogant Chia – had summarily evicted Old Hsiang and Little Ko from their rooms in the spindling structure. She had wanted the whole tower to herself, to work whatever perverse practices she wished on Xanthippe's body. Chia had locked herself in with the Egyptian, and no one had caught a glimpse of either in the last four days. The doors remained locked, the windows shuttered.

Ming-kai had protested to Sung, but Sung had simply shrugged in impotence. What Chia wanted, she got, and the T'ao-tsang help anyone who stood in her way. Ming-kai eventually agreed to give the sorceress three days. This was the fourth day.

He turned on his heel and splashed a determined path to East Tower. No more, he swore as he thrust open the tower door. Not one hour more will I give that beautiful devil. 'Not one hour more,' he muttered as he ascended the steps.

'It ends now.' He pushed open Sung's door and strode into the room. The Teacher glanced up from his chair by the Lao Tzu shrine.

'Three days,' snapped Ming-kai. 'That's all I promised. The three days are up.'

Sung stroked the iron chain weighting his shoulders and pulled a wry face. 'All right, the three days are up. So *you* go and drag her out of South Tower.'

'What about your promise? It'll take the whole community banded together to stand a chance against her.'

'Oh, *that*.' Sung waved airily, rising to his feet. 'I lied.'

'You swore on the spirit of Lao Tzu!' the war veteran thundered, pointing at the camphor-wood figurine of the revered sage in its wooden shrine.

'Oh, I've lost all love for Lao Tzu,' declared the Teacher, his heavy tread creaking the floorboards as he crossed to the painting of an angular mountain with empty slopes. 'Ever since seeing Chia again, I've rediscovered my first and last love. What's a shrivelled old sage next to a goddess like Black Dragon?' He stroked the vacant slopes of Black Dragon Mountain. 'Ah, Chia,' he sighed. 'You have no idea how much I love you. No idea.'

Digusted by the Teacher's behaviour, Ming-kai fought an impulse to grab the scrawny throat and squeeze it till it popped. He knew that he couldn't take on Chia alone and, truth be faced, the handful of hermits wouldn't join him in an attack on the sorceress even at the Teacher's urging. War veteran though he was, he felt close to shameful tears.

He had made a vow, long ago. A vow to his dead wife and daughter – dead by Chia's hand. He'd stayed his own hand for as long as he thought the she-devil might frighten away whatever ghosts were haunting the temple. He had waited – dying of patience. But Chia had exorcised nothing. She had added fear on to fear. Now his patience was ended; the waiting was over. It was time for action. And yet – he couldn't bring himself to do it. Even if Chia had her back to him and his knife was ready in his hand – he couldn't do it. Not unless she admitted her crime. Now that the sorceress was a flesh-and-blood reality instead of a phantom of imagination, he found that the roles of judge and executioner were too heavy for his shoulders.

What he wanted was to put her to the torture. He wanted to wrench the truth out of her. She must confess her crime. *Then* he could strike the blow. And Chia, he had discovered since her arrival, wasn't as invulnerable as legend made her.

One good blow and the immortal would be mere remains.

He suddenly realized that Teacher Sung had been speaking.

Ming-kai cleared his thoughts and met Sung's even stare. 'I wasn't listening. What were you saying?'

'I asked if there'd been any sign of Lung-ch'i.'

'Not that I know of. My bet is that he's run away. Pretending that he was passing on your summons was a sick joke even by the cook's standards. I doubt he'll ever show his face around here again.'

'Strange joke,' mused Sung, fingering his wispy beard. 'It resulted in Xanthippe's destruction. Didn't it strike you as odd that I should pass on a summons to the Hall of the Immortals via an intermediary like Lung-ch'i?'

'You've done it before.'

'Have I? Oh, well. I've done it before, then.'

A previous doubt resurfacing, Ming-kai looked askance at the Teacher. 'Are you *sure* you didn't say something to the cook about the hermits gathering in the Pavilion Hall? Something he may have misconstrued?'

'Of course I'm sure. It was some stupid prank he was playing before running off to wherever he's gone.' The Teacher paused, his gaze lowering. 'And I've never encountered a prank with such tragic consequences. Poor Xanthippe . . .'

242

'Yes,' came the heavy sigh. 'If only she'd been slower in answering the summons, or the rest of us quicker.'

'Yes. If only.'

Ming-kai's vision slanted to the painting of Black Dragon Mountain. 'Chia,' he breathed through clenched teeth. 'She might not be guilty of stealing Xan's face-soul, but somehow I know that she's implicated in the deed. She makes things happen. And Fen-chou – I've little doubt of who killed him.'

The Teacher's mouth bent in an ambiguous smile. 'Beauty doesn't blind Ming-kai. Is that how you see it?' When no response was forthcoming, the Teacher shrugged. 'If you're so on fire to bind Chia in chains, why don't you call on Aklo? I'm sure he'd be willing to oblige.'

The offhanded remark made Ming-kai's heart miss a beat. The Teacher, he presumed, had been indulging in a piece of mild sarcasm. But – it *was* an idea. Aklo – dangerous, smiling Aklo. Whatever the Rainbow-Robed preacher was, he was more than human. And dealing with the Woman in Black required more-than-human assistance.

Aklo.

'You seem to be in a dream world.' Sung's voice cut into the other's speculation. A frown formed in the narrow brow. 'What were you thinking about?'

Ming-kai assumed a bland mask. 'Nothing. Nothing that concerns you.'

Now that the idea was firmly planted, he made for the door. 'Let me know if you hear anything about Lung-ch'i,' he said casually.

'Hey – where are you rushing?' Sung called out, but the war veteran was already bounding down the stairs.

Teacher Sung rubbed thin fingers over his sharp chin. 'You've got Chia-hate in your eyes, Ming-kai,' he murmured. 'Your hate's almost the equal of my love. Or perhaps it's more than equal.'

Then, on reflection, he rejected the notion. It was impossible to hate Chia more than he loved her.

The round room at the top of South Tower was shuttered from the light, locked against intrusion. Its air was thick with candle-smoke and incense. The room contained two breathing women. They both looked as if they belonged with the dead.

Xanthippe's white lion robe had been unclasped and spread out as a rug for her immobile body. Lines of needles, tracing the ch'i paths, decorated her nakedness from foot to head. A yellow square had been painted on her stomach, and a silver moon on her brow.

Around her inert shape was a profusion of candles: red candles to the south, white to the west, black to the north, and green to the east. The perfumed candles emitted the scent of a hundred flowers – wax-preserved memories of spring and summer in the autumn room. Metal talismans festooned the raftered ceiling, tingling fragile chimes that mingled with the rhythmic vibration of rain on roof and shutters.

Po-shan-lu censers, each modelled in fanciful imitation of the Five Sacred Peaks, wafted clouds of incense from the bronze fairy hills, the metal inlaid with gold, silver, turquoise and carnelian. The aromatic cloud hung in the air like a manifestation of the spirit world, almost obscuring the Egyptian-Chinese mythic scenes that Chia had painted on the walls in her first day of frenzied activity.

Before applying paint and brush, she had attempted what she'd sworn never to attempt.

She had tried to summon the terrible power inside her body; tried to turn the key of that locked dungeon door in her heart. To save Xanthippe, she was willing to become a monster. Chia would have damned herself to save her love.

But each time she turned the key in that door, she knew that what waited on the other side was the same kind of monster that had taken the Egyptian's face-soul. Releasing Thzan-tzai power would make her fully one of the enemy – a creature that would damn Xanthippe deeper, if that were possible.

So all Chia had left was the natural magic of her own faculties: simple Chia magic.

In the midst of incense smoke and flickering candles, Chia knelt, black overcoat belted tight around her, arms hugging her waist as she rocked back and forth. She hadn't slept for four days. She hadn't eaten for four days. She had barely entertained a human thought for four days. And after the talismanic painting of the walls, she hadn't moved from her kneeling posture. She just rocked back and forth, reciting all the summons of the soul to be found in Egyptian and Chinese necromancy. The constant repetition had dwindled her voice to a croak.

'Return, O Spirit! Why have you deserted your home
        for the distant corners of the world,
    abandoning the house of content to confront all that
        is evil?
Return, O Spirit! In the East you can not stay . . .'

The lambent aura of candles highlighted the joints and curves of Xanthippe's dark, shining body. But the nothing face seemed to absorb the wavering candlelight. The facial absence was without reflection.

The clouds of incense thickened to a dense, aromatic fog, making a hazy profile of Chia as she continued to rock backwards and forwards, throatily intoning the shaman chant from the remote Chou dynasty:

'Return, O Spirit! You risk eternal loss.
Return, O Spirit! In the north you cannot abide . . .'

The black candles north of Xanthippe's head spluttered wildly in the swirling mists of incense.

'Return, O Spirit! Do not ascend to High Heaven . . .'

245

The gold, silver and bronze talismans bedecking the rafters rained jangling sounds on the figure of Xanthippe below.

'. . . Its gates are guarded by tigers and leopards, their
    mouths hungry for mortals . . .'

Chia's chanting tone had become a raw exhalation.

'Return, O Spirit! Do not descend into the Lands of
    Night.
There the Earth Power reclines in his nine coils . . .
Return, O Spirit! You risk damnation.
Return, O Spirit! Return through the open gate of the
    city . . .'

Chia's strained throat finally failed her. Having delivered the warnings to the wandering soul, she was unable to pass on to the enticements that would lure the spirit back to its body in the living lands. She struggled to force the words out of her mouth: her vocal cords refused to obey.

She slumped forward, arms squeezed tight round her waist. Her long, disordered hair swung over her drawn features and dull green eyes. Everything in her crumpled posture suggested defeat, a final submission to circumstance or destiny.

*Never*, she whispered in the dark behind her bleak stare.

*Never give in.*

Forcing up her head, she gazed at the spirit carnivals she'd painted on the eastern quarter of the wall. They were the carnivals of Chinese heavens and hells, the immortal celebrants tenuous shades behind the fragrant veils of incense. Murky red, orange and yellow held sway on the lower section of the wall where the ten hells were depicted, merging gradually into green, blue, silver and gold as the eye ascended to the exalted realms of the heavens.

*Where are you, Xanthippe? Where is your face?*

The ten hells of T'aoist lore, animated by the dance of candle-flame, were astir with the malign bustle of blue-skinned demons and the frenzy of kwai spirits. Red-robed Yen-lo, Lord of the Sad Dead, took his ease on a red lacquer throne as he surveyed his ten regions of afflication. In the hell of desecrators and cannibals, yellow-eyed demons and black dogs drove the condemned souls into a river of boiling blood. In the hell of dismemberment, the guilty hung in bits and pieces from hooks and chains. In the upside-down hell, the damned were suspended by their heels from the ceiling, their condition reflecting their scale of values in life.

The torments of Yen-lo's underworld were intended to purify the souls and lift them up to the Chung Kuo of China, or even to the heavens of Shang Ti, Hsi Wang Mu, or the August of Jade.

Raising her eyes from the hells, Chia scanned the cloud-swaddled peaks of the celestial realms. Hsi Wang Mu presided over Mount K'un Lun and its peach trees of immortality, attended by mountain and tree spirits. Tung Wang Kung, god of the East, lord of Mount P'eng-lai, dispensed benisons to the dwellers in his Eastern Paradise. Yu Ti, the August of Jade, reigned over the Blue Palaces of high heaven. And –

Chia's gaze moved left of the Blue Palaces to Cheng-o's kingdom of the moon, the lunar domain hovering above the summit of Mount P'eng-lai.

For an instant, she thought she'd glimpsed a small figure beside pale Cheng-o under her cassia tree. But, strain as she might, the figure failed to rematerialize to keep lonely Cheng-o company. All the goddess of the moon had for company was the hare that pounded the stolen herb of immortality with pestle and mortar. Just Cheng-o and the moon-hare in the lunar Palaces of Ice.

Chia had hoped to catch sight of Xanthippe's image in the hells or in the heavens, but there was no hint of her soul in either low worlds or high.

If the Egyptian's soul-image had appeared, however fleetingly, in the pictorial spirit world, then the sorceress would at least have known where to look for Xanthippe's lost face. To find her in one of the hells, even the hell of dismemberment, would be far preferable to not finding her at all. Chia knew a way into the hells – and a way back. She hadn't only travelled across the face of the earth.

But there was no sign of her love in the spirit world. *Don't give in. Never give in.*

Chia swerved her vision across to the western quarter of the round room, its imagery even more misty with incense than the eastern stretch of wall.

To the west, framing Xanthippe's denial of a face, was the Egyptian after-life in reed-green, corn-yellow, Nile-blue.

Above the Hall of Judgment and white-faced Osiris's golden throne was the Hall of Waiting, its ceiling lost in clouds and its walls covered with the mosaics of eternity. And beyond the Hall of Waiting, where souls played the game of a thousand years on boards of ageless wood, lay the blessed realm of the undying, the beautiful Amentet.

To one side of the Judging and the Halls of Eternity she had painted several representations of Isis and Osiris. In one picture, she had recalled the birth of the celestial sister and brother from the union of Earth god Geb with Sky goddess N't. She had portrayed the twins as emerging from the fission of the original hermaphrodite birthed by N't, Isis-Osiris separating into Isis *and* Osiris. In another portrayal, the twin brother and sister were shown in state after their marriage.

Before executing the wall-paintings, Chia had placed herself under a trance. And in a trance, unconscious of self, or other, she had taken brush and paint to the wall. She had painted, not knowing what she painted. She had painted, not knowing *that* she painted. The Chinese and Egyptian spirit worlds had sprung from her brush like the creation of the Ten Thousand Creatures from the unthinking interaction of yin and yang. Such unknowing was the prerequisite of all spirit painting: it was the art of the shaman – the exposition of the unknown by the means of unknowing. It was the way known as 'the wise inner dark'. And that was the essence of magic. It presented the shaman painter with images proceeding from the heart's darkness. And from that dark, dreams appeared on the wall. Dreams that illuminated, perplexed, surprised.

Chia gazed at the Egyptian resurrection dreams, trying to decipher their mythic cryptograms.

Moon-silver – the magic unguent looked like moon-silver. And while Osiris's face was merely a white daub, the face of Isis was a fusion of two women's faces. Nefertiti's – and Chia's own features.

Hints from painted dreams – clues from the dark. . .

But grief has its natural rituals and observances, its intrinsic ceremony. And grief held sway in Chia, magnified to a pitch that could barely pass as human emotion. Grief shadowed her wits as the incense cloud dimmed the painted scenes. Grief insisted on the humdrum track, precluding sudden jumps of the imagination.

So while Egypt held out its teasing lures of enlightenment, Chia was restricted to the narrow search for a face-image in the halls and chambers of the after-life.

*Xanthippe – where are you?*

Turning east once more, she scanned the Chinese heavens and hells, her weary vision shimmering like heat-haze and flashing like sun-sparks. She gripped the ankh tight and struggled to focus on the mythic moon of Cheng-o. Had she seen a figure there or had she imagined it. . . ?

It was there again, a tiny figure seated beside pale Cheng-o. And this time it didn't disappear.

Ignoring the cracking protests in her stiff joints, Chia forced her rigid muscles to push her upright. She crossed the room with wavering steps, praying that the figure wouldn't vanish. It was still visible when she came close

249

to the painted moon and peered at the small shape of a man.

At this near distance, the man's clothes and face were clearly distinguishable. He wore the red Kang-i robe of a T'ao Seeker, partially draped by long hair. And on his brow she could just discern what appeared to be a blue half-moon. As she noticed the blue crescent, the image started to fade. But she had seen enough.

She had seen this man before on at least one occasion – sitting on the beach, mumbling to himself.

The man had vanished from the moon, but the brief apparition had served its purpose. It was the first and only guide she had to Xanthippe. And that guide was a hermit here in the temple.

Chia staggered to the window, light-headed and bone-weary from the long vigil, and threw open the shutters to the sea wind and the vigorous downpour. The fresh flare of hope restored her taut vocal cords sufficiently for one, loud summons:

'SUNG!'


The sun, a watery yellow smear, made a poor excuse for noon as Ming-kai approached Forest Bell Village under glum clouds and the drub of rain. Any pretence that the village was a thriving fishing port had long since been dropped in favour of its grim side-show – the cult-shrine of Aklo, avatar of the god Tung Wang Kung.

Forest Bell Village was no longer a village in the true sense. It was the goal of pilgrimage for Eastern Paradise Seekers – a pilgrimage from which, these days, no one returned.

The hermit hadn't visited the community for two months, but as he rounded the headland and the small curve of Forest Bell Bay came into sight, he was taken aback at the swift dilapidation of the dwellings in so short a time. The houses, which were erected on four natural tiers of rock, breathed neglect and decay. If there was one word that summed up the sorry village, it was –

250

'Damp,' he muttered, eyeing the huddled, dark-timbered dwellings with distaste. 'Damp.'

As if the sea had got into the wood.

There were few people out of doors, and those few wandered aimlessly, seemingly oblivious to the downpour, and all dressed in the green smocks favoured by Aklo's cult.

Ming-kai needed someone dangerous. He needed a dangerous young god to bring the Woman in Black to her knees. As bad as Aklo was, he couldn't be as bad as Chia. No one was as bad as Chia Black Dragon.

Ascending the stepped central lane of the village, the hermit wrinkled his nose at the dank, rotten smell from the houses on either side. It reminded him of the stench of timber fetched up from the belly of the sea. And – he frowned his puzzlement – there was a faint glow in the small, square windows. A glow like moonlight. It was as though each house was a sea house, with a small moon inside.

A willowy man in a green smock brushed past him, heading down the steps with unhurried, graceful paces. He smiled a crooked smile at the hermit, the corner of his mouth tilting up to the right. Ming-kai nodded, then continued the upward plod, his gaze straying occasionally from left to right.

In some of the windows there were faces, staring out at the autumn rain. All of the faces were smiling. All the smiles were crooked smiles. All the smiles tilted up to the right.

Ming-kai took a deep breath and averted his gaze from the surrounding houses, fixing his attention instead on the bay's upper slope and the goal of his journey. The Old House. The House of Heaven.

High above the village, its winged roof almost reaching the rim of the cliff, the four-storey mansion rose, surrounded by a small wood of weeping willows. There had been a time when Ming-kai had wondered at the growth of weeping willows where no such willows should

251

grow, just as he'd been amazed at how the weeping willow known as the Tree of Bells could flourish at the tip of Sea Rock, but the other prodigies of Silver Music Bay had long since overshadowed the curiosity of the unlikely trees.

The House of Heaven itself overshadowed the willows, in all senses of the word. If timber had been cut from the trees of Hell and transported here to be erected into an edifice, it would not be more daunting than the Old House. The willow from which the mansion was constructed – an willow so dark it remembered ebony – was cracked and weathered. The numerous shutters were ramshackle lattices, some of which hung loose and stirred the way of the wind. The broad verandah was thronged with weeds and bramble and a cluster of blue tiles that had tumbled from the lofty roof. No birds had ever been seen nesting on that high roof, nor had any fox or squirrel been sighted in the willow wood that wrapped the mansion in a kind of silence.

If Ming-kai hadn't loved his murdered wife and daughter so deeply, he would have turned tail and run at first sight of the identical smiles in the quiet village. But here he was, ascending to the House of Heaven, a far worse prospect than the interior moonlight and crooked smiles of the houses he was leaving behind.

And inside the Old House he would find Aklo, if he was lucky.

Despite the eerie gloom, he almost laughed. Lucky! It didn't say much for his present circumstances if meeting Aklo could be called lucky.

Following the snaky trail through the willow wood, he kept his gaze fixed on the ground in front of his booted feet, afraid that if he stared his goal straight in its oak face, his resolve would crack and his wife and daughter go unavenged. One foot in front of the other, he told himself. Don't think of what's ahead. Keep on. One foot in front of the other.

Scaling the steps to the tall verandah, his skin

252

contracted as he heard a long, loud creak from the door above.

He forced his unwilling feet to the top of the verandah steps. In front of him was the huge double-door. Both doors were wide open, revealing a square of yellow lantern-light. The tall, slim figure of Aklo leaned on a door jamb, his silky Robe of Rainbows a wild splash of colour in the drab surrounds.

Aklo's features were hidden by the wide conical hat on his inclined head. 'A visitor. How nice,' whispered a voice from the shadow of the hat's down-curling brim.

Ming-kai caught the glints of needle-nails as the youth unfolded his arms. He forced the words from his constricting throat before Aklo took it into his head to test the sharpness of those nails on the hermit's chest.

'My name's Ming-kai. I'm from Melodious Temple . . .'

'I know that perfectly well.' Aklo sighed with the heavy patience of a god dealing with a crass supplicant. 'Why do you trouble my ease?'

'I've come to – ask for help.'

The youth's face was still in shade from the wide straw brim. 'I sense a dark lying on you. Ah yes. The dark of a dragon.'

Ming-kai struggled for breath. 'Do you know why I've come?' he asked.

'I know everything,' came the soft breeze of Aklo's voice. 'I understand everything. The shadow of the Black Dragon blights your soul. You want me to rid you of Chia Black Dragon.'

Ignoring Aklo's astonishing prescience, Ming-kai nodded vigorously. 'I want you to force the truth of a crime from her, then assist me in ridding the world of her evil. Would you do that? *Can* you do that?'

'You wish me to torture and kill her. Not so?'

'She'll need to be put to the torture to confess. And – I would wish a part in her kill – her execution.'

'Ah, so little compassion in the world,' sighed Aklo.

253

'So little compassion. But if this woman has done wrong then she must of course be punished – for her own good.'

The hermit, eager, leaned forward. 'When will that be, great Aklo?'

'Tomorrow night, come the Hour of the Rat, it will be the fifteenth night: the full moon. The night when the White Lady displays her entire naked splendour to earth and Heaven. The night of the Ceremony of Deliverance from Guilt. That's when Chia Black Dragon will be brought to judgment and truth. That's when Chia will cease to be Chia.'

'And I?' enquired the hermit. 'What shall I do?'

'You will lead her to judgment.'

'How shall I lead her to judgment? What means shall I use?'

Aklo slowly lifted his head, and the shadowed features emerged into the rainy daylight. The light revealed a crooked smile on his lips, tilting up to the right. The crooked smile whispered its answer:

'Be her friend. Hate her enemy. And – tell her a story.'


Hua Shan.

The hermit with a crescent-moon scar on his forehead was called Hua Shan.

'Why didn't Sung tell me about Hua Shan?' Chia muttered hoarsely, her throat still raw from days and nights of chanting the soul summons.

Chia sat cross-legged in the lotus asana, beside the naked form of Xanthippe with its patterns of chen-chiu needles that glinted in the tremulous light of green, red, white and black candles. The flower-scent in the candles mingled with the pungent incense that made a grey-blue fog of the round room. China and Egypt were hazy on the walls. Chia tried to look anywhere but at the non-face of Xanthippe. She struggled to think of anything but her grief, now that a faint chance of saving the young girl had materialized on the wall in the shape of Hua Shan.

Hua Shan. When Teacher Sung had finally responded

254

to her call from the window, she had locked the door of the top room behind her and met the temple master in the room below. She had enquired of a hermit with a crescent scar. And he had told her of Hua Shan. He was scarcely into his narrative before she felt wrath boiling within. Why hadn't he told her about Hua Shan the moment she arrived? she wanted to shout in his gaunt face, but her vocal cords forbade such voluble expressions. Instead she had clenched her right fist, gritted her teeth, and glared.

Hua Shan. He had been in or near the Forest of the Ancestors on the night she sent Nyak's poisoned spirit back to destroy his hidden and guarded body. He had been there.

And when Ming-kai found Hua Shan near that same forest, some months later, the hermit was a shell that continually echoed the same refrain: *mountains of the moon, plains of the moon, valleys of the moon*. Hua Shan was living on the moon: not the sphere that rode the night sky, but the mythic moon, the dream moon, the moon of Cheng-o, the White Lady in her Palaces of Ice.

Hua Shan. The Forest of the Ancestors. The moon.

Too many coincidences. Far too many; a tangle of coincidences. And she had to untangle them and weave them into a pattern. Hua Shan was a man she needed to talk to.

She glanced at the dull light filtering through the shutters. It would soon be dusk, and still the hermits hadn't located Hua Shan. His searchers had prepared her for that. The moon-hermit, a couple of the hermits had informed her, was sometimes impossible to find, as if he had disappeared into thin air. Chia had a strong suspicion that she knew why Hua Shan was sometimes impossible to locate. If he could appear from time to time on a painting of the moon, then he might have learned to live inside a moon dream.

'But I wish you'd hurry and find him, all the same.' She said, gently rubbing her throat.

*And why didn't Sung tell me about Hua Shan straightaway? Why wait for me to ask? Surely even his addled head must have comprehended the significance of the moon-hermit . . .*

Shaking her head, Chia let the moon-hermit slide out of focus for a while. There was nothing she could do until Hua Shan was located and brought to her. And she certainly wasn't leaving Xanthippe's side to join in the search.

'Xanthippe,' she sighed, resting pale hand on dark hand. 'I'll find you. Wherever you are, I'll find you. I can't use my Thzan-tzai powers, but I still have one special art at my command.'

She squinted through the perfumed smoke to the hells and heavens of China and the god halls of Egypt. *Yes, I have one special art . . .*

'I can still dream.'

*And I can attempt, if I dare, to summon the long-dead.*

Glancing at the door to check that it was securely bolted, Chia slid the silver chain off her neck and dangled the ankh in the candlelight. The ankh, the Egyptian symbol of life, had been forged from her silver dagger sometime during her years with Nefertiti. It should establish an affinity between her spirit and the soul of one exiled among the stars for fifteen centuries.

If it was true, as Xanthippe claimed, that Nefertiti visited her in sleep, then perhaps – just perhaps – Nefertiti could be summoned through Xanthippe's body. The likelihood was that 'Nefertiti' was a ruse concocted by Nyak or his servants, but still – there was a slight chance . . .

She threw a swift look at the dimming light behind the shutters. The sun would be sinking behind the forest now. An auspicious time for the summoning of spirits.

Averting her gaze from the nothing face, Chia placed the ankh around Xanthippe's neck, then rested the point of the dagger on the ankh lying between the girl's breasts. With her free hand she positioned the Night-Shining Jewel on the Egyptian's navel.

256

Then she turned her eyes to the images of Isis on the wall, an Isis whose face was compounded of Nefertiti's and Chia's features. She took a deep breath, and commenced the summoning.

'Nefertiti, Daughter of the Nile, Queen of the Upper and Lower Kingdoms, I give you your name.

'Nefertiti, Daughter of the Nile, if your soul wanders lost among the boundless stars, let the utterance of your name call you back so you may walk once more in the Black Land of Khemet.

'Nefertiti, Daughter of the Nile, if you walk among the delights of beautiful Amentet, visit, I implore you, this body of the Black Land of Khemet. Enter its heart so that it may know affection. Enter its head so it may speak.

'Nefertiti, reborn Daughter of Isis and Osiris, I call you by the dream of my breath . . .'

As she spoke, she formed an image of Nefertiti in her mind, an image sharp and clear as the Diamond Body of the Buddha. She breathed in, holding the image firm. She opened her mouth wide, preparing to release the ch'i in her body in a long exhalation. Charging the Nefertiti-image with the power of ch'i, she breathed out.

A dream floated out of her mouth with the condensing breath. A dream of Egypt drifted between her lips, visions swam in limpid colours. A rippling dream of Nefertiti flowed with her breath across the room. It glided to the portrait of Isis resurrecting Osiris. It sank into the figure of Isis.

Then all sign of the dream-breath was gone. But it had worked its will. The Isis-figure which had absorbed the dream now wore only Chia's features: all trace of Nefertiti had vanished from the painting.

Nefertiti's dream-spirit was ready for the *mdw ntr* – the Egyptian Word of Absolute. Chia's voice resonated with renewed power as she recited the words from the Scroll of Life:

'Arise, thou sleeping one, and cast off the bindings of

dreams. Arise, thou sleeping one, and come forth by day from the halls of Amentet. Arise, thou sleeping one, and walk once more in the Black Land of Khemet. Nefertiti – arise. Arise . . .'

With the naming of Nefertiti, the Night-Shining Jewel, resting on Xanthippe's midriff, began to glow with a calm blue radiance. The blue light intensified as the ankh gave birth to a silver luminescence. The blue and silver auras formed an image above Xanthippe, an image of the moon reflected in deep water. Then the blue and silver radiance descended into the curves and contours of Xanthippe's body.

And a spirit swam up inside the skin of the Egyptian's face. And Xanthippe's face was truly a face for a time, although it was no longer hers.

A silver-blue spirit emanated from the girl's facial profile – the starry spirit of Nefertiti. Nefertiti was just below the skin. Yet she was also a million li away, under the daylight stars and silent hymns of Amentet's gardens.

The simultaneous nearness and remoteness of her first love wrung Chia's heart. She ached to reach and touch the untouchable, retrieve the irretrievable. And she knew that what she witnessed was an emanation of Nefertiti's soul, not the wholly present spirit of the queen herself. It was more akin to a ghost than the true Daughter of the Nile. That profound sense of the unattainable almost deflected Chia from her purpose, but she controlled her hopeless longing. She was enduring this for Xanthippe. For Xanthippe, the questions must be posed:

'Daughter of the Nile, what was the secret name you gave me? It is Chia Green-Eyes who asks you this.'

The silver-blue spirit moved Xanthippe's mouth. It was Xanthippe's voice, not Nefertiti's, that Chia heard softly murmuring the answer to the question.

'Chia . . . I called you Nefer – the Beautiful.'

Tears stung Chia's eyes. What little doubt lingered was swept away. This wasn't Nyak's conjury. This was

258

Nefertiti, albeit her distant ghost. Chia heard the tremble in her tone as she put another question:

'Nefertiti, do you still love me?'

'I love you. But sometimes I forget. Sometimes it's hard to remember your face. There are too many stars here. It's easy to forget the time of walking in the Black Land of Khemet when you wander the vast halls of night. There are too many stars.'

Chia felt a phantom chill, deep in her body. 'Don't you walk in the immortal gardens and courtyards of Amentet?'

'There is no Amentet here. No gardens. No court-yards. There is no one. I drift among the stars. The stars do not speak.'

Chia fought against the sobbing from within, the sense of desolation from without. 'Oh, Nefertiti . . . golden Nefertiti . . . why are you still an exile among the stars?'

'I don't know – hard to remember . . .'

The spirit-radiance was beginning to dim. The voice was starting to fade. Chia realized that her private grief was distracting her from aiding Xanthippe. She sought to make good her error before it was too late.

'Nefertiti, do you visit Xanthippe in her dreams?'

'There is a girl of Khemet who dreams she is me. I think the dream draws my spirit. Someone calls to me.'

'Where is Xanthippe now? Can you see her?'

'She is on the other side of where you are now. But the moon is too near to her. And there is a false paradise.'

'Nefertiti, my first love, tell me how to reach Xanthippe . . .'

The fading spirit seemed not to hear. 'Too many stars. Take care, Chia-Nefer – the moon is too near. Remember the golden time, Chia-Nefer. Remember the golden time . . .'

'Nefertiti!'

The voice, like the spirit-face, was receding, receding into the huge silence of the stars. 'Forgive me, Chia. Forgive me for being mortal . . .'

Chia couldn't contain the grief any longer. Her eyes streamed and sobs shook her shoulders. 'Nefertiti,' she whispered. 'Come back . . . Come back, my love.'

With the final flicker of the silver-blue spirit, a faint whisper issued from unfathomable depths: 'Forgive me for seeking immortality . . . Forgive me for being mortal . . .'

The voice echoed into silence. The luminescence died. The Night-Shining Jewel and the silver ankh lost their radiance. And Xanthippe once more wore the nothing face. Incense and candlelight resumed sway over the circular room.

And Chia cried like an orphaned infant.

Time passed.

There was the sound of footsteps on the stairs . . .

Chia instantly straightened up. Swept her overcoat sleeve across swimming eyes. Froze her heaving shoulders. Adopted a stern mask.

In a few moments, Chia-Nefer became Chia Black Dragon.

Replacing the ankh around her neck, she crossed to the door and slid back the bolts.

'Stand clear,' she ordered. 'I don't want anyone seeing inside.'

Opening the door a crack, she slipped through and shut it behind her. Leaning against the red panels, she scrutinized the two men on the stairs. One of them was Ming-kai. The other was Hua Shan.

'I heard you were looking for him,' said Ming-kai, indicating his companion. 'This is Hua Shan.'

Chia appraised the vacant-eyed, slack-jawed figure lolling against the stocky war veteran as she pondered her next move.

Ming-kai broke into her thoughts. 'Black Dragon, you have no cause to trust me after the way I condemned your conduct during the Yellow Headband Wars, but I ask you to give me a hearing. We have a common enemy: Nyak. That is solid ground for friendship to take root.'

260

She gave an abstracted shake of the head, concerned only with that lonely place beyond Hua Shan's eyes. 'Your friendship I neither need nor want.'

'Nyak murdered my wife and daughter simply because I once had sight of a book – a very special book.' His head sank, as if recalling grief and rage.

'He's murdered many wives and daughters,' she began, then gave a slight shrug. 'Book – what book?'

Ming-kai's gaze lowered further. 'I wish I had never set eyes on it. It was thirteen years ago, when I was a history student in Chang'an. I found the ancient manuscript misfiled in the library's Exalted of Jade Room . . .'

'Did you, indeed,' she responded vaguely, her attention centring on Hua Shan.

'It was an account of the history of what the book called "the black and the silver" – Chia and Nyak. And not just a history. It was also a prophecy.'

Chia gaped for a few moments, then frowned her suspicion. 'I've never heard of such a book.'

Ming-kai lifted his head, straightened his shoulders. 'It was called *Mortal Wound*.'

'Rubbish,' she said. 'I'd have heard of it if – ' Her disbelief wavered at the associations of the title. Her father's head, tumbling . . .

' "We were a wound in nature",' Ming-kai said.

'What!' she exclaimed, glaring at the hermit's stolid face.

'That was the first line of the book.'

She masked her surprise. Whoever had written the book must have known something about the Thzan-tzai. And a little extra knowledge was always useful.

'I'll meet you in Sung's room in a few minutes,' she decided. Ming-kai nodded and left, holding Hua Shan by the elbow.

Chia walked back into the room and stood over the inert figure of Xanthippe. A slow smile curved her lips as she looked down on her beloved Egyptian. 'I'll save you, Xanthippe – I'll save you.'

She glanced at the painting of Isis raising Osiris; Nefertiti's features had returned to the goddess's face, melding with Chia's. And her smile faded a little as she recalled Nefertiti's words:

*Forgive me, Chia . . . Forgive me for being mortal.*

## 17

Deep lamp reflection in a mica mirror.
The Silver River sinks in heaven, drowning the
    morning star.
Does Cheng-o now regret stealing the immor-
    tality herb
As she ponders endless nights, above the green
    sea, below the blue sky?

              Li Shang-yin: *Cheng-o*

Chia rocked a goblet of rice-wine in her hand as she stared across Sung's room to the burly figure of Ming-kai seated on a chair painted with clouds and dragons. Preferring to sit on the floor, she looked up from a corner of the room to the short, thin shape of Teacher Sung and the tall, thin shape of Lao the Mad Hermit, both raised above her by wooden stools. Hua Shan sat cross-legged on the mattress, mumbling quietly to himself.

Night was a square of black in the unshuttered window, and a presence in the lantern-lit room. The breath of the ocean sighed in through the window's black square.

Since entering the Teacher's chamber, she had probed the deeps behind Ming-kai's eyes. Perhaps wishing made it so, but she saw what she hoped to find. As the war veteran started to explain more fully his hatred of Nyak and the Silver Brethren, she had discerned genuine hatred in his eyes. Yes – it was there – anguish for the wife and daughter killed by two Silver Brethren under orders from Nyak; unremitting vengeance for the destroyer of his family. Chia, accustomed

263

to people treating Nyak as a figment of her imagination, couldn't resist a sense of companionship with Ming-kai. After all these years, here was someone who not only believed in Nyak's existence, but who hated him almost as much as she. After all these years, a faint reflection of her own hatred. It didn't matter that he had blamed her for staying aside from the recent war. As the war drew towards its bloody conclusion, she had blamed herself more than he ever could. In fact, his open hostility at first meeting made her trust him all the more now. And she could make a good guess at the depth of remorse he must feel for noising abroad his reading of *Mortal Wound*. Nyak's servants had come to hear of Ming-kai's sight of the ancient manuscript. Ming-kai had succeeded in destroying it before the Silver Brethren could put their hands on it. Ming-kai had escaped Nyak's wrath, but his wife and daughter had taken the brunt of his vengeance.

Ming-kai was sitting, chunky fingers fidgeting, in his chair near the window. He had just finished describing his reason for vengeance, and evidently the act of describing had unearthed two shallow graves in his soul. He cleared his throat as he resumed speaking, the narrative switching from Chang'an to Silver Music Bay:

'I came to this bay because of what I read in *Mortal Wound*. Although the manuscript was an incomplete, early Han copy of the original Chou account, I read enough to discover where I should look if I wanted to find Nyak at his weakest. Here. Here in the bay . . .'

'Just tell me what you recall from *Mortal Wound*,' Chia broke in.

The hermit's wide brow furrowed, presumably in concentration. His tone was low, and somewhat hesitant. 'I remember its introduction very clearly . . . "I, Feng Yellow-Cloak, Wu Shaman of Spirit Hill Cave, in this year of tan-wo in the reign of King Wu, on the night of Full Pearl in the ninth moon, was first visited by the spirit of the hill. And the hill spirit took over my head and hand and set my fingers to spirit-writing. Thus I

264

wrote, not knowing what I wrote, in the dreams of each night from the ninth moon to the eleventh moon. And this is the account that the spirit wrote through me – the history of the black and the silver, the Twilight and the Owl, Chia and Nyak. This is the history of the Mortal Wound . . ." '

He glanced up from his narrative, an uncertain smile twitching his lips. 'I only read the manuscript a few times. Also, the Han copy I had was *very* incomplete. So you'll have to make do with a rough outline until I've had time to sit down and recall a more substantial – '

'A rough outline will suffice,' Chia assured with an impatient flick of the hand. 'Just summarize the beginning – and the end.'

Teacher Sung was leaning towards Ming-kai, mouth gaping in fascination. 'This is going to be very, very interesting,' he breathed softly, hand stroking the links of his iron chain. But there were lines of anxiety in his forehead that belied his words.

The Mad Hermit munched a handful of magic mushrooms, apparently lost in his own bizarre dreams.

' "We were a wound in nature," ' recited Ming-kai. 'Those were the first words of the actual history. As for the rest, you'll have to be content with my own clumsy words. So, a short, clumsy history . . . It seems that there were two types of humans living on earth in a time before tools were fashioned and speech invented. One of these human races was our own. The other – alike to the first in all respects but one – was called the Thzan-tzai. What was different about the Thzan-tzai was their ability to greatly lower their temperature when too hot, or raise it when too cold. This control over the body extended with the coming and going of generations and the passing of centuries. They learned how to alter the thickness of their skin by will alone, to stretch their limbs and elongate their torsos as a way of frightening enemies, or to compress their frames to half their normal size if evading a foe by hiding in foliage. With the coming of

265

speech, the power of thought was vastly enhanced. And this power of thought over flesh progressed apace. They no longer needed to live in fear of beasts, for they could become the beasts. They became shape-changers. And – here's one of the many things in the *Mortal Wound* history that I don't understand – it's written that they returned to the sea from which we all came. Did we all come from the sea? It's the first I've heard of it. Anyway, for an undisclosed age, they lived in the sea. When they came back to the land again, any resemblance to humanity had long since disappeared. They had become what I think the book called "the infinite flesh". And – yes, now I remember – the history stated that the Thzan-tzai were able to change from shape to shape by means of some faculty called "the flesh dream". "What they dreamt, they were." That's the way the book put it. So the Thzan-tzai could be what they wanted, do what they wanted. And sometime, either in the sea or when they returned from it, they conquered death. Now – now here is a strange event in a strange history. They conquered death by a joining of what the book termed the light-of-moon and the water-of-moon . . .'

'Male and Female,' murmured Chia. 'Hermaphrodite.'

'Male and female, yes,' Ming-kai nodded. 'But – what was that word?'

'Greek. Never mind. Go on.'

'Ah – ' He faltered for a moment, then resumed the narrative. 'The males and females joined to form single male-female entities. These male-female, yang-yin beings were self-regenerating; immortal; and with infinite potential. It is from this time of sexual union that these beings are properly called Thzan-tzai. The name "Thzan-tzai", in an old, forgotten tongue, means, literally . . . oh, what was it the book translated the name . . . ?'

'Literally,' cut in Chia, not wanting the narration to get bogged down in linguistics, 'the name means "power of not-light-of-moon-not-water-of-moon". The power of

266

no-thing. The power of the unlimited male and female. You can loosely translate it as the Nothing Masters.' She gulped a deep breath as Xanthippe's empty face made a hole in her thoughts. 'Now, as we're sitting in a haunted temple in a haunted bay with hardly a clue as to what's going to happen next, I suggest you make your promised outline even rougher than intended. You've told me nothing new so far.'

Ming-kai's fist tightened, then relaxed. 'I'll make it as short as I can. These male-females – these Thzan-tzai – became what the book calls "wounds in nature". As immortal male-females, not only did they possess a limitless store of flesh transformations, they could also tranform flesh into thought, into a living dream. In this living dream, they could even travel to the moon. Apparently, the infinite flesh of the Thzan-tzai warped all matter that came into contact with it. If a man came near to a Thzan-tzai, his flesh would flow and merge into its strange male-female nature. Anything that propogated its kind by sex was liable to alteration and absorption by the Thzan-tzai – humans, animals, fish, insects, even certain trees . . .'

Chia gave an imperceptible nod. *Like weeping willows . . .*

'. . . anything remotely sexual was vulnerable. And – now here's another difficult part of the book – the Thzan-tzai secreted something known as moon-milk, moon-silver, or sometimes quicksilver. This secretion had some similarity to the ordinary quicksilver we're all familiar with. Ordinary quicksilver is both liquid and metal; it has the shapelessness of liquid with the capacity to take on metallic shape below a certain temperature. It can form an amalgam with any other metal – except iron. It is highly corrosive and poisonous – '

'I think you're labouring the point,' Sung snapped, scratching his thin beard.

Ming-kai shrugged off the interruption. 'Shapeless and shaped; liquid and metal; interacting with all metals

267

excepting iron; poisonous; corrosive. And – I almost forgot' – he threw a quick glance at Hua Shan mumbling incoherently on the bed – 'quicksilver has always been a symbol of the moon. Moon-liquid. Moon-metal. But – as for moon-*milk* . . .' He shook his head, then slanted a quizzical look at Chia. 'That foxes me. Do you have any idea what that means, Black Dragon?'

On the verge of telling him that it was for him to speak and her to listen, she suddenly remembered Ming-kai's wife and daughter, dead at the bidding of Nyak. She realized how empty the hermit's years must have been since that day. She inclined her head in assent.

'Yes, I know what it means. Thzan-tzai quicksilver – let's call it moon-silver to avoid confusion – has all of quicksilver's properties. But it has many more properties of its own. Moon-silver can pass as a liquid into the human body, then congeal in solid form. In its liquid form it is moon-milk, and actually smells like sour milk. That sour-milk scent is still strong in the solid state, if your sense of smell is acute enough to pick up the scent in the first place. Once inside the human body, it tends to congeal, but traces of it will enter the bloodstream, flowing in liquid form. But, whether liquid or metallic, strong- or weak-scented, it has one property which makes it deadly.' Momentarily, she blinked as the image of the wu-hsing statue glinted its bronze at her from the murky Hall of the Immortals.

*That scent. That moon-silver scent. It was strongest in the wu-hsing statue. Xanthippe lost her soul face beside that statue. And – a week ago – in front of that same image, there was what Ming-kai called a stab of silvery light . . .*

Chia nodded slowly. 'Yes,' she murmured. 'Yes.'

Teacher Sung, thin arms folded, planted himself firmly in the middle of the floor, his feet straddling the wu-hsing circle he had painted on the floor. The painted wood creaked under his slippered feet. 'You were about to tell us of the one property which, I quote, "makes it deadly". Moon-silver, that is. Or moon-milk. Or what-

268

ever. If you're going to start an account, then you may as well finish it.'

Chia gazed at the creaky wood of the wu-hsing circle, and stroked a finger across her wide mouth. 'Yes. I may as well finish it.' She rested her head against the wall, still staring at the wu-hsing circle. 'Moon-milk. One property deadly. That property is sentience. The residue of the Thzan-tzai is like a living legacy – a physical memory of their presence on earth, long ago. And there is a cult – a Thzan-tzai cult – headed by Nyak, that makes use of that living memory. The Silver Brethren are made into what they are by drinking moon-milk and sharing in Nyak's flesh. That residue – that moon-milk – can be forced down someone's throat in a much faster, cruder fashion. When that occurs, the moon-milk totally usurps the mind and body of the victim. It makes the poisoned body serve the purposes of the Thzan-tzai cult. It makes the victim a slave of Nyak.'

Her hand moved from her jaw to the lapel of her overcoat. 'Fen-chou died with my needles in his chest,' she said softly.

'And Lung-ch'i's missing too,' chimed in the Mad Hermit, suddenly deciding to join the conversation.

'Ah yes,' she smiled grimly. 'That would fit. Fen-chou and Lung ch'i. Words were put in their mouths. Alive, they would have contradicted those words.' She glanced at Ming-kai. 'The moon-milk scent is rank around that Five Faces statue in the Hall of the Immortals. Why should that be? Perhaps there was something inside the bronze mould, something inside the hollow of Five Faces. Something hard, like metal. Something soft, like liquid. Something "like a stab of silvery light" '. Her hand slid inside the black overcoat. Her gaze was still centred on the floorboards creaking under Sung's feet. 'Imagine,' she said in a voice barely above a whisper, 'moon-silver instantly transforming from metal to liquid, pouring down a man's throat as moon-milk

269

before partly congealing as metal in his body and partly flowing as liquid in the veins.'

She raised her eyes to meet Sung's steady stare.

'Ordinary quicksilver,' she said, 'forms an amalgam with any metal – except iron. That's why it's carried in iron containers. Moon-silver is likewise limited only by iron. Without iron to contain it, moon-silver would go wild in the body, causing unchecked transformations. And moon-silver is very heavy in both its metallic and liquid forms. A large quantity would add considerable weight to a man – enough to make the floorboards creak while he's standing still. And, of course, an iron chain planted on his shoulders might explain the sudden increase in weight, but I doubt your chain is *that* heavy, Teacher. I suspect that you drank something which disagreed with you as you stood by the wu-hsing a week ago. Something that lay heavy on your stomach. Something that could only be kept in check by iron – *enchained* by iron . . .'

Chia whisked the silver dagger from her overcoat and sprang across the room in a single motion. But Sung – Sung-silver – was faster. He flipped the iron chain over his head and hurled it out of the window, simultaneously jumping back on his heels.

The swipe of Chia's blade met empty air as she skidded to a halt in the wu-hsing circle, one foot planted on a green dragon's face.

The Teacher was changing even as she looked at him. Released from the stricture of iron, the moon-metal in his stomach and the moon-milk frothing in his veins celebrated their sudden freedom in a transformational display. The skin acquired a silvery sheen, palpitant as snake-skin. The eyes were instantly drowned in thick milky fluid. And the flesh rippled in waves from head down to foot. He wept white tears; dribbled white saliva.

'Cover your faces!' she yelled at the stunned hermits. 'Especially your mouths.'

Before she had completed the command, the red-

270

robed silver figure launched itself at the ceiling, cracking roof-timbers as its palms slammed on to the surface and thrust it back down with superhuman force. It dropped like a dead weight from the sky and blasted through the floorboards, disappearing in a swirl of red and blur of silver into a ragged crater in the floor.

Chia instantly leapt in pursuit, plunging feet-first into the jagged hole. As she jumped, she heard a crash from below as Sung's shape smashed through another floor. She plummeted through the second hole, falling two floors before impacting on the bent floorboards of Kang's former room. Ignoring wrenched muscles and jolted spine, she instinctively rolled well clear of the landing point before springing to her feet in a low crouch, dagger weaving, eyes probing candlelit shadows.

He wasn't in the room. Or if he was, he had made himself invisible. The door was locked; the window was shuttered. Nowhere, amongst the guttering candles on the floor, was there a sign of moon-silver-Sung.

The silver head suddenly appeared in front of her face – upside-down. White froth bubbled inside the gaping mouth as it exhaled its milk-breath: 'The moon's over your head, Chhhiiiaaa . . .'

She threw herself back as the silver shape returned to its inverted roost on the ceiling, squatting there as if it were a floor.

Keeping her hand firmly cupped over mouth and nose, Chia craned her neck at the rippling form on the ceiling. The revelation of Sung's poisoned flesh had been so swift that she'd been left no time to think, or remember. Now she remembered, all too lucidly. Moon-silver had dual poles of attraction: earth and moon. It could bear down on the ground with its full weight, or transfer its liquid metal activity to the moon's attraction.

'Feeling thirsty, Chhhiiiaaa?' asked the inverted, milky mouth.

271

Disregarding the implied threat, she glared at the viscous eyes. 'Give Sung's body back to him, you pool of talking pus.'

'Ohh,' bubbled the mouth. 'Can't do that, Chhhiiiaaa. Got to keep Sung tucked up nice and warm inside. He's part of me now. He's mine. His memories – affections – loves – hates – hopes – fears – are all mine. Ahh, Chhhiiiaaa . . . you should know better. I don't *possess* this body. I *am* this body, metamorphosed by moon-milk. Lovely, lovely moon-milk. Care for a small drink?'

She aimed the point of her blade at the thing that grinned down at her. 'I'm going to destroy you,' she growled, voice muffled by the covering hand.

'And how, precisely, do you intend to do that, dear heart?' frothed the inverted mouth. 'You seem unaware that I *know* about *you*, lovely lady. Oh yes, you're in a sorry, sorry state. Not yourself at all. You haven't been *quite* yourself for a couple of years now, have you, lady-love? All your powers went – puff – in the wind. No more hin-kung leaps to soar over your enemies. No more long moment for you to dart about in while the rest of the world is moving so slow. No more descending from great heights like a feather that takes no hurt in the fall. No more . . . but enough of no more. You are now what you've always wanted to be: just like everyone else – or as near as makes no difference. *How does it feel?*'

'What makes you think I've lost any of my powers?'

'I am the scent of the Master's flesh. What he knows, I know.'

Chia tensed at the disclosure. If this was the scent of Nyak, and this embodied scent had exploded from under the hollow bronze image, then Nyak's smashed body had at one time been placed inside the wu-hsing statue. Perhaps he was still there . . .

'Why so averse to my proximity, Chhhiiiaaa?' rippled the silvery voice from above. 'I love you as the Master loves you. I love you as all moon-silver loves you. We mean you no harm. We mean you all good. Why so distant, Woman in Black? Come close. Be intimate. Be with us. Be in us. Be us.'

'I'd sooner be in Hell.'

'No – you'd sooner be in Paradise. Come – let us take you there. You have no power left to oppose us. You've been stripped of all your powers. Why protract the painful struggle? Be with us.'

'You just try and take me to your Paradise,' she hissed softly, 'and you'll soon see how many of my powers remain.'

'Oh, *really*? I'm *so* frightened. Bluff on, dear heart, bluff on. You can't stop the resurrection.'

Behind Chia's stern expression, her thoughts sped. Nyak was coming back by way of the wu-hsing. He was returning as Five Faces. And the faces stolen in the past months were the flesh and soul substance of his resurrection. But was he fully resurrected, or did he wait for one last element before body and spirit breathed as one? And Xanthippe – had he already absorbed Xanthippe's soul?

*No. He hasn't taken her soul yet. I don't believe it. I won't believe it. She is on the border of Nyak's world, but she's yet to step inside. Xanthippe's not lost. I won't let her be lost.*

She glared up at the poisoned body on the ceiling. It was time to throw away caution, time to declare hostilities. From now on, it was a long, unremitting battle.

With a disdainful gesture, she dropped the protective hand from her face as she raised the dagger aloft. The moon-silver thought that she had lost all her powers. But it was wrong. She retained her greatest power.

She could still dream, still form an image in the air.

And, if even that failed, she would fight like a wild cat.

'I,' she snarled, 'will stop Nyak's resurrection. My brother won't be coming back.'

'Ahh, Chhhiiiaaa,' bubbled the milky mouth. 'Wrong again. Wrong, wrong, wrong. It isn't just the Master. They're *all* coming back.'

The dagger wavered in her hand. 'What are you talking about?'

'The Thzan-tzai. They're all coming back. All of them. This is the Great Year of Resurrection.'

'Liar,' she whispered, but hearing the uncertainty in her own tone. *It could be. I knew that if Nyak came back, he would be stronger. And if he's strong enough he might find a way to resurrect the Thzan-tzai, the Nothing Masters. Where would I then find a place to hide? Where would anyone in the world find a place to hide?*

But again, she whispered, 'Liar.'

Silvery laughter trickled down on her. 'Just wait until tomorrow night's full moon, Chhhiiiaaa. When the Ceremony of Deliverance from Guilt is concluded, the not-light-of-moon-not-water-of-moon will entrance the world as they once did many thousands of years ago. You can't stop him. And his regenerating body is where you will never look. Where you *cannot* look. Where he is, he could sleep for ten thousand years and no decay would mar his body. Long after China is dust in history's tracks, the Master will still be.'

Chia could hear the muffled sound of footsteps on the stairs. Two of the hermits were descending to investigate the trouble under their feet.

'Come on!' she challenged the moon-silver shape above her head, trying to distract it from attacking the men. 'Drop down on me, you lump of sour milk. Take me on, if you dare.'

'Oh yes,' rippled the airborne liquid metal. 'I dare. I dare very much.'

It detached itself from the ceiling, arms spread wide, milky mouth gaping.

Chia thrust the silver dagger into the descending shape – and was astonished when it screamed and steamed as if scalded by the blade. It flattened itself back on the ceiling, a perturbed mess of liquid and metal in a red robe. Then, elongating as it stretched for the window, the tortured moon-silver flooded across the

274

room and smashed through the shutters. By the time a knock resounded from the door, there was nothing in Kang's chamber but Chia and the wind that blew from the wrecked shutters.

A small smile slanted her lips as she gazed at the glitter of the dagger in faint moonlight. 'So,' she breathed, 'you're still able to surprise me after all these years, my little silver killing thing. And Nyak is in for a bigger surprise. He doesn't know that I can still dream up a vision in air. And he doesn't know that you're like poison to moon-silver. Oh yes, my brother's in for a big surprise.'

She returned the dagger to the sheath sewn in an inside pocket, then opened the door to admit Ming-kai and the Mad Hermit.

The stamp of shock was deep in Ming-kai's features. 'What happened . . . ?' he gasped. His anxious eyes zigzagged about the room. 'Where's Sung? What – what happened to him?'

'He's gone.' She shrugged. 'In every sense of the word.'

'Gone?'

'Out of the window.'

Consternation was scrawled in every line of his face. 'Out of –' He glanced at the smashed shutter. 'I don't – What do you mean?'

Still inwardly rejoicing at the discovery of a new potency in the silver dagger and the prospects it offered for dealing with Nyak's planned mass resurrection, she simply smiled and gave another shrug. 'Sung's body was saturated by moon-silver a week ago. After that, although he looked like Sung, he wasn't really Sung any more. He killed Fen-chou. And he's killed Lung-ch'i too, I think. So don't waste your time grieving. That wasn't really Sung who flew out of the window.'

His heavy lower lip quivered in suppressed rage. 'But it *was* Sung who was eaten up by this – this moon-milk a week ago. Think of that. Surely you grieve for his fate.'

'Yes, of course,' she responded in a flat, wholly unconvincing tone, brushing past the war veteran on her way out of the room. 'But there are things to do, you know.'

Ming-kai held his wrath in check as he watched Chia ascend the stairs with a chuckling Mad Hermit dogging her steps. When they were out of sight he murmured to himself, somewhere below a breath:

'Be her friend. Hate her enemy. Tell her a story.'

Repeating Aklo's words reminded Ming-kai to keep his anger under iron control. Aklo had given him the weapon to destroy Chia: a story based on the few fragments of *Mortal Wound* saved from the great burning of books under the Ch'in emperor Shih Huang Ti. It sketched a rough outline of Chia's ancestry, history and future. And there were 'one or two falsehoods' included in the narrative that would lure the Black Dragon to destruction.

Ming-kai had carried off the deception so far. He mustn't fail now. In Chia's eyes, Ming-kai must be her friend.

'Yes,' he breathed softly, assuming command of his anger. 'I can do it because I must do it. I'll be Chia's friend – until tomorrow midnight.'

He closed the door gently behind him, as though there wasn't a trace of rage in his soul.


Chia slammed the shutters together and locked out the night.

'Well,' she said, sauntering across Sung's erstwhile room and flicking a quick glance at the gaping hole in the floor. 'We'd better make good use of what little time we've got left. Once the moon has set I'll be heading north along the bay.'

'And I,' said Ming-kai, shifting on his stool, 'wish to accompany you.'

She slumped down on the floor, rested her tousled head against a wall, and stroked a finger over pursed lips. 'Possibly . . .' she murmured. 'Possibly.'

Her gaze wandered to Hua Shan, still sitting cross-legged on the mattress, slack lips mouthing silent words. The Mad Hermit squatted beside him, his spiky grin like an open man-trap, staring vaguely at the moon-haunted survivor of the Forest of the Ancestors.

Ming-kai cleared his throat. 'Black Dragon – shall I resume my account of *Mortal Wound*?'

She waved a silencing hand as she stood up and moved to Hua Shan. 'Not just yet. I'll have to create what little security I can for Xanthippe before I leave the temple.' Kneeling in front of Hua Shan, she drew out her dagger and rested its hilt inside his curled hand. 'You're heading for safety, Hua Shan,' she said quietly. 'You're heading out of the forest.'

Slowly, the man's twitching mouth became still, and a distant glint of clarity showed in his eyes.

She extracted the Night-Shining Jewel from a pocket and held it so it touched the centre of his brow. Closing her eyes and breathing in the yoga rhythm of pranayama, she made herself an empty vessel.

An empty vessel ready to be filled with a dream.

'Give me your forest dream,' she whispered gently.

At first there was nothing in the blackness behind her eyelids.

Then a burst of black trees with silver leaves exploded in her head . . .

*She is running, running through the forest, with a wind-devil at her back and her name is Hua Shan . . . She tumbles out of the forest down a steep slope . . . A Silver Brother descends the slope, a green sign on his mask brow . . . The Silver Brother whispers, 'Fly to the moon' . . . The East Face of the monolith, glowing green, is a green moon, its pouting mouth ready to receive her, ready to take her face for the Master. . . .She tumbles, head over heels, into a glowing green moon . . .*

*. . . and then, she prays, she prays to Cheng-o, the gentle, lonely goddess of the moon, the White Lady of night . . . tumbling head over heels, tumbling into a nightmare shaped round and coloured green . . . 'Chengo-o, moon goddess of the Ice Palaces, save me*

*from the nightmare moon. Take me into your Ice Palaces, kindly Cheng-o. Take me into your dream of the moon, White Lady. Cheng-o – hear me – fly me to your moon.'*

*She still tumbles, head over heels . . . but now she has tumbled over the green moon with its open mouth . . . She tumbles upwards to a night sky of snowflake stars on black velvet . . . In the midst of the stars, a white and silver dream of the moon . . . Falling now, falling to the silvery disc . . . Ice Palaces rise to meet her . . . and there is the figure of Cheng-o, tiny in the distance, sitting under her cassia tree with the white hare pounding the herb of immortality . . . Cheng-o, growing larger as I descend . . . Cheng-o, her pale face growing larger as she looks up at me . . . Cheng-o is – familiar . . .*

Chia arched backwards as she wrenched herself out of the dream, her heart drumming its dread. Cheng-o – familiar? No. She'd been bedazzled by dream's magic bag of tricks, that was all. She'd almost become as lost in the moon-dream as Hua Shan.

She shook her head free of visions. Hua Shan's vacant face swam back into focus. Perhaps it was illusion, but she thought she glimpsed a touch of warmth in the hermit's eyes, as if someone had fleetingly visited him on his moon.

Chia glanced at the dagger that still lay in his palm. Its unknown metal, so deadly to moon-silver, was a welcome touch to Hua Shan. She gave a faint sigh. She had just found a guardian to watch over Xanthippe.

'What were you doing?' asked the Mad Hermit, his bald head lolling from the mushroom visions in his skull.

She ran long fingers through her unruly mane of hair. 'I visited Hua Shan on the moon.'

'Oh, is that all,' he grimaced, manifestly disappointed. 'I do that all the time.'

'Really?' she smiled, rocking back on her heels. Then she studied the tattooed face more closely. Lao lived very much in a world of his own. He was mad as a noon midnight, but that could be a talisman against Nyak's influence. A man so thoroughly engrossed in his own

278

mad world might be impervious to the deadly madness distilled from moon-silver and spread by the whispered words of the Silver Brethren. It was even possible that he was able to enter Hua Shan's moon-dream.

She shifted the dagger from Hua Shan to Lao. 'Here. Hold this tight. No – not the blade, the hilt.'

His gaunt fingers tightened round the hilt and his smile widened. 'Yes,' he breathed. 'It feels good – expansive, enriching. Yes. Can I keep it?'

'No,' she scowled, instantly retrieving the dagger. 'Just answer a few questions.'

He spread his tattooed palms. 'Anything you say.'

'Can you tell the difference between reality and illusion?'

'Not at all,' he promptly replied.

'Does that bother you?'

'Not in the least.'

'Good.' She nodded, a brief smile flickering her lips. 'And how do you feel about Xanthippe? Does she arouse you sexually?'

He shook his head. 'Nobody arouses me in any way.'

'Then do you find her repellent?'

'What sort of question's that?' he complained. 'I know I'm mad, but I'm not *crazy*.'

'All right,' she conceded, rising to her feet. 'If I have to trust anyone to keep vigil over Xanthippe, then two moon-fools are my choice. Go and take over from Chen-pao, and don't leave Xanthippe's side until tomorrow night's moon has set.'

'All right,' the Mad Hermit grinned, rising up and gently lifting Hua Shan from his cross-legged posture. 'Come on, Moon Hermit – that's it.'

Vaguely complying with Lao's pressure on his arm, Hua Shan wobbled to his thin legs. The two started to move towards the door.

Chia was pulling the silver ankh chain from her neck as she watched the men's departure. It seemed to cling to her hand as if it were part of the flesh. Her blighted memory was highly unreliable, but to the best of her knowledge she had never parted with the ankh since the unremembered day of its making. Letting go of the ankh was almost tantamount to tearing her heart out and handing it to a stranger.

But Xanthippe – Xanthippe lay under the roof of South Tower with a void at the front of her head. A girl who had never done or even intended harm to anyone had her soul-face ripped from her as if she were an unwanted doll in the hands of a spiteful child. She deserved something. She deserved –

' – the ankh,' Chia said. 'Take it and put it around Xanthippe's neck.' She dangled the Egyptian sign of life in front of her. 'Go and do it quickly – it might help restore what was stolen from her.'

As Lao plucked her ancient amulet from her hand she experienced a sharp pang of loss. Nyak had stolen most of her powers; now she was giving up one of her two essential talismans. For Chia, it was like disposing of armour and weapons in the middle of a battle. But she kept her feelings to herself as she watched the door close on the hermits.

The terminal rattle of the latch had the note of a death-knell for Chia. It was almost as if the shutting of the red door had locked out Xanthippe forever from Chia's life.

*Nyak: he always plays the same refrain . . . If Chia loves a woman – kill her. If she has a dog – kill it. A cat – kill it. A squirrel – kill it. Always the same refrain: 'You-will-live-alone.'*

'I am the Death-bringer,' she murmured.

'Indeed?' rumbled Ming-kai's deep voice.

She whirled round, instantly masking her love and her grief. 'I'd forgotten you were there,' she remarked casually, strolling over to the shutters. 'I was merely quoting one of my titles.'

Ming-kai immediately lowered his head and she was unable to observe his reaction. Wanting to ensure that he regarded her as the deadly sorceress of legend and not the lonely woman she actually was, she added salt to the broth: 'Surely you're familiar with all the names they call me? Chia the Death-bringer, Mad Chia, Chia the Vampire.' She turned up the collar of her overcoat and smiled a crooked smile at Ming-kai. 'I'm the most evil woman who's ever lived – and I'm the only hope you've got.'

She lifted an eyebrow at Ming-kai's sharp response as he sprang up and turned his back to her. 'I've heard all I wish to hear about you, Black Dragon,' he said in a thick tone, as though talking through a mouthful of grit.

'Must have overdone it,' she said to herself. *But if it's a choice between hate and pity – give me hate.*

Whatever emotion had seized Ming-kai, he quickly mastered it. He swung round and waved in the direction of the stools. 'Shall I conclude my outline of *Mortal Wound*?'

She reached for the ankh – and was momentarily shocked by its absence. Quelling her disquiet, she gave a curt nod. 'Finish it. But not here. We're going to the Hall of the Immortals. I'll listen to your account in there.'

Seeing his puzzled frown, she vouchsafed a brief explanation. 'When I was talking with that moon-silver-Sung downstairs, it occurred to me that Nyak's body was probably placed inside the wu-hsing statue when his remains were first brought to the bay. And it also struck me that the body might still be there. On small reflection, I realized that was very unlikely. If his body was still hidden in the hall, the entire temple would be swarming with Silver Brethren. However, I'd be a fool not to look . . .'

Flinging a long grey cloak over his Kang-i robe, Ming-kai looked askance at the sorceress. He appeared to be mulling something over in his mind. 'Chia,' he began. 'A true friend, they say, is one who isn't afraid to speak his mind.'

'They say all sorts of things,' she sighed, starting for the door.

281

'May I speak my mind?' he persisted.

'If you must.'

'As far as I know, no one in Silver Music Bay has ever seen any of these "Silver Brethren". Teacher Sung used to – ' He halted for a moment, quietly handling his sorrow. 'Sung used to quote your descriptions of them. It would be hard to miss men wearing helmets of solid silver.'

Midway to the door, she paused for a moment, pondering whether she'd be able to stop talking if she decided to start. 'A few words won't hurt,' she finally mumbled. Staring away from her companion, she spoke swiftly and quietly.

'They are – or were – men. And men only; Nyak detests women. Through a prolonged moon-milk ritual and a sharing in Nyak's diseases, they achieve a greatly lengthened lifespan. Their hands share four different colours of plague: red, white, black and green. If they touch you – you're dead. And if you wonder why you don't see them, that's because they don't want you to. Whenever they congregate in a small area, like this bay, they cover it in a whispered web of words that acts like a spell of selective blindness. It's a kind of trance they impose, similar to a Wu shaman who persuades you that you are seeing something when there's nothing there or, more to the point, that you can't see something that really is there. Do you know what the Silver Brethren whisper more than anything else: "I'm not really here". But, believe me, they *are* really here. Scores of them.'

She was on the verge of telling him that the 'Watchers' were the Silver Brethren, but decided against it. No point disturbing the man further.

Ming-kai scratched his beard. 'Hm . . . you wouldn't think they'd need to wear silver masks.'

Chia halted by the door, hand hovering over the latch. 'Well, they don't have a choice. *They* call them silver masks, so *I* call them silver masks. But they're not actually mask-helmets, nor are they actual silver. They're organic.'

282

'Organic?'

'They're shells. They grow out of their heads. Carefully administered, moon-milk can make shell grow anywhere on the body, but particularly the head.'

'Shell,' muttered Ming-kai, brows knitting in a frown.

Chia's mouth bent in a grim smile. 'Sorry you asked?'

The frown was instantly expunged. 'No. It's – it's just a disturbing image, that's all.'

The grim smile grew grimmer. 'If you haven't seen the mask-faces that form on those head shells, you have no notion of what the word disturbing means. The masks are faces within faces. And sometimes, they move –' She stopped herself in mid-flow. 'No,' she said, shaking her head as she opened the door. 'You wouldn't want to know about that. You really wouldn't.'

'If Nyak has such servants,' he remarked, 'what is *he* like?'

'The Silver Brethren are pale imitations of Nyak,' she said as she descended the stairs. 'That should tell you something.'

'And Nyak's your brother,' Ming-kai observed silently. 'That should tell me something, too.'

## 18

Understand what is male
But play the part of the female. . .
Understand what is white
But play the part of the black. . .

Lao Tzu: *T'ao te ching*

Five Faces cast its glittering eyes down on Chia's upturned face. The wu-hsing statue, its tall profile a continuous shift of hopping shadows and agitated glows, dominated the hall with its scented presence.

'Can you smell that curdled odour?' Chia asked, turning to the man at her side.

Ming-kai sniffed the air, then shook his head. 'No – just the smell of old wood and candle-wax.'

'Not surprising,' she said. 'Thzan-tzai scent, even at its strongest, is hard to detect.' The sight of Five Faces made her blood hot with anger. It was by means of this image that Xanthippe's soul had been ripped from her face. The wu-hsing had stolen Chia's love within hours of the birth of that love.

'Might Nyak still be inside the statue?' she heard Ming-kai whisper in her ear.

'A remote chance,' she shrugged. She planted her foot on the image. 'Let's find out.'

Breathing deeply, summoning the dormant ch'i force in her body, she prepared to deliver a vicious kick at the huge bronze shell. When the power was near to brimming over, she lashed out.

Her foot slammed the statue back from its base. It reeled. Toppled.

284

The thunder of its impact reverberated around the murky Hall of the Immortals, resonating in the metal of two hundred bronze images smiling in the fragile play of candlelight.

Ming-kai's eyes widened in horror as he saw the monstrosity previously hidden inside the shell of Five Faces. 'Spirit of Lao Tzu, protect us . . .' he gasped.

Before the last syllable left his lips, a sound exploded in the air above them. The hermit recognized it as the raucous melody of the Tree of Bells, but so loud that he almost believed the eerie tree had materialized inside the hall.

As Chia raised her dagger to the monstrosity revealed on the wu-hsing pedestal, she flicked a glance upwards and saw that the source of the jangling cacophony was swooping down.

'I should have known,' she groaned. *I should have known.*

*Now, now, now,* intoned Quicksilver, bursting into the House of Heaven from the golden doors of Paradise.

The speed was Quicksilver.

Quicksilver was the speed.

It swerved violently from left to right in its downward rush through the stairs, halls and corridors of the House of Heaven.

The willow doors of the mansion slammed open and shut as Quicksilver swept into the misty airs swirling above Forest Bell Village, tearing rents in the gauze of the air with the wind of its passing.

Night sky and sea and land tilted sharply to the east as Quicksilver veered around the pine-clad spur south of the village and hurtled across the shingle-littered beach of Silver Music Bay, aiming in a straight line for the far end of the crescent bay.

*Now,* exulted Quicksilver as its straight path took it from sand to sea. It brawled its way across the waves, streaking like an arrow for Melodious Temple.

The liquid velocity slowed as it neared the temple. Quicksilver had no wish to burst the temple in pieces by ramming its timbers at full velocity. It wanted the temple intact, just as it wanted the Woman in Black intact – for now.

*Ah – Woman in Black*, sighed Quicksilver as it streamed like airborne liquid to the upper storey of the Pavilion of the Immortals.

*Easy now*, whispered Quicksilver.

*Slow and easy.*

Peripherally aware of the approaching roar of the thunder-wind, Ming-kai shrank back from the descending figure of bells.

A figure of bells: that was the only name he could find for the swooping shape of flowing silver. Suddenly he felt Chia's hand thump into his shoulder – and he was hurled down the aisle, skidding to a halt at the foot of the ruby-eyed Lord of Fourth Hell.

A swift glance showed Chia that the hermit was clear of immediate danger. And she was free to act un-impeded. She swerved her blade to meet the silvery downrush. It instantly halted and hovered clear of the blade's bite.

Moon-silver-Sung floated over her head, naked now of the red robe, and bereft of any significant resemblance to Teacher Sung.

She wanted to taunt the rippling apparition, challenge it to test her dagger a second time; but its noise drowned out everything but the approaching thunder-wind.

Like the atoms of Democritus, the entire shape suggested a mass of infinitesimal metallic spheres jiggling together in manic chimes. The silver shape rang like a million bells. And it flowed like moonlit water.

Chia understood the import of the deafening peals. It was a sign of moon-silver's excitement before an impending release of energy. What manifestation threatened she wasn't sure. But she made certain to be alert to the first hint of attack. And she fought the temptation to glance at what she had revealed from under the Five Faces statue.

Footsteps – she sensed faint tremors through her feet. Ming-kai . . .

'Keep back!' she yelled, waving him back without taking her eyes off the ringing, streaming figure. The noise swamped her voice but the cessation of foot-tremors in the floorboards told her that the hermit had stopped his advance at sight of her warning gesture.

The liquid shape of bell-music suddenly darted at her face. Before she could slice its strange flesh it had withdrawn with the speed of moonlight.

Despite her growing unease at the magnifying growl of the thunder-wind, she struggled to devote her whole attention to the rippling figure. Moon-milk frothed inside that figure. And moon-milk was sentient. It was also quick – quick as thought.

And it was singularly attracted to the human head. She sensed the need in that sour-scented milk. It wanted to stream into her mouth, her ears, her eyes.

It darted again, flicking a silvery tongue at her face. She ducked and parried with the blade, just in time. The frothy tongue retracted and the shape resumed its airborne stalking.

Her eyes followed its sinuous movements with fren-zied concentration. *I can't keep this up much longer. One more time – and it might take me. Have to make a move. One throw. But dare I risk it?*

She bent her wrist back. *Have to throw from the hilt. Not easy. Have to be fast. But it's faster than me.*

Chia released the dagger with all the speed in her.


*Easy now*, sighed Quicksilver, gently opening the door to the Hall of the Immortals.

*Slow and easy*, it whispered as it quietly shut the door and slipped among the sullen bronze images.

Be silent. Be subtle.

Like a silvery fish.

The shape streamed away from the streaking blade.

But not quite fast enough.

The dagger seared into the milky mouth. And silenced the singing bells.

The shape suddenly didn't know what to do with itself. One moment it had too many arms and legs – the next it had none. It was dull metal. It was sparkling liquid. It was burning gas.

It emitted a high-pitched screech as it gave up all pretence to form and function and fled from the woman who had launched the terrible metal into its substance. The dagger dropped at Chia's feet as the moon-silver grotesquerie escaped into the dark.

She slipped the blade inside her black overcoat as Ming-kai rejoined her. The total silence signified that the thunder-wind had reached its destination. She hoped that the destination wasn't too close at hand; the night had troubles enough.

'Lung-ch'i,' she heard her companion mutter, mouth working in spasms as he stared at the bizarre spectacle on the wu-hsing pedestal.

Scanning the amalgam of flesh and three-tiered crucibles, Chia wasn't sure whether she was looking at a man wearing a bronze tan-t'ien, or a tan-t'ien wearing a man. There were no legs to speak of – just raw appendages with what might have been feet dangling some distance above the pedestal. The groin had been opened up to reveal a crucible containing sulphur, the dragon of alchemy. A hole had been excavated in the stomach: inside it could be glimpsed the central crucible of quicksilver, the tiger of transmutation. Lung-ch'i's head rested on a crucible sprouting from his neck.

The cook's entire body had been miraculously impaled on Hsiang's tan-t'ien.

Stepping up close to the plump head on the upper crucible, she peered into the gaping mouth.

'His mouth's been crammed with immortality pills,' she observed, arching an eyebrow. 'A mordant touch.'

And a message had been carved into the waxen brow: *It's all in the head.*

She could hear Ming-kai choking out the words: 'Did – did Sung do this? And why – why not kill him cleanly?'

'Moon-silver Sung did it – under Nyak's guidance. And the manner of death? A message. Nyak flaunts his resurrection method in front of my face. The tan-t'ien is sexual alchemy – male sulphur and female quicksilver mixing in the "inner copulation of the dragon and the tiger". Nyak is achieving full resurrection through sexual alchemy.'

Ming-kai unclasped his grey cloak and flung it over the grisly union of man and metal. 'We must carry Lung-ch'i from here and – '

Chia shook her head as she caught hold of a candle. 'We leave him where he is. There's too much to do between now and tomorrow moonset. After that, you can build a golden mausoleum for him, for all I care.' For the moment, there was a clue to follow – the message cut into Lung-chi's forehead. *It's all in the head.* The wu-hsing's head?

Brushing aside the hermit's protests, Chia strode round the pedestal and knelt at the open base of the toppled wu-hsing statue. She played the candle-flame on its smooth interior, but was unable to throw light on the shadowed hollow of the head. The curdled scent of moon-silver from inside the bronze shell nearly dissuaded her from exploring further. What if there was a lump of active moon-silver inside the head?

But a small clue was still a clue. She couldn't ignore it. Like it or not, she had to crawl inside the wu-hsing's head.

Holding candle and dagger in front of her face, Chia eased her body into the dark recess of Five Faces.

*Easy now*, whispered Quicksilver, touching each statue as

it glided down an aisle between austere bronze Immortals.

Where Quicksilver lightly trod, it left evanescent footprints of moonlight, and where its fingers touched, a smear like a luminous slug-trail.

The temporary sentience it imparted to the bronze images was no more than a mollusc might possess; but it was sufficient to create a small stir in the candlelit hall. A mollusc can open its shell, and close it; a mollusc can feed.

*Softly now*, exhaled Quicksilver, oozing into the fourth aisle to stand behind the stocky figure of Ming-kai. *Whisper softly* . . .

*I'm not really here*, Quicksilver whispered into Ming-kai's ear.

Quicksilver laughed its silent laugh as the hermit spun round, sensing something behind him – seeing nothing. The Watchers – that's what the hermits called the unseen presences. And that's what Ming-kai thought stood near him – one of the Watchers.

*Ah no*, smiled Quicksilver. The Watchers are the Silver Brethren, hiding themselves inside a few whispered words. Your subtle ghosts are the Silver Brethren – the children of Quicksilver.

*And I*, rippled Quicksilver, *am the Master.*

*I'm the Dark Woman's brother.*

*And I've come to visit my sister.*

Quicksilver slipped between the shadows and alighted on the tumbled wu-hsing statue.

It caressed the five-faced head with munificent hands, bestowing silver gifts to the bronze head.

The deeper Chia forced her shoulders and hips into the wu-hsing statue, the tighter the squeeze. She was eventually reduced to a series of small undulations as her boots slipped on the metal and the wavering candle neared the crown of the effigy.

'Any further and I'll have to rely on Ming-kai to pull

me out,' she muttered, squinting forward into the agitated patchwork of light and dark. 'Perhaps it's time I started to rely on someone.'

Her stretching fingers were already inside the curved metal of the head.

There was something there, inside the bronze head: a white blur at the edge of the candle's aura.

Wincing at the thickening scent of sour milk, she gave one last wriggle that pushed her fingers within touching distance of the white blur –

– and got stuck fast inside the metal mould.

'Hell's blood,' she groaned. 'Just my luck.'

She flexed her shoulders against the bronze embrace – still caught fast.

There was nothing to be gained from bewailing her predicament, she decided. She might as well satisfy the curiosity that had lured her into the trap.

Her brow contracted as she peered at the white blur in the crown of the head. It was becoming less of a blur. It acquired form – a rounded shape.

A skull? she speculated, goose-pimples prickling her skin. *His* skull?

No, too small. Although the curdled smell in the effigy held all the pungency of Nyak's after-scent, and it was evident that her brother's body had been interred in the image, the scent had faded too much for the interment to have lasted long. Too short a time, and too long ago, for any real knowledge to be gleaned here. Another blind alley; and one she'd have difficulty in retreating from.

The white, rounded object in the crown came slowly into focus. It was not a skull, but a conch – a seashell with its mouth gaping at her face. Inside its spiral throat there was a trickling sound – and tiny flashes of silver reflected on lustrous shell.

Instinctively, she covered the conch's mouth with the point of the silver dagger and steadied the shake of the candle with an effort of will.

291

Moon-milk. The conch was full of moon-milk. Not the Mad Hermit's absurd concoction, but the real thing.

This was the little memento that Nyak's servants had left in the wu-hsing: a shell brimming with Thzan-tzai residue, a substance forever toing and froing between metal and liquid. And always ready to form an amalgam with anything, except iron.

'And seashell.' Her voice was a muffled murmur in the bronze confines. 'Yes.' From somewhere in her shattered memory, she retrieved a hazy recollection. Whimsical moon-silver – limited by shell.

*The Nothing Masters, aeons ago, returned to the sea from which we all came . . . Did they grow shell, in all those millennia under the waves. . .?*

Moon-silver, contained in a conch, had been the active agent in the stealing of Xanthippe's soul-face. It had summoned her face to the moon.

'And now my head's stuck inside Five Faces' head, sharing its hollow with a deadly brew of moon-milk.' Chia's wide mouth formed a wry twist. 'I've been in better places in my time.'

The conch, she noticed, clung limpet-like to an upper surface of the bronze, defying gravity.

'Ah,' she breathed softly. The moon-milk was compelled towards the attraction of the moon, carrying its shell with it. And the silver dagger, apparently so deadly to the substance, was aimed directly at the shell's mouth. At least she wasn't likely to be splashed in the face.

On the other hand, she was still trapped in the statue, and the dying flame of her candle showed that the air was running out.

The fading of the candle-flame revealed an incongruity. As the flame lowered, the illumination heightened.

As the candle guttered, she became aware of a presence. A familiar presence – familiar from long ago. It filtered through the bronze of Five Faces, curdling the air.

292

Her brother was standing outside the statue. She sensed the nearness of his spirit eating into the bronze.

Frantically, she kicked her booted feet against the metal, drumming up aid from Ming-kai. It was unlikely that the hermit was even alive, out there with Nyak's spirit, let alone capable of rendering aid, but unless someone pulled her out of this trap very soon, there would soon be nothing left to pull out.

The candle-flame flickered and vanished, but she wasn't left in the dark.

The interior of the bronze head ignited into bright life. Bronze blazed to radiant gold.

And faces bulged out of the bright gold. One face swelled out of the crown, four faces protruded from each side of the head. Five Faces statue looked inside its head, all ten eyes fixed on the trapped Chia.

Lashing her feet against the metal, Chia fought a battle with panic. Panic was poised for a swift victory. Her head was caught within a haunted head that was wearing its faces on the inside. And if she let her blade stray from the open mouth of the conch, she knew what was waiting to spring out.

'Ming-kai!' she screamed. 'Pull me out of here! *Ming-kai!*'

A distant murmur resonated from the sea shell: cold, metallic, pristine. It sighed a vast whisper into her face from the whorled mouth:

'*Chhhiiiaaa . . .*'

'Ming-kai! Get me out of here!'

'*Chhhiiiaaa . . .*'

'MING-KAI!'

The whisper was swiftly drowned by the rising tingle of bells. The moon-silver was starting to play its music from the depths of the shell. Anticipating an outburst of energy, it was stirred to excitement, and when the moon-silver excitement reached a jangling climax, it would erupt from the shell.

The faces surrounding her head, like five gleeful moons, beamed a baleful welcome to her terrified eyes.

Muscles straining in agonized frustration, Chia gave a scream that almost swamped the racket of bells in the brazen head.

She was living inside the head of a madman. And who could stay sane for long inside a madman's head?

Through blurring vision, she saw her knife-hand wavering, glimpsed a lump forming between thumb and forefinger – a throbbing lump that expanded and contracted rhythmically. With each fleeting second, the bulging lump burgeoned.

*It's starting again.*

Trapped and crazed inside a madman's head, she had to get out, no matter what the consequences.

To break free, she would do anything.

*Be* anything.

Her right hand was transformed into a pulsing mass.

Be wild flesh.

Infinite flesh.

'No!' she yelled, as a little light broke into her tormented wits. Her hand reassumed human shape, gripping the silver dagger.

And in a blast of inspiration, she buried the point of the blade into a part of the conch near the metal, close to where the moon exerted its magnetism on the moon-silver. She snarled as she wrenched a section of shell free.

Moon-silver erupted as moon-milk from the crack in the conch, and soared to the attraction of the moon. A beaming bronze face loured between the quick liquid and the moon. The moon-milk splashed on to the bronze face. Bronze had none of the properties of iron – or seashell. The moon-milk burned into the bronze face. And the brazen visage lost its smile. It writhed in exquisite torture as the silvery liquid formed nightmare amalgams in its metal features.

The moon-milk's violent frenzy to ascend to moonlight lifted the statue clean off the floor. Chia felt the shift of gravity in her body as the effigy tilted upright.

'Now or never,' gasped Chia, preparing herself for one of her more painful tricks.

A deep breath.

Four of the faces loomed in on her, mouths opening. *Now.*

With a sharp wrench of shoulder muscles, she yanked her shoulder-blades out of their sockets.

The dislocated shoulders weakened the bronze grip. And the weight of gravity pulled her down to the floor.

As her feet thudded on to the floorboards, she realized that the screaming she heard was her own.

A second deep breath.

She slammed her right shoulder on to the metal at an angle that slotted the shoulder-blade back into its socket.

A final deep breath. She restored her left shoulder to its proper form with an equally powerful slam against the bronze. Still distantly aware of her own screams, she picked up her dagger, gave a savage push to the effigy, and rolled under the gap as it rocked momentarily on its base.

She sprang into the tiger stance the instant she was clear of the wu-hsing statue. Left hand hooked in the action of the tiger claw, right hand weaving the dagger before her, her long, slanted eyes warily roved the shadowy hall.

'Right,' she challenged hoarsely. 'What's next?'

Hua Shan swayed in the grey-blue fog of the po-shan-lu censers, his bowed head hovering over the brown contour of Xanthippe's body stretched out on her white lion robe.

Hua Shan was fully aware that he sat cross-legged in the round room at the summit of South Tower. He was also conscious that he sat on the moon, outside the tall Ice Palaces of Cheng-o. He could never see the goddess properly – she was always at the edge of the eye, never quite in sight. But that didn't matter. Here he was safe, on Cheng-o's moon. Safe from the whispering silver masks, safe from the green moon, and safe from the Nothing Man.

There was one place – that place beyond the dreams – that he was beginning to fear. It had only become visible of late, and then for mere moments at a time. It was a barren moon, a desolate lunar landscape devoid of dreams or goddesses. And above it hung a shimmering green-blue sphere. This lifeless moon had harsh ridges and deep craters under a black sky with never a twinkle in its starry eyes. He called it the Hard Moon – and it wasn't a dream.

So Hua Shan knew he must stay quiet and safe in Cheng-o's dream moon with its Ice Palaces, in between the earth and the Hard Moon. Step one way and the Nothing Man would seize him; step another and the Hard Moon would kill him.

Stay quiet, stay still, trust Cheng-o, and vacantly observe the earth-visions that constantly paraded before his eyes. That was the way to survive. Preserve the verity of the dream moon in a litany of its magical heights and deeps:

'Mountains of the moon . . . Plains of the moon . . . Valleys of the moon . . .'

'Doesn't the white hare ever get fed up with pounding the herb of immortality all the time?' he heard the Mad Hermit enquire.

But he didn't answer – mustn't answer. Answering questions would bring him too close to the earth, and the earth was almost as deadly as the Hard Moon. Keep chanting. Keep affirming the magic moon of Cheng-o . . .

'Oh well,' the Mad Hermit grinned. 'No harm in asking.' He scratched his tattooed scalp and tried to peer at the nothing face fronting Xanthippe's head, but his attention kept sliding past the facial void; it was like curved ice, impossible to get a grip.

He held up the silver ankh, which he'd so far neglected to place around the girl's neck as Chia had insisted. The rise and fall of the thunder-wind, less than a minute ago, had reminded him that Xanthippe was in danger, and people in danger needed protection. In this case, the protection of a silver talisman.

He looped the chain over her head, leaving the ankh to rest on the breast-bone, then sat back on his heels. He was glad that he'd remembered to fulfil Chia's instructions. He liked Chia Black Dragon. She was the only person he'd met who was madder and badder than himself.

For a few moments he stared at the ankh, then he realized he wasn't staring at it anymore.

The tattoos on his brow distorted as he leaned forward with a puzzled frown. The ankh and the chain hadn't exactly disappeared. It was just that it was impossible to look at them; his gaze slid past the silver in the same way that it skidded without purchase on the empty face. The silver had become – *nothing* silver.

He glanced back at the front of Xanthippe's head.

There was a hint of something in that nothing face: a silver hint.

'Interesting,' he mumbled.

He stretched a hand to the void metal. And missed it, his fingertips contacting instead the cold skin of the motionless girl. He tried to touch the silver by sliding his fingers over the skin until they reached the metal, and found that his fingers unaccountably hopped over the object of his search.

'Weird,' he murmured appreciatively. 'So weird.'

His fascination was instantly quelled by an un-accustomed foreboding. There was something in South Tower: a presence. A presence that had started to climb the stairs with footsteps soft as moonlight.

It suddenly struck Lao the Mad Hermit that there might be someone even madder and badder than Chia. And it surprised him to discover that there might be someone mad and bad whom he didn't like at all.

Perhaps there were limits, after all.

And as Lao's heart beat out the slow seconds he became increasingly sure that whatever was ascending the stairway of the tower was definitely beyond the limits.

The seconds were passing quicker; no — it was his heart that was beating faster. He'd forgotten the sound of fear in his ears, its taste on the tongue. His gaze darted round the incense-clouded room, barely taking in the Chinese and Egyptian spirit worlds that peeked intermittently through fragrant fog. The bronze chimes dangling from the rafters directly above Xanthippe struck up a few chimes of warning or welcome to whatever was mounting the stairs.

'Hide inside the Ice Palaces,' he urged Hua Shan.

But Hua Shan required no urging. He sensed what was coming. Already his thin shape was acquiring the translucency of a phantom as he wrapped his body deep in the folds of his moon-dream. Soon he was all but invisible, a wraith in the smoke of incense.

Lao pursed his lips and nodded. So that was why the Woman in Black chose Hua Shan to be one of the watchers over Xanthippe: when the enemy came, he could slide sideways into his dream of Cheng-o, hide himself in the bosom of the White Lady of the moon.

'But what am I supposed to do?' he muttered.

It had been a long time since he last experienced fear. How to deal with it?

Instinct told him to keep his back to the door. Against all reason, his heart advised that if he couldn't see the intruder, then the intruder wouldn't see him. So he didn't turn round when he heard the first complaint from the panels of the door. Instead, he fixed his gaze on Xanthippe as he fingered his necklace of rat skulls.

And when he heard the first crack resound from the door, he decided to go mad.

Chia's glance darted about the statues and shadows of

the Hall of the Immortals. Left hand still hooked in the tiger claw, dagger still sweeping to and fro, she twitched at each creak of wood and resonance of metal.

Despite the eerie atmosphere of the hall, she gradually relaxed her arms from combat posture. Nyak had been here, and added an extra tinge of haunting to the bronze images. But his scent was fading: he had left the hall to its haunted effigies and jumpy candles. Anyone who didn't know Nyak might suspect that the battle was over, but Chia knew that she'd merely survived the first skirmish.

Of Ming-kai there was no sign.

A grim smile brushed her lips.

He was probably still running.

She slanted her gaze to the wu-hsing image. It stood upright, rocking occasionally on its base with the furious activity of the moon-silver in its bronze head. Nightmares were enacted on the five faces of the wu-hsing as the moon-silver performed its bizarre alchemy on the constricting metal. Each visage underwent increasingly rapid tranformations as silver and bronze simultaneously allied and warred with one another, the two metals joined together in the unhappiest of marriages. Five Faces was virtually eating its own head.

Chia spared the statue a last scornful glance as she moved down the aisle, leaving the image to its auto-cannibalistic feast. 'That's one for Xanthippe,' she hissed. 'There'll be more.'

As she passed beneath the eight ruby eyes of the Lord of Fourth Hell, she thought she caught an echo from the bronze lord. She might have imagined it, but it sounded like 'I live.'

'So what?' she muttered. Chia had already sensed that Nyak's visiting spirit had conferred a touch of haunted life to the ranked images of the Immortals. Small displays of that transitory life were to be expected. So long as she didn't tarry too long in the hall, the bronze effigies offered no threat.

'I live,' tingled the metal of Chu Jung, god of fire, as she walked by his tall shape. The voice was like a delicate bell, small but clear.

She ignored the florid image of the god of fire and kept her eyes fixed firmly ahead.

A few steps further and she drew opposite Kou Mang, god of wood and wind. 'I live,' resonated the metal statue. 'I'm nothing, but I live.'

The percussive tone struck up a chorus of reverberations from the surrounding statues. 'I live – I live – I live – I live – '

'That's right,' Chia murmured wryly, displaying an indifference she didn't feel. 'Just talk amongst yourselves.'

There was a certain timbre to the metallic echoes mounting in the hall, a timbre suggestive of the chime of moon-silver.

As the brazen percussion swelled in volume, the unique resonance of moon-silver became unmistakable, seemingly vibrating from all two hundred Immortals. Gods of wood, metal, fire, water and earth all rang out Nyak's triumphant declaration: '*I live.*'

It was as if her nightmare brother's spirit lived in all the five elements of the wu-hsing. As if Nyak lived in everything. Five Faces . . .

A stark realization blasted all thoughts of the wu-hsing from her head. There could never have been enough moon-silver in the hall to set all the bronzes ringing so loud. She would have known. She would have felt its presence. The agitated moon-silver was a new gift from Nyak's phantom hand.

The chiming voices abruptly exploded into a thunderous bellow.

'I LIVE,' roared a metal multitude.

The floorboards under her feet seemed to bounce back the deafening words as Chia raced towards the door of the hall. The din suddenly ceased as she slammed the door shut and took the stairs three steps at a time, not

300

pausing until she kicked open the pavilion door and stood under the night sky. A glance to her left revealed the stocky figure of Ming-kai sitting by the stagnant fish-pool. She walked up to him, pushed her hands deep into her overcoat pockets, and arched a sardonic eye-brow.

'My hero,' she said in a flat tone.

He shrugged his broad shoulders, and said nothing.

'At least you stopped running once you were out of the pavilion,' she finally conceded, starting to move away. 'And we've both found out that you're unfit to face the House of Heaven. If what happened up in the hall frightened you so much, then the House of Heaven will kill you. Once the moon has set, I'll head for Forest Bell Village – alone. You stay here.'

The hermit shook his head. 'I'm coming with you, whether you like it or not. If you try to get rid of me you'll never know the final secret of *Mortal Wound*.'

'What final secret?'

'The secret that may show you the way to destroy Nyak. There's a great deal that I can tell you right now. But the final secret – not until we're inside the House of Heaven. Agreed?'

Her lips curved slightly. 'I could torture it out of you.'

His head lowered. 'I was once taken prisoner by General Tsao's army. They learned nothing from me. And I was tortured by experts.'

'Compared to me,' she said quietly, 'every torturer's an amateur.'

'And every tortured man is a liar,' he responded, rising to his feet. 'Not until we're inside the Old House. *Agreed*?'

'A pity you weren't so brave in the Hall of the Immortals,' she said sharply. She stepped up to the edge of the pool and gazed at the reflection of the moon on its scummy surface. The reflected moon was green in the lambent lantern-light. The colour was mirrored in her brooding eyes. 'Agreed.'

Ming-kai nodded. 'Good."

'Bastard,' she swore under her breath.

'According to *Mortal Wound*, your father wasn't human,' the hermit remarked.

'He *became* human,' she snapped, right hand tightening to a fist. Just as quickly, the fist relaxed back into an open hand. 'In the end, he became human.'

'Yes, but in the beginning he was Thzan-tzai – one of the Nothing Masters.' Ming-kai's wide brow was deeply furrowed as he concentrated on recalling the account. 'As such, he was a male-female being. But he was torn apart into two separate entities. The male entity gradually became human, and named himself Glak-i-kakthz . . .'

'The separation' – she cut in – 'how did it occur?'

'In a flesh dream,' he replied. 'Thzan-tzai would sometimes travel between earth and moon in flesh dreams. Somehow, he became caught between the two – trapped midway in a dream. The opposing attractions of earth and moon eventually split the being in two. The female entity was drawn to the moon, while the male fell to the earth.'

'A woman on the moon,' Chia murmured, staring at the green moon in the pool. 'Cheng-o.'

'Yes,' the hermit nodded. 'According to *Mortal Wound*, that's where the myth of Cheng-o came from. A primordial being split in two; one was transformed into the goddess Cheng-o, the White Lady of the night, the other became Glak-i-kakthz, your father.' He halted, studying her pensive expression. 'Didn't you know about Cheng-o?'

Chia gave a slow shake of the head. 'No. I never knew what happened to the female aspect. Alone on the moon . . .' Her slim frame shuddered as her hand sought the solace of the ankh, only to find it missing. 'Enough . . . enough . . .' she mumbled. Then she recovered her composure and motioned the hermit to continue.

'Well, the rest is very sketchy. After a huge lapse of

time – some seven thousand years – Glak-i-kakthz mated with a woman called Chi of the Huan Tribe. She gave birth to twins, Nyak and – and you. When the twins were twelve years old, Glak-i-kakthz told them of his Thzan-tzai origins. You started to hate him because of those origins, while Nyak hated him for casting aside all Thzan-tzai power. So, for opposite reasons, you and Nyak joined together and murdered your father.'

'That I remember all too well.' Her voice was heavy with the past.

'After your father was killed, something strange manifested itself on the body. The head grew a shell.' He paused momentarily as Chia tensed, then, at a nod from her, he continued. 'When Nyak revisited his father's remains, he discovered that a silver shell had grown out of the head. The head had already been sliced from the body so – '

Chia stopped listening. She remembered. ' – so the silver shell became the mortal mask,' she whispered below a breath.

The memory was at first a tableau: two heads framed by an arch of rainy daylight – frozen imagery. Then the images began to move . . .

*A green-eyed youth, his face the mirror of her own, stands just inside the arched mouth of Black Dragon Caverns. His smile is wide and friendly. He holds up a head by its long grey hair. For a moment she thinks it's her father's head. Then she sees it's made of silver. Its mouth is a twisted gash and its features contorted, as was her father's when she hacked through his neck.*

*'A cunningly wrought silver mask, Nyak,' she says. 'But I'm trying to forget that night – and the look of agony on his face.'*

*His smile softens to a wistful curve. 'Ah, my beautiful sister, it's not silver. It's scale. It grew out of his head, growing around each individual hair. His brain is dust, his skull rotted fragments. But his flesh is silver shell. This is father's death mask. It is also father's head.'*

*She steps back, tasting bile on her tongue. 'Destroy it. It's the Thzan-tzai legacy in his flesh. Take it out and destroy it.'*

303

'It can't be destroyed, lovely Chia. It's eternal. This mortal mask is immortal.' His smile grows strange. 'Why must you and I grow old and die, beloved sister? We've inherited a longevity that makes other mortals less than dragon-flies. But longevity is not immortality. We won't live to see this mountain crumble with age, or witness the death of the moon. In ten or twenty thousand years we'll be old, Chia. Old. Our bones will be sticks and our skin will be rags. Do you know what the human story is? It's a tale simply told: white teeth, black hair – black teeth, white hair. The essential tragedy of human life is that it's too short for tragedy. It's a joke. A bad joke.'

She shakes her head. 'Given so much, you now want everything.'

He sighs that characteristic long-suffering sigh of his. 'Twenty years or twenty thousand years – we always want more than what we're given. But you know that, Chia. You're like me. We want nothing less than everything: immortality, infinite flesh. We want the Thzan-tzai birth-right our father denied. He made us what we are; neither mortal nor immortal. We must now make ourselves into what he once was.'

She tries to keep the tremble out of her voice. 'I killed him for what he once was – and might be again. I killed him because he coaxed Mother into drinking moon-milk, not caring how it was altering her, but only concerned with keeping his mate by his side for as long as possible. He didn't do it for her sake. He did it for fear of his loneliness, for his needs. Thanks to him, Mother has lived almost two centuries, but she doesn't look like Mother any more. She doesn't even recognize us. She doesn't even remember her name.'

She can see how much that hurts him. He glances out of the cave to the hut in the rainy valley. 'Oh, I didn't know that. That last time – I thought it was a passing illness. My mother – never recognizing me. Never knowing her name. It's like a small death – for us all. I didn't know, Chia. I didn't know.'

Hiding her emotion makes her tone hard. 'You should visit more often.'

He takes a deep breath. 'Or not at all.' He glances at the hooded black cloak that muffles her from the chill of late autumn. She *knows that he is trying to distract himself from their mother's affliction. 'You used to hate black.' His flippant disguise is too thin: behind it, clearly visible, are knives and night. 'Now you dress like the Dark Woman of the North Winter.'*

*He wants her to state the old and the obvious, she realizes, because he has something new and subtle to say. She obliges. 'We both wore hooded black robes as we merged with the night, lying in wait for our father. Those black robes hid our knives. When the killing was over, I wanted to hide in the night, forever. I wanted to be one with the winter, when the nights are long. I wrapped myself in comforting darkness. I wear black because it's the colour of night. And now I' – she hears the shake in her voice – 'I am of the night.'*

*He nods gravely. They are the closest of twins, and each understands the other. 'I carried the guilt, too,' he says. 'Every day of forty years. But now' – he grasps the grey hair and brandishes their father's shell-head from a high hand – 'now we're free of the night. This is a silver dawn. This mortal mask is more than a relic. It is resurrection. It is immortality. While he lived, father denied me my Thzan-tzai birth-right. But in his death, he gives me the Thzan-tzai legacy. My father's head has become a silver crown – and I will wear it as a god-king.'*

*For the first time in her life, she perceives an alien strand in her brother's character. It comes from the mortal mask. He can't have possessed their father's silvery death-head for more than two moons, yet already it's changing him. All of the lingering Thzan-tzai memories of their father were incarnate in that shell. And whoever wore it would be slowly poisoned by those memories.*

*Nyak lifts the mortal mask above his head. He starts to lower it.*

*'Think what you're doing!' she begs. 'That silver scale embodies everything father hated in himself. You'll become everything he hated.'*

*'I'll become everything he* feared,*' he says with a crooked smile. Then the smile is blotted out as the mortal mask, half as large again as her father's living head, comes to rest on Nyak's shoulders. Long, dead grey hair swirls to his waist.*

*Her heart drums with dread as she stares at her father's head on*

305

Nyak's body. Her father's death-agony, immortalized in shell, mouth like an open wound, features convulsed, confronts her with her crime. It is a frozen death scream, realized in deathless substance.

'Look at me,' she hears him saying, his voice muffled by the shell-head. 'I'm living inside my father's head.'

A shudder runs through her. 'Nyak, please – take it off.'

He refuses to listen. His hand slides beneath his light grey mantle. 'Do you remember,' reverberates his imprisoned tone, 'that father once confided how he would sometimes stretch out his right hand and touch his sister on the moon? He called it his "flesh dream". It was more than a dream, Chia. It wasn't only his head that turned to silver.' Nyak extracts a silver hand from under his mantle. 'His right hand grew a silver shell too. Here, take it. It's yours.'

He throws the hollow hand of silver scale. She seizes it with an instinctive catch, then almost drops it in revulsion. The fingers are hooked in the death-spasm. She remembers them reaching for her face as she sliced through the sturdy neck.

There is an eerie note in Nyak's loud whisper. 'Ah, Chia,' he exhales softly through her father's screaming mouth of shell. 'Ahhh, Chhhiiiaaa. I feel it flowing into my head: quicksilver, liquid moon. And there are so many stars, Chia. So many stars. They blot out the night. The moon is silver. The stars are silver. The night is silver. And I am Quicksilver. I am solid and liquid. I am neither solid nor liquid. I am the Nothing Man. For the Nothing Man, everything is possible. Oh, if only you could see what I see, Dark Woman . . .'

She hears herself screaming. 'Take that shell off! Take that filthy shell off!'

For a stretched moment he fails to respond. Then he surprises her by lifting the mortal mask off his head. His dazed expression quickly clears. He smiles his tilted smile. He is the same Nyak she's known all her life. Almost. There is a dreamy lilt to his lips, a hint of distance in his eyes, that wasn't there before. It would make her happy to laugh it off as a passing aberration, a brief trip to a dream world, soon forgotten.

But what Nyak had experienced he would never forget. It would

306

*grow in his head, like a disease. She knows this in the dark of her
heart, where premonitions are born.*

*This is the beginning. This is the first crack of an impending
schism. They would split apart until they became strangers.*

*'Chia,' he grins. 'Don't look so worrried! I've had stranger
visions with a single gulp of ling-chih. The mask must have made
it seem worse than it was.'*

*She puts a smile on her lips. 'Yes, I know. It just came as a
shock, that's all.'*

*'Well' he shrugs. 'It's all over now. I'm glad there's no harm
done.'*

*She sees clearly how they are already drifting apart. He should
have seen through her fabrication at a glance. But now she can hide
her heart from him. Strangers – already they are becoming
strangers.*

*And one day, when he is Quicksilver and she the Dark Woman,
they will be mortal enemies.*

*She looks down at the hollow silver hand resting in her grasp.
Her hand is trembling. No – the* silver *hand trembles.*

*Its scale fingers are hooking round her hand. Squeezing.
Pulling.*

*She returns the pressure, crushing the silver . . .*

Flesh fingers. Flesh fingers caught in her contracting
grip.

'Chia!' groans Ming-kai. 'Let me go, for the ancestors'
sake!'

He was sprawled on the ground, her foot on his chest,
her grip crushing his right hand. Releasing her grip she
stood back and folded her arms.

'You're mad,' he muttered, struggling to his feet.
'Mad.'

Watching the hermit flex his bruised fingers, Chia
impatiently tapped her foot. The revelation she had just
received made her eager to head north for the House of
Heaven, regardless of the high moon over the bay. A
high moon, exerting its fey attraction on moon-silver,
meant danger every step along the beach. She had
delayed entering the Old House long enough.

She glanced up at the moon. 'Cheng-o,' she murmured. Pensive lines creased her brow.

*Cheng-o is not alone on the moon.*

Brushing aside the sudden, disturbing intuition, Chia fixed her attention on Ming-kai. 'How long was I in a trance?' Her tone was brusque.

'Not long,' he mumbled. 'Less than a minute.'

'Were you telling me about the mortal mask?

'The mortal mask? – yes. I *tried* to tell you that your father's head-shell became Nyak's mask. It – it altered your brother's head in some way. And it gave him visions, and powers. But before I could tell you any more, you suddenly attacked me. You looked like something out of hell . . .'

'Don't take it personally,' she sniffed. 'I'm usually demented when coming out of a trance.' Her hand reached for the familiar touch of the ankh, finding nothing but absence.

*'Xanthippe . . . mustn't think of Xanthippe. Just destroy Nyak. Thoughts won't help her. Actions will.*

She threw a sidelong look at Ming-kai. 'Was there anything in the account about scale growing on my father's right hand? Anything about a hollow silver hand?'

He shook his head. 'Not that I remember. There was only the head of scale. The – what was it? – mortal mask. After Nyak covered his head with the silver mask, the story becomes very sketchy. Over the centuries, Nyak increasingly identified himself with the colour of silver, which he sometimes dubbed "the white" – meaning love and truth. You, on the other hand, associated yourself with the black of night.' A hollow chuckle escaped his bulbous lips. 'It's even said that you became a vampire in the late Chou dynasty. A vampire in the Forest of the Ancestors.'

'And if I did,' she remarked distantly, 'what of it?' Her attention slid past the uneasy hermit into the clogged shadows of North Tower. 'Being a vampire isn't so terrible.'

Nyak was still in the temple. She could feel his nearness in her flesh. Nyak was likely to linger wherever she stayed. Perhaps she should distance herself as rapidly as possible from Xanthippe, and draw Nyak with her. It would be best not to wait until moonset. The sooner she left for a hiding place far along the beach, the less risk for the Egyptian.

Her eyes strayed up the spindly silhouette of North Tower. And froze at sight of what stood on the summit.

A Silver Brother, mask glinting in the moonlight.

'Do you see him?' she asked, indicating the figure. 'On top of the tower?'

Ming-kai peered up at the roof. 'I can't see anything – '

She nodded. 'They made a good job of whispering invisibility commands into everyone's ears.'

'Who's up there?' he queried.

'One of your Watchers.' She considered for a moment. Then, mind made up, she turned to leave. 'We can't do anything now about the Silver Brethren. The Old House is where we've got to go. Right now.'

When the first crack had resounded from the door in the topmost room of South Tower, the Mad Hermit had decided to live up to his name. He had decided to go mad.

Easier said than done.

Hua Shan, enfolded in his moon-dream, was barely a phantasm in the incense-clouded room. He was safe on the moon. Lao must find his own safety – in his madness. If you lived inside your own world, nobody else could make you live inside theirs.

And whoever or whatever was forcing a way through the door wanted Lao to live in its world. It wanted *everyone* to live in its world. Whether Lao sensed that wish of the intruder through the inspiration of madness or the clarity of fear, he neither knew nor cared. All he knew, with profound conviction, was that he'd rather be buried alive than enter that proffered world.

Lao reassured himself with mad logic: *If I can't see him, he can't see me. So don't turn round. Don't look at him, and he won't look at you.*

He heard the door give way with an odd, crumbling sound; heard steps, gentle as moonlight, at the threshold of the door. But the hermit kept his eyes fixed on the floorboards in front of him.

A presence filled the smoky room, the presence of someone very old, very subtle.

And a long, thin shadow slid across the pine floorboards. It stretched to the far wall and ascended its wooden surface.

Lao listened to the blood-thud in his ears. *Don't turn round. Don't turn round.*

The head of the elongated shadow neared the rafters, then halted, towering over the two hermits. An arm of shade reached down to the supine body of Xanthippe. Shadowy fingers groped for the silver ankh lying between her breasts.

But the shadow fingers were no more successful than Lao's flesh-and-bone fingers in seeking the ankh. The ankh's metal had become non-silver. It was an ankh-shaped absence in the world, beyond reach.

The dark arm returned to the tall shadow.

Lao had the disquieting feeling that the silhouette head near the ceiling was staring at him. Whatever cast the shadow was mad and bad beyond Lao's most rampant imaginings.

Finally, the shadow retreated down the wall as the intruder softly departed. It shrank out of the room as faint footfalls, real or imagined, descended the stairs.

Hua Shan gradually emerged into visibility. And Lao released a breath of relief.

Then he noticed a long outline on the floor, and apprehension made a swift comeback. His eye travelled the length of the outline to where it met the wall and stretched up its pine surface.

310

The shape of the intruder still lay on the room in the form of rotted wood.

Where the shadow had rested, green mould grew.

A figure of mould stretched up the pine wall.

Lao felt his thin frame quaking. His voice was a hoarse whisper: 'If that's what his mere *shadow* does, then what is *he* like?'

## 19

That next world beyond the sea – a hollow tale.
Now this life is over, and afterlives cannot be
foreseen.

Li Shang-yin: *Ma-wei*

At first Chia thought she was back in Black Dragon
Caverns, safe in her ancient retreat.

Then her bleary vision cleared and she discerned the
unadorned walls of the cave overlooking the shingled
beach. Rubbing the sleep out of her eyes, she sat up and
peered out of the cave mouth to the dull expanse of the
sea. The troubled waves were grey under the slate
canopy of clumped clouds.

Ming-kai stood half-way between cave and tide, his
figure drab in the fading light.

Chia, suddenly alarmed, jumped to her feet. How long
had she been asleep? She had told the hermit to wake her
before dawn, and this was later than dawn. Her gaze swept
the horizon as she emerged from the cave. There was no
hint of the sun behind the massed clouds. She looked for
faint shadows on the sand and shingle. And found them.
They pointed east. This wasn't the dim light of dawn, but
of sunset.

Enraged, Chia swung the man round by his shoulder.
'You broke your promise, you bastard!'

Unruffled, he gave a light shrug. 'You were obviously
exhausted. It seemed wrong to disturb your rest.'

'Seemed wrong?' she snorted, right fist clenching.
'Wrong?' Her glance darted to the spur of rock that hid
the Forest Bell Village just five li to the north. 'Do you
know what you've done? Tonight's the full moon, Full

312

Pearl – the time of the Ceremony of Deliverance from Guilt. The most propitious time for Nyak to achieve full resurrection. And you've left me mere hours to find the mortal mask before the full moon rides high.'

She whirled away, resisting the impulse to plant her fist in his wide face, and strode north towards the village. 'Idiot,' she muttered. 'Stupid idiot.'

Ming-kai followed her long strides, trying not to smile. He had pondered how he might delay Chia's arrival at the Old House, and came up with no solution. But the sorceress had solved his problem for him in the hour before dawn when she decided to rest in the cave, on the firm understanding that he wake her before sunrise. As sunrise came and went and the day waxed and waned, his spirits rose ever higher. Aklo had wanted Chia brought to him when the full moon assumed sway over the bay. And that, thanks to the woman's long sleep, was precisely what was going to happen. He had almost fulfilled his difficult task, continually fighting the temptation to bury his knife in Chia's back, and brought her to Aklo's judgment.

There were times when Ming-kai could hardly believe what he was doing. Five months ago he had spent a night in the House of Heaven, and never had morning been more welcome. He had embraced it like a long-lost friend, vowing never to return to the shifting shadows and croaking wood of the ancient mansion. But now here he was, heading straight back to the Old House. The Old House – and Aklo – whom he still feared despite the pact against the Woman in Black. He had no illusions about deadly, smiling Aklo. Aklo was sweet-tongued poison. Aklo was the Holy Man from Hell.

But Aklo hadn't murdered Ming-kai's family, and Chia almost certainly had. And that was all that mattered. Even if the mysterious Nyak was a far worse prospect than the sorceress, and Ming-kai's actions resulted in the unleashing of horrors on China, nothing would deflect him from bringing Chia to trial. Justice for

313

his wife and daughter. That was all that mattered, even if it destroyed the world.

His eyes narrowed as he stared at Chia's back. A few more hours and this evil woman would be tried and condemned. He had already decided on the punishment: live burial. It seemed appropriate to visit upon his enemy that which he most dreaded himself.

Chia threw a brief look over her shoulder at the man who tracked her steps. 'Don't you think it's time you told me the final secret of *Mortal Wound*?'

He shook his head. 'Not until we stand inside the House of Heaven. That was the agreement.'

She grimaced, twisting the corner of her mouth. 'You agreed to wake me before dawn. So what's your promise worth?'

Lengthening her already long stride, she scanned the eastern horizon as she followed the curve of the shore. The longer she looked the more sure she became that an unusual mist was gradually dimming the numerous peaks of the Ten Thousand Islands. Sea mist in autumn was no rare sight, but the vapour that was smudging the sea's rim had a green tint she hadn't witnessed before. If drowned spirits had breath, they would exhale such mist.

'It'll be tonight,' she murmured. 'Whatever's going to happen, it'll happen tonight.'

'Now,' whispered Aklo, stroking a needle-nailed hand over the bark of the Tree of Bells. 'Ah yes, at last. No more waiting. Now.'

For a moment his gaze lingered on the involute trunk, its configuration like two coiled snakes joined in love or war. The Tree of Bells was two weeping willows united by time and the moon, trunks interwoven, boughs intermingled. And it bore strange fruit: bells of rare silver.

The silk of Aklo's Rainbow Robe rustled gently as he turned with outspread arms and smiled benevolently at

314

the small group of villagers kneeling at his feet, their green smocks damp from the spray whipping over the flanks of Sea Rock.

Aklo tilted his smile to the left.

In unison, fourteen villagers' smiles tilted to the left. Two, however, hesitated momentarily before slanting their lips in accordance with the young god. Feng, and Wua, her features bruised from the kicks that her lover had been forced to lash at her face, had still not learned to love Aklo completely.

'Ah, so sad,' Aklo mourned softly. 'Two of you have refused me to your hearts. You give your obedience, but not your hearts.' With one magisterial sweep of his arm that took in the small curve of Forest Bell Bay, he spoke in a tone of reproach. 'I have won the love of all but two. I have gained hundreds of hearts, but two eluded me. One young man and one young woman chose to give their love to each other rather than to me.'

He beckoned the nervous young couple forward. 'Don't be afraid to come to me,' he reassured them. 'Aklo, avatar of the Lord of the Eastern Paradise, does not punish. Aklo only gives people what they most desire.'

The sixteen-year-old youth and girl trudged reluctantly up to the tall young preacher, the two making a determined effort to keep their limbs from shaking. They stood with bowed heads in front of the lithe figure of Aklo as if awaiting the fall of the executioner's axe.

'I mean you no harm,' sighed Aklo in a tone as silken as his robe. 'You love each other. I give you each other.'

With a fluent motion he pressed the glittering tips of the needle-nails into the throbbing temples of the two lovers. Liquid light flowed like quicksilver along the nails into the punctured flesh. 'There,' Aklo breathed faintly, stepping back as he withdrew his fingernails. 'I've joined you in marriage.' His smile widened. 'Make love.'

There was a new kind of obedience in the couple's

eyes: unthinking obedience. Their movements were vacant as they doffed the green smocks and lay naked on the ground. Legs encircled legs. Arms wrapped round waists. Lips met. The rhythms of passion began.

And the small congregation of villagers witnessed the scene with crooked smiles and indifferent eyes.

Aklo waved an airy hand at the lovers. 'For this,' he wryly observed, 'they rejected Paradise. For this brief joining of flesh, they refused Aklo's gift of salvation.' He hooded his eyes. 'In Paradise, there is no passion. If there was passion in Paradise, Paradise would no longer be Paradise.'

The lovers at Aklo's feet were in the last throes of lovemaking. Warm lips grew warmer with moist contact. Heaving backs glistened with sweat. Muscles tensed as the two bodies neared union.

'*Now*,' Aklo whispered.

The lovers' lips, seeking sensual union, found physical union. The flesh of their lips became one flesh as the mouths were sealed with a lovers' kiss. Breastbone cleaved to breastbone. The tangle of legs fused, skin to skin, bone to bone, like coiled snakes. Joined mouth to mouth, the lovers breathed frantically through dilated nostrils as muscles and skeletons merged.

'Flesh alchemy,' sighed Aklo. 'Ah yes.'

Lungs laboured as face joined with face. Four arms threshed as one in panic and pain. If there had been a mouth to scream, it would have rung loud across the bay.

All breath was smothered as the lovers' faces fused. A last spasm of union, and the amalgam of flesh and bone lay still and quiet, head to head, heart to heart.

Aklo ran needle-fingers through his long hair. A chuckle escaped his full lips. He flung out his arms. His laughter tripped down Sea Rock promontory.

'What Aklo has joined together let no man pull asunder,' he declared, shaking with mirth. Amusement subsiding, he gave a wistful shake of the head. 'It's a pity there aren't any Christians left alive here to appreciate the joke, but one can't have everything, I suppose.'

He returned his attentions to the small congregation in front of him. 'Go back to your brethren,' he ordered quietly. 'Go back to the village and ready yourselves for the coming of the Tung Wang Kung, Lord of the Eastern Paradise of P'eng-lai. It will be tonight. Paradise will come to you tonight. It will come with the sea and the moon.' He waved a dismissive hand. 'Go now. Go.'

He turned his back on the departing villagers and faced the Tree of Bells. He fondly scanned the graceful fusion of two willows, one male, the other female, into the serpentine shape of a single androgynous tree. A male-female weeping willow with liquid silver for sap.

'A memory.' Aklo sighed gently, his eye following the tracery of branch and twig. 'A memory – and a promise. Birth. Resurrection. Paradise.'

His gaze slid past the tree to the dimming horizon. A faint green mist, like the visible musing of a sea god, rose from the ocean's edge. An observer might conclude that the green mist was growing larger. Aklo knew that it was coming nearer.

Aklo's voice soughed like the tide. 'Nearer. It laps nearer, that sacred sea. And above it, the ancient moon, where the ancient glories sleep.'

He uplifted reverential hands to ocean and moon. 'Born in the sea,' he intoned softly. 'Reborn in the sea.' And then, softer still. 'Green moon.'

'Tonight,' Chia murmured. 'It'll be tonight.'

She glanced at the green mist ghosting in from the sea, and tried not to think of Xanthippe. She listened to the crunch of the shingle under her booted feet, and tried not to hear Xanthippe. She glanced up to where the uneven tiers of the Ancestral Gallery clung to the upper cliff, and tried not to see Xanthippe.

The Egyptian girl's fate had clouded Chia's mind for five days. Four days of necromantic summoning in

317

South Tower had robbed her of precious time. Now, thanks to Ming-kai letting her sleep the day away, she had only a few small hours to recollect her wits, a little time to think . . .

. . . The tan-t'ien in the Hall of Transformations . . . Flesh alchemy . . . Proteus . . . Hermaphroditus . . .

Chia halted in her tracks. 'Flesh alchemy.' She exhaled sharply. Her gaze strayed to the mist-bordered sea. 'Protean.'

'What was that?' queried Ming-kai, drawing to her side.

Oblivious to the man's interruption, her lips continued to voice her thoughts. 'Proteus was an older ocean god than Poseidon or Nereus. He was known as the Old Man of the Sea. When Menelaus, returning from Troy, was stranded on Pharos Island beside a bay that would later become the East Harbour of Alexandria, he encountered the god Proteus. Eidothea, the daughter of Proteus, showed Menelaus how to bind her sleeping father. To escape from the bonds, Proteus went through innumerable transformations. He changed into all manner of animals. He became a tree. And finally – he became water. As water, he almost escaped.'

'I still don't understand,' Ming-kai snorted.

'Proteus, the shape-changer from the sea,' Chia continued, ignoring her companion. 'Each of the god's appearances was a mask. A mask from the sea.' She glanced at the glimmering, green mist wafting towards the crescent shore. Then studied a rock pool garlanded with rank green seaweed. 'Hermaphroditus,' she mused in a pitch barely above a breath, 'son of Hermes and Aphrodite. His father was the rider on the wind, bringer of dreams to mortals, and the guide of souls to the underworld. His mother was born from the foam of the sea.'

'Chia . . .'

'Be quiet!' she snapped, shutting her eyes. 'I'm trying to think. When Hermaphroditus left his home on Mount

318

Ida and went to Halicarnassus, he came to a sacred pool and looked into it, admiring his handsome features. A water nymph called Salmacis lived in the pool, and the naiad Salmacis pulled him under the surface, intending that she and the youth would be united for eternity. The two bodies were fused into a single shape – a woman's body with male genitals. A hermaphrodite – an undying hermaphrodite.'

'*Chia!*' Ming-kai's outburst was underscored by the thump of right fist into left palm. 'Your mind's rambling. Why waste time standing here when we should press on to the House of Heaven?'

She opened cold eyes on the warrior-hermit. 'I'm trying to outwit the most intelligent and devious man who's ever lived' – her eyes clouded – 'or died.'

Unperturbed, he folded his arms. 'The sooner we get to the Old House, the sooner you'll hear the final secret. That should give you the weapon you need to outwit Nyak.'

She looked askance at the hermit's scarred features. 'Perhaps – perhaps. But I'm not so sure about that as I was.' Her gaze once more strayed to the incoming mist. Her voice was quieter than the lap of a distant wave. 'The day my Sentinel Tree rang, I dived into my pool. And something changed in me – I remembered the sea.'

Chia watched a crab scuttle from the rock pool near her feet. The surface of the rock pool settled as the crab scurried to another lair. Her thoughts drifted from the pool to the sea. It was in the sea that the Thzan-tzai had their second, terrible birth – the sea from which we all came. *Born in the sea. Reborn in the sea.* Hermaphrodites, with Protean faculties of transformation.

And Nyak had been brought to the edge of the sea to achieve resurrection because –

'Because this is where he was born,' she murmured, her glance sliding along the bay. A muscle spasmed in her cheek. 'This is where *I* was born.'

Inside her head, her voice continued. *He was born in the*

*sea. We were born in the sea. He will be reborn in the sea. He will absorb Xanthippe, and rise as an undying Hermaphrodite. And then he will summon back the ancestors, the terrible ancestors. My ancestors . . .*

'My ancestors.' The words caught like brine in her throat. Her green eyes, wayward with the onset of panic, darted to and fro. Her right hand clenched and unclenched in a habit ingrained by fear. 'No,' she choked out. 'Not my ancestors. My father was human – had been human for thousands of years. Human.'

She grabbed the shoulder of a startled Ming-kai. 'I'm human, Ming-kai. Human. I remain within myself. I always remain within myself.' Dimly aware of the crazed note in her voice, she fought to subdue her tone, calm her twitching muscles. 'Look at me,' she pleaded. 'Look at my face. Look *into* my face. It's not a mask. It's a human face, isn't it? *I'm* human.'

Chia's wits had cleared sufficiently to perceive the man's stony glare. His voice was like gravel. 'Yours is a face of blinding beauty. Your eyes are from Heaven.'

Confused by the disparity between granite tone and flowery words, Chia blinked her vision back to clear focus. The hermit was wearing a smiling expression: no sign of hatred.

*My madness again,* she concluded. *It makes me see enemies everywhere. It makes me make enemies everywhere. And I need a friend. I need a friend.*

'Are you – quite recovered?' he enquired hesitantly.

She nodded, withdrawing her hand from his shoulder. 'Yes, I think so.' A thin smile bent her lips. 'Until the next time. You'll have gathered that I'm not the sanest woman that's ever lived.'

'No need to explain,' he reassured her, turning away as he started to move towards the village. 'I went a little mad myself after the Silver Brethren used their knives on my wife and daughter. More than a little mad.'

'I suppose so,' Chia began, then frowned at the man's wide back. '*Knives?*' she questioned under her breath.

She must have misheard. 'Your family was knifed by the Silver Brethren?' she called out.

He turned, nodded.

Her frown deepened. 'I've never known the Silver Brethren to use anything but their plague hands in killing,' she muttered under her breath. 'Never.'

Ming-kai caught the drift of Chia's faint words, and slanted his eyes to the sea before speaking in a measured manner. 'It may not have been the Silver Brethren themselves. Some of their servants, perhaps? I try not to remember my family's death, but I'm unable to forget.'

Chiding herself for lack of trust, Chia inclined her head in recognition of the man's loss.

The hermit's tone was hollow as he looked out to sea. 'Thirteen years ago, in Tung An, the better part of my life died with Mai-lo and Fu-lai.'

Chia looked up sharply. She had been in Tung An, forty li inland from the bay, some thirteen years ago, attempting to track down a Silver Brother named Providence and a mysterious companion of his called House. And in Tung An, she had stayed under the roof of a woman called Mai-lo with her small daughter Fu-lai. She also recalled that Mai-lo's husband was absent throughout her stay. As far as Chia's blurry memory could recall, a score and more women and girls had been murdered by the oddly-named House. But not one man had been killed in Tung An, which made the townsfolk's suspicion of her all the more inexplicable – she assumed it was common knowledge that Chia killed only men. For all her long list of crimes, she had never killed a woman in her entire life.

Her mouth formed a bitter line at the news of the murder of Ming-kai's family. It must have happened the day she left on what proved a false trail in her search for Providence and House. She never did find them. And she never went back to Tung An. Mai-lo and Fu-lai had obviously fallen victim to House. House had sliced open his victims with what must have been the sharpest of knives, extracting the liver, heart, spleen, lungs and kidneys and nailing them to the walls of his victims' houses.

But it was the fate of Ming-kai's wife and daughter that brought back Chia's old friend: guilt. Mai-lo had welcomed Chia into her home. For that act of kindness Nyak had marked her for death. Chia should have stayed away, remained alone. She was responsible for the death of Ming-kai's family.

Ashamed to meet Ming-kai's curious glance, she fixed her eyes on the way north and focused her thoughts on Nyak's resurrection, pushing guilt and memory to the back of her head.

'One face at a time,' she murmured, surveying the scree and shingle and sand that stretched ahead. 'Look at the wu-hsing one face at a time.'

A short time before, she had been granted a revelation, a strong conviction that she and Nyak were born in this bay. It wasn't part of her conscious memory – the childhood images of her life were all of Twilight Owl Village by the upper Yellow River. She had always assumed she was born in that village, and no one had told her otherwise. The certainty of the twin birth on this shore seemed to come from the salt in her blood, a saline affinity with the tides that surged at her birth. The blood remembered the sea.

This bay, she reflected, was once called the Wound. A wound in nature?

Nyak had returned to his birthplace for a second birth. All the signs indicated that this second birth would take place tonight. In the Old House?

'Chia!' Ming-kai's cry of alarm and upward-pointing finger jerked her attention up the rumpled slopes of the cliff to the zigzag line of the Ancestral Gallery.

Fear shook the hermit's voice. 'The dead have risen.'

She peered up at the ranks of distance-dwarfed figures that stretched as far as the eye could see along the wooden lanes of the dead. The intermittent glint of silver from the masked heads convinced her of what she had already guessed.

'Not the dead,' she said. 'Silver Brethren.' Her gaze swerved north to south, south to north. 'Hundreds of them. Hundreds. All the Silver Brethren in China, gathered in one place.'

'I can't believe what I'm seeing,' Ming kai exclaimed hoarsely.

'What's hard to believe is that you're seeing it at all,' she responded grimly. 'Many of them must have been here for two years, guarding their Master's mortal body and his mortal mask. Their whispered incantations hid them from your sight for two years. Up until now, they've blinded you. They've blinded everyone.'

The man looked frantically up and down the empty beach. 'Which way shall we run? North or south?'

Slowly, she shook her head. 'There's nowhere to run.' Her slanted green eyes grew thoughtful as she scanned the masked host lined high above. 'And there's no need.'

'No need?' he echoed in disbelief.

'I thought they'd trapped me when I was up on that gallery,' she said quietly. 'But it was a false trap, and a false escape. They only wanted to delay me from returning to Xanthippe before the wu-hsing could take her soul. They don't want to kill me. They only want to see me suffer.'

'Are you *sure* about that?' asked an unconvinced Ming-kai.

She gave a curt nod. 'Look at them. Look how many there are – five hundred, at least. They could have flung me into Hell with plague five hundred times over. No. They don't want my death. The way they're gathered up there, standing sentinel by the funeral houses, it looks like – like a ritual gathering. They've come as witnesses.'

'Witnesses to what?' Ming-kai's eyes were still large with fear. 'The resurrection of the dead on the Ancestral Gallery?'

'Not those dead. All the rituals in the world won't

bring those corpses back to life. They may not lie down. Moon-milk would make them move. But they would still be dead in heart and head. That's what it means to be mortal.'

'But their spirits might return,' he persisted, still eyeing the gallery with dread. 'They might flock back as birds from P'eng-lai.'

A ghost of regret showed in Chia's eyes as she started to move north once more. 'There is no P'eng-lai. There is no Paradise beyond the sea. There is no god Tung Wang Kung ruling a deathless haven of the blessed. It's just a dream we have.'

Still viewing the Silver Brethren with trepidation, Ming-kai followed in Chia's tracks. Every few steps, he glanced up at the silent figures overhead. Not once did he catch a hint of movement. They just watched. And waited.

As his feet covered the last few li to the rocky spur that hid the village, the presence of the Silver Brethren seemed to add a sombre depth to the silence of the deserted bay. And – it may have been imagination – the watching figures seemed to draw the green sea mist ever closer to the beach.

Most of all, the tall black figure of Chia in front of him dominated his world. Even if all in the world were demons and Chia was the solitary saint, he would bury his knife in her back for the sake of his wife and daughter. Too many witnesses had seen the Woman in Black butcher Mai-lo and Fu-lai for there to be any doubt of the woman's guilt. She had sliced out the Five Organs and nailed them to the walls of his home. For that, Chia must die, even if the whole world died with her.

As they reached the promontory of Sea Rock and the village emerged into sight, he silently rehearsed the final words that Aklo had commanded him to pass on to Chia after entering the Old House: 'Use the hand against the head.'

Aklo had told him what the hand was. Ming-kai

couldn't see Chia's silver dagger, hidden inside her bizarre overcoat, but he knew what it was.

Use the hand against the head.

Then he switched to an old, familiar refrain: *Beauty blinds – beauty blinds – beauty blinds –*

He was steeling himself to follow through the plan agreed with Aklo: bring Chia to the House of Heaven, and then she would be subjected to that darkest of deaths – live burial. But Ming-kai's resolve to carry out that agreement was dissolving each hour that he shared with Chia. She wasn't quite the monster he wished her to be. More and more, he was tempted to exact justice with a swift jab of his knife to the heart. Once she was in Aklo's hands, such a merciful death was out of the question. Chia would never confess under Aklo's torture; her spirit was too resilient. That much he had learned about her. Wouldn't the souls of his wife and daughter rest easier with Chia's swift execution rather than a prolonged, breathless agony?

Hovering between alternatives, he didn't notice at first when Chia turned east and speeded her pace as she headed along Sea Rock promontory. He ran to catch up with her, his breath misting in the darkening air.

'We should go straight on to the Old House,' he panted. 'What do you expect to find here? There's no answer in the Tree of Bells.' He threw a backward look at the dark mansion that squatted above the village. 'The answer must be in the Old House.'

As she peered ahead at the tree's silhouette, her exquisite features seemed to absorb the moonlight. Her green eyes had a feline glow. 'This bay is a wound in nature,' she muttered, 'a crescent scar left by a primal violation. I can sense an ancient violence – in the marrow of the rocks, in the deeps of the sea.' Her vivid green stare could have come from either Heaven or Hell. Her low voice vibrated in his skeleton. 'Echoes have no ending. Did you know that? This wounded bay is full of ancient echoes. There's even an echo of that violence in the old name for the bay: the Wound.'

325

His long hair swayed with the shake of his head. 'A true sage of the T'ao might understand you, but I can't. And I don't hear any echoes.'

'You wouldn't. They're right on the edge of my hearing. They come from the east.'

'From the mist?' he ventured, staring at the luminous green vapour that had advanced more than halfway from the horizon.

'Higher than the mist,' she said, raising her eyes to where the white-silver full moon sailed high and free of the green fog. There was both wonder and dread in her uplifted face and low voice. 'The Thzan-tzai once flew to the moon in flesh dreams. They were wounds in nature that the T'ao of the earth inevitably rejected. Where would they fly in their flesh dreams?'

Awed, despite himself, Ming-Kai gazed up at the scarred, silvery sphere.

'They went to the moon,' Chia said softly. 'Expelled by the T'ao of the earth, they were wrenched from this coast by the power of the moon, leaving a scar where they were ripped from the world, and the echoes of their strange music.' A spasm in her right hand made her pause for a moment. When she resumed, a slight tremor unsteadied her voice. 'They flew to the moon from Silver Music Bay. This region was their gate out of the world. And now they sleep on the moon, dreaming moon dreams.' She reached for an ankh that wasn't there, and dropped a lonely hand. 'Perhaps that long sleep ends tonight – here. The way out is the way in.'

Chia abruptly withdrew herself from lunar absorption. 'Why would my father bring my mother to give birth in such a place?' she pondered, a frown troubling her brow. 'The only reasons I can think of are bad ones.'

They had reached the desolate patch of earth fronting the Tree of Bells. The few stunted plants that grew under the eaves of the weeping willow had a harsh, metallic appearance, reflecting a silver lustre back to the moon. Chia studied them for a moment, then turned towards her companion. 'No one has ever seen a plant die in this desolate little garden, have they?'

Ming-kai pursed his heavy lips. 'No, they haven't. It's said that they've never lived, and that they'll never die.'

'Not while they soak up moon-silver from the soil,' she observed. 'Whatever subsists on moon-silver never lives and never dies.'

He shifted his feet uneasily. 'There's moon-silver under the soil?'

'It smells like a pool of sour milk to me,' she remarked, wrinkling her nose. 'Can't you catch its scent at all?'

He sniffed the air. 'Now you mention it – faintly.'

Wariness slowing her steps, she walked up to the tree, her gaze roving over its drooping branches. 'Moon-silver nurtured and preserved this tree for thousands of years,' she stated. 'Moon-silver grew metallic fruit on its boughs. Silver bells.'

Ming-kai backed away. 'If it's moon-silver, it might attack – '

'Not these tree bells. They are of and for the tree. They just play mad music in sympathy with the coming and going of Nyak's spirit, and perhaps also in memory of the Thzan-tzai on the moon.' Her brow contracted as she caught sight of a shape lodged in the branches. She studied it for a long breath, then lowered her eyes. 'A man and a woman fused together and hung from a tree,' she murmured. 'The metaphorical beast with two backs – made literal.'

Ming-kai didn't look. He didn't want to look. Instead his attention slid past the willow to the luminous green surge out over the waves. 'It's getting nearer all the time,' he heard himself mutter.

Chia didn't react to the comment. The configuration of trunk and bough, the intermixing of male and female catkins, plucked a sharp note from her taut nerves. 'A male-female tree. A special tree.'

He gave a slight lift of his shoulders. 'The Tree of Bells has always been a male and female union,' he said. 'It

327

was the jangly music that made it remarkable, not its dual sex.'

'I've got a Sentinel Tree that makes jangly music' she sighed indifferently. 'A touch of moon-silver applied to wood can make a useful alarm. But these two trees grew into one like lovers – or Thzan-tzai, below the waves.'

Gradually her stare moved upwards, responding to the attraction of the moon. Her lips moved in the frailest of whispers: 'Thousands of years before my birth, a Thzan-tzai was caught between earth and moon in a flesh dream. It was torn in two. The male fell to earth. The female fell to the moon. Glak-i-kakthz remained on the earth, Cheng-o on the moon. They never grew together again.' Her thoughts drifted back to her sharing of Hua Shan's moon dream. 'I saw the Cheng-o of Hua Shan's dream, and she looked familiar to me. She looked like my father's twin. She looked like me.'

At length, her vision descended to the green phosphorescence of the sea fog. It appeared to be less than a few li from the shore. And it had acquired a fluid quality – like a phantasmal sea. Her voice sounded distant to her own ears. 'A sea mist that's perhaps more sea than mist, and more ghost than sea.'

As she turned round to Ming-kai, the Tree of Bells exploded into life.

A jingle-jangle cacophony resounded in her skull as the moon-silver fruit on the trailing boughs was stirred into an agitation of toneless music.

She covered her ears against the din, but the Tree of Bells lapsed into silence as quickly as it had mounted into celebration. Moving swiftly from the tree, she waited for the ringing to stop.

But the ringing didn't stop. Suddenly realizing that the distant peals were coming from the bay and not from inside her head, she scanned the southward sweep of Silver Music Bay.

It took a little time to discern the lambent lights in the windows of the funeral houses. The lights were soft and subtle like the glow of the moon, as if there was a tiny moon inside each house, a tiny moon that sang in a voice of silver bells. The moon-chimes, however, didn't come solely from the Ancestral Gallery.

Bells also rang in the high forest.

Delicate peals and chimes fell from the entire stretch of trees and the long line of death houses along the curve of the bay.

A silver waterfall of sound descended in a majestic cresent.

And a procession of lights wound from Forest Bell Village, gradually bending south.

The villagers were all but invisible in the night as they headed in single file for the north stair of the Ancestral Gallery. Over three hundred lanterns moved through the dark, each a little moon.

Mouth agape, Ming-kai watched the spectacle for innumerable thudding heart beats. His tongue eventually framed articulate speech.

'Those lights – has the moon come to earth? And the villagers – what are they doing?'

Chia, hands thrust deep into the pockets of her black overcoat, spoke in a murmur attuned to the cadence of the tide: 'It's in the trees. The moon is in the trees. Every building in the bay has been constructed from the trees above: the temple, the Ancestral Gallery, the village, the Old House. Moon-silver rules the whole bay. And moon-silver gives Nyak power. Each part of Silver Music Bay has a touch of Nyak's spirit.'

'But the villagers,' he persisted. 'Why are they heading for the Ancestral Gallery?'

'They're going to keep the dead company for a while – or forever.' A grim smile curved her lips. 'And it's no flickering flame they've got in those lanterns – the villagers are led by the lanternlight of the moon. Living quicksilver.'

To the exquisite accompaniment of silver chimes, the line of moon lanterns threaded its way up to the glowing windows of the gallery.

Chia threw a glance at the full moon. 'The night of Full Pearl,' she remarked, then swerved her gaze to the procession of lights. 'And a string of bright pearls in the night.'

Ming-kai, observing the tail of the procession leaving the village, tugged Chia's sleeve. 'The Old House, Chia. We can't delay.'

She expelled a long breath that misted in the chilling air, then took the first step towards the House of Heaven.

Five hundred paces took them to the emptied village. The houses smelt like timber rotten from the sea. An open door somewhere tapped gently on its hinges.

Chia's booted feet hardly made a sound as she climbed the central stair that ascended to the willow wood encircling the mansion. Never speaking to the man at her back, she searched her memory in the short space left before entering the huge, wing-roofed edifice.

Her memory was candles in the dark. One candle, however, made a hazy image of her father's face from the shadowed centuries. The face was linked with an echo of words:

'I once built a house by the sea, but the wood was bad and the moon came too close.'

'What did you say?' Ming-kai's baritone broke in on her reverie.

Not aware that she had been thinking aloud, Chia reached for the comfort of the ankh, then remembered, and lowered her hand. 'I think I've just realized why this mansion is called the Old House,' she said quietly as the shadow of the willow wood closed in on her.

Ming-kai didn't ask her to elucidate. His hand was on the hilt of his hidden dagger and his eyes were on Chia's back. Better a swift stroke of justice than Aklo's untender care. But it was hard to bring himself to accomplish the act. Now that the time had come, it didn't feel like execution: it felt like murder. But he had made a vow, thirteen years ago . . .

He chanted the old litany in his mind. *Beauty blinds –
beauty blinds –*

The shadows of the willow wood dropped away as
they came to the cracked steps of the verandah. Chia
looked up at the looming bulk of the house wrapped in a
special kind of silence.

She startled Ming-kai by swinging round abruptly.
'Once inside the door, you tell me the final secret of
*Mortal Wound*,' she quietly insisted. 'That was the
promise'.

'A promise I'll keep,' he nodded, meaning what he
said. He owed her that at least, before he summoned up
the will to thrust sharp steel between her shoulder-
blades. And that quick death was itself a mercy,
compared to putting her in Aklo's hands.

Chia turned back to the wooden steps and climbed the
boards, wincing at every creak. Brushing past the weeds
of the verandah, she stood for a long moment, shoulders
slumped, staring at the black square of the open doors.

As Ming-kai nervously mounted the steps behind her,
he tried not to remember what he had once seen inside
the House of Heaven all those months ago . . .

The florid swirl of Aklo's Rainbow Robe in candlelight at the end of a dark corridor; a living shadow;
impossible footsteps; bad memories in the grain of the
wood; voices that croaked from dark, carved timber . . .

And Chia. He had seen an image of Chia. She lived in
the memory of the old House.

Ming-kai halted directly behind Chia. His fingers
tightened on the bronze hilt of his knife.

Chia shivered as she peered into the dark behind the
open invitation of the doors. There was a hint of the child
in her soft whisper:

'I'm home.'

## 20

When did the moon first shed its light?
I ask of heaven as I raise my cup.
I wonder what season it is tonight
In the Celestial palaces and pavilions.
I would ride up to them on the wind
But I fear the domes of crystal and halls of jade
So far above are cold past enduring.
So my moon-shadow is my partner in the dance
Of moonlight on the earth.

Li Yu: *Shui-tiao ko-t'ou*

It had been a long walk, from the dark of her body to the light of the moon.

There had been times she wondered whether she was dead or dreaming, but mostly she just walked.

Before the long walk, she had gone up to the Hall of the Immortals to meet Teacher Sung and the rest of the temple hermits. But she had met Five Faces instead.

She had wanted to start the walk then. She had yearned to walk north to the heaven inside a house. But a woman made her lie still in a little wooden temple. Sometimes the woman who kept her still and quiet was Nefertiti, sometimes she was green-eyed Chia.

Then the woman went away, and two men tried to keep her quiet and still. But they weren't as strong as the woman. So she got up and walked.

She walked through a wooden world: a world of halls and corridors and stairs and bridges and balconies. She had walked through a room with erotic carnivals on the walls – men with women, men with men, women with women, men and women with animals, animals with animals. There was a dab of silver magic in the paint and the wood, and the magic made the pictures jump off the walls and talk to her. They stopped talking when the full heat of sex sealed their mouths in a final union, head to head, heart to heart.

It had taken her a long time to walk through the painted rooms, but at last she found the way out. She stepped off the top of a tower and walked on the trees. The trees asked her to join them, but she didn't listen. She told them she was going north to find a man she had never met: the man who was her lover. Then the trees stilled their silvery voices and let her pass.

And then she had come to a long, wooden lane of merry houses high above the sea. There were hundreds of faces smiling at her from the windows, and she would have smiled back if she had a face.

So she just kept walking north to find the heaven inside a house. She walked straight to where her lover was waiting, in the house by the sea.

Inside the little houses on each side of the wooden lane, she heard the remote laughter of people making merry by moonlight. She was tempted to share their festivities for a little while, but her lover was waiting, her face in his hands, and she didn't want to disappoint him.

It had been a long walk, from the dark to moonlight, but she was near the end of the lane to her lover, and her short steps changed to strides, then to long bounds. The woman who was sometimes Nefertiti and sometimes Chia had kept her from her lover for a long time.

But the end of the lane was in sight, and she and her lover would be united.

And she, who had lost her name, would be given his.

Lao scratched his tattooed scalp and squinted at Xanthippe's needle-decorated body on her white lion robe between the four sacred candles.

For a while he had thought that hopping lights and

shadows were tricking his vision, but now he was sure that his eyesight was reliable.

'She's fading, Hua Shan.' The Mad Hermit frowned. 'If this goes on, she won't be there any more.'

Lao couldn't yet see the lion robe through the woman's body, but it seemed it wouldn't be long before the fur became visible beneath flesh and skeleton.

The dark brown had been fading from Xanthippe's skin for more than five hours. The richness of her colour had been drained to a drab grey.

Now that drab body was becoming gradually less opaque. Her prone form looked like grubby glass. And that murky glass was growing clearer by the moment.

'She's fading,' he mumbled again. 'See what you can do for her, Hua Shan.'

Lao had already decided what he was going to do. Chia must have chosen him because he was so mad. So to aid Xanthippe, he must be as mad as possible. And the maddest thing he could think of was to deny the reality of what was happening, discount the evidence of his own eyes, and pretend that the girl was perfectly normal – normal dark colour, normal everything . . . no fading at all. It was a simple matter of imagination conquering his senses.

So he set himself about the task of imagining Xanthippe as he remembered her when she once lay on the beach, peacefully asleep: dark brown skin, glistening sweat, chest rising and falling.

*That's* what she looks like now, he slowly convinced himself. And, as reason fought a losing battle with imagination, reason's banner faltered when it noticed that the faintest tinge of colour *had* returned to the girl's skin.

Hua Shan, looking out from the mountains, valleys and plains of the moon, perceived that slight reassertion of colour. But he knew it wouldn't last. The Mad Hermit had delayed the fading for a brief space, that was all. He had slowed the girl's spirit walk to the House of Heaven, but she was already near the end of the Ancestral Road.

And moonlight – bad moonlight, like milk gone sour – was steeping her spirit-body in its potent glamour. She was going to meet her lover in the moonlight. And if she fell into his arms, he would never let her go.

Hua Shan looked in the direction of Cheng-o, whose form and face he could never quite see, deep in ageless sleep, her image splintered into a thousand facets by her Palaces of Ice.

'Cheng-o,' he pleaded. 'You dream forever inside a moon of dream. Send out a living dream to Xanthippe. Protect her from bad moonlight. The green moon is too close to her. The old sea is too close. I can't reach her. Save her with a living dream.'

Cheng-o's voice was more than a voice should be: it charmed the heaped snowflakes off the ground to dance in the air. 'She can save herself with the strength of the white lion and the memory of love.'

'But what can *I* do?' he demanded. 'How do I help save her?'

'By sitting still. By staying quiet on the mythic moon, where you have hidden from my brethren for years.'

Puzzlement creased his brow. 'Your brethren? Who are your brethren?'

'The ones who sleep below the surface of the Hard Moon, the sphere that circles the earth.'

He heard a bitter note in Cheng-o's unearthly voice. 'Are your brethren not your friends?' he queried.

'My brethren are the friends of no one.'


'I'm home,' Chia whispered as she gazed up the tall face of the house. Its black timbers and blind eyes seemed to be sealed against the outside world. This house only looked inwards.

'I'm home. And that's what frightens me most.'

Repressing a shudder, she stepped into the black square of the door. Ming-kai's gruff tone drew her to a halt within the doorframe. 'I'll tell you the last secrets of the *Mortal Wound* now. I thought I could go in there again, but I can't. It's worse than last time. It would be like – like walking into the head of a madman.'

Chia nodded her understanding. 'Just tell me the last secret – then go and find peace.'

Ming-kai steadied himself, then, face averted, spoke quickly and quietly. 'There's little to tell. Nyak wore the head-shell you call the mortal mask more and more often. Eventually, he couldn't take it off – the shell grew into his head. It altered him physically. And it poisoned his spirit. He lost all human passion, becoming something close to pure intellect. And he had a kind of hunger – which he called love – to make everything like himself. His contempt for all human emotions became so great that he convinced himself that he was born pure Thzan-tzai. He blacked out all memory of his real father, and his sister – and the murder of the father. He believed himself to be unalloyed immortal: no father, no mother, no sister.'

'I, also, forgot my father and my crime,' Chia said softly. 'I couldn't bear to think that my flesh was of Thzan-tzai descent, however distant. I lived for my passions, my loves and hates. They made me human. Then I remembered my crime. I passed on that knowledge to Nyak. I thought it had destroyed him. But it hasn't. He's coming back. And now he knows that all he has to do is absorb a woman's flesh and spirit to become what he always longed to be – pure Thzan-tzai, undying hermaphrodite, capable of anything . . .' Her green gaze settled on the moon above the willow wood. 'Capable of raising the dead.'

Ming-kai fidgeted nervously. '*Mortal Wound* stated that Nyak can be defeated if his sister uses the silver hand against the silver head.'

Chia instantly recalled the waking dream outside the Pavilion of the Immortals. Nyak had given her the silver shell that had grown from her father's right hand. And there was a legend – a legend that the metal of her dagger had fallen from the moon. 'My dagger,' she breathed. 'I made it from my father's hand. Use the silver hand against the silver head. Use this dagger against the mortal mask. *That's* why moon-silver is so averse to the bite of my dagger.' She drew out the blade and smiled. 'Now I know what kind of weapon I hold.' Throwing a grateful glance at the hermit, she replaced the dagger. 'And the last secret?' she prompted.

His nervous eyes slanted up to the sky. 'The last secret is – a prophecy, a warning. I recall the exact words: "In the time when a man and woman walk on the moon, they will awaken the sleepers, and the sleepers will bring us their dreams." '

Chia raised her gaze to the full moon. 'No mortal man and woman could ever walk on *that* moon. Death would come in an instant. That's one prophecy I'll not trouble over. It'll never happen.'

She turned and faced the black door.

Ming-kai stepped up to a short pace behind her. His knife was slowly pulled back.

Now was the time, if ever there was a time.

He hovered on the brink of decision. Which way? Let her go and be buried alive by Aklo? Stab her in the back, hard between the shoulder-blades? Was he absolutely *certain* that Chia had murdered his family? The third choice – he could join forces with her, truly be her friend, at least for the time it took to defeat the evil in the bay.

'Moonlight.' Chia was sighing, staring into the house.

He made his decision. He plunged the knife-point straight at the bitch's back.

'Moonshadow,' Chia said.

Before the last syllable was completed, there was a stab of silver light, like the deadly flash of moonlight he'd glimpsed in the Hall of Immortals. His knife-hand went sideways, the wrist firmly in Chia's grip. And he perceived that the silver lightning stab was Chia's dagger pointed straight at his throat. He felt it prick a trickle of blood from the skin.

He gaped at the cryptic smile on Chia's lips.

337

'How – how –' he gasped.

'Moonshadow.' She shrugged. 'There's a full moon right behind you. Your shadow is quite visible inside the door. It was reasonable to presume that your shadow was doing what you were doing.' She twisted his wrist, forcing him to drop the knife. 'Besides,' she remarked, 'I could hear your movements, your fast breath, the creak of boards as you poised yourself to lunge. Clumsy. And so slow, so painfully slow – compared to me, that is.'

Ming-kai wanted to sob. For the first time in years, he wanted to sob. This terrible woman had made nothing of him, treated him like a child.

Fighting the tears, he backed away. Chia knelt and picked up his knife, then slipped it into one of her numerous pockets.

'By the way,' she said, twirling the silver dagger between two fingers. 'Why did you try to kill me?'

'You butchered my wife and daughter.'

She dropped her nonchalant facade, lowered the dagger. 'Oh – I see. That's what you think. In that case, you can go. But don't try to do it again.'

Ming-kai found himself walking away. He had meant to ask for death. He'd tried and failed. He shouldn't be alive. But he was walking away. Chia had broken him. He was no longer a man.

Chia stared at Ming-kai as he broke into a run and disappeared into the dark of the willow wood.

She gave a pensive shake of the head. 'Everywhere I go there are people trying to kill me. Can't blame them, I suppose.' Then she straightened her back, turned up her collar, and faced the tall mansion once more.

'I may be able to do you an undeserved favour, Ming-kai. I can't find House and Providence, but I can find the one who gave the orders.'

She took a last look at the dark, soaring walls. 'At least – I'll find his head.'

A final deep breath, and she stepped into the house.

\*

338

Ming-kai didn't stop running until he was clear of the willow wood. Then he dropped to his knees and wept out his remorse.

He had failed his wife and daughter. He had failed to execute Chia with a clean stroke of the blade. He had failed himself.

Finally he forced himself to his feet and raised a parting look at the grim outlines of the House of Heaven.

What he saw pumped raw dread through his veins.

There was a glowing face in each of the windows of the house. Twelve windows. Twelve faces. And all the faces were identical.

Aklo looked out from twelve windows.

Aklo whispered to him from twelve mouths:

'Ah, such folly, my child, to run away within sight of your goal. Ah yes. But still, it was an ill-considered mission, little one. You chose the wrong target. It wasn't Chia who killed your warm wife and your cuddly daughter.' Twelve mouths smiled. 'It was someone known as House, accompanied by a Silver Brother called Providence.'

Ming-kai shook his head. 'No, no . . .'

'Ah yes, yes. Providence cloaked House in Chia's image, and House explored the insides of your loved ones. He took the ch'i of their Five Organs, and Chia took the blame.'

Ming-kai backed away from the taunting faces, his heart racked with anguish. 'It's not true,' he heard himself gasp.

'House nailed their insides to your wall. Ah yes. Believe me *now*?'

The hermit lowered his gaze as his retreating feet came to a halt. Yes, he did believe it. Yes. 'Chia – forgive me,' he breathed softly.

Then, softer still: 'Kill me.'

'Oh, come now,' chided the faces in the twelve windows. 'There's no need for such barbarity. This is a night of rejoicing. A new world – and an old world – is coming tonight. You must join the festivities on the Ancestral Gallery. In fact, I *insist*. Or rather, Providence insists. He'll take you to your wife and daughter. We've invited them to the merry-making. Providence will escort you to your family's new little house. As for me, I have more urgent business in my own home. Be happy, Ming-kai – after all, you'll never really die.'

The twelve faces vanished, leaving blank windows.

'Follow me,' resounded a deafening whisper at his back. It bounced endless echoes in his skull, reminiscent of the silvery chimes descending along the bay.

His mind rebelled but his body obeyed. He wheeled round to confront a tall, grey-mantled figure in a silver mask draped by long, grey hair. The name *Providence* glowed a luminous white from the wrinkled brow of silver shell. The face itself was a maze of lines that drew the eye inwards. Faces appeared on that inward voyage, then faces within faces.

'Share the loving flesh,' commanded a huge whisper.

Suddenly, the mask became beautiful to Ming-kai. It became a face of absolute perfection, impossible not to love.

He needed no bidding to follow the face wherever it led.

The end of the wooden lane was in sight, and her lover was waiting.

He loved her because she had dark skin, because she was alien, because she was from far away.

And she loved him because – because he loved her.

She would bear his name. And perhaps she would wear his face.

And that would be heaven, in the house by the sea.

She wanted to fly to him with one great leap.

But something dragged her feet.

There were two men, somewhere south of the world, who slowed her steps. One of the men was mad, and cast a little cloud on her love. The other was on his own small moon, and spread a slight mist on her world.

But the two men were weak, and her lover was strong. They could only delay her. They could never stop her joining her love.

There was a weight round her neck. At first, she hadn't noticed it.

Now, with each step, it grew heavier.

And heavier.

If she had a face, she would have frowned.

As the weight thumped painfully against her chest, a tickling sensation troubled her skin.

The sensation felt like the caress of fur. A fur robe that also increased in weight. It reminded her of strange places and strange experiences on the other side of the world. It smelt of strong animal. A comforting animal. She recalled a name:

Lion.

White Lion. Egypt. Alexandria. Christos.

Mother. Father.

The weight round the neck felt like a ponderous chain of iron. And the leaden sign that banged on her breast was an agony.

But she shuffled on, down a lane denuded of its flamboyant flags and brave banners, willing to endure any agony for the sake of her lover. There were no more happy faces in the windows. Fingers ceased to pluck plangent chords from the moon-lutes. Hands stopped beating the chieh-ku drums.

Except for a silver rain of sound, there was silence on the drab Ancestral Gallery.

She gripped the weight that thudded on her chest. It burned her hand and she would have screamed if she had a mouth.

Holding up her palm, she stared at the sign seared into her skin. The sign formed a word inside her head:

Ankh.

The sign of life.

Nefer – Beauty.

Nefer –

Nefertiti.

*Nefertiti – meaning 'The Beautiful One has come.'*

The name hovered in the air, bright and sharp. Nefertiti. *Nefertiti.*

'Xanthippe.'

Although the neck-weight became light and easy and the lion robe soft and reassuring, her feet came to a halt. She became aware of the moon above, and far below, a green sea.

The diaphanous green sea lapped frothy tongues of foam up the walls of the cliff. *The coastline was different then,* she thought. *Thousands of years past, the sea was nearer. Now the old sea returns. And it's filled with ghosts.*

'Xanthippe,' sighed a phantom voice from the ancient tides. 'Hold the ankh, and I'll bring you my dream.'

Her fingers closed round the ankh. Her flesh tingled as a spirit entered the metal . . . the spirit of an Egyptian queen – Nefertiti's spirit. And it spoke in the metal with a silver voice. 'Chia took the hand and formed a knife. I took the knife and with alchemical art formed an ankh from the hilt. Ask her to forgive me.'

She nodded her agreement. She knew that Chia would forgive Nefertiti anything.

Chia is my lover too, she wanted to say, but she lacked lips to frame the words.

*Chia is my lover.*

Then who is the man who waits in the house? He can't be my lover. Who is he?

And who is Xanthippe? I think that I should know her. Who is she?

Who is Xanthippe?

The man in the Old House became remote, hazy.

*Where is my face?*

Two sad ghosts rose from the ancient green sea. Their breath was damp on her skin. Familiar voices surged into her head.

*Mother. Father.*

Her parents spoke as one.

'Don't look for Paradise, daughter. Aklo misled us into the sea with a vision of P'eng-lai. He wanted you alone. He wanted you lonely. Reject the false Paradise. Remember your name, Xanthippe. And remember that we love you.'

Her mother and father dwindled back into the foaming green sea, awash with ghosts.

*Xanthippe. Who is Xanthippe? Me?*

'Xanthippe,' resonated the spirit from the ankh. 'Reclaim your name. Take back your face.'

*Xanthippe? Yes – I* was *once called Xanthippe. But now?*

'Xanthippe,' sighed Nefertiti. 'Say your name. Speak your name and take back your face.'

*But*, thought the girl, *I have no mouth to speak.*

*And my lover needs me, in the house by the sea.*


In the House of Heaven, she held her breath, listening in the dark.

She took a few tentative steps from the door, and stumbled over an obstacle.

Wincing at the noise, Chia spread out her arms, blindly searching out the height of the obstacle. Her hands contacted nothing.

She shrugged defeat and reached into a pocket for the Night-Shining Jewel. Showing a light was an option she was reluctant to take, but there was no sense in blundering around in the blackness.

The luminous stone distilled blue radiance; that was its nature. But the aura of the house had altered its nature. It shone with the baleful light of the moon.

'All right!' she yelled out, thrusting the stone into her pocket. 'I know you're waiting for me. Show yourself. Don't hide in the dark.'

Even as she challenged the hidden occupant, she experienced a lightening of the murk that enveloped her.

As the illumination increased she gave a wry nod.

343

'Moonlight. Interior moonlight. What a surprise.' She gleaned some consolation from the note of weary indifference in her tone. For all that she was trembling inside, she put on a brave show for the invisible enemy.

Inside, in the pulsing heart, the percussion of dread underscored the silver chimes falling outside the house. Her fear threatened to shrink her to childhood size.

She was in the house that her father built, three thousand years ago, from wood that was bad at heart. The house in which she and her brother were born. They must have fled its walls when she was in infancy. A house made from bad wood is a house born bad.

'I'm home.'

Moonlight slowly emanated from the walls. The outline of a stair emerged in front of her. It was the lowest step that she had stumbled on in the dark. In the small entrance hall, doors led off on either side, but her attention was drawn by the stairway that ran straight up to darker moonlight.

*When I was small, that stairway looked as if it led all the way up to Heaven.*

Her feet wanted to back away, wanted to run out of the house, and keep on running.

Shaking her head, she stayed still as an effigy, fighting the fears in her skull. Her memories of this house were dimmer than the moonlight at the top of the stairs. But, dimly or not, she recognized her home. And as far as Chia was concerned, home is where you run from.

*It's been waiting for me. Waiting for three thousand years.*

Expelling a sharp breath, she reminded herself why she had come. Nyak was on the threshold of resurrection. The moon of Full Pearl was arcing towards its zenith, marking the time of the Ceremony of Deliverance from Guilt, the time of sexual alchemy. Her brother would absorb Xanthippe's flesh and soul, and become the Thzan-tzai he had always aspired to be. And then he would call down his brethren from the moon.

'And I'm here to stop it,' she muttered. 'I've come for

you, or your mask.' She readied herself to climb the stairs. 'And I've come for Aklo, whoever he is.'

One last breath, and she planted her booted foot on the first step. The sound of her footfall made her hesitate for a moment.

In that moment she heard her footfall on the second step. And the third. And the fourth. She froze at the bottom of the stairs, listening to her footsteps preceding her up the stairway. The footsteps sounded in quiet creaks all the way to the top of the stairs.

There was a short spell of silence. Then the footfalls returned down the stairs with the speed of an angry charge, each board bending under the crash of heavy impact. When the lowest step cracked with the fury of the downward rush, Chia flung herself to one side and skidded across the dusty floorboards.

Raising herself on to one elbow, she scanned the hall and stairs as if there were something to see. There was only moonlight from dark wooden walls. Crossing to the stairs, she gingerly placed her foot on the step. No preceding footfall.

She tried the second step. No ghostly herald walked before. So with the third step. And the fourth.

It wasn't until she was halfway up the stairs that she lifted her eyes to the landing and discerned the tall, robed figure standing with his back to her at the top of the stairs.

Completing the ascent with slow, deliberate steps, she halted behind the black-robed figure. Her right hand closed over the dagger in her pocket. Her left hand spun the man round by the shoulder.

Shock almost flung her backwards down the stairs. It wasn't a man's face that she confronted, but a demon visage. It was a face turned inside out, like a facial expression left in wax: a face that looked inside its own head.

A low chuckle trickled from the inside-out face. Then

the face was pulled off by the man's hand. He twirled the waxen mask in his hand, then tossed it aside.

Chia stared into the youth's handsome, golden features. The longer she looked, the more certain she became. The young man bore a strong resemblance to her brother as a youth. He nodded, with a slow smile, seeming to discern her thoughts.

And as he nodded, the amiable, beautiful face aquired a rigid, unforgiving quality. The long, slanted eyes glittered like polished black stones. His expression hardened into a stern, relentless stare.

A loud whisper escaped from the unmoving lips: 'You see the family resemblance. Ah yes. So you should.'

'Who are you?' she demanded, cursing the tremble in her tone.

The youth's mouth bent into a wooden smile. 'Ah, Chia, lovely Chhhiiiaaa . . .' He slipped the black robe from his shoulders. 'Can't you guess? I've been waiting for you so long, so very long. All of three thousand years.'

Realizing his implication, she gave a slight shake of the head. 'You're not Nyak.'

His black mantle had fallen to his feet, revealing the extravagance of his Rainbow Robe. The silk of the garment swished as he spread out his wide-sleeved arms. 'Ah, there's no fooling you, is there, Black Dragon? You're right, of course.' Flourishing needle-fingered hands, he gave an exaggerated bow. 'I'm Aklo. And I'm so glad you've come back home.'

She glared at the insouciant youth. 'Who are you, Aklo?'

'Oh, come now,' he taunted. 'I imagined greater insight from Nyak's sister. Who would wait here for three thousand years? Work it out for yourself, Green-Eyes.'

'I've better things to do,' she muttered, brushing past the youth and peering down a long corridor lit by moonlight from the wood. 'Where's Nyak?'

Visibly irritated, the youth folded his arms and pursed

his lips. 'You've just met Aklo, *the* Aklo. What about my appearance? Don't I impress you?'

Chia glanced at his fingers. 'Well – you could cut your nails. And if you improve your manners, you might even find a girl one day.'

Irritation dissolved into a sly grin. 'These fingernails come in useful – very useful. And as for a girl – I've already got one.' He looked towards the south wall. 'She's coming right now, walking the spirit path. Walking along the wooden lane to meet her lover.' The grin became crooked as he looked back at Chia. 'She's just what I've always wanted. Someone very different from myself. A dark-skinned girl from far away. Someone who'll broaden my horizons.'

Chia felt her skin grow cold. 'Who are you to call Xanthippe?'

'Watch,' he instructed. 'And learn.'

A door swung open and a bright beam of moonlight flooded out, bathing Aklo in its glow and throwing his long shadow on the wall. He lifted his arms and clasped his hands, interlacing the fingers to form a shadow-face on the wood. It was Xanthippe's profile, painted in shadow, steeped in her soul.

'I have her face in my hands,' he sighed ardently. 'So she comes to me to offer her heart.'

As if in response, Xanthippe's shadow-face spoke.


Providence led him up the high stair above the surging green sea with wraiths that rose and fell like foam.

There, high above the sea, was a bright lane of happy moonlight and ancient song. In the lighted windows there were cheerful faces. His wife and daughter waited for him behind one of those windows. He had thought they were dead, long ago, but they were alive. Providence had told him that they were alive. And Providence commanded absolute trust.

Such a beautiful face couldn't tell a lie.

*Beautiful – face.*

347

*Beauty*.

The word started to echo in his head, bouncing back and forth. It hurt his head, and he tried to shake it free, but the echo wouldn't have an end.

*Beauty – beauty – beauty – beauty –*

He followed Providence down a lane of wood painted all the colours of the rainbow, skirted by cypresses, weeping willows, and cassia trees. He walked past the House of Autumn Dragon, where merry-makers poured silver wine from white jade jars into green dragon cups. He came upon the House of the Hsia Emperor Chuan Hsi, where the yellow-robed Son of Heaven reclined in the k'ung-sang, the Hollow Mulberry Tree, playing chords on moonbeams.

And everywhere, there was laughter, like jingling crystals or distant bells, an omnipresent tintinnabulation of festivity.

Providence guided him through the festive throng beneath the eternal moon, the White Lady of the night, to a house garlanded with white orchids and bright with the radiance of living pearl.

This, he understood from beautiful Providence, was where his wife and daughter waited in the home where they would live forever. The House of Bright Pearl.

'Beautiful,' he breathed to the orchid-scented air.

The painful echo rebounded all the more insistently in his head. *Beauty – beauty – beauty – beauty –*

Providence escorted him into the house where friends – he was sure they were friends – clapped his arrival.

And his wife and his daughter, gowned in white silk, cheeks flushed with joy, rushed to him with open arms.

Time had a magic length here. It was a length of silk from the solitary Mulberry Tree of the East where the ten suns were born. It could be stretched. Or folded.

He lay in bed with his wife, her shapely body and ever-smiling face warm beneath his weight. She hadn't aged a day in thirteen years.

The echo returned, louder now: *Beauty – beauty – beauty – beauty –*

He glanced at the window. A small girl looked out of the window, a huge, beautiful pearl resting on her neck in place of a head.

He moved his face back to his wife's smiling mouth, her teeth as white as the girl's pearl head.

'Unite with your beloved,' whispered Providence from amongst the perpetual smiles of his friends. 'Seal your love with an immortal kiss.'

*Beauty – beauty –*

He bowed his head to kiss the white crescent mouth.

*Beauty –*

Lips touched.

*– blinds.*

Something obdurate, an obstinacy ingrained by long years of repetition, pounded a remorseless percussion in his skull.

*Beauty blinds – beauty blinds – beauty blinds –*

The kiss went stale. The scent of orchids grew a little sour.

When he wrenched his lips away from his wife's wooden grin, blood ran where the skin had been torn from his mouth.

If she had a face, she would wail.

Nefertiti was hurting her. The spirit in the ankh that she clasped was burning her hands. The Egyptian queen's voice was paining her head.

'Xanthippe, say your name.'

Xanthippe: it was the name of pain. To hear it was hurt enough. It separated her from her lover waiting in the house by the sea. To say it was impossible. Even the sound of the name was making her see terrible things in the windows of the little houses of the wooden lane. She saw living men making love to dead women, and living women making love to dead men. And she saw them growing into each other, head to head, heart to heart.

Worst of all, the children were included in the dire sexual alchemy.

She yearned to escape, to run to her lover in the house.

'Xanthippe, say your name. Reclaim your face.'

But her lover wasn't a man.

*Chia is my lover.*

*The man in the Old House is not my friend.*

'Say your name.'

She sensed where her name was: it was with her face, in the shadows. A ghastly glamour of moonlight bathed her, told her to forget her name, to listen to old melodies on antique lutes, but the moonlight made the shadow all the sharper.

The shadow writhed and formed her face. And it spoke her name.

Her face flew down the Ancestral Gallery between the funeral houses. Her face hit her head and swept her off her feet.

No wind could have matched her as she hurtled backwards down the lane of the dead.

'Xanthippe,' she said, now that she had a mouth to speak. 'I'm Xanthippe.'

'I'm a nonsense in the night,' she laughed, rejoicing in the sound of her laughter. 'I'm flesh-of-wind, breath returning to the body.'

The funeral houses blurred by as she roared down the lane, the wind of her flight cracking the air.

She soared over ringing trees and plunged down to the towers of Melodious Temple.

She was coming home.


His family was dead.

He remembered that now. Dead and buried in Tung An cemetery, thirteen years ago.

The blood from his torn mouth dribbled on to the seashell-splinter smile of the wooden mask a faint breath away from his face.

He sprang back on to his feet, stomach lurching. The

pathetic female corpse that twitched at his feet was Wu-li, one of the women from the whore house below the temple, her death-white flesh still whole on the bone. The wooden mask covering the face savaged by Kang's teeth glowed with a silver aura. And it seemed to breathe.

Moon-silver: a touch of magic silver had been added to all the masks.

Head swimming in horror, he reeled round to witness the spectacle in the shabby room.

He was in House Tsin, where he had brought the beheaded girl, all those months ago. Perhaps that was why Providence had chosen it as his final home of rest. Not that there was any rest in this funeral house.

The living and the dead lay in each other's embrace, united by passionless instinct that made the living like the dead and the dead like the living. It was like a puppet performance in Hell. Faces merged into moonglow masks, masks ate into facial flesh.

It was a denial of both life and death. It was a fusion of the sexes so that neither existed.

This was Aklo's new world; a world where nothing was ever born and nothing ever died; a world of paradoxical flesh.

'And what will happen when the sleepers awake?' he gasped hoarsely, retreating to the window. 'What will happen when they come down from the moon?'

His shoulder touched the conch-head that he had fixed on the girl's neck on what now seemed a distant spring dusk. The scent and gurgle of moon-silver inside the head of shell warned him to keep his distance.

Shaking with grief and fear, he closed his eyes. 'Oh, Chia, if only you were here.'

Chia . . . Chia had said that the magic silver was limited by iron – or shell. And it was singularly attracted to the head.

Moon-silver had been applied to the corpse's body or mask, and it had passed into the symbolic head of shell.

351

That was why so much sentient liquid frothed inside the sea head. It had been drawn into it, and perhaps not only from the mask and body.

He grimly reflected that if his head had come too close to the conch-head, the moon-silver would have discovered its mistake and poured out into the real thing.

'But what difference does it make?' he groaned softly. 'I'm lost. The world's lost. This is just a foretaste, a puppet performance before the real Puppet Masters walk on to the stage.'

In the light of the sour moon, his bleak gaze moved out to sea.

The green ghost sea, superimposed on the ocean, washed up the sides of the cliff like a phantom aspiring to higher things, only to fall back on itself before it aspired once more.

He felt it in his blood, in the salt he shared with the sea. He felt the presence of innumerable ghosts, out there in the swirling green. Something in the bay drew them, offering them – what? Company? He would have warned the ghosts, if he could.

But there was nothing he could do. He was defeated, utterly. A giant hand had swept up the sum of his life and squeezed it dry.

The mind often recalls the most inappropriate images in times of despair. The image that flew into Ming-kai's mind was a paper kite – a paper kite on the ninth day of the ninth moon, the festival of Ch'ung Yang. He held on to that kite as if its cord was a lifeline, an easy flight out of grief.

His mouth creased into a humourless smile as he realized that kite-flying on Ch'ung Yang wasn't quite the idle fancy he had supposed. On Ch'ung Yang it was customary for people to retreat to high places for kite-flying. It commemorated the legend of a sage of old who warned that the sea would flood the land. He had fled to a peak and escaped the tidal wave from the sea.

For all he knew, the legend was a memory of an

ancient flood on this coast, and the phantasmal sea was its green ghost.

The hollow gaze rested on the reflection of the moon on the spectral green tides.

The moon in the sea.

'Green moon.'

The gurgle of moon-silver in the conch-head drew his eyes back to the shell.

Anger instantly exorcised grief – anger on behalf of the beheaded girl; anger for the sad puppets on the Ancestral Gallery; anger for his wife and child; anger against – Providence. Providence had connived in the murder of his family.

His wide, scarred brow contracted as he stared at the head of shell. It sounded as if there was an abundant amount of moon-silver in that shell.

Moon-silver. Shell. Head. Providence.

Stretching his arm to its furthest reach, bending his head away from the reaching arm, Ming-kai placed his hand on the conch. And waited.

He didn't have to wait long.

Providence strode into House Tsin, surveyed the merging bodies, then looked across at the hermit.

The garment of flayed human skin showed beneath the Silver Brother's grey mantle as it swirled in his swift progress towards the mortal who had dared to reject his command.

Providence stood in front of Ming-kai, and pointed a gauntleted hand at the unquiet body of Wu-li. 'Seek love,' he whispered. With the whisper, his monstrous mask became a beautiful face. 'Share the loving flesh.'

Ming-kai stared Providence in the face. Such exquisite beauty commanded love and obedience.

'Beauty blinds,' the hermit grated between his teeth.

He wrenched the conch-head from the dead neck stump and thrust the open mouth of the shell over the left eye of the Silver Brother's mask.

Ming-kai heard the moon-silver pouring into the

353

small opening, trickling with glee on finding a real head in which to go wild. He had learned from Chia that the Brethren became what they were by taking small amounts of moon-silver.

Hopefully, the lively liquid that flooded from conch into head would prove a little too much for Providence.

So it proved.

The exquisite face was swallowed up in the grotesque mask. As the last drop of liquid silver drained from the seashell, the hands of the Silver Brother gripped the sides of the head mask. And a bellow of agony issued from the ornamental lips of the rounded mouth aperture.

Providence staggered close to the window, roaring his torment as the inventive liquid played havoc with the inside of his skull. For as long as moon-silver remained in your head, you never really died. And this moon-silver was contained by shell – forever.

'That's for my wife, and my daughter,' growled Ming-kai as he walked past the threshing figure of Providence.

He shut the door of the funeral house behind him, leaving Providence within, trapped forever inside his own head.

Ming-kai expelled a deep breath, then spied out a tangle of vines dangling from the rim of the forest overhead.

The rest was animal instinct: the prey fleeing the hunters.

A scramble up the vines . . .

A race through trees that sang silver songs . . .

At length he tumbled to his knees, fighting for breath.

It was a long time before his lungs eased and his vision cleared. Gradually his surroundings came into focus. Tall pines stretched in all directions, the spaces between filled up with nothing but long grass and quiet dark.

It was a scene that resembled peace. The resemblance was close enough. He relaxed into a gentle sigh and closed his eyes.

He would rest, just for a little while.

He fell asleep.

When his eyes flickered open, he grimaced at the stiffness in his joints, and wondered, as he stretched his arms, where he was and how he had got here.

Then he remembered. He remembered it all.

He leaned against a tree trunk and quietly dealt with his memories, hugging the red Kang-i robe to his sides.

Then he noticed something strange moving through the trees. It was green, and luminous, and it flowed like mist.

'Or the sea,' he murmured. 'A green sea.'

The luminous green sea advanced through the trees, lapping softly against bole and bough. The slow waves on its surface splashed phantom foam on the tops of the pines. Spray added a glimmer to the green of the leaves.

The ghost sea glided over Ming-kai's head. It was like breathing moist air.

The green sea surged on into the forest as his mouth formed a wistful curve. 'Ch'ung Yang,' he murmured. 'The memory of an ancient flood.'

Then a spectral fish of sullen gold flickered its tail past the hermit's head.

He thought it a rare and remarkable fish, but then he saw others. Ghostly golden fish glided in the sea between the trees.

Entranced, he watched the fish that swam in the forest.

Finally, he lifted his gaze to the lazy waves of the surface overhead. Through the green sea, he saw the disc of the moon.

He smiled a slow smile as he whispered below his breath:

'Green moon.'

## 21

The cries of the geese are first heard. No sound of
 cicadas.
Marriage of water and sky south of the hundred
 foot tower.
The Dark Woman and the White Beauty share
 the cold,
Rivals in grace on the icy face of the moon.

Li Shang-yin

The shadow spoke on the moonlit wall.

The mouth moved on the shadow projected by Aklo's
clasped hands.

It spoke a name. Its own name:

'Xanthippe.'

And Xanthippe's shadow image was suddenly empty
of the girl's soul. The resemblance was still there, in
shadow-play of moonlight, but the shade cast by Aklo's
interlaced fingers had lost the Egyptian girl's spirit.

With a wry grimace, Aklo lowered his hands.

'Oh,' he responded philosophically. 'I thought I had
her in my hands.'

Chia, bemused by shadow games, started to move
down the corridor. 'I'm not impressed by your conjuring
tricks. I have a brother to find.'

Aklo was staring at his needle-fingered hands. 'I
thought I had her. A gift from the Master.'

She shook her head. 'Your Master wants her for
himself.'

'What?' he exclaimed, arcing a painted eyebrow. 'Oh

356

yes, of course. Yes, he wants her. He needs her. And now' – a deep sigh – 'we've both lost her.'

She glanced down the corridor. Unbidden, a flash of memory enlightened the green of her eyes: colours, many colours . . . paintings . . . colours on the walls . . .

'There were wall-paintings in this house, long ago,' she reflected. 'Pictures on the walls. I suppose three thousand years will wipe any wood clean.'

Aklo chuckled. 'It wasn't the work of time. It was more a touch, like a touch of silver – and a dash of something else. The pictures just' – he waved his arm – 'jumped off the walls.'

'Where's Nyak?' Chia cut in, grimly aware of the moon rising high above the roof to its zenith, indicating the beginning of the ceremony of sexual alchemy. 'All I want is to get my hands on Nyak.'

Aklo smiled a secretive smile. 'If you want Nyak, you'll have to go through me.'

'Whatever it takes,' she hissed, drawing her dagger as she leapt.

She landed on the spot where he had been standing. Whirling round in a low crouch, her darting glance probed the light and shadow of the house. There was no sign of a youthful face or a florid robe. Aklo had vanished into the air.

But his words echoed eerily from the mansion walls: *You'll have to go through me.*

'He's delaying me,' she finally concluded, straightening up from her combat stance. 'Whoever he is, he's using the old delaying tactic.'

Finding Nyak: that was all that mattered.

Her eyes studied the sharp tip of the silver dagger. 'Sometimes,' she whispered, 'sometimes it points the way.'

Eyes hooded, she poured her soul into the metal as she thrust it into moonlight and moonshadow, her hand tight on its hilt. In her mind, she roved the rooms of the house, seeking a hint of Nyak's presence. All, however, was dark.

Sparks of memory, tantalizing fireflies, intruded into that dark.

*Sunlight on the mask of the Silver Brother called Reproach as he confronted her in Black Dragon Valley. His words . . . 'The Master is where you will never look.' And moon-silver Sung, perched on the ceiling . . . 'Where he is, he could sleep for ten thousand years and no decay would mar his body. Long after China is dust in history's tracks, the Master will still be.'*

The dagger shook in Chia's hand as she weaved it to and fro, seeking Nyak as she resisted the memory.

Her hand twisted as a shock ran up her arm from the silver metal. Eyes springing wide, she stared at the dagger's point.

The dagger was weeping tears. Red tears.

Tears of blood spilled from the tip of the blade and splashed on the dusty floorboards.

Glowing a luminous red, the mystical blood flowed in the moonlight.

The knife came from her father's hand, and its strange substance remembered the crime of Chia the parricide. And it remembered Nyak.

The dagger was pointing directly upwards.

Nyak must be somewhere in the upper floors.

*Soon*, she thought, *soon I'll find you, Nyak. Resurrected or resurrecting, I'll find you.*

What exactly she would do when she found her brother was another matter. She tried not to dwell on it too much.

Reaching the second floor, she aimed the dagger at the ceiling. It spurted fresh red. Two more floors to go. Nyak had to be on one of them.

Wincing at the low groan of old willow under her feet, she slowly mounted the third stairway. Now she could hear her pulse thump in her ears. The palm that held the dagger was clammy. It took a conscious effort to relax her tightening muscles.

The further up the house she moved, the more likely she was to encounter Nyak at the next step, round the next sharp corner.

Chia jumped the last two steps on to the landing and spun low in the tiger stance, her nervy gaze flickering down corridors that lost themselves in darkness.

'All right,' she challenged the silent passages and stairs. 'Come on. Show yourself.'

Her challenge thickened the surrounding silence. Her own blood sounded in her ears like a drum beating a retreat. The liquid life in her veins sang a persistent refrain: *get-out . . . get-out . . . get-out . . .*

She aimed the dagger upwards. It bled richly. Her eyes swerved up to the ceiling. One more floor left.

Her gaze probed the murk of the top stairway. The lunar shimmer of the walls was less evident on that final flight of stairs, and the upper reaches were steeped in dark.

Chia ascended the stairs one slow step at a time, eyes fixed on the hidden head of the stairway. Her outstretched dagger arm trembled with the pulsing of her blood. The red tears of the silver blade spattered the steps in slap-dash patterns.

*He's waiting for me. Up there in the dark.*

The landing above was the soul of shadow.

The dark began to lift as she covered the final steps, afraid that at any moment she'd precipitate an avalanche of bad soul on her head.

The moony glow from the walls was stronger here than downstairs, pushing the dark back to the far ends of the passages. A wry smile twisted her lips as she glanced down at the silver blade.

'Treacherous blood,' she whispered. 'Where are you leading me?'

Then the blade twisted in her palm and aimed at the most leftward of the passages, seeming to tug at her hand. She jumped at the loud slam of a door at the dark end of the passage. And from that door, hidden in shadow, she heard the approaching pad of running feet.

She pressed her back to the wall, still struggling to control the wilful tug of her dagger as the light footsteps raced out of the shadows and into the moonshine, where Chia saw –

– nothing. No outline of pursued or pursuer showed in the moonlight. Even the dust on the floor was undisturbed by the passing of the invisible feet. As the light, short paces sped past Chia, she felt her skin contract with a touch of cold.

And she heard – or thought she heard – the plaintive wail of a child from somewhere deep in the house, or far in the past.

As the padding feet receded down the corridor, the remote cry came again, and words flew back to Chia like frightened little birds . . .

*No, Father. You mustn't. It hurts. It hurts.*

Then there was nothing in the corridor but silence – and Chia, trembling in every limb.

There was something about that faint, desolate voice; its terrified protest. Something that stripped Chia of all that carefully cultivated nonchalance, deprived her of the courage forged in the hot blood of the world.

She glanced left, wiped a trace of sweat from her temples, and allowed the tug of the dagger to guide her down the passage. After several paces, her narrowed eyes discerned the outline of a closed door. As she approached, the door swung open. The pull of the blade virtually wrenched her over the threshold.

Stumbling into the black ink of the interior, she tried to guess the size of the room from the echo of her footsteps. At first she received the impression of a low ceiling, close walls.

Her paces were shortening, and the room –

– the room was larger than she'd thought.

She walked into the past.

The silver metal was a comforting warmth in her grip, like a friendly hand. A hand that now gripped her fingers. A guiding hand.

A hand from the past.

A room from the past.

It was a large room, and she liked to be led into it.

Led by her father's hand

She was a small girl now, but one day she'd be big, like Father.

Her little steps could hardly keep pace with her tall father's long strides.

'Come on, Twilight.' He smiled down at her. 'Time for sleep.'

Mouth compressed in a sulk, she looked at the paintings on walls that were even taller than her father, pictures of animals playing on hills and in rivers beneath blue skies thronged with rainbows. She liked the pictures on her bedroom walls. The rainbows were best.

She climbed into her bed before she realized that she'd forgotten to keep sulking. Immediately, she made an angry face. 'Why doesn't Owl have to go to bed early?' she grumbled. Her twin brother was still playing on the beach. It wasn't fair.

'Stop that,' her father ordered, a stern glint in his green eyes.

He leaned down to kiss her goodnight.

She winced at the kiss. She hated him kissing her goodnight. He always took such a long time over it.

Tonight was longer than usual. She squirmed, wishing he'd stop. His large mouth was smothering her.

Her father's hand moved from stroking her hair to stroking her chest. His breathing sounded strange, strong and fast. 'No, Father,' she gasped, mouth struggling to escape his wet lips.

'Just – a touch,' she heard him mumble.

His large hand moved down her stomach. Her hair was gripped tight in his other hand, forcing her head to stay still as he persisted with his stifling kisses.

'Let me – touch.'

*No, Father.*

His bulky fingers were forcing between her legs now . . . pressing in . . . pushing upwards.

*You mustn't.*

The pain was hot and sharp. She wanted to scream, but his mouth stopped her.

*It hurts. It hurts.*

'You and me, Twilight,' he breathed into her mouth. 'When you're older – just you and me.'

She couldn't breathe, could barely move. Fear poured into her mouth and filled her up from toe to head.

*No, Father. You mustn't. It hurts. It hurts.*

She was breaking free as the fear expanded her body. She tore loose, started running.

As she ran, her strides lengthened. Her height increased. The room shrank as she grew larger.

She pushed open a door that led to another world.

The world of the present.

Chia raced down the dark passage, terrified that her father's spectre was gliding at her heels. Not until she reached the stairway did she slow to a halt and lean on a wall as she recovered her wits. The thump of her pulse subsided. Her breathing eased.

'I remember,' she breathed. 'Now I remember.'

*That was the first time. After that, he did that to me every night when I was small. Father was always happy to put me to bed.*

'I must have forgotten what he did,' she murmured, 'once I was out of childhood. Must have thought it was a dream. I never remembered. Or' – her brow furrowed '– *did* I?' Her grip tightened on the hilt. 'Is that why I killed you?'

Chia's wild eyes darted about the smudged outlines of the house her father built. 'Is that why I killed you?' She raised a fist aloft. 'You *bastard*! I'm glad I killed you, Father! Do you hear me? I'm glad I cut your filthy head off!'

A hundred heartbeats drummed by as she stood quivering at the top of the stairs, fist uplifted. Then she lowered her arm and drew long, deep breaths. No matter what, she mustn't be distracted from her purpose.

Tonight was Nyak's night. He was wearing her father's face.

Her gaze descended the stairs.

'Sister's coming.'

She stole down the steps, eyes flicking in every direction for signs of Nyak, ears alert to any tell-tale creaks in the house that was twice as old as China.

At first she thought the increasing illumination came from the moon sailing aloft, but as the silver glow heightened she realized that the moon-silver in the willow timbers was shining its light on her. The House of Heaven was lighting up.

'All the better for my eyes to see by,' she muttered.

Muscles tensed for trouble, she quietly opened the first door she encountered, easing her shoulder past the door-frame as she peered into the room.

The third room contained a single item. It covered half the floor space.

It was a replica of the House of Heaven, in painstaking detail.

Warily, she approached the imposing doll's house, its blue-tiled roof overtopping Chia's head, and peered through one of the windows. No miniature furniture or dolls. Skirting the house, she glanced at each window, seeing nothing of note. Until she turned its far corner. There was a little figure in one of the third-floor rooms. It was herself.

It was a stylized, two-dimensional figure, like a cut-out, or a painted portrait peeled off silk. Her image had a lively look, the liveliness of a dab of moon-silver added to paint.

Her little self in the doll's house was staring at a house barely bigger than itself: a miniature replica of the doll's house.

Chia pressed her eye close to the window. It was a brief moment before she perceived that the animated portrait of herself was imitating her actions, pressing her eye close to a window of the tiny house inside a house –

' – inside a house.' She frowned, pulling back from the window. Simultaneously, the portrait Chia pulled back from peeking into the minuscule window.

Steadily, she backed away from the replica House of Heaven. She was in no mood for games, magical or otherwise. Shutting the door on the curious house, she continued down the passage.

The next room revealed nothing but dust.

The next room likewise.

The last room was a little different. There were double-doors on the opposite wall. As she entered the room, the moonlight-by-willow spread a bright welcome about her. Every detail of her surroundings became clear in sharp blacks, keen whites, and all the shades of grey.

She saw, beyond the double-doors, another pair of open double-doors, framed precisely by the square doorway. And beyond the second pair of doors, another set of double-doors. Beyond that, another double-doorway. Beyond that, another. And another. And another. She couldn't identify any point where they ended. The doors seemed to stretch forever. Or – her perceptions took a sharp tilt – the rooms were boxes inside boxes, with doors that got smaller and smaller.

Then she tensed as she perceived a shape on the near wall. A shape that hung on the wall.

The naked victims had been nailed face to face, groin to groin. An old, old man pressed tight to the body of a young woman. And their heads had been exchanged: a young female head was sewn on to a grey, withered male body; and on the woman's young shoulders, a man's old, old head.

It was a sight Chia had witnessed many times before. It was an example of Nyak's 'sharing love'.

Reaching up she yanked the man's shrivelled arm off one nail, then freed the rest of his brittle limbs. The body toppled backwards and crashed on to the floor, releasing a cloud of dust. It was then Chia saw that the decrepit corpse had been attached to the woman in more ways than one.

A scaly cord linked the wrinkled stomach to the young woman's vagina. His cord of life had never been severed at birth.

'Young mother. Old son,' Chia intoned bleakly. 'How my brother likes his flesh games.'

The woman's insides had been scooped out.

Chia's eyes narrowed as they discerned five nails in the shadows on the wall above the dangling woman: five nails for five viscera. Four of the nailed organs were difficult to distinguish, but the wu-hsing cross pattern of nails was grimly familiar. And the heart, nailed to the symbolic south of the wu-hsing cross, was clearly visible.

'Liver, heart, spleen, lungs, kidneys,' Chia recited, recalling all those homes where a killer had performed his morbid wu-hsing magic.

*'House'*.

Gritting her teeth, she wrenched the nails from the woman's feet, then, at full stretch, worked the nails free from the wrists, pocketing each as they came loose. Task concluded, she stepped back, expecting the corpse to tumble to the floorboards. But the body stayed put, fixed in its crucified posture. Chia moved to the woman's side. The moonglow revealed the woman's back where it adhered to the wood. Chia peered closer. No – not adhered. Merged. The grain of willow showed beneath her flesh. And the luminous patch of wall near her back had a fleshy texture like a slug in its slime.

'Hell's blood,' she exclaimed, backing away from the woman. 'The wood must be crawling with moonsilver.'

Her gaze flicked up to the nailed viscera, their shapes now displayed in stark relief. And she saw that a message had been written above the wu-hsing cross, its faded characters doubtless scrawled in the paint that only the heart can supply. It was the simplest of messages:

*Welcome home*

Chia gripped the four nails in her pockets, rolled them around her fingers. And moved slowly toward the double doors. Her hands shook. *Think about Nyak*, she told herself. *Think about destroying Nyak. Nothing else. Don't get side-tracked – just think about Nyak.*

She jumped as she heard the distant pad of running feet issuing from the depths of the apparently endless tunnel of doors, or from deep inside rooms within rooms. As the thump of racing feet grew louder, she also heard the periodic slam of doors, which also increased in volume.

Soon the sound of the invisible oncomer was a low pounding, surpassed only by the crash of slamming doors.

Chia crouched and pointed the dagger at the door-way, her throat trying to swallow from a dry mouth.

Her dagger hand twitched as she caught sight of slamming doors, far in the distance. One by one, the doors whacked shut as the yet-to-be-seen runner approached with astonishing speed.

The racer and the doors sounded like two kinds of thunder: a deep rumble punctuated by loud bursts.

The thunder of speeding feet and crashing doors hurtled towards Chia with a ferocity that made her heart drum with dread.

'Five doors to go,' she counted in the faintest of breaths. A moment later. 'Four.' Another moment. 'Three.'

'Two.'

A moment. 'One.'

The double-doors slammed shut with a thunderous roar and a blast of wind.

Chia, wits spinning, was slammed to the floor.

She shook her head, trying to focus on the floorboards, inches under her nose. They swam in and out of vision. When they finally steadied, she leaned back and sat on her heels. She was facing the single door by which she'd entered. Her dagger lay just to the right of her.

A few seconds after she'd retrieved the blade, a shadow slipped over the spot on which it had lain.

A long, thin darkness spilled over the floorboards and skimmed up the wall. As the blurred head halted near ceiling height, the shape spread out two narrow arms as if in greeting.

Where the shadow rested on the wood, mould sprouted in abundance, silver in the moonlight. A figure of shade and mould lay across floor and wall, its shady fungus arms outspread.

'*Welcome home*,' whispered a voice at Chia's back.

She was already turning to face what was behind her. The voice of welcome had a characteristic ring. It was a perfectly orchestrated chorus of voices rather than the utterance of a single tongue: stolen voices, from stolen face-souls.

Her brother spoke in multitudes.

Completing the turn, her eye travelled the length of the shadowed mould. It terminated under the rim of the double-doors.

Panels of wood were all that stood between her and Nyak.

Swiftly rising to her feet, she launched herself at the doors, blade ready to slash. The impact of her leap flung the doors wide. Her dagger was slicing to and fro before she landed on her feet.

There was nothing to slice but air.

The shadow extended to the next pair of closed doors.

Moments later she kicked the doors open.

The shadow stretched on, the one who cast it still hidden behind panelled wood.

Cursing out loud, she smashed open the doors.

More shadow.

Another pair of doors were kicked wide.

More shadow.

Crashing doors.

More shadow.

Doors.

Shadow.

Doors.

Shadow.

Chia threw up her arms in frustration, a frustration that rang in her yell. 'Damn you, brother! Damn you!'

Whirling round, she stalked back along the thin

stretch of mouldy shadow. Arriving at the wall crowned by Nyak's shadow head and crossed by his shadow arms, she sheathed the dagger and thrust her hands deep into her pockets.

'*Welcome home*,' repeated the chorus of Nyak's stolen voices.

Chia's fingers contacted cold metal in her pockets. She recalled the treatment handed out to the mother still linked by the birth-cord to her ancient son. She withdrew her hands from her pockets. In each hand she now grasped one of the nails used to crucify the young mother and the aged son.

She raced across the room and leaped at the looming shadow with its outspread arms of shadow-mould. And plunged the steel nails into the shadow's wrists.

Dropping to the floor, she rolled back to her feet and, with a crooked smile, awaited the outcome.

The shadow writhed on the wall, blood spilling from where the nails impaled dark wrists on the wood. The crucified shadow, nailed to the willow, screeched as it struggled to tear loose.

Chia folded her arms and shook with mirth. 'Hung up and bled dry, dear brother. A little homecoming present from your devoted sister.'

A savage contortion ripped Nyak's shadow arms from the crucifixion nails. His shadow fled, wailing, back to where it had come from, leaving its visible memory in a crucified silhouette of mould.

'Oh well,' she shrugged, a smile twitching the corner of her mouth. 'It was fun while it lasted.'

Blood still trickled from the pierced willow, smearing two trails down the wall. Squinting her eyes, she looked closer at the spilling liquid. In the glaring moonlight emanating from the timbers, everything was painted in black and white. Her own hand was as white as death. So she had thought nothing of the grey hue of the liquid that oozed from the nails.

Chia almost reached out to touch the grey dribble

from the punctures in the willow; was on the verge of coming into contact with the slimy streaks. She hurled herself back just as two jets of moon-silver spurted from under the nails. Rolling clear of the poisonous liquid, she sprang for the door and raced into the passage.

Aiming for the stairs, she slowly shook her head. 'You know what you are, Chia? You're an idiot, that's what you are.'

Taking the stairs down to the second floor at an easy pace, she guided her thoughts back to her mission: Nyak's destruction.

She had given his shadow a couple of pin-pricks back there, a small jolt to the system. That might give her a minute's pause to search the house in peace. But after that – he'd be back. In full flood.

Halting on the second floor, she scratched her head as she surveyed the plethora of passages.

He could be anywhere. She might search for days and never find him. And she didn't have days.

'Hide-and-seek.' She exhaled sharply. 'Hide-and-seek.'

Memory instantly transformed the house from a black-and-white nightmare to the colourful home of three thousand years ago . . .

*'Hide-and-seek!' her twin brother yells excitedly. 'Hide-and-seek!'*

*She is still upset because Mother and Father let him play on the beach more than they allow her to. She pouts and shuffles her foot. 'Don't want to.'*

*'Oh, come on, Twilight,' he pleads, holding her hand as they tramp up the big, adult steps to the second floor. 'We'll hide-and-seek on the second floor.'*

*'Don't know,' she mutters, still thinking about the beach.*

*Still, a game was a game. And it wasn't really her brother Owl's fault about the beach.*

*'I'll tell you what!' Owl exclaims. 'I'll hide – you seek. You like that best, don't you?'*

'You hide – I'll seek,' she sighed, sad with memory.

'You'll have to go through me,' murmured a silken voice.

Whirling round, she was confronted by Aklo leaning on a wall beside her. What struck her wasn't so much his impossibly sudden appearance; it was his Rainbow Robe, his conical hat fashioned in imitation of a blue-tiled roof, the light gold hue of his skin.

Inside the house, it was a black and white world of moonlight. In this black and white world, Aklo appeared in full colour.

Her hand slid inside her overcoat, fingers curling round the hilt.

'What are you, Aklo? A dream?'

He inclined his head. 'Why should you think me a humble dream? I'm clearly made of sterner stuff than such night-time gossamer.'

Hoping to distract him as she drew the dagger, she nodded at his robe. 'Colours in the moonlight, Aklo. Colours in the moonlight.'

The ploy failed. His gaze remained on her face. 'You can talk, Cat Woman. Those luminous eyes of yours add a little green shimmer to this grey, grey world of ours. Your father's eyes. Your brother's eyes.'

'I'm my mother's daughter.'

The youth's eyebrows lifted. 'Why so proud of that side of the family? Your mother was human. Ordinary. Your mother was nothing.'

Rage heated her heart. 'My mother was more than I'll ever be. And my father was less than nothing.'

'Is that what your mother thought when she mated with him?' queried Aklo. 'Your father was special. Ah yes. So special.' His dreamy eyes slid shut. 'He was once the male half of a god. When that god was torn in two while dreaming a flesh dream between earth and moon, the male half fell to the earth and eventually became your father. The female half was drawn to the moon and wove her world of dreams on its lonely surface, becoming

370

in time the lovely Cheng-o, White Lady of the night.' A chuckle escaped his lips. 'You know – in a way, Cheng-o is your aunt.'

Aklo's eyes were still closed. She could ram her dagger down his chuckling throat right now, but she hesitated for an instant, recalling Ming-kai's words:

*Use the hand against the head.*

The advice had seemed sound at the time, given moon-silver's aversion to her blade. But do you heed the advice of a man who's tried to stab you in the back?

Aklo's eyes opened. His gaze lowered to the dagger. He stepped back, fear showing in his face. He gave vent to an uncertain laugh. 'What do you intend to do with your knife, Green Eyes? Slice onions?'

The youth's reaction did nothing but increase her doubt. His response was too extreme, the look of fear too evident.

Her gaze moved to the wall.

The walls were all of old willow soaked in moon-silver. She plunged her blade deep into the wood.

Instantly Aklo gasped with pain. The youth gripped the side of his chest for a few moments, then flashed her an awkward smile. The needle-nails that had sprouted from his fingers in unison with the sharp cry were swiftly retracted.

With a soft *shush* of silk he glided down the passage. 'Such wanton damage,' he scolded as a corner swallowed him from sight.

Pursing her lips in puzzlement, she returned her gaze to the dagger. It was then she noticed the patch of wood around the blade. It glowed an even brighter silver. It rippled in lively waves. As she watched the activity, it was soon apparent that the silver sap in the willow was flowing *towards* the knife.

The silver dagger was *attracting* the moon-milk.

Grasping the hilt, she pried it loose from the willow. The sap in the willow didn't want to let go of the metal. It took a violent wrench to pull the blade free. Prepared for

371

the sudden gush from the wound, she had already thrown herself to one side as the cut in the wood bled the sourest of milk.

Panting heavily her troubled gaze wandered the black and white world of the unheavenly House of Heaven. 'Am I playing my brother's game?'

*Hide-and-seek.*

Shoulders shrugging in resignation, she stepped on to the stair that angled down to the first floor. 'His game or mine, it's the only game going.'

The creak of her footfall sounded from the second step. But her foot hadn't touched the step.

A footfall from the third step. The fourth. The fifth.

Her footsteps descended the stairs ahead of her, as if leading the way. After a short hesitation, she started in pursuit of her footfalls. In a madhouse like this, perhaps it made perfect sense to follow in your own footsteps.

The footsteps led her down to the first landing before turning sharp right into a wide passage that ran straight towards imposing double-doors. The preceding footfalls halted abruptly. There was the creak and slam of opening and closing doors, although the doors stood immobile.

The corridor suddenly tilted, flinging Chia forwards. What had been a level floor suddenly became the steepest of slides. Arms flailing, trying and failing to gain purchase on the door frames that flew by on her downward plunge, she sped head-first to the double-doors at the bottom of the slide.

Covering her head with her arms an instant before she hit the end of the slide, Chia crashed through the doors and skidded some distance over bumpy floorboards before the floor righted itself as quickly as it had gone askew.

The speed of her tumble rolled her several feet over the level floor before she finally came to rest. On her feet in seconds, she circled in a crouch. She was near the centre of a long, low hall. The lunar shine gleamed dimly here, leaving the corners of the hall in shadow.

From one of those shadows walked Aklo, his robe resplendent with all the colours of the rainbow in the midst of the dulled moonlight. Chia reached for her dagger, then thought better of it.

Smiling thinly, Aklo sauntered to a stop almost within reach of Chia. Stretching out his arms, he swayed languidly. 'The moon's almost overhead, Dark Woman,' he sighed. 'The moon's so – attractive. Didn't you feel its attraction just now? It was responsible for your rather hasty entrance.'

Glancing round the hall for signs of Nyak, while being careful to keep the strange youth always in the corner of her eye, she disdained to respond.

'Ah, the moon,' he murmured. 'The White Pearl in the shell of night. Cheng-o. The pale goddess in her Palaces of Ice. My one, true love. The love I see every night, but whom I can never touch. The one, perforce, I worship from afar. Tonight's the night she comes close, but not close enough to touch. So sad. Ah yes. So sad.' Surfacing from his brief reverie, he bent a smile at Chia. 'But you know about love, don't you, Green Eyes? You came here to find a friend of mine. A very intimate friend. And you also came to save a love of yours, a luscious Black Skin, delicious enough to eat. A lovely, lovely girl. I quite understand what you see in her.'

Needle-nails started to sprout from Aklo's fingertips. 'Of course,' he remarked, 'your love must remain unrequited. You do realize that, don't you? My friend – my intimate friend – promised her to me. And I want the Black Skin. I want her to come live with me in the moonlight, in the house by the sea. She slipped out of my hands a short while ago, but I can grasp hold of her any time I wish.' He flipped his left hand over. 'Look what I've got in the palm of my hand right now.'

A portrait-Chia shimmered in Aklo's palm, its formal profile rippling slowly across the skin. 'I slipped into the temple and peeled her off the wall,' he chuckled. 'Then I

373

put her in a doll's house. I gave her a little stack of wood and three tiny pots of paint. I made her construct an identical doll's house with an identical little Chia in it. My wish would drive this tinier Chia to construct a yet smaller house, with the most minuscule of Chias in it. And she would paint and animate a yet smaller Chia, who would make another, and another – and so on. Smaller and smaller and smaller. An entertaining notion, isn't it?'

Chia sensed the light of discovery thrilling in her veins. *A house inside a house.*

'Not much,' she answered vaguely, still probing the shadowed hall for any hint of Nyak. 'Quite childish, really.'

*A house inside a house. Aklo gasping in pain when she stabbed the willow. The five wu-hsing organs nailed above the crucified mother.*

The youth's brow frowned in disapproval. 'Childish? Is that how you dismiss a feat of imagination?'

'Yes. Childish – except without the imagination of a real child.'

Aklo's exquisite features were suddenly ugly with rage. 'Childish? No imagination? How dare you? No one can scale the heights or plumb the deeps of my imagination. No one can – '

'Either tell me where Nyak is, or shut up,' she snapped, anxious about Nyak, Xanthippe, time slipping away . . .

'You want to know about Nyak?' he sneered. 'Use your *imagination.*'

Chia's right hand spasmed with the rage that suddenly raced in her. 'Damn imagination. I know who you are. I know *what* you are.' She nodded at the thousand tiny pictures, all interlaced with rainbows, in the whispering silk of Aklo's robe. 'Your robe carries all the pictures my father once painted on the walls. I remember the rainbows. The pictures must have peeled off the walls quick with moon-silver, thousands of years ago,

374

like that portrait-Chia in your hand. And that doll's house. A house within a house.'

She felt her right hand throbbing with fury. 'A house. That's what your willowy figure is, Aklo – a house within a house, your nails a little rusty with the passing of centuries. You said I had to go through you if I wanted to find Nyak. That was true enough. I had to go through the house. What were you born of, willowy youth? The marriage of willow and moon-silver over three thousand years? Oh yes – I know what you are. You're the flesh dream of the House of Heaven.'

A jolt ran up her right arm from her pulsing hand. 'You're the living wood of the house. And you're House the wu-hsing killer. One and the same.'

Aklo's wide mouth creased into a smile of pure pleasure. 'Ah yes,' he murmured, 'a house woke up one fine morning, stretched its timbers, dressed itself in pretty pictures, and went out walking in the wide, wide world.'

The youth tilted his head so that the blue-tiled roof hat obscured his face. 'Ah yes,' he mused, finger-needles stroking his shimmering robe, 'a very special house dreamed inside its walls, fed on moon-silver and moon memories, century after lonely century. A house became a ghost. A ghost became a man. A man became a god. And the more five-element organs the god could pluck from bodies, the further the god could walk abroad. A house-ghost is exalted to a house-god. And now' – he expelled a vast sigh – 'I'm the god of the bay, ready, at last, to heal the Wound in the shore. I'm Willow, Wild Willow, merry with the music of the moon.

'Like my intimate friend, I have many names. Two centuries ago I was Master Willow, and Master Willow built a house of his own, a temple by the sea. You know – I think of the temple and this house as the two hands of arms outstretched in welcome, ready to receive the lost gods back, ready to heal the Wound. This is the spot where the T'ao of the earth rejected the five-faced gods,

leaving them to the mercy of the moon's attraction. Ah –
but the way out is the way in, like the House of Heaven
with its single entrance. Ah yes, the way out is the way
in. And tonight the old gods will step back in by the way
they went out. This is a magic night, the night of Full
Pearl.'

Aklo's laughter was a chime of delicate bells. 'I'm so
glad you were able to attend.' He squeezed the hand that
held the portrait-Chia. Squeezed it tight. A streak of
painted moon-silver dribbled from his fist to form a tiny,
unquiet puddle on the floor. 'My intimate friend has
such plans for you. You'll never be quite the same again.'

Chia fought to subdue the wild energy that shook her
right arm. 'Where is he?' she yelled. 'Where is your –
intimate friend?'

'Why, he's in the house, of course. He never leaves the
house. When the house goes walking, he goes with the
house. When the house flies like thunder through the
sky, he flies with the house.'

Aklo's laughter subsided to mild mirth. 'Oh, but he
wasn't himself at all when they first brought him to the
bay; just a head with bodily aspirations. A head,
protected by the mortal mask, and bits and pieces of
exploded anatomy, that was all that was left when the
Silver Brethren brought him to the temple and installed
him in the wu-hsing statue, blinding the hermits to the
visitors' presence with whispered words. Unseen, they
tried to restore their Master in the tan-t'ien I made
myself two centuries ago. No use. I could have told them
that. Then they brought him to me, to the house. Deep in
the house, safe in the house, he started to grow again. A
child in the womb grows from the head. My friend was
like a child in the womb, growing a new body out of his
head.'

The youth gave a reverential sigh. 'Ah, and the head
was fed, with faces of flesh and faces of spirit. The head
grew strong. The head grew a new body, more subtle,
more strange than the old. Ah yes, Nyak's back. And

he's come back stronger. Thanks to House. Thanks to Master Willow.'

'Where is he?' she roared. 'Tell – '

Chia reeled at a sudden, radical alteration in the hall. In the blink of an eye, the shadowed hall seemed to turn upside-down. A fleeting glance at the ceiling above proved the perception false. But false or not, the perception persisted. The floor she stood on seemed to be above the ceiling. She felt as though she was standing upside-down.

'Ah,' sighed the Holy Youth, 'Lady Moon comes close, so very close.'

'Where-is-Nyak?' she ground between her teeth.

'Ah yes,' smiled Aklo the House. 'It's time you talked with my intimate friend.'

The youth's features hardened into a mask as rigid as wood, the eyes like black windows. His willowy body slowly ascended from the floor.

As he ascended, he touched the sharp point of a fingernail to the side of his neck. And sliced a line clean across his throat.

The severed throat opened two ripe lips – a second mouth below the youth's hard smile. Moonlight flooded out of the second mouth. Moonlight – and an old, familiar voice. It was not the multiple voice he had used for so many centuries, but the melodic tones of the brother she had known in the age before China's birth.

'Welcome home, sister.'

A wild tremor ran up her right arm. Biting her lip, she fought against the errant flesh of her arm. *It's starting again – for real.*

'I wanted you to come, dear sister. I flew on the silver thunder-wind and filled your valley with moonlight as I killed your dogs. You loved those dogs. I didn't like that. It's me you should love. Only me. A sister should love her brother. But you responded to the killing as you responded to what you believed was the menace of my silver-masked children. You left your valley. You came

377

home – home to your loving brother . . . back to where it all began.'

A shudder sped through her body. 'It was me you wanted. Me. Not Xanthippe. Oh gods – you want to mate with me. Not Xanthippe. She was only an extra lure. You want to mate with your sister.'

'Ay yes, beloved Twilight,' resonated that familiar voice. 'House Aklo wanted Xanthippe. I wanted *you*. Owl and Twilight will soon be back together again, forever. And when we become one, the Thzan-tzai will flow back from the moon.'

'I'll never mate with you,' she managed to croak, shaken by the wildness spreading in her body. 'Never.'

'But dear sister,' vibrated the voice of moonlight, 'look at your flesh. Our mating has already begun.'

Chia raised her right hand. It pulsed like a fingered heart. She hardly heard her brother's quiet invitation:

'Welcome to Paradise.'

## 22

'Green seas haunt the skies.
White Lady of the Moon has changed her colour.
Fish swim in the forest.
Ghosts surge upon the shore.
The Dark Woman and the Nothing Man kiss
In the Full Pearl of Paradise Home.
The lost gods resume their reign.
The time of man is over.

Master Willow

The green orb of the moon, like a full-cheeked monarch, beamed sovereignty over the bay.

Ming-kai caught frequent glimpses of the green moon as he ran through the phantom sea in the forest, past spectral golden fish that swam round the trees.

He saw a wide gap in the drowned trees, and headed straight for it. The sight that greeted him when he emerged from the forest was awesome.

Gazing out from the brink of the cliff, he saw that green didn't reign supreme in Silver Music Bay. Green shared equal sway with silver in the long crescent of the shore.

The Ancestral Gallery was a lane of silver light below him. The sands of the beach looked like heaped moon-dust. And Melodious Temple, not far distant, gleamed like an open oyster shell.

But it was the threads between moon and shore that took his breath away. Silver filaments, fine as cobweb, were being spun between earth and the green sphere in the sky. Earth and moon were being linked by spidery strands. Two worlds were being woven together.

And unearthly music thrilled along the bay, uniting rock, tree and sand in silver harmony.

His body responded to the summons of bells. His foot moved over the edge of the cliff, his muscles flexed to soar like a kite over sand and sea.

*Be with us. Be in us. Be us.*

'No!' he exclaimed, jumping back from the sheer drop. 'I won't be with you. Not ever.'

He thrashed along the brink of the cliff as he aimed for the temple. The occasional upward glance showed the silver strands multiplying and tightening their fibres between coast and moon. And the moon was almost overhead.

As he ran, he experienced an increasing lightness of limb. He seemed to speed past the trees in long paces. Soon he felt virtually weightless. He glided towards the temple, his light feet barely touching the earth.

He threw a last look at the moon.

The green moon was massive. It filled a quarter of the sky, like a head leaning down to peer at the world.

And he thought he saw a face in its huge circle.

A round face with round eyes and a rounded mouth aperture with pouting lips.

The silver cobweb path extended from the gaping mouth to the bay. Something – something he didn't want to see – was streaming down that silvery path.

And his body, his feather-light body, almost left the earth to greet what flowed down from the moon.


Hua Shan watched the paintings shimmer on the walls. There was moon-sap in the walls. It made for lively wall pictures.

The Land of the Nile rippled on one wall. The Empire of the Dragon Throne trembled on another.

As the Moon Hermit watched, white-faced Osiris stepped off the Wall of Egypt.

Xanthippe was shrinking back from the apparition, shivering as she hugged the white robe to her body and

380

grasped the silver ankh tight. Lao the Mad Hermit was observing the spectacle of moving pictures with a spiky grin.

At least we got Xanthippe back, reflected Hua Shan. Her face had suddenly filled with soul. She had sat up and rubbed her eyes as if waking from a dream. Yes, they had got Xanthippe back. For a little while.

The moon was close now, very close. It was starting to open its mouth and lick the bay with its silver tongue. Already he could feel the upward pull of the green moon. He almost floated from the floor.

'Mountains of the moon, plains of the moon, valleys of the moon,' he chanted.

He slipped sideways and sat on the mythic moon of Cheng-o. The elusive face of the goddess, hidden in a charm of whirling snowflakes, seemed to turn from her elaborate Palaces of Ice and look up at tiny China on the earth high above.

'My brethren are flooding back to your world by the way they once left it. The way out is the way back in,' Cheng-o said in a voice that was more than a voice. 'They flood down the silver path in a flesh-dream. When Twilight and Owl mate, my brethren will rule again. And humankind will cease to be.'

'Can't we stop them, goddess?' pleaded Hua Shan.

'It all depends on Chia – Chia Twilight,' Cheng-o sighed. 'And there's little hope for Chia. There never was.'

'Is there nothing you can do?' he implored.

'I can only wait.'

He shivered as he sensed a vast desolation nearby, a jagged lunar landscape with yawning craters and the blackest of skies sprinkled with diamond dust: the Hard Moon. The airless sphere that circled the earth. The lifeless, godless Hard Moon.

'The Hard Moon,' he shuddered, pulling his red Kang-i robe close about his thin frame. 'It's so close tonight. So close.'

381

'I know,' murmured the huge voice of the goddess. 'It's just a thought away.'

The Moon Hermit slid sideways again and sat in the upper room of South Tower with his two companions, who stared in amazement at the pictures jumping off the walls.

A green phantom sea started to pour through gaps in the shutters. A golden fish swam through the air.

Xanthippe, eyes wide with terror and wonder, gripped the silver ankh with both hands as a golden fish swam past her head.

The door opened and Ming-kai stepped into the room, followed by a flood of ghostly sea.

At first sight of Ming-kai, Xanthippe sprang to her feet.

'Where's Chia?' she demanded. 'Where's Chia?'

Before he could answer, the walls went wild.

The old wood bled milk. Inventive milk. Energetic milk.

The silvery milk clouded the ghostly green sea.

Chia fell to her knees on the floorboards, struggling to gain control of the wild energy that made deadly play of her right arm.

Above her head, Aklo hovered like a wooden effigy, the rent in his throat a mouth of moonlight that repeated her brother's invitation in the softest, most affectionate of tones:

'Welcome to Paradise.'

'The worst of all possible paradises,' she muttered, trying to restore normal form and function to her throbbing arm.

The arm had swollen to twice its proper size. And her pulsing hand – her hand had too many fingers. Teeth grinding blood from her lip, she shut her eyes and imposed her will on the skin and bone.

*Thought over flesh*, she intoned in her head. *Thought over flesh. I am what I think myself to be. My arm is what I wish it to be.*

382

Feeling the swelling subside, she opened her eyes to witness her arm shrink back to normal size. Superfluous fingers receded back into her hand, leaving the customary five in proper shape and order.

Chia slanted a smile at the second mouth in Aklo's throat. 'I'm what I think myself to be,' she declared. 'Just another woman – albeit with a few extra tricks up her sleeve. Just a long-lived mortal.'

As she spoke, she saw, out of the corner of her eye, the double-doors swinging wide.

The sea surged in through the open door. A ghostly tide slowly flooded across the hall, frothing a luminous green over the floorboards.

The phantom of an ancient sea, it filled her with dread. Rising to her feet, she started to back away from its advance.

A deep sigh streamed with the ray of moonlight from Aklo's throat. 'Can you feel it?' whispered the throat lips. 'The pull to the heavens? The attraction of the moon? It's come near, lovely Chia, drawn close by silver threads. The moon draws an ancient sea to the house and forest. And it draws you upward. It was like this for the Thzan-tzai when they fell from the earth, long ago. Their world turned upside-down: forest above, moon below. And they fell into the sky.'

Phantom green waves washed over Chia's booted feet. She spared them a swift glance before swerving a watchful gaze back on Aklo's figure overhead.

The mouth of streaming moonlight, ringed with pouting lips, resumed its melodious speech. 'When the old gods were wrenched from the earth, the agony of their departure tore a wound from the shore and threw the ocean into turmoil. A mighty tide deluged this entire coast. Thousands of years later, when we were born, you and I, we drew in the phantom of that ancient sea, the spectre of that moon of antiquity. Father had built a special house for the birth, a house constructed by willows quickened by moon-milk, because he wanted a very special child.'

Dread raced quick blood in her veins. 'I don't want to hear this,' she mumbled.

'We were born,' said the moonlight voice, 'on the night of Full Pearl in the ninth month, and the sea and moon mingled at our birth. We came from our mother's womb like a pearl from an oyster. A single pearl, a pearl born into a phantom, moonlit sea.'

'Born in the sea.' Chia heard her words as if they came from a stranger.

'Yes,' breathed the voice from the gaping throat. 'Born in the sea. Born as one. We were born as one being, male-female. Self-procreating. Self-knowing. Undying hermaphrodite. That is the secret I have learned in this house.'

She shook her head to fend off the revelation. But she knew, in the salt of her blood, that Nyak was speaking the truth. The truth had made him strong. It would probably drive her insane.

'Father named the magical child "Twilight Owl",' the moonlit mouth murmured. That is who we are: Twilight Owl. One being. As Twilight and Owl, Chia and Nyak, sundered twins, we don't really exist. When Twilight Owl was born, you didn't exist.'

'I was reborn in the sea,' she asserted, her pitch shrill. 'Father must have repented. He must have realized what kind of monster he'd brought into the world. A Thzan-tzai born on earth would draw down its sleeping kin from the moon. So he separated us.'

'Yes,' mourned the mouth full of moonlight. 'He trapped Twilight Owl between two trees at the edge of the sea – two weeping willows, one male, one female. As the tide washed over the two willows, Father's power and the nature of the trees worked their sundering magic. We were torn apart between a male and female willow. As the sea spilled over us, we were born between two trees.'

Chia finally dragged her enthralled gaze from the

throat mouth and forced her legs to move away from the body dangling in air. 'And now,' she whispered, 'the two willows have grown back together and become the undead Tree of Bells.'

'Just as we must grow back together,' Nyak's voice declared. 'But not with the passing of centuries. We're not trees. We are two halves of the mightiest being under the sky. I am you. You are me. Let's unite, dear sister. Let's both be born again, as one. Full Pearl.' The moonlight speech became reverential. 'Ah, Paradise. Paradise as only the Thzan-tzai can know it, self-enclosed, inviolate. Free of all passion – and pain. Paradise. Come join me in Paradise, sister.'

Chia assumed a brave face, lifted a cynical eyebrow. 'Together again – after all these years? I'm touched. But not in the head. Be seeing you.' Green sea swirling round her legs, she headed for the double-doors, her mind set on one course:

Flight.

She had to escape the hall. Get out of the house. Run from the bay. Flee from China, as far as possible from her loving brother. She wasn't the potential saviour of Silver Music Bay – she was its greatest threat. She was yin to Nyak's yang, and joined together they would form the darkest T'ao in history.

'Get out, Chia,' she muttered under her breath. 'Get out before all paradise breaks loose.'

Nyak's voice flew in her wake. 'Why choose mortality, Chia? Mortality, with its passion and pain and loss.'

'I'll pay its price,' she responded.

Nyak's soft tones pursued her down the hall. 'Ah, but you don't pay the price. You age like everyone else, but every few years your nature rebels against mortality and your flesh goes wild with Thzan-tzai power. It isn't any death sleep that rejuvenates your body, Chia. It's your Thzan-tzai flesh, asserting its immortality. And each time, you lose a little more memory. Forgetful, aren't you, Chia? But you can't forget that you're not human.

385

You're not mortal. Mortality is just a face you wear. But the mask doesn't fit, and it makes you the mad, sad woman you are. Throw off your mask, Chia, and come into the arms of your loving brother.'

She raced out of the hall, running from her brother's tormenting voice, luminous green waves swirling round her black figure as she sprinted down the corridor.

Her brother's voice echoed down the walls of the corridor:

'You hide. I'll seek . . .'

Memories streaked through her head as she ran:

*Sunlight on the mask of the Silver Brother called Reproach as he confronted her in Black Dragon Valley. His words . . . 'The Master is where you will never look.' And moon-silver-Sung, perched on the ceiling . . . 'Where he is, he could sleep for ten thousand years and no decay would mar his body. Long after China is dust in history's tracks, the Master will still be.'*

The Master *was* where she would never have thought of looking – in a house inside a house. And inside that strange, walking house, he could rest forever if he wished, ouside China, outside time.

The moon-silver light was back in full force by the time she reached the stairway. Except for the luminous green of the sea that flooded up the steps, the House of Heaven had plunged her into a black and white world again.

Chia all but flew down the stairs, the ghostly sea a mere damp caress as she dived into its currents. The instant her feet thumped onto the landing she swerved on to the next stairway, taking the steps five at a time.

*Hide-and-seek.*

Her strides were even longer as she hurtled down the third flight of stairs and leapt with a crash onto the landing.

She drew to an abrupt halt, and gazed around her.

There was no green sea lapping the dark wood. And she was suddenly aware that there should have been only one flight of stairs before she faced the front door of the

mansion. She had descended three. And there was still
another flight below her.

*Twilight hides. Nyak seeks.*

Recognition dawned in her darting green eyes. This
was the top floor, the floor that contained what had once
been her bedroom. Nyak was two floors below, eager to
renew an old acquaintance.

*I am you. You are me.*

Baffled, she ran nervous fingers through her hair.
How could she have run down to the top floor?

Heaving an anxious breath, she turned to descend the
stair once more.

It wasn't there.

Where the stair should have been there was a replica
of the House of Heaven. She glanced around. Somehow,
she was back in the second-floor room with its head-high
doll's house.

The black and white illumination died a sudden
death. Chia was steeped in blackest night, as if someone
had smothered her eyes in wet soot.

Then the colourless light blazed again.

And was quenched once more.

The light returned. Then the dark.

Light.

Dark.

The alternation of moonlight and darkness accelerated. Light. Dark. Lightdark. Lightdark. Lightdark lightdark lightdarklightdark.

The room was transformed into a flickering black and
white image which pounded its pulse into Chia's brain.
Disorientated, she stumbled for the door, and found
instead that she had staggered up to the doll's house.

In the maddening blink of moonlight, she gradually
discerned twelve faces in the facade of the doll's house,
twelve faces in the twelve windows that fronted the
house. Twelve Aklos stared out of the windows, their
features barely distinguishable in the vibrating light.

'The way out is the way in,' said the twelve Aklos. 'By the front door. Quite simple, really. Having problems, are we?'

'Damn you!' she screamed, aiming a kick at one of the windows.

The kick landed on the face of a kneeling Xanthippe. The blow cracked the bridge of the girl's nose.

'Again,' Aklo's light tone ordered, somewhere at her back. She whirled round, vaguely aware that she stood in a different, larger room, illuminated by a steady light. Aklo wasn't there, but she heard his voice resound from a far wall:

'Again. And again. And again. And again.'

Swerving back to Xanthippe, she saw nothing but dusty floorboards.

The floor fell away like a sheer cliff. She fell headlong down the wooden cliff. And crashed through a door into utter dark.

As she fell, she grew smaller. As she grew smaller, her fall slowed. When she was very small, she slipped into bed. Her father was a huge presence in the dark, with big hands.

*Let me – touch . . .*

Her father's head lit up like a bright moon. She beheaded the moon. It tumbled from the shoulders of night.

And rattled like a hollow shell on the floor. Her brother picked up the shell and lowered it over his head.

*'I'm living inside my father's head.'*

Her father's head spoke to her in her brother's voice:

*'You hide. I'll seek.'*

She ran from her father-brother, seeking a place to hide. But there was no hiding-place. His face was on every wall. In every corner.

'Mother!' she cried out, spotting the door to her mother's room. 'Mother! Help me!'

Chia flung open her mother's door and ran into –

– Black Dragon Caverns, their recesses dark in the glum light of a rainy day out in Black Dragon Valley.

Her mother was huddled in one of the recesses, her lumpy form partially obscured in shadow.

'I'm sorry I took so long,' Chia apologized, letting drop her shoulder-bag. 'The Hu Tribe were stirring up trouble again. Here – I've brought you some wine.'

Her mother ignored the proffered wineskin. It was then Chia noticed the empty bowl at her mother's feet. The inside of the bowl had a silver liquid shine – a moon glow. And the glow moved inside the bowl.

A gurgling sound resonated from her mother's malformed throat. 'I've had – a little drink. Nyak came – brought me a little drink.' The dumpy shape moved slightly, emitting the creaks and squeaks of shell-patches rubbing together on the flesh.

Chia's skin prickled. 'Nyak brought a whole bowl of moon-milk? You drank an entire bowl of moon-milk?'

The lumpy shape creaked and crackled as it nodded. 'A good boy, Nyak. Not like you. He knows what I need.'

'Gods, what was he thinking of?' Chia groaned, kneeling down by her mother. She touched her mother's bumpy head.

And the head sprang up out of the shadows. The face was a patchwork of skin and shell. The eyes swam in milky liquid, weeping white tears. Sour milk dribbled from the pendulous lips.

The mouth opened wide, and a flood of moon-milk spouted out and blinded Chia . . .

. . . Chia staggered back in the dark, fingers clawing at her face, tearing at the skin, and stumbled out into the corridor.

It took some moments for her to recover from the memory. It was a lifelong haunter of her dreams.

Slithering down a wall, she slumped to the floor. She leaned her head back, with a low moan. What was the point in running? She was chasing round in a maze with no exit. Nyak was the master of the maze.

389

She couldn't oppose Nyak. She hadn't a chance. He had all the advantage. She had none. She was powerless.

'I want my powers back,' she all but sobbed. 'I want my powers back. I'm defenceless without them. I'm nothing without them. I want my powers back.'

And a little, taunting voice in her head threw the words back at her, adding a few choice observations of its own.

*You always wanted to be human, to be mortal. You always wanted to be like everyone else. You didn't want to be special. Well, you're not special now . . . How does it feel?*

Numbly, Chia saw that her right hand had started to pulse again. She barely heard her slurred answer to the mocking voice:

'I want to be ordinary, and I want to be extraordinary. I want to be mortal, and I want to be immortal . . . Just like everyone else.'

At length, she forced herself to her feet and gazed up and down the passage.

Rather than stand still, she progressed down the corridor, struggling to subdue the throbbing lump that threatened to make her hand go wild again. Power lay in that wild flesh, but its price was too high. Better to seek a way out, even if the search was condemned to failure. She turned a corner. And there was Aklo, a vibration of colours in the grey shades of a passage, standing with folded arms and wide grin. Behind him, she swiftly realized, was the front door, the way out of this madhouse that was her home. She quickly brushed past the smirking youth.

'Going so soon?'

She aimed directly for the front door, walked under its lintel.

And stood on the first landing, where she had originally encountered Aklo with his inside-out mask.

A long breath escaped her lips. 'Can't say I'm overwhelmed with surprise.'

Aklo blasted up through the floorboards in front of her

and landed gently to one side of the ragged hole, which was already snapping back its planks, healing the wound in the wood.

'Ah yes.' He sighed dreamily, tipping his roof-hatted head. 'It's time we finished our little game of hide-and-seek. There's nowhere to hide – I think you realize that now. Time to stop pretending. You've always been one of us.'

'I'm one of no one.'

The youth's wide lips compressed into a thin line. 'Do you seriously believe that you can refuse my intimate friend? He loves you, you know. He loves you so much that he won't let anyone near you. I understand that kind of deep, caring love. Yes I do. I'm much the same myself. I'm in love too, you know. Not with Xanthippe – that's a purely physical thing. I love – I *adore* – the White Lady of the night, exquisite Cheng-o. And, who knows, one day . . .' He stroked his hairless chin. 'I've become a god, after all. Who's to say I'm not worthy of a goddess?'

Chia hid the thought that suddenly sprang to mind, and retained an impassive mask. She chose her words carefully.

'One thing puzzles me, Aklo.'

'Yes?'

'Why do you choose to be Nyak's servant?'

'What!' he exclaimed. 'Me? A servant? Don't be ridiculous.'

'Oh.' She shrugged. 'It's just that I don't understand why you're refusing your single chance to join Cheng-o. I assumed it was loyalty to your master.'

'He's the master of the house,' Aklo snapped. 'But he's not the master of me.'

Chia gave another shrug. 'Same thing, surely?'

'This,' he waved an imperious hand about the interior, creating a small eddy in the ghostly green sea, 'is just a mansion soaked in moon-silver. *I*' – he tapped his chest – 'am a god.'

'Oh well,' she remarked. 'I merely wondered why you

were passing up the chance of leaping up to the White Lady on the one night that she leans down so close. You have your reasons, I suppose.'

The youth's smooth brow formed lines of thought. 'But it can't be done, can it? She's just out of reach. Isn't she?' The frown deepened. 'Do you know something I don't?'

She spread her palms. 'What can I tell a god about moon-silver that he doesn't already know?'

Leaving that thought in his head, Chia walked past him and mounted the second flight of stairs. This time, the house didn't play tricks on her. For the time being, it behaved itself. But as she ascended the old mansion, she found her feet occasionally leaving the floor. With each upward step, her body lightened.

By the time she neared the top floor her body wasn't sure which was up and which was down.

'Moon-silver,' pondered Aklo, sitting near the front door. 'What does she know about moon-silver that I don't? Was she bluffing? Hmm – hard to tell. Moon-silver – secretion of the gods, attracted to earth and moon. Attracted' – he jumped to his feet – 'attracted to the moon. That's it! And the secretion is attracted to the gods returning from the moon. As the gods glide down the silver path, I can float up it on moon-silver! The way in is also the way out. Of course!'

Cheng-o, he thought ardently. Radiant goddess. We'll soon be together on your mythic moon, encircled by your palaces of living dream.

'Ah yes, soon,' he sighed, spreading his arms. 'Tonight's a night of love.'

Aklo had existed three thousand years in the Wound of the bay. For millennia, he had harmonized its liquid melodies into a crescent of silver celebration – a labour of love for the gods. His labours were concluded. The gods were descending. Twilight and Owl were merging.

It was time for Aklo to take his reward.

Time to ascend into Heaven and live with his love in the moonlight.

Aklo inhaled.

He inhaled as no living lungs could inhale.

Like a void in the heart of the world.

*Flow, moon-silver. Flow into me. The moon is high, and time is fleeting.*

In the dark behind his closed eyes, friendly silver flowed to him like rivers to the sea.

It seeped from the pores of the house and tripped down the stairs.

It streamed from the trees overhead and rained down on the young god's head.

It sped along the bay, from temple to village.

It raced a liquid path along the Ancestral Gallery, draining its aged timbers of whimsical life.

The moon-silver of Silver Music Bay showered its blessings on the divinity called Aklo.

He soaked them all in, every last drop.

Chia tripped over a step on the third flight of stairs.

And fell up the stairs.

Her fingers momentarily scrabbled for purchase on the walls, then retracted at the touch of seeping moon-milk. The silver-white liquid frothed from the willow, spilling down the stairs as she fell upwards, drawn by lunar attraction.

Despite her fear, Chia smiled. There was nothing more stupid than an upstart god. Aklo had fallen for her trick. He was drawing vast quantities of moon-silver to himself, aspiring to rise to his love in the moon. She wished him every success.

Her smile faded as she rolled up the stairs. Whether Aklo succeeded or failed, there was no hope for her. She was headed for oblivion – the oblivion of Bad Paradise.

She tumbled off the top of the stairs and slammed against the ceiling, the impact whooshing the air from her lungs. Spreadeagled on the rafters, she awaited the arrival of her brother.

He would come soon. Tread softly up the stairs. Take her in his arms. And drag her kicking into Paradise.

The beat of blood sounding in her ears, her gaze flickered over the head of the stairs. Soon, very soon, Chia would cease to be Chia, and become one half of an abomination. An immortal abomination.

In the last minutes of her existence, Chia's bedevilled mind reached out to the one sacred face of her long, long life: the unique deity of Chia's personal idolatry . . .

*Nefertiti.*

At that name, whispered in the mind, her fingers twitched, instinctively reaching for the ankh even as she remembered that it lay around Xanthippe's neck, wherever that gentle girl was. Chia sent up a brief prayer to Xanthippe's man-god that the Egyptian was safe.

If Chia's plan failed, no one would be safe, ever. Not even the ghosts.

Nefertiti's image flowed back like the Nile at spring, inundating Chia's spirit, forcing tears from her eyes.

*'Forgive me, Chia.'*

'I'd forgive you anything if there was anything to forgive.'

She winced as the edge of a rafter dug into her spine. The lunar attraction was intensifying. Moon and earth were mingling auras. So little time left. So little.

The moment of sexual alchemy must be imminent.

Her anxious gaze probed the dark stairway, seeking hints of her brother.

Her brother bulged out of the wood next to her head.

The planks screeched in protest as they were moulded into a head that sprouted from the ceiling.

Dangling crown downwards, the wooden head grew faces. Five faces. The head could instantly view the world from every angle.

The five willow mouths cracked open. 'Up to your tricks again, sister? Your wits must have dulled with age.

Aklo won't ascend to the moon – not with me inside him. That I could never permit.'

'It's time,' the mouths said. 'Time to merge in Full Pearl. I can feel the gods approaching across the bridge of dreams from the moon. We must ensure they reach us. You must become wild flesh. You stubbornly resisted the urge to transform into a flesh dream as you blundered about the house, in spite of all my efforts to drive you towards your true nature. You wouldn't join with me of your own will, as I hoped. Now, to my regret, I must take you against your will. It's time for us to unite in Paradise.'

Chia raised an eyebrow. 'Isn't there a more seemly way to draw ancient gods to earth? How about a mystic incantation on a mountain top?'

The five smiles widened. 'You always did hide behind sarcasm when you were frightened. And you're frightened now. Very much so. But there's no need. You are about to shed the burden of your false human identity. You are on the edge of entering undying bliss. As am I. We will cease to exist. Yet we will live forever, a deathless hermaphrodite, a divine paradox.'

Her lips formed a dubious slant. 'And how do you suggest I have sex with a wooden head?'

The smiles died on the mouths. 'You've been walking inside my head since you entered Old House. Aklo is House. But I am the Master of the House. When you scaled the stairs, you ascended to the crown of my head. The corridors you ran down and the rooms you explored were the tunnels and chambers of my head. Those who walk in this house walk in me.'

Chia refused to show her profound disquiet. 'Oh well,' she sighed nonchalantly. 'I'll be having sex with a house then. So long as the point is clear. I must have got it all wrong, as usual. I thought there was an actual head inside a tangible mortal mask. Too literal-minded, I suppose.'

The wooden mouths creaked laughter. 'Oh, there is

indeed an actual head – and body. As for the mortal mask, after I put it on it grew into my head. The mask became my head. My head become the mask. The silver mask I wear, fashioned in the image of Father's death-face, is purely ornamental, for show. True, the mask grew back out of my head when my body was destroyed. It became the protective shell it was in the beginning, but that protection is no longer required, and head and mask are merged again – a head mask; a mask head.

'Where are you, exactly?' she queried. 'Where's your physical form?'

'Inside Aklo, of course,' said the faces. 'Inside the world of House Aklo.'

'And that's where we unite – inside Aklo?' she enquired.

'*That*,' said the mouths, 'was your plan. Persuade Aklo to rise to the moon, then enter his body to keep me from stopping his moonflight. You intended all three of us to fly to the moon, with no chance of return. But really, sister, you shouldn't have thought me so gullible.'

*Damn*, Chia swore to herself. He's seen straight through me. *Damn, damn, damn*.

The wooden head retreated into the ceiling. 'It's time I stepped out of Aklo's world, sister. It's time we met face to face. What appearance do you wish me to adopt?'

'You choose.' She shrugged. 'It's all the same to me.'

The boards of the ceiling cracked back into place.

'How do I look?' asked a melodic voice from below.

His appearance temporarily robbed her of speech. She had expected an extravaganza of visual novelties, a carnival of horrors. But he looked like the Nyak she had known in youth, before the mortal mask ate into his head.

He looked like her, her male counterpart. His mouth curved into a pleasant smile. 'Ah – I've surprised you, sister. That's good. You used to enjoy me springing surprises on you when we were children. Remember?'

Chia couldn't suppress a wince at the sight of him.

Memories came back. Good memories. And nothing hurt more than good memories of times long gone.

'We've been enemies for too long, Twilight,' he said, his voice loaded with regret. 'We used to be friends – once.' His green eyes shone with passion in the dark. 'There's one thing I've learned from the long lesson of my life – the futility of trying to exist in separation from my one and only sister. We were born to be together, Twilight. Any other form of existence is unimaginable, unendurable.'

He stretched out his hand. 'Will you come to me freely? Accept the flesh alchemy with a willing heart?'

Chia was about to deliver a barbed retort when the house shuddered. It reminded her of the shudder of a lover in sight of his quest.

Nyak's young face, framed by long, flowing hair, gazed up as if seeing above the ceiling. 'They're coming,' he whispered. 'The ancient wonders, they're coming.'

Looking for wonders above, he was unprepared for a prodigy from below.

Nyak was hurled aside as Aklo blasted through the floorboards like a shooting star returning to the heavens. Trailing a luminous wake of silver celebration, he hurtled through the ceiling in his heavenly progress.

His voice was a million bells. 'Cheng-o!' he rang out, bursting through the roof. 'Your love flies to you on silver wings!'

Chia retained her wits through the sudden astonishment. Her thoughts raced as fast as Aklo's ascent.

*If Twilight and Owl are reunited, the five-faced gods are certain to return. But if Twilight and Owl can never be joined – if worlds separate them . . .*

'I can always dream,' she murmured.

She turned herself into a dream.

A flesh dream, linked to aspiring moon-silver.

Her flesh went wild as it sprang on the shimmering tail of Aklo's flight.

She became an impossibility. Flesh-of-wind, moon-bound.

She became a wound in nature, and soared clear of nature's realm.

As she roared through the shattered roof, she cast wind words in her wake:

*Goodbye, Nyak. If you stay, then I must go.*

With eyes of liquid velocity, she looked her last on the earth. Transfigured by a moonward urge, she saw the earth hanging above her, while the moon waited below.

'Chia,' whispered Xanthippe. 'Where are you?'

Amidst the sudden quiet of the temple since moon-silver had drained from the walls and spilled out into the night, Xanthippe gripped the silver ankh and prayed for Chia's return.

The looped cross seemed to resonate in her palms as if the metal caught distant echoes.

'Chia . . .'

Dread was holding the Egyptian's heart. Its fingers squeezed.

Her hand tightened about the silver metal. 'Chia . . . Where are you?'

Flesh-of-wind, he flew into the sky, a dangerous non-sense in the night.

He hated Chia. But he loved her more.

Better to exist like a stone on the moon than to live without Chia.

*'Sister!'* he called out as he neared her speeding presence on the moon-silver trail. *'Come back!'*

Nyak flew to her side and tried to merge with her subtle wind-flesh. He spoke words to the wind.

*'We'll both fly to the moon, beloved sister. We'll live there together.'*

Glancing ahead, he saw the moon-silver storm that was Aklo blasting up the fragile bridge of dreams. And the storm blew the distant half-shapes of the gods back along the bridge to the pouting green face of the moon. The delicate link with earth was broken.

398

Even as he watched, the silver webs between earth and moon untangled. The intricate patterns unravelled into dissolution. The bridge of dreams was undone.

There was no way back for any of them. Not for the gods. Not for Aklo. Not for Nyak. Not for Chia.

No way back.

'Nefertiti.'

Chia's last thought was of love.

*Nefertiti.*

A last memory. . .

*Golden fingers plucking an Egyptian lute behind glass-beaded curtains. The golden fingers of Nefertiti, fingernails painted silver. 'Remember the golden time, Chia-Nefer,' she whispers. 'Remember the bright, mortal hour.' The warm brown eyes of Nefertiti in a face grown older. The full, moist mouth. Mouth parted, murmuring, 'Forgive me, Chia.' She holds out the ankh on its silver chain. It sticks to the dagger like a sundered twin . . .*

The flesh-wind that was Chia faltered in its flight.

The dagger – the ankh, were sundered twins.

*'Forgive me, Chia. Forgive me for being mortal. And forgive me for seeking immortality in your silver dagger. My alchemists took a portion of the hilt and made an ankh for me. It didn't make me immortal. It poisoned my flesh. Here, take back the ankh that came from your dagger . . .'*

The ankh, the dagger – of one substance, of one spirit. Sundered twins, seeking reunion . . .

She formed a many-fingered hand and held out the silver dagger. Swerving it to the earth above, she reached her fading mind along a glittering thread that extended from the blade to the shrinking shore above.

A fragile call tingled down that thread.

A call of like to like.

Chia wheeled round from the moon and fell to earth.

Nyak, tumbling moonwards with Aklo and the lost gods, wailed out his loss. *'Sister, why are you deserting me? I love you. Why are you deserting me?'*

She sent back one final message to her swiftly receding brother: *'Because you killed my dogs, you bastard.'*

Then she threw all her energies into assuming human shape as she plummeted to earth, dagger aimed directly at Melodious Temple.

Cheng-o scooped miraculous snow from the air as she watched, through a square window in her lunar dream, the fall of the lost gods that were her brethren.

They rained down on the Hard Moon like boulders. And, inert as stones, they rolled to rest in the cave from which they had issued on their voyage to the earth.

They had been sleepers for ten thousand years. Now they were sleepers again.

She turned away from the square window on the Hard Moon, and thought no more of her nightmare brethren.

The White Lady of the night rolled the radiant snow in her hands as she looked up at the living wood that plunged towards her Palaces of Ice.

The descending shape was part man, part house. The figure had manlike outlines, but it had timber for flesh, twelve windows for eyes, and a door for a mouth.

Inside one of the windows was an anguished face she recognized: Nyak, son of her other half – her male half. She had witnessed Nyak flee into House Aklo's mouth after the departure of Chia, hiding from the terror of the Hard Moon. He cowered in there now, breathing the dream air of the house, doubtless hoping for acceptance in the goddess's visionary moon of snow and ice.

Sacred snow clasped tight between her hands, she observed House Aklo open the door of its mouth in joyful greeting:

'White Lady of the night, your love comes to live with you in the moonlight!'

She flung the snowball at House Aklo as he flew near the square window, her aim the true aim of a goddess.

The snowball, half the size of the house, knocked

Aklo off course, propelling him through the window on the Hard Moon.

Cheng-o watched House Aklo crash on to the cratered surface of the Hard Moon.

Then she shut the window.


Silver power blazed from the ankh. Wild power.

Xanthippe shrieked in pain as she dropped the looped cross. For a moment the hands that had held it throbbed rhythmically, emitting a silver sheen. But the pulsing subsided and the glow faded.

Shaking, she turned to Ming-kai. On the verge of voicing her confusion, she suddenly caught the sound of a fury in the night. An approaching fury.

Instinctively, they all backed away to the door, breath held as the thunder-wind resounded in the chamber.

'Get out!' Ming-kai ordered as the roar mounted. 'Out of the door!'

Alarmed into action, they hurried out of the room and slammed the door behind them.

Moments later the door was blown off its hinges.

Coughing in the swirling dust, they each looked at the other, wondering who should go in first.

Ming-kai finally summoned up the courage. He squared his shoulders, moved to step forwards, and was halted in his tracks.

The tall figure of a woman in black emerged from the shattered doorway. Her green eyes lingered on Xanthippe for an instant, then moved away.

Chia dangled the silver cross in her hand as she strode on to the landing.

'Thanks for taking care of my ankh,' she said. Then she pushed past them without another word.


The afternoon light sparkled the ankh as she swung it to and fro from her fingers. The tide frothed close to her booted feet, occasionally splashing the hide.

401

A lump pulsed between the thumb and forefinger of the hand that swished the ankh.

'Bad flesh,' Chia murmured, her gaze hidden behind black glasses. 'The last of a bad breed.'

She glanced up and down the empty beach.

No one came near her now, except for the Mad Hermit, who was blithely indifferent to her calculated coldness.

Chia had cut everyone dead since returning to the temple. She had gone out of her way to be cruel. It had been a convincing performance. She had even fooled Xanthippe. The Egyptian girl was afraid of her now.

That was good. Chia wanted no more lovers. Her flesh was poison to the touch. She only wanted to be touched by enemies.

What enemies she had were gone. The Silver Brethren, bereft of their Master's will, had departed unseen.

The bay was largely drained of moon-silver, thanks to Aklo.

Chia was left to herself.

She stared at the beating of her tainted flesh.

'I must live alone.'

Beside the cave that hid the massive, stony forms of the lost gods, he sat with arms folded over his silken Robe of Rainbows.

It was unlikely that the lost gods would be stirring again. They depended on the activity of sex to ignite the flare of life in their bizarre bodies.

*And there's no sex on the moon*, Aklo reflected sullenly, cut to the quick by Cheng-o's response to his amorous advance.

From under the brim of his conical-roof hat, he glumly scanned the harsh ridges and craters of the lunar landscape: his new home, for a long, long time.

As Aklo had only pretended to be a living, breathing man, he had no need to breathe.

But he could dream. He could always dream.

He ignored the voice that resonated inside his strange body. Let his guest lay down commands as if he was still lord and master. Aklo took no notice. He hadn't asked Nyak to leap inside his body of wild willow. Nyak could pace about in Aklo's mystical rooms and corridors until the sun cooled to ice, for all the Holy Youth cared.

Nyak was obliged to stay indoors, breathing the dream air of Aklo's willow-flesh walls. He was confined to the house for the rest of his days on the moon.

So much for Nyak.

As for his accursed sister –

He glowered at the huge blue sphere of the earth hanging in the utter black of the sky. It looked enticing, with its fleecy wisps of clouds.

But here he would have to sit, gazing up at the unreachable prize of earth.

He thought again of Chia, and shook with fury. *Nasty trick, Green Eyes. You knew I'd finish up on the Hard Moon. Nasty trick*

House Aklo sat on the moon, and mused on a prophecy.

Then he glared once more at the earth above. *You haven't seen the last of me.*

His mind returned to the prophecy.

Dwelling on the prophecy, he started to smile.

*One day,* he reflected. *One day.*

# Epilogue

Chia didn't wave as the ship slipped out of port.

Xanthippe and Ming-kai waved from the port rail, but she forced herself not to respond.

Wearing a hard face would make the parting easier for Xanthippe, on the first leg of her long journey back to Alexandria. Only Lao the Mad Hermit, standing at Chia's side, was privy to the knowledge that she had secretly provided funds for the voyage.

As the ship dwindled into the horizon and the moon rose over the dusk sea, Lao scratched his shaven, tattooed head and turned to the moody sorceress.

'Where are you going to now?' he asked.

She didn't hear the question. The rising moon and a prophecy engaged her thoughts:

*In the time when a man and woman walk on the moon, the sleepers will awaken . . .*

'You've got the moon in your eyes,' the Mad Hermit reflected. 'It's a mysterious beauty you have, Chia.'

She slipped black glasses over her eyes, hiding behind twin black moons.

Slowly, she shook her head. 'I'm not what I appear to be.'

He shrugged narrow shoulders. 'Who is?'